Low Road in High Country

A Smoky Mountain Mystery

by Mike Due

More of Mike's books can be found at:

Main Characters

Dedications

I am dedicating this book to several people. First, to my oldest friend, Doug Powers. Doug passed away late in 2018 during the writing of this book. He and his brother, Steve, are present in my earliest of memories. We discovered a new world together, and listened to a lot of great music in their room with the awesome stereo their dad bought from Swallen's department store. I've chosen to honor Doug by using his last name for my main character.

This book is also dedicated to Tom and Joan DiLullo, the parents of a good friend of mine, Michelle DiLullo Painter. While writing this book, I spent an hour with this married couple who travelled to the Smoky Mountains several times a year spanning their entire married life, with the goal of traversing every trail they could find. In the past, the Great Smoky Mountain National Park has had as many as 900 miles of official trails open to the public. Keep in mind, some of the trails are "out and back" trails meaning you're hiking the same miles twice. They could have hiked well over 1,000 together. I'm not sure if the couple ever accomplished their goal of hiking every trail, but that hardly matters. The important thing is that they shared many adventures together that spanned most of their lives together. They encountered bear poachers, were stalked by wild hogs, and viewed sights that most people will never see. What a fantastic way to share each other's lives as man and wife! Tom and Joan DiLullo are now into their 80's and are no longer hiking, but images of the trails still remain firmly in their memories, and in several crowded shoe boxes. Note: the honey incident in this book was taken from their real-life exploits.

Lastly, this book is dedicated to anyone who has ever enjoyed vacationing in the Great Smoky Mountains National Park. It's a place shared by roughly 12 million visitors every year, yet I still think of it as a little slice of paradise that God reserved just for me (although I certainly didn't feel that way when I recently visited during the Memorial Day Weekend). Thanks, mom & dad, for picking the Smokies as our frequent vacation destination.

— Mike Due

Doug Powers   Tom and Joan DiLullo

Chapter 1

Central Tennessee, early autumn, in a year not too distant from now.

There was a chill in the air as Mark Powers, a ranger for the Great Smoky Mountains National Park, began recording a video with his smartphone. He was a well-known web celebrity, having recorded over 20 videos on YouTube where he documented the day-to-day activities of a park ranger. He had never counted on such success, and had only begun producing the videos as a way of helping the public have safe and enjoyable visits to the Smoky Mountains. With heavy web traffic, and the addition of ads on his YouTube channel, he was now making a nice side-income. This gave him a greater incentive to keep making more videos.

Unlike his others, this installment had personal significance to him, and he was finding it difficult to gather his thoughts for what to say.

Video Transcript:
Wandering Ranger #28
(YouTube Channel)

Visual Description:

START VIDEO: Special Agent Mark Powers of the GSMNP talking to camera, poolside, sitting on a deck chair. It is night time, pool area is illuminated by above-head lighting. Other evidence collection personnel are seen in the background, examining the scene of the crime.

Audio Script:

Hello everyone, welcome to the latest Wandering Ranger video. My subscribers know that I do my best to show what the life of a park ranger is like, day to day, and I tend to get a little nostalgic about the Smoky Mountains in the process. But this time we have a situation that is definitely out of the ordinary. It's really gotten me to thinking about life, a little bit. Let me do my nostalgia thing first, then I'll pose a question for you to ponder.

When I was a kid, my family vacationed in the Smokies every year. I thought it was the coolest place on earth. That's why I moved here, and started my career here. I was even married here, right in the middle of the park.

Between the ages of maybe five to fifteen years old, or so, swimming pools really had a hold on me. Every campground had a pool, and they were all different. I loved a good pool with a slide, or diving board, and I especially loved swimming at night, when the water was lit up. I can remember the smell of the chlorine, the irritation I felt from opening my eyes under water too much. Then there was the memory of shivering as I got out of the pool at night, and running to my mom to get a towel before I froze to death. I remember the sound of those cheap diving boards bouncing against the rubber thing on the underside, after my sister would execute a perfectly graceful, backward dive. And then me and my brothers, we'd get up there and do a bazillion cannon balls, jack knifes, and crazy, uncoordinated flips. Man, I'm telling you, there was nothing on this planet that welcomed me like seeing that illuminated aqua-blueness at night, with slightly lighter and darker shades of turquoise dancing around on the bottom of the pool, making the surface look like wobbling, blue Jell-O.

Streams were my daytime fascination. On a hot day, there was nothing like going ankle- or knee-deep in a mountain stream, fighting the force of the rapids, or just swimming out into the calmer areas. Sometimes dad would go to the gas station before we left our little town of Erlanger, Kentucky, and load up on inner tubes that us kids could use to ride down those streams like some natural amusement ride. I remember jumping off of rocks into a deep pool of clear stream water, over and over again. I loved streams so much I even got married at one. I have so many great memories of streams.

So that's my nostalgia trip. But what does it have to do with this Wandering Ranger video episode? Well, maybe this time I should say this is a 'Wondering' Ranger video, because I am 'wondering' about something and I don't have an answer. It ties into the crime that took place here last night, which I'm about discuss.

Maybe you can see I'm sitting next to a pool. Notice the crime scene tape, twisting in the breeze. I'd like to tell you about what happened here last night.

Visual Description:

Mark pans the view of the camera to show the swimming pool area.

Audio Script:

By the time I've posted this video, I will have made sure this information is safe to release. At this very moment, though, there's an ongoing investigation which I'm not at liberty to discuss. So, you may be seeing this video long after it's been recorded.

About 24 hours ago, the manager of this roadside motel heard one of his customers' trucks pull into the lot. He recognized the distinctive growl of the muffler and knew that customer liked to park around the back of the building. He didn't even bother to get up from the chair he was lounging in behind the counter.

Twenty minutes later, though, he heard a lot of commotion coming from the pool area on the far side of the parking lot from his hotel office. He thought he might have even heard someone light off a firecracker or some kind of fireworks. He finished a phone call to his wife and then looked out his window. He saw two people in dark clothing running from the pool toward the woods. There was also a third person in the pool. The manager thought maybe they were a bunch of drunks, messing around, because he'd seen plenty of partiers at his motel in recent months. He almost ignored all of this, but decided to walk over to remind the person that the pool had closed for the season, even though he'd yet to place a tarp over the water. That's when he noticed the person floating in the water, and blood mixing with the pool water. Oddly, there was a wooden baseball bat floating next to him, as well. A nice Louisville Slugger, barely used, as it looked like to me, when I inspected it.

The manager was still pretty shaken-up by the time I got to speak to him. Seems this man and I have a similar life experience. Some of you who know me, are aware I lost my wife at a stream... over at...

Visual Description:

Extended pause, Mark appears as if he's breaking down emotionally. He regains composure and continues.

Audio Script:

Sorry for getting a little choked up, it's always hard talking about Laurie. But let me get to the point. Have you ever had a great memory overshadowed by some other horrible experience? You just heard me go on and on about how great streams were when I was a kid, but later in life, my wife was murdered at a stream. I'm telling you, it's a real effort to keep the horrors out of my head so I can get in touch with those childhood memories. How on earth can we expect to reach old age without being jaded by the darker moments of our lives? Will this hotel manager ever look at a pool again without imagining a dead body floating in it? I'm telling you, for as much as I love nature, and streams, I still find it hard to go back to where I lost Laurie. I can barely think of my great childhood memories without the anguish coming back to ruin it all. What can we do to protect those shreds of child-like innocence we carry with us through life from being trampled by the ugliness of the world? That's what I want to know. If you have an answer to this question, or just anything else to add, please leave a comment below this video. That's all I've got this time. Peace.

Visual Description:

END VIDEO: Fade to black

Mark Powers was an attractive, middle-aged man of 54, with the dirty blonde hair and crystalline blue eyes. He also had a cleft chin that gave him a rugged look, but that was only when he was clean shaven. He sometimes grew a beard, then got bored and shaved it off. Presently he had quite a growth going, but it had gotten to that itchy phase and he was considering a shave in his near future. He was of normal height, but had broad shoulders and muscular legs, a trophy from years of hiking all over the United States and Canada before joining the park service in Tennessee. While mostly clean-cut in appearance, he did sport two tattoos, one on each forearm. Each was a 6 digit number, the meaning of which he kept to himself. He was a gentle man, but the tats gave him a bit of a rough look.

A Northern Kentucky boy with a love of the Cincinnati Reds, Mark's happiest days of his youth were spent in Gatlinburg, Tennessee. The Smoky Mountains were very impressive to him, so much so that he would later choose to spend the rest of his life there.

The Great Smoky Mountains National Park, half of which is located in Tennessee, the other half in North Carolina, transfixed him in awe as a kid. His family spent all of their time on the Tennessee side, simply because that was closest to home, and because that's where Gatlinburg was located.

Tennessee seemed like another country to Mark. It had, in fact, been a part of a foreign country (The Confederate States of America during the Civil War). People talked differently there, the landscape was far more vertical than Erlanger, Kentucky, and he was hard pressed to see anyone playing a banjo or mandolin at home. Erlanger felt more like a southern suburb of Cincinnati than it did southern. Comparatively, the young Mark Powers found Tennessee to be truly representative of southern culture.

His parents had been hard-working people. His mom, Bernice, had forever tried to get rid of that pile of laundry on their basement floor, or applied Bactine on scraped knees. She spent a lot of time cleaning, cooking, and keeping Mark and his four siblings out of trouble. Mark, more so than the others, was a rebel who needed taming. For that reason, it was quite a surprise that he was the one to take after his father by pursuing a law enforcement career.

Bill Powers was a no-nonsense police officer, who worked long hours to provide for his family. The family was firmly positioned in the middle class, never left wanting for what they needed, but seldom getting what they merely wanted. They had never vacationed at a fancy inn in the Hamptons, or a resort in the Caribbean, but they were able to trek to the Smoky Mountains every year.

For young Mark, it felt as if the annual vacations would never end. They were a given, like knowing school would start every August, or knowing Santa would not forget his annual pilgrimage to his family's rooftop. They witnessed their father worrying about the financing of each trip, but Papa Powers always made it happen. Their mother did her part by cutting costs during the trips, telling them *no* when they asked for a useless souvenir or an adult-sized entree at a restaurant. They felt their economic reality every day of their childhood, but that never diminished their happiness. They always knew somehow, some way, they would get to the Smokies each summer.

They were not a hotel family, generally, because they had the big canvas tent (that forever smelled like mold), which kept them mostly dry for over a decade and a half of camping. This afforded them a great number of adventures they would never have had in a motel. One example was the time a bear visited their campsite while they were away. The large mammal literally shredded their Coleman cooler to feast on butter, eggs, and milk. They returned to find their camping neighbors in a fluster over the incident and discovered food related trash scattered a long way up a trail, into the woods.

After wrapping up his duties at the crime scene, Mark returned home, He was feeling drained of energy for having spent so many hours driving to and from the south end of the park, with a good 16 hours in the middle. He undressed and took a long, hot shower before going to bed. Once horizontal, it took less than a minute for sleep to find him. In time he was carried into a vivid dream where he was hiking along a powdery dirt trail atop a mountain ridge, well worn, with roots exposed.

It was mid-day with the sun directly overhead, sheltered by a canopy of green and a wispy cloud cover. It was an idyllic cool hike at about 70 degrees. He looked behind him, and saw his wife walking with his parents. Still further back were his siblings. They were not interested in the hike, and let him be the trailblazer.

As his dream continued, he surveyed the mountains around him. He spied a few jagged cliffs, where he knew others had died while repelling or climbing. He also spied beautiful meadows filled with wildflowers, and a distant waterfall which glistened in the shards of sunlight slicing through the clouds. There were snakes and rabbits, falcons and sparrows, ticks and ladybugs. He could actually feel the blend of danger and peacefulness everywhere he looked.

He turned once more, to ask Laurie to walk beside him, and she was gone, as were his parents. Far behind him he saw his brothers and sisters, walking off trail, seeking different destinations. Suddenly he was alone. He turned once more and noticed the trail branched into two separate paths. He had no map, and no knowledge of which branch he should follow. He did, however, have a sense that one of those trails would lead to destruction, and the other would lead to safety.

Wild pigs could be heard somewhere behind him, audibly making themselves known with their snorts while turning up insects and grubs in the soil. He knew well that they are not mild critters (called 'Rooshins' by generations of locals because of the Russian boars that were bred with local swine). They were armed with dangerously sharp tusks and he was concerned that he had no weapon with which to protect himself. It was time to move forward. Mark wanted to blaze his own path, off trail, but could not make his legs move accordingly. He was hopelessly stuck, until he woke up. He thanked God for a full bladder, nagging at him to urinate, which saved him from his own dream.

Chapter 2

Central Tennessee, several months earlier, late spring.

Mark was stationed at the Little River District Headquarters, located behind the Sugarlands Visitor Center. It looked like a typical suburban house, complete with office space above a one-car garage. He'd not been there much recently, as he had been working on a few cases of illegal lumber theft near Cosby. Locals were entering the park, cutting down live trees, and transporting them outside of the park to sell as firewood. This always amazed Mark as there was plenty of timber outside the park they could easily cut down without breaking the laws of the federal government. These laws came with stiff sentences, yet thieves would do it merely for beer money. He knew it was because some people just loved to get something for nothing, and had no respect for authority. To them, the law was dispensable if it stood in the way of them making an easy buck or two.

These cases required Mark to install motion sensor cameras in hopes of getting visual identifications of the culprits and their vehicles. If they were stupid enough to go back repeatedly, as they often were, rangers would succeed in putting an end to the theft. This use of technology was something Mark had introduced into the law enforcement playbook years earlier, as was his enthusiastic adoption of the Global Positioning System (GPS).

It was his first day back at Little River in more than a week and he was happy to have a paperwork day, as well as a short meeting about Echo Ridge. Mark found a shared desk and computer to do his work. The facilities were small, and the infrastructure was aging. While he waited for the system boot up, he was joined by two female rangers, Talia Manaia and Belle Whittle, who were arriving for the meeting.

"Well, look who's back. We've missed you around here, Powers," said Talia Manaia, with flirtatious overtones. She arrived with a thermos filled with coffee, and a desire to stir up trouble in the Echo Ridge meeting. She was not a fan of the development.

"Why thank you, good to see you too," Mark said. "But I won't be here for long. I've got to get a few more cameras to catch those lumber jerks out at Cosby."

"At least you have lumber jerks. We have hippies," said Belle, who had grabbed an open desk and was logging in to get her email using the shared computer she found there. "Talia and I found a small pot field in a bald up on your mountain."

Mark felt his stomach drop. He would insist he be involved. His position as a special agent was viewed by many to be like a detective, although he also tended to routine cases like wood theft, public intoxication, speeding, and the like. In this case, he had a personal investment in catching the pot growers.

"My mountain?" he asked, for clarification.

"You know, where you're going to be spending most of your time over the next two years," said Belle.

'Oh, THAT mountain, Thunderhead. But you said pot? What was that all about?"

"Yes," said Talia. "California Sensimilla, maybe about 2,000 plants, about two weeks shy of harvesting."

"Anyone apprehended?"

"Nope," said Belle, now giving Mark something of a ping-pong effect as he talked with both women to his left and right.

"It was just tucked into a little bald up on the Tennessee side," added Belle. "Pretty far off trail. Got a tip from some AT through-hikers who had a permit for backcountry. I was going to Thunderhead Mountain to check on a few things for the groundbreaking when we heard the call come in. We were closest, so we responded."

"You called them hippies," said Mark. "I get it, but never forget these pot growers can be violent thugs. They'll do anything to protect their crops." He was doing his best to keep a cap on his emotions. He wanted to say more, but he preferred what happened after his first big pot bust stay in the past.

"I calculate the going street price for this bust is just shy of a million," said Talia.

"The DEA's doing the seizure?" asked Mark.

"As we speak," replied Belle.

"I got a few hundred photos of the crops, tire tracks, boot impressions, the works," said Talia. "I sent them to both of you, so Belle, use what you want for the news media. Hopefully they'll cover it. It would be nice to see some park news other than the stupid lodge."

Talia was a vivacious and attractive brunette of Samoan origin, with a muscular build. She had her master's degree in

Botany and worked in the Biological Resource Division, with her main responsibility in Landscape Restoration and Adaptation. She had played a key role in gathering data for an environmental impact study for Echo Ridge, and she was vehemently opposed to the lodge's development. She was 29 years old, which was about 25 years younger than Mark Powers. She didn't seem to care about the difference in their ages. She had no reservations about flirting with Mark, or any other man, at any time. She once joked that when the HR department gave the sexual harassment class, she was not required to go because she had already proven her proficiency in that area.

Belle Whittle was the Executive Assistant of Public Affairs, and as such, was responsible for coordinating the groundbreaking ceremony for Echo Ridge. She also handled all communications with the public, including the media. Unfortunately, this meant Belle handled all the press inquiries and the onslaught of social media hate-posts from environmentalists who were opposed to the Echo Ridge development. Representing the park service in the Twittersphere was a new twist to her job that she longed to delegate to someone else.

Belle was focused on remaining professional in the workplace rather than making comments to Mark about how 'hot' her cup of coffee might be — such a remark would be more Talia's style. Belle had spent years in law enforcement before moving to the PR division. With her experience, Belle was quite handy with a gun and was quite familiar with other law enforcement rangers like Mark Powers.

Their meeting was not set to start for another 15 minutes, so Talia decided to continue socializing with Mark, although now in a more direct, one-on-one manner. She took a seat on a blank portion of Mark's desk, next to his computer monitor and keyboard, as if suggesting she was setting up for a long conversation. This up-close-and-personal posture had increased in frequency over the past few weeks. Mark was reluctant to tell her he was not interested in a personal relationship, again, as she had been told this already, and many times.

Mark's computer had finally booted up, and he began to log in, thinking that might indicate to Talia that it was time to get some work done. It did not work out that way. After logging in, he glanced over and noticed she was holding her phone at an odd angle, up in the air.

"Selfie vid, Marky Mark!" she said, now pulling the phone back in front of her face to watch the video she'd just taken. He hated it when she used that teen-aged voice, and equally despised being called Marky Mark. "You're too old to be a part of the selfie generation, Talia," he told her, with no impact.

"Nothing wrong with being young at heart! Don't be such a grouch, Mark. Live a little."

He had heard such comments before, and he knew she had a valid point. Before he could counter an objection, Talia once more changed the subject.

"So Mark, how's the Echo Ridge debacle going, anyway?" crossing her legs at her ankles and cupping her hands between her knees. The intention of her posture was to let him know she was hoping for a long and engaging conversation.

"The Echo Ridge project is going just fine and is not a debacle," replied Mark, slightly annoyed at her politics creeping into the conversations. He also thought it was funny she asked him this question, since the details of Echo Ridge were more of Belle's responsibility.

"Are you going to share with us when the groundbreaking ceremony is going to take place?" asked Talia.

"That's being kept a secret," replied Mark.

"What's up with that? I'm on the team. If you want me to be there, I've got to put that on my calendar. A girl needs to know a date so she can make herself presentable, you know."

"That's not my call. Belle, what do you have to say about that?

"I will let everyone know when they need to know," said Belle. "For now we don't want protestors to show up, so we are keeping it hush-hush."

"Gotcha," said Talia." They do have a right to protest, you know."

"Never said they didn't," replied Belle.

Sensing she was ruffling some feathers, Talia turned back to Mark for more casual conversation.

"So, Marky Mark and the Funky Bunch... I saw one of your YouTube videos the other day. Pretty interesting. So how many people check out your videos anyway?"

"Enough," replied Mark.

"What's that supposed to mean?" she asked.

"I don't want to come off as bragging. I do it as a creative outlet, and to give people some insight about what life is like as a forest ranger. I don't do it just to be able to say how many views I'm getting."

"Okay, fine. So what, you have a maybe a thousand subscribers?"

"I can tell you it's a lot more than that."

"Really? How many?"

"The last time I looked at my metrics, I had about 12,000 subscribers, but my views have gone over 100,000 for some of my better posts."

"Wait," said Talia in a moment of disbelief, "are you saying the same number of people that can fit in Neyland Stadium have watched one of your videos?"

"Yes, and they are from all over the world," successfully hiding a prideful smile for such impressive statistics.

"Damn, you're like hot shit, aren't you? Well... at least maybe just... hot." The latter comment was delivered in a hushed tone so only Mark could hear.

"Hey, both of you," said Mark, ignoring the whisper, "we need to get to the meeting room in just a few minutes, but before we go, when the two of you were out there taking the photos of the pot field, were you alone?"

"No," said Belle, "we were with each other."

"Right, but neither of you are law enforcement. Did either of you take a GPS beacon with you?"

"Noooo, I did not have a beacon," said Belle, "not on my belt, but I did have GPS on my phone and in my cruiser."

"Not a good answer. Your phone can't be trusted out there and you know it. One cold night and your battery will be dead as a doornail. I don't want to be a jerk about it, but the handbook says when handling dangerous situations in remote locations, you need to take a beacon."

"Guilty as charged," said Talia, in a tone that dismissed the importance of Mark's message.

"It's not just all creeping purple phlox and baby deer out there in the woods," continued Mark. "Remember Curtis Jones? He lost his leg from explosives when he triggered a trap those so-called hippie's left to protect their crops."

"Got it, Mark. No need to get all preachy," said Belle, wishing his lecture would end. She really liked Mark, but knew he could come off as 'fatherly' when it came to following procedures.

"Marky Mark," said Talia, "just for the record, I think your private developers who want to build a lodge in the middle of our wilderness are more dangerous to humanity than pot growers."

"Seriously? Go talk to Curtis about that," replied Mark. "Look, you have to stop bringing your politics into your job, Talia. I think it's great that you're concerned about conservation, that's why we are all here. But our own organization sanctions Echo Ridge, so we just do our job and move on. Right?"

"Dr. Martin Luther King once said 'our lives begin to end the day we become silent about things that matter.'" said Talia.

"Yup. He was a wise and great man," replied Mark. "But my voice rings loud and clear in the voting booth where nobody else has to be annoyed at hearing me." This was a subtle jab at Talia, as Mark knew she was on the side of the protesters, and knew she financially supported their cause.

"Different strokes, I guess. Sometimes a vote is not enough. Dr. King used civil disobedience to achieve change. You say he's a wise man, well then, get on board and try a little civil disobedience sometime."

"I don't have time to march in the streets. I'm too busy doing my job," replied Mark, now very much annoyed by the political discussion.

"Okay, you two, simmer down," said Belle. "Politics in the office is never a good idea."

"Agreed," replied Mark.

"I don't know about that," said Talia. "I kind of like it when a man gets all passionate about something," said Talia, with a flirtatious smile.

"C'mon you two, it's time for the meeting," said Belle, logging off of her computer and rising from her desk.

Later that afternoon, Mark had positioned additional motion sensor cameras near Cosby. He had a few remaining, so the next day he hiked to the location where the pot field had been located, and placed the devices in nearby trees. He had not yet been assigned to this case, but knew it was easier to gain forgiveness than approval, and believed timing was of the essence to get footage of the pot growers on their first return to their garden. And most importantly, he needed to know if the people in charge of this crop might be the same people who had all but destroyed his life ten years earlier.

His excursion to the hillside of Thunderhead Mountain was filled with solitude, and he enjoyed this aspect of his job. Nothing filled him up like the sound of a strong wind blowing through the forest, or varied bird calls echoing through a wooded glade. But the precious calm he felt on this day would not last. There was no way of knowing it, but both of the women he'd met with earlier in the day would be shot by a sniper on this very mountain in a matter of days.

Chapter 3

It was a cold spring day that found a group of political leaders gathered in southern Gatlinburg. The past few days had been unseasonably warm and many of those in attendance had forgone a heavier jacket in favor of their suit coat or light jacket. They found themselves wishing for their heavier coats and were finally relieved of their shivering once they were met with the warm interior of the Bearskin Lodge.

One important attendee, an older man in a forest green suit, slipped through the back door and was led by a receptionist to a private room where the luncheon would commence promptly at 12:30 pm. It was an unconventional place for such a meeting, by not taking place in a government building. Instead, the committee thought it would be nice to finalize their plans just a block or so away from the entrance to the Great Smoky Mountain National Park.

There was an air of security about this meeting to which the older man was not quite accustomed, with Tennessee State Troopers in the parking lot and inside the small reception room. This was mainly due to the presence of Tennessee Governor, Janet Goodwyn. She was in her early 40's, with a sharp gaze and a frame most would consider mildly obese. Her smart business attire hid the weight well, and communicated to all onlookers that she was serious about her job. Goodwyn was raised in nearby Cocke county and fully supportive of any effort that would bring jobs to the region. She was eager to get this project underway and had brought a small contingent of handlers with her for support and show.

The topic of the meeting was to make final preparations for the groundbreaking ceremony, to discuss funding issues, and other logistics. Anyone who had a role to play in the project was in the room, several whom would soon put their signature on paper to seal the deal. Belle Whittle would be there too, although she would arrive late and leave early due to other commitments. Mark would endure the full meeting.

Janet Goodwyn had arrived first, and when she saw the man in the forest green suit coming toward her, she reached out to shake his hand.

"You must be Craig Banister," she said with a smile, "I'm pleased to finally meet you."

"Yes, that's me, and ma'am, the pleasure is all mine. Congratulations on your victory last fall."

"Why Thank You. I've had a while to settle in, and I'm still thrilled. It's my pleasure, and honor to serve the people of the volunteer state."

"I understand completely," said Banister, "I love serving in Tennessee, too. It's such a beautiful part of our country. I have a history of managing parks out west, but my-oh-my, the GSMNP is my favorite. It is so lush and green here. I almost feel as though I should not have worn this suit... I feel camouflaged!"

His comment was greeted with a chuckle from the governor, as well as from others gathered nearby, listening in on their conversation. Banister was a personable older fellow. He was in great physical condition and chopped wood to stay in shape. Despite this, he had a weathered facial appearance that made his age difficult to surmise.

As the superintendent, Banister held an impressive position of power. He was the top dog within the Smoky Mountains National Park. You'd never know it based on his pleasant demeanor. He simply did not come across like an authority figure. He looked more like the retired guy who lived next door and took care of his yard all day long.

"How does one aspire to become a superintendent of a large national park anyway?" asked the governor.

"That's a good question. Most people assume it's because of my infinite knowledge of the natural sciences," joked Banister. "And while I do know a thing or two about some of that, I can't ignore the importance of networking. It's all about greasing the right palms," he said, modestly.

"Yes, it helped to have the president fly down for a rally just days before my election. I owe him a great debt of gratitude."

"That's what I'm talking about. Speaking of the president, those protesters outside are the same ones who are calling for his impeachment, and now they are after me, too, all because of this resort! I suppose that makes us strange bedfellows, he and I."

"Ah, yes. Well, everyone has a voice, Mr. Banister, and I keep reminding myself of our nation's great history of free speech. But just because your voice is loud and abusive does not mean you will get your way. I don't subscribe to greasing the squeaky wheel. Protest culture churns my stomach. My base won the majority vote, and they want

Echo Ridge, so that's what I'm going to give them, protesters or no protesters. And besides, the project plan is set and the contractors are all in place to begin construction, so it's too late to be protesting at this point anyway."

"Well, Governor, there are some final details we need to agree upon today before we give our autographs on the bottom line. Did you get my revisions to the documents?"

Janet's face grew flush. She had not seen the edits, and was angered by the lack of professionalism by her personal assistant, Isabella Lopez. In reality, it was the governor's fault that she had mishandled Lopez's email, but she blamed the assistant anyway. "I'm sorry, my assistant has been overworked lately, and neglected to share those changes with me. She's just back at the hotel, I can call her..."

"No need to worry," interrupted Banister, "I have extra hard copies, and we can review once the meeting starts. The edits are but a few in number. Let's sit down and have our lunch first, before we talk business, shall we?" Goodwyn agreed, but was worried to think Banister could possibly delay the start of construction. Such a move would lead to cost overruns which could easily devastate the project's budget.

On the far side of the room sat Mark Powers. Technically, Banister was his boss, his big boss, sitting at the top of the ladder of command. While they'd spoken many times on the phone, Mark had never met the elder statesman. While Belle Whittle would be the local liaison for the development of Echo Ridge, Mark had been tasked to regularly monitor construction to look for any violations to park rules, and be in constant communication with Banister once construction was underway. Mark walked over to Banister, and exchanged greetings. Their banter was brief, commenting on the chilly weather, before Mark returned to his seat.

Mark was in a slight minority amongst park rangers, with most of them vehemently opposed to the new development.

Mark had more of a centrist approach. On one hand, he believed in doing his job, and if he was instructed to participate in the project, he would do so. On the other hand, he knew mankind had a rather abysmal track record of maintaining a man/nature balance. His knowledge of major man-made disasters was long: the Bhopal gas leak, the North Pacific garbage patch, the BP Gulf Coast oil spill, the Exxon Valdez oil spill, the Chernobyl nuclear meltdown, and other catastrophic failures of man at the expense of nature. He also witnessed this phenomenon on a micro level in the visitors who left trash lying about the park on a daily basis. In the end, he decided to support Echo Ridge, but he would take a *trust but verify* approach where he'd be the first one to blow the whistle if there were shortcuts or mistakes that would be bad for the environment.

There were many different backgrounds among the park ranger rank and file. Many rangers were naturalists. Mark came from a law enforcement background. Still others specialized in search and rescue, fire prevention, public relations, administration, or other backgrounds. Together they functioned as a team to protect the country's federal park lands, its wildlife, and their visitors. They all had a place within the park service. But when it came to any kind of new development within the park, even the development of new roads, the naturalists' voices were usually the loudest. It was almost sacrosanct to consider developing any square inch of the Great Smoky Mountain National Park, and many rangers were less likely to side with Mark Powers.

Mark knew it was possible to succeed with Echo Ridge, and there was historical proof that man could have a presence in the mountain tops without being destructive. This came in the form of a famous lodge that stood atop LeConte Mountain, situated halfway between Gatlinburg and the North Carolina line. It was this lodge that had sparked the controversy surrounding the Echo Ridge Resort, which would be built on the side of Thunderhead Mountain.

Mark had visited LeConte once while he was in college. The lodge was, and is, legendary because of its remote location, with two primary modes of transportation readily available for reaching the place: the human foot, or by llama. It is a hearty breed of visitor that's drawn to the lodge, as the shortest of several trails is 5.5 miles long, and it is also remarkably steep. It is so remote that supplies need to be delivered via llama, on the famous Llama Trail.

The lodge is not really one building, as the name might suggest. It is a collection of cabins and one main dining hall, all of which sit upon the upper reaches of the mountain. The resort had been built in the 1920's, and began a long history of being managed by the park service. It has long been loved and revered as one of the great excursions for nature lovers in the park. Mark was quick to point out there were never any protests about that older lodge when it was being built. Time had proven that the lodge posed no significant threat to nature, and Mark saw no reason to believe Echo Ridge would either. This was assuming the job was done right. It would be his job to keep mankind from doing anything stupid, and he took that responsibility seriously.

LeConte had been well cared for over the years, and time had provided the wooden exterior of the buildings an invitingly rustic appearance. Still, there was talk of what may become of the place over the next century. Some feared the resort would eventually succumb to the ravages of time, others argued it could be maintained in perpetuity. Regardless, enterprising minds came up with an idea to build a new resort which would continue this tradition of LeConte in case LeConte ever ceased to be. This new resort was to be called the Echo Ridge Resort.

Somewhere along the line it was decided this new resort would not only provide free showers and cheap restaurant fare for hikers on the Appalachian Trail, but also cater to significantly higher net-worth clientele. Echo Ridge plans included spacious and luxurious guest cabins, a four-star restaurant, a spa, a mirror pool, and a long list of expensive amenities. There would even be helicopter ferrying services for the upper-elite who were incapable of hiking, or who perceived the physicality of the hike to be unattractive. The belief was that Echo Ridge would generate an attractive revenue – in the long run – rather than drain the park budget. This income would help fund other conservation efforts throughout the park for decades to come. On these grounds, even staunch environmentalists could be swayed in favor of the development.

One snafu in this plan was construction. There was simply no way to use modern earth-moving equipment in that location, and thus it would be built by hand, the old fashioned way, with shovel, hammer and saw.

Mark had seen the environmental impact studies, which included partial data from his co-worker, Talia Manaia. He was surprised at the measures being taken to make the lodge a *green* structure. Roofing would consist extensively of solar panels, with additional wind turbines positioned along the ridge. There would be waterless toilets, localized composting, and dozens of other measures intended to minimize man's negative impact on the mountain. There would also be a new observation tower constructed and used for fire prevention and environmental studies.

Environmental action groups perceived all of these plans as concessions, designed to keep them quiet. After all, how could they possibly be opposed to a new climate change research station? But that did not change the fact there would soon be a man-made structure on the mountain where once there was none. And the fact that the lodge would partially cater to the rich did not help assuage the ire of protesters who were apparently infused with class-warfare dogma.

Perhaps the most vocal in their opposition to this development was a new and extreme group called EarthForce1 (EF1). Not widely known, the group consisted of faculty and students from several southern universities, intent on protecting the forests and wetlands of the southern United States – at all costs. They claimed Echo Ridge was just the first of many new developments to follow, and claimed they had inside knowledge of condominium developers who were bidding for rights to add housing near the proposed Echo Ridge facility. The government denied such rumors vociferously, as that would require clearing the land of trees which was a long standing violation of laws established for the park. EarthForce1 did not wish to see Thunderhead Mountain turned into a ski resort community and were ramping up their new, and powerful, protest machine.

While Mark waited for the meeting to commence, he thought about the protesters he'd seen outside of the Bearskin Lodge. He could also hear them, slightly, from his position near a window inside the hotel. He thought about the report he was asked to create. Mark had been asked by the head of law enforcement to produce a fact-finding report about EarthForce1. This would become the single-source document within the organization detailing what was known about the Eco activists. They had staged smaller protests in the months prior to Echo Ridge being finalized, and many of the EarthForce1 protesters had nearly taken over several campgrounds in the park, turning them into environmentalist pep rallies, of sorts. Law enforcement thus tasked Mark to find out all he could about who they were, how they were organized, funded, etc. It was a daunting task as the group took great measures to keep their leadership invisible.

During the meeting, it was confirmed Belle's team, including Mark, would serve as guides and security for the groundbreaking ceremony. That is when his involvement in the Echo Ridge project would escalate, meaning longer hours on top of his already hectic schedule.

Mark thought about the logistics of the groundbreaking ceremony, and found them nearly laughable. He could hardly wait to see Governor Janet Goodwyn – slightly chunky in build – wearing her fashionable duck boots as she labored uphill for five-plus miles to the Echo Ridge site on the northern side of Thunderhead Mountain. He had warned the group it would be strenuous, but they insisted it would make for a better public relations statement if they trekked to the exact spot where Echo Ridge would soon exist. Mark considered ordering helicopters to ferry folks up to the site, but would have a hard time justifying the expense. Little did he know Belle had other plans.

Throughout the meeting, Governor Goodwyn pressed hard to put ink on paper to cement the deal but Superintendent Craig Banister pressed for extended oversight from the Environmental Protection Agency. From this point forward, Goodwyn and Banister were not on such friendly terms, as they had been, when they first met earlier that day.

Finally, all parties on the committee signed the authorizations, contingent upon securing additional EPA oversight. The governor had yielded to Banister's demands, but still considered the meeting a success since the project would begin on time. She took a sigh of relief that the intense political battle was over. Others, like Mark, sighed in relief simply because the meeting had ended.

One detail the press had not been privy to during the meeting was the specific date, time and location for the groundbreaking ceremony. When asked, they were told the details were still being worked out. Once the meeting was adjourned, key players gathered in another room to agree on those details and all present were warned not to speak in public about them. All were reminded it was imperative they keep things quiet, for their own safety, and the success of the project.

On the streets in front of the hotel the protestors shifted into high gear anytime a new media outlet arrived to cover their actions. Some shouted rhymes about Echo Ridge being the next step toward climate change annihilation. Others protested on the grounds that the resort would scar the beautiful view of Thunderhead Mountain, visible from the Cades Cove area. They opposed the presence of *any* man-made structure built on one of the most majestic mountains in all of the Great Smoky Mountains, despite assurances that most of the development would be obscured by the tree line when viewed from the valley. Still others were protesting the disruption of black bear habitat. Not only would the presence of humans be disruptive, but frequent helicopter traffic would drive wildlife from the mountain and impact untold ecosystems. Indeed, it was well known by naturalists that balds in the Smokies were ecologically peculiar for their flora and fauna, and losing even one of the balds was a significant loss.

Signs carried by the protesters were both serious and hyperbolic. "Kill the Rich," "Eco not Echo," "Bear Lives Matter" and other sentiments were displayed for local media to offer viewers on the evening news. This instance of civil disobedience annoyed many local business owners, visitors, and police, and carried on long after the meeting within the hotel had ended. The protesters cared not one bit, knowing they had to take a stand to protect the forest from development.

After the meeting, the dignitaries returned to their vehicles across the street, with police officers assisting them so they would not be accosted by protestors. There they found black spray paint had been applied liberally to their vehicles, across painted surfaces and glass. "BEAR KILLERS," "NATURE NAZIS" and "CAPITALIST PIGS" adorned the cars there, including

Banister's BMW. The car's headlamps and windshield had been smashed out but he remained unemotional.

"What the hell?" asked Mark, of the Sevierville police sergeant who had been inside during the meeting. "I thought you had uniforms out here in the lot?"

"We did. But that was the longest damned meeting, and at one point they came in for coffee."

"You've got to be kidding me. What about the State Troopers? Weren't they watching the lot too?"

"Nope, they explained when they got here that they were explicitly to provide security for the governor, meaning, if she was inside, they were inside. I'm sure the chief will be hearing about this any time now."

"Yup. Get ready to lose some weight, 'cuz he's gonna chew you a new asshole."

Unknown by many park visitors, a trail leaves the southern edge of downtown Gatlinburg and leads to the Sugarlands Visitor Center. This is known as the Gatlinburg Trail. It is the first trail hikers can take when leaving Gatlinburg city limits, and entering the protected lands of the Great Smoky Mountains National Park. Being mostly flat, and just under 2 miles, it's a pleasant and fast hike.

An unkempt man in his late 30's stood silently near the start of the Gatlinburg Trail with his bird-watching binoculars, inspecting the fruits of his team's labor. No doubt it was his comrade who had coordinated local teenagers to perform their spray painting mischief for a generous price. He was as anti-establishment as one could get, and he laughed out loud at the damage he saw viewing through his binoculars.

The man was wearing old, stinky garb, hiking boots, sunglasses and a trail-worn backpack. He had also grown a substantial beard since the last time he'd encountered Mark Powers. His latest endeavors near the southern part of the park had required a lot of back-country hiking, and his attire reflected his activities. He did not, however, identify himself as a thru-hiker, like the type of people who walked the Appalachian Trail. His reasons for being in the woods were nefarious; he was not there for exercise, entertainment, or bragging rights.

Just before finishing his reconnaissance with his binoculars, he spotted Mark Powers, as well as the governor. Instantly he formulated a risky idea. He withdrew a map and marched toward the parking lot.

The man began alternating his gaze between the map and his surroundings. His act was to give the impression he was lost, while trying to make sense of his map. He hoped in this way he would not be viewed as a protestor. He casually strolled into the throng of politicians who were angered at their vehicles having been spray-painted and awaiting backup transportation. At last, he found himself face to face with Powers and the governor.

He was risking a lot by placing himself face to face with Mark, but with the beard, hat and sunglasses, he knew he could pull it off. He also opted to try a fake accent. Why he was taking this risk, he did not know, except for a need to play games with Powers, as he had been doing so for more than a decade.

"Pardon me, sir" he said, with a well-executed Boston accent. "I've gotten myself lost. Can you point me to the Visitor's Center?"

A Tennessee State Trooper now stepped up as if to usher the hiker away from the governor who was but a few feet from

Powers. She motioned that she did not need security, and wanted to interact with the public.

"I saw you standing over there," said Mark. "That's called the Gatlinburg Trail, and it will lead you to the Visitor Center, but going that-a-way, not coming this-a-way."

"Oh, great," said the man. "Thanks. Looks like I was in the right place after all." He was laying the Boston accent on thickly, hoping to mask his slight Latin American accent as one more measure of keeping Powers from recognizing him.

"So you passed through here once already?" asked Mark.

"Uh, yeah, maybe twenty minutes ago. Had a little lunch across the street about an hour ago."

"Say, did you by any chance happen to see anyone near this parking lot, anyone who might have vandalized these vehicles?"

"Na, sorry. Wasn't paying attention."

"Well, as you can see, we've had a lot of damage to our vehicles. If you should happen to run into someone on the trail who's toting a bag of spent spray-paint cans, please be sure to report that at the visitor's center."

"Oh, most definitely. Looks like that's going to be expensive."

The governor had been listening in. "Are you from Boston?" she asked the hiker.

"You might say that. A couple of hours away from there. Enfield, Connecticut." The man was proud of himself for being so quick with an answer, having heard that town's name in a recent news clip on the web.

"Well welcome to my state," she said, offering a hand to shake. "I'm Janet Goodwyn, the Governor of Tennessee, and we are very proud of these mountains. Have you ever hiked the Appalachian Trail?"

"Yeah, a long time ago, when I was a boy," said the man.

"The whole thing?" asked Mark, impressed.

"Most of it," faked the man, thinking he should have simply denied ever having hiked the AT, as it would have invited fewer questions.

"My relatives live along the trail just northeast of here," replied Janet, "and they are regular providers of trail magic."

"Magicians, how nice!" said the stranger, feeling as if he was beginning to venture into unknown conversational territory.

"What was your trail name?" said Mark.

"My what?" asked the man.

"You know... your trail name? It's a..."

"The, uh, name of the trail was the Appalachian Trail. But it's actually made up of a bunch of smaller trails, too," said the man, doing his best to sound like he knew what he was talking about.

"No, well, uh, never mind, it's a long story," said Mark.

"Well, it's been nice meeting you. I really need to go, I'm supposed to meet someone and I'm already late," said the man, now looking for a way out of the confusing conversation.

"Have a great time in the park!" said the governor.

"I will. Thanks. Nice meeting you two, and good luck finding the little shits who painted the cars!" With that the man was off toward the trail.

While the governor seemed to have missed it, Mark found the conversation very unusual. "That was a little odd, don't you think?" he said after the man was out of earshot.

"Why do you say that?" asked Janet.

"He's never walked the trail, although he said he did. I can tell you that for sure. He's probably just one of those people who likes to brag about hiking the AT but never set foot on it."

"Now how do you know that, Ranger Powers?"

"It's obvious. He had no idea what we were talking about when we mentioned a trail name or trail magic."

"I thought he was joking when he said *magicians*."

"I guess that's possible. But that's not how I read him. If that man walked the Appalachian Trail, well then I'm... Farrah Fawcett."

"Where's the red bathing suit?" joked the governor. This brought a smile to Mark's face, which was nice in the midst of this moment where all the cars had been vandalized.

"Why on earth did you think of Farrah Fawcett?" asked Janet.

"It's a long story. My wife. She looked like Farrah. Really, she did. Just like her."

"She must be a beautiful woman, then."

"She's no longer with us. Gone to meet her Maker. But yeah, she could have been a body double for Farrah in Hollywood, for sure."

"Oh, Ranger Powers, I'm terribly sorry. I didn't know. That's so sad. When did it happen?"

"Just about ten years ago, now."

"You have my condolences," said the governor.

As the conversation ended, Mark glanced toward River Road, and could see a vanishing glimpse of the faux hiker as he made his way to the trailhead. There was something familiar about that man, but Powers could not place it. Had he known the man's true identity, their conversation would have ended quite differently.

The faux hiker caught a glimpse of the protesters nearby as he left the edge of town. He eyed them with disdain. Granted, he was in league with them now, but he did not share their world view. In his home country of Venezuela, if you went to protest the government, you might never return home that night. There, 75% of the people were living below the poverty line, eating rats for sustenance. Here, they protested for trees, and had three square meals a day.

He hiked until he came to where the Gatlinburg Bypass rejoined Route. He approached his rendezvous point by the side of the road, and sent a text to his coordinator, with a mention that he had gotten a very good look at the governor. A smiley face emoji was sent in return.

He was glad he hadn't stopped at the ranger's headquarters since he'd been questioned there many years earlier, before he had been sent to the Sevier County Jail, and later, prison. He turned his gaze to the road and waited for the purple Prius. She was there promptly, but coming from the wrong direction. As she did a U-turn, he noticed the license plate. He had to think about if for a moment, and then it made him laugh. **N8TR1ST**. It was so predictable.

Together they departed, driving toward town. They discussed next steps. With the kind of money he was going to make working with her group, he was planning a very expensive dinner, and asked if she cared to join him. She turned him down, as she was somewhat involved with another one of the team leaders. Soon he was dropped off at his motel and his contact returned to work. Their plans had been executed to perfection, and an expensive steak house was his next target. It was a nice way to prepare for the day when he would kill the governor.

Chapter 4

When President Calvin Coolidge moved to establish the Great Smoky Mountain National Forest, there was one small problem with the plan. The land was still occupied. Families were scattered all across the 300,000 acres (which eventually grew to 522,000 acres), and negotiations were initiated to buy the land from these folks who, for the most part, knew no other way of life than living off the land. Some were happy to cash in on their property, and seized the opportunity to start a more prosperous life somewhere else. Some relocated with great reluctance. And some chose not to go at all, and concessions were made to allow them to remain in the park until the land owners passed away.

For those who stayed, they found their way of life would not remain the same, despite their victory over forced relocation. There were new rules created by the Department of the Interior which many found difficult to observe, if not downright impossible. No longer was it permissible to hunt or trap. The maple trees that once provided fresh syrup in the Sugarlands, could no longer be tapped. Property owners were not allowed to use their firearms to protect their livestock from wild animals. Nor could they cut trees for firewood. For many who remained, these rules simply could not be respected, and their remaining days were spent fighting with the government to reinstate their personal freedoms.

The felling of trees was one of the rules that would be cited as reason enough to prohibit the creation of Echo Lodge. Opponents argued the scope of the development would certainly require trees to be cut down, but the developers argued otherwise. There was a large meadow (bald) upon the proposed site, on the side of Thunderhead Mountain. The blueprints suggested the full lodge would fit within that tight area and would include a 20 person shelter for thru-hikers, and deluxe accommodations for elite visitors. Proponents also remarked the park service had planted hundreds of thousands of saplings over the years for the ongoing preservation of the park. Even if a few trees needed to be removed during construction, the net result of man's presence within the park was exceptionally positive.

Governor Goodwyn had requested that her personal assistant have an adjoining room to her own at the historic Gatlinburg Inn, near the center of town. She wanted the young woman to work with her throughout the day and evening, and the shared door would make things easier. This would have been an ideal arrangement had Janet's husband, Shane Goodwyn, not decided at the last minute to come along for the trip. While his presence was not so disruptive as to require they change their reservations, it did mean Janet and Shane would need to be conscious of the adjoining door between the two rooms if they were to enjoy each other's company without the assistant's eavesdropping.

How it was that a hardcore environmentalist, feminist, leftist college student came to be the personal assistant of a republican governor was an anomaly of American politics.

The truth was, Janet had barely looked at Isabella's rcsume, which masked the depths of Isabella's social justice affiliations. Had Janet been more stringent, she might have realized Isabella was not suited to work for a Republican. But then, there was that one, solitary recommendation in favor of Isabella that came from Janet's largest campaign contributor. Isabella had slept with him while in college, and he was more than happy to repay those good times by recommending Janet hire Isabella. This all came at a time when Janet's other assistant had quit without notice, and she was in a bind. Janet had blind faith in her chief financial supporter and hired Isabella with little due diligence having taken place.

Chameleon-like, Isabella put on a good face and learned a lot about how Republicans thought, spoke, and acted, incorporating those things into her daily demeanor. She never gave reason for Janet to fire her. Even the speeches Isabella wrote sound as if they'd been penned by Rush Limbaugh. The two connected as professionals, and as women who strove for upward advancement. Or at least that's what Isabella wanted Janet to think. She had learned how to apply her world-view in a subtle dose while conversing with her boss, and in some cases, succeeding in changing Janet's position on certain issues, or at least tempering them. Her ambitions, using her words, were to 'save the environment from capitalists who believed in prosperity over sustainability.' She had to bite her tongue on a number of occasions, wanting nothing more than to engage in full-blown debate with Janet, but she had succeeded in curbing those impulses, and learned a whisper could be more effective than a sledge hammer. Given her long-term plans, this was just the perfect place for her to be.

On this particular day, Isabella Lopez was busy finishing the speech the governor would present to a conference of bankers the day after the groundbreaking ceremony. She cringed as they cobbled Janet's bullet points into coherent sentences. It was all about establishing fiscal policy, implementing quantitative easing, and Keynesian recessionary aggregate demand something or other blah blah. As she stressed over the speech, Isabella heard the Goodwyn couple in the other room. The adjoining door was slightly ajar. It dawned on her the couple were not aware of this, yet her curiosity was too great to get up from her desk and close the door herself. If it came to a point where they began fooling around, Isabella would close the door, but until then, she was content to listen in. She was always alert to learn something new, something that might benefit her and her social justice friends.

"I'm beginning to enjoy these little road trips," said Shane as he wrapped his massive arms around his wife. They stood on a balcony facing the famous Gatlinburg SkyLift, mechanically transporting tourists up a mountain on the west side of town. "I sure as hell don't want to be called a house-husband, and that sure as hell doesn't apply when we're not home!"

"House husband? Please!" replied Janet, staring up at him. "You wouldn't know how to keep a house if your life depended upon it."

"Well of course not. I'm the man of the house, and you expect me to be cookin' and cleanin', forget about it."

"And apparently you're the sexist of the house, too," she said playfully, knowing his remarks were intended to amuse her.

"Sexist, no. Sexiest, yes," he replied.

She tippy-toed to give him a quick kiss as he bent down to meet her half way. Shane was about the same age as his bride, having met her in college at the University of Tennessee. He was a hulk of a man, standing 6'7" with big arms and broad shoulders. He had been an intimidating figure on the front line of the UT Volunteers football team, and was still as strong as an ox. He was also bald and preferred shaving off any remaining red hair rather than looking like bozo the clown with wrap-around locks. He compensated with a sugar-n-cinnamon goatee: white hair mixed evenly with whiskers of rusty red. Presently, Shane was employed as a spokesperson for the National Rifle Association (NRA), despite his propensity to rub people the wrong way. He was the kind of guy one might enjoy knowing for a brief period of time, but whom would get on one's nerves with repeated exposure.

Shane was a lady's man, but had been tamed, for the most part, by Janet. They truly loved one another, despite his propensity to boast about past conquests and gaze at other women like a deer in the headlights. That did not sit well with Janet. She also struggled with taming his comments when he accompanied her on official business; he simple had no filter and had embarrassed her on many occasions. She'd never thought of how important decorum would be in a mate when they fell in love years earlier.

"Maybe we can get that little Snowflake in the other room to do all the housework, too!" he said. Just as those words left his lips, Shane noticed the adjoining door was opened slightly. He was amused, knowing Isabella must have heard him use the nickname he reserved for her, and which she hated. She had told him many times that the snowflake term was an insult, but he did not care.

Shane was in one of those moods and took this opportunity to have fun at Isabella's expense. He walked over to the door and peered through the thin opening, spying Isabella, sitting at her desk. The young woman was not only pissed off at having heard the insult once again, but now she was disturbed at how he was invading her privacy. He closed the door as he said to his wife, "Better shut this. We don't want the heat from our room to get in there and melt our little Snowflake." He laughed hysterically. "She needs to keep her igloo nice and cool over there!"

"You are terrible!" said Janet, hoping his comments had not been heard by Isabella. "That's what I mean, honey, you can't go around insulting people on the left! You'll give conservatives a bad name if you keep doing that!"

"If the shoe fits!" countered Shane. "Besides, they call us deplorables and worse, what the hell do I care if they get their feelings hurt when I call them snowflakes?"

In the other room, Isabella rolled her eyes, unseen by anyone. She hated the nickname, and wished she could think of a nickname to call him in retaliation. No matter what she came up with, he laughed, producing the wrong result.

Shane rejoined his wife. "So where were we? I think you were telling me what a great chef I am," said Shane, snuggling with his wife after her playful scolding.

"Well, I'll admit, you do a good job in the kitchen, even if you think the only form of protein is venison."

"Now what are you talking about? We've had elk, bison... even wildebeest!"

"You know," added Janet, "when we were in college, you had a game every Saturday. Now we eat game every night!"

"Very funny, you rabbit. You'd be happy with a Cobb salad every night, wouldn't you? Just like a damned rabbit."

"You know that's not true. I like meat, just not... wildebeest."

"Ungrateful. There's nothing quite like wildebeest-kabobs!"

Janet disengaged from her husband and went to sit on the bed. "You need a cookbook. Go slip into one of these gift shops around here and pick up a cookbook and learn how to make something that's not just a slab of meat."

"Baked potatoes. I do baked potatoes!"

"That's a side, not a main course. You need to work on some new entrées."

"Yeah, maybe. But you know I'm a meat and potatoes man."

"How about a good quiche. Or a zesty Alfredo pasta dish?"

"That's chick food."

"And... I'm a chick. When do I get what I want?"

"You get your wine with every meal."

"Ah... so you think as long as I have my Pino you can cook whatever you want, and I'll just eat it without complaining?"

"You're on to me. That's why I give you a big glass a half hour before supper time, to get you a little saucy so you don't care what I'm fixing."

"So *that's* your strategy, is it?"

"Been working for me for a while. I'll skip the cookbook. But you know, this is a cool little town. Out on the east parkway is a great little gun shop I found. The owner has some big guns at a great price. I might just have to pick up a little something for my trip to South Africa next year."

"Oh, well, there goes the budget. Besides, you get so many guns for free, why buy one? And do you really *need* another gun?"

"Stop," he said as he joined her on the bed, only resting back to stare at the ceiling. "This guy's a startup, and a member. Got to treat our members right, you know. A sale or two might make a big difference to him and his family."

"You and your guns. I've got to say, though, I think the NRA vote really helped my campaign."

"Helped? Damn, woman, you've got to be kidding me. You owe me big time. My connections carried your tired ass across the finish line and that's for sure."

"Tired ass?"

"A sexy one, at that, but yes, that was a long, costly, exhausting campaign. And you have to admit, the gun lobby contributions made all the difference there at the end."

"I'm not going to admit that, I'm an independent woman," she said, smiling. "An independent woman who's supporting YOU right now, for the most part, while you play with guns all day."

With that, Shane sprang into action, turning quickly to begin tickling his wife. She shrieked with delight as the two began wrestling, which led to more hijinks on the comforter.

In the other room, Isabella could hear a filtered version of what was transpiring in the other room, thankful that the hotel walls were not as paper-thin as they could have been. She was perplexed. It sounded as if the two were having a great time, yet that was not what she had witnessed during the campaign. In fact, she would have bet money on a divorce, sooner or later. Shane had put his neck on the line by asking the NRA to support her, and they did. Then, during her acceptance speech, she commented on the need to increase government regulation on assault-style weapons. Pressure was brought to bear on the shoulders of the massive ex-footballer, and weeks later, he was temporarily suspended from his position with the NRA. This led to crazy arguments between the two, but apparently, judging from their folly in the other room, all that was behind them now.

In the fallout, Shane blamed Isabella for convincing Janet to shift her position on gun patrol, a near unforgivable sin for the man who received his paychecks from the NRA. He had no intention to back down from his harassment of Isabella, not as long as she was threatening his livelihood and the first amendment.

Chapter 5

**Video Transcript:
Wandering Ranger #24
(YouTube Channel)**

Visual Description:

START VIDEO: Mark, talking to camera using a selfie stick, walking through open field deep in the park, upon a Thunderhead Mountain.

Audio Script:

Hello, all, and welcome to video #24 in my Wandering Ranger video series. Today, let's talk about ticks and drug dealers. Many people who come to the Great Smoky Mountain National Park are well aware of ticks, but you'd be surprised at how many are not. We recommend after spending a few hours out on a hike or after horseback riding, that you check yourself and your family for ticks. And look for them everywhere on your body. They like to find your hairy areas, and the cracks of your body where they think you won't find them. If you don't protect yourself against ticks, and they bite you, you can get Lyme Disease, Rocky Mountain

Spotted Fever, Anaplasmosis, Powassan Virus Disease, and many other illnesses you've never heard of and should be thankful you haven't. Ticks are parasites, living off of other living creatures by taking something that doesn't belong to them... your blood. Nobody likes ticks, although, it should be mentioned they are a natural part of the environment, and so are those diseases I just mentioned, but that doesn't mean you shouldn't protect yourselves against their negative effects. That's right, folks, just because something is natural, does not automatically make it a good thing. Other examples include bear attacks, snake bites, botulism, and death by lightning strike. Yes, they are natural, but I suggest you avoid them.

Visual Description:

Mark turns camera so he's not in view, seeing only open patch of dirt surrounded by trees.

Audio Script:

Now, look over there, and you'll see this small patch of open space up here in the backcountry. We're way up in the mountains, a good ways from any trail, and far from other people or roads. Because this area lacks trees, Some people call these open areas 'balds', bare patches where the sun gets in. Normally we'd expect to see a lot of undergrowth here, such as thickets, brambles and briars. But notice this patch is just a lot of upturned dirt. This is because rangers found a substantial marijuana patch here, enough to make someone a whole lot of money. Those plants have since been removed, and we have a small piece of our forest that has been ecologically damaged, by greed and misuse.

Some of you watching this video might think growing pot is okay, although, at this moment in time, it's still illegal in Tennessee, and it is a federal offense to grow it in the Great Smoky Mountain National Park. These mountains belong to the people of the United

States, whose elected officials have declared it illegal to grow pot here. So if you are an American citizen, these numbskulls are cultivating illegal crops on YOUR land and keeping the money for themselves. In my mind, they are like ticks, or parasites, making their livelihood off of someone else.

Visual Description:

Mark turns camera so it's pointed directly toward his face and torso, with trees in the background.

Audio Script:

Something has happened with how people think about the law these days. Back in the day, it was just common sense to follow the law. It seemed as if criminals were few and far between, as they say. When I was a kid back in the 70's, I caught a glimpse of the coming disregard for the law on one of our camping trips.

As usual, our family was on a trip to Gatlinburg. Back then, they had these T-shirt artists up and down the main strip, using their airbrushing skills to sell souvenirs to people from all over the country. I remember getting a T-shirt one time, and when I put it on, I could smell the paint the artist had used. It was a really cool thing. I was wearing an artistic creation. So anyway, there was this one artist who tried to sell my sister on the idea of having her name airbrushed with a marijuana leaf growing up and around the letters. Man, I thought my dad was going to kill that guy. I was just a kid, and remember thinking to myself, *why would he try to sell a T-shirt with a pot plant on it if that's illegal?* I suppose some people see the law as dispensable when it's in conflict with their own beliefs or desires. But let me remind you, the law is not dispensable, it is mandatory, and those of us law enforcement rangers in the National Park Service believe the law is the glue that holds our society together. I'm not the only one who feels this way. So, if you break the law in our park, you will have to deal with us, and maybe even a judge or jury somewhere down the line.

Now, if you just happen to be one of the parasites who was growing these crops right here, and you have not yet checked on your garden in the past few days, I hate to inform you that you have just experienced a little something I call 'unexpected profit sharing.' That's right, you have now shared *all* of your profits with the Drug Enforcement Agency, who have destroyed each and every plant you had cultivated so carefully. Thanks for sharing, bloodsuckers. Peace.

Visual Description:

END VIDEO: Fade to black

Before placing his phone in his pocket, Mark looked at the time and realized he really needed to get moving if he was to get back to his patrol car before dark. He quickly gathered his gear and realized his movements were triggering the video equipment he'd placed in two trees around the field's perimeter. He waved to one of the cameras, knowing soon he would be the one watching that footage.

He followed his self-marked trail back through the woods to where he would connect with the Bote Mountain trail, which would then connect to the Anthony Creek Trail to carry him back to the Cades Cove parking lot. The trees in this area were rather large and far apart, and there was only moderate undergrowth. Visibility within the forest was good. He felt fairly confident he would not surprise any wildlife along the way. At least not any wildlife that could kill him if suddenly startled.

Then there was smoke. While he could not see it in the limited light of dusk, Mark could smell it. It was the last thing a park ranger wanted to smell out there, away from the places where people normally roamed. He could not just let this go. It was his duty to identify the source given the serious threat posed by forest fires. No longer was he making a B-line back to his car, but he removed his radio from his belt and called it in. Within a few minutes he learned nobody had filed a request to be camping in the backcountry, on this mountain, at this time. That's when he caught a glimmer of light further up the mountainside.

As he approached, he spotted a campfire, still burning, with several short pieces of wood in the center to keep it burning for at least a half-hour. The fire was unattended; no one was in sight. Next to the fire was a backpacker's stainless steel coffee pot, sitting just close enough to the fire to keep its contents warm. He glanced about, looking for more details to help him piece together an explanation. He circled the fire, and on the other side he found a joint, still smoldering, producing the undeniable fragrance of marijuana. There wasn't much left of it, but it was there. He mused if this fire belonged to one of the pot farmers, scared off at the sight of an approaching ranger. That seemed like a good theory for the time being.

While he nearly missed it, he also found black cable, the kind used to recharge electronic devices. It was almost completely invisible in the dim light, betrayed only by the campfire's flicker upon a silvery USB jack on one end of the cable. He picked it up with a bandana in hand so as not to get his own fingerprints on the surface. He had a similar cable at home, which he used to recharge the batteries of a Bluetooth boom box. Carefully he placed it in his pocket.

Lastly, Mark found one more item next to the fire. He found it by stepping on it. Once he felt it under his boots, he squatted to inspect. At first it looked like the kind of chain one would find on a motorized chain saw, but then he noticed it had wooden handles on each end of the chain's length. It was a poor-man's chain saw, used frequently by backpackers for cutting branches off of trees for firewood. This was probably the tool that had been used in the gathering of some of the smaller deadwood that was burning in the campfire. *At least they had the common sense not to cut from a living tree*, he thought. From the looks of things, the individuals who had abandoned the site were regular, seasoned hikers, since novice hikers generally did not possess such tools.

Now walking further from the fire, he removed his flashlight and examined the ground that was partially shrouded in small ferns, ivy and grass. There, in somewhat of a clearing, he found two yellow, plastic tent stakes, with attached pieces of rope. It was thin rope, the kind used for tethering a tent to the ground. It appeared that whoever removed the tent, did so in a hurry or clumsily. The stakes and ropes were gathered, and they joined the electronics cable in Mark's jacket pocket.

The ranger used his boots to topple the stacked wood at the center of the campfire. The stack fell down, sending embers spiraling into the air, glowing brightly, as orange as molten steel before fading to gray. With the logs dispersed, he removed a small canteen from his belt and used the remainder of its contents to douse the fire as best as he could.

Then came the waiting game. He sat down next to a very thick pine tree that stood ten feet from the dying fire. He sat there, motionless, for a long time. This gave the fire a little more time to die down before he extinguished it once and for all. He also wanted to see if, perhaps, whoever had built this fire, might return from gathering more firewood, or after taking a squat in the woods. But he waited in vain, as no one returned.

He formulated a few hypotheses about the camp site. It was quite probable, he thought, that someone had caught sight of him as he was on his way to or from the site of the marijuana patch. If they were scared off by Mark, it would mean he had just missed them. The smoldering joint suggested this was the most likely scenario. He realized they could be watching him right now, from not far away. He smiled at the prospect of them being angered at his willingness to just sit against that tree, waiting as long as it took for someone to return. As he waited, he listened, carefully evaluating every noise so as not to be surprised if someone did, in fact, return.

After well over 45 minutes, it was completely dark. Mark decided to kill the fire once and for all before returning to his vehicle. He did not trust that the water had been sufficient to extinguish the coals. There had been more than one forest fire started by campfires that had been presumed extinguished, only for the glowing coals at the heart of the fire to reignite once the campers had gone. With that in mind, he used his hands to wipe away leaves and twigs from a patch of ground where he was now kneeling. He removed his trusty bowie knife from the sheath on his belt and began stabbing at the earth, repeatedly, until he had enough loose dirt to serve his purpose. After cleaning the knife and returning it to its holster, he cupped his hands and tossed dirt, free of any flammable debris, onto what remained of the fire.

Knowing his work was done, he retrieved his GPS beacon and saved the location's coordinates for future reference. He knew he might want to return again in a couple of days, to look for evidence of someone having returned to this very spot. He took his index finger and traced a perfect circle in the dirt around the fire. If he returned to find the circle had been disturbed by foot traffic, he could feel relatively certain the perpetrator had returned to the site. This would rule out that the site was hastily used by misguided travelers on the Appalachian Trail who would not return to such a spot.

Mark reluctantly turned to leave the site. Not only would this drive him crazy with curiosity, but he was also angered in knowing the camper or campers could have started a forest fire by leaving their campfire burning unattended.

And, to a much lesser extent, they were likely camping without a backcountry permit and had been cutting wood illegally. These were the kinds of people that tested Mark's patience as a ranger. He had just mentioned it earlier while filming one of his videos, that some people had no problem breaking the law when it suited their beliefs or desires.

His anger at this moment was nothing, however, compared to what he'd feel within 24 hours, as he'd contend with multiple murders on this very mountain.

Chapter 6

The morning after Mark Powers' campsite discovery up on Thunderhead Mountain was the day of the groundbreaking ceremony. This meant he was going to spend his time going right back up that same mountain he had visited the night before. Unfortunately, he would not be able to break away from his group to go check on that site to see if his circle in the dirt had been disturbed. Nor would he be able to check on the motion-sensor cameras near the pot site. He would be fully committed to leading the dignitaries and camera crews up the side of the mountain for the groundbreaking ceremony.

The event was to be mostly for show as construction crews would not begin digging for a few more days. Recently, surveyors had been making final preparations, but all that work had finally been completed. The site was now ready for the groundbreaking ceremony, whether Mark was enthused about it or not.

Those traveling up the mountain gathered bright and early at 7 a.m. Right up to the last minute, Mark insisted, to anyone who would listen, that this was a bad idea. The park service had rated the trail as strenuous, and there would be an elevation gain of 527 feet per mile hiked. While he and his team of rangers were in great shape, and could easily handle the steep grade lasting a five-plus miles in one direction, he was not so sure about several of the others. In particular, the governor did not appear to be very athletic, but what she lacked in conditioning, she made up for with enthusiasm, determination, and new hiking attire.

The governor insisted her husband, Shane, attend as well, to serve as her own personal security force, as evidenced by the holster under his left arm. While Shane did regularly work out in a gym, Mark doubted the man's cardio conditioning could have prepared him to move his 290 pound frame up such a steep grade for such a long distance.

Shane walked past Mark, spying the ranger's rifle that was strapped across his back. The glance revealed Shane's mild amusement. He was a true gun snob, and his smirk suggested he thought Mark's weapon was old, in disrepair, and inadequate. Mark was not intimidated, but the look was noted.

Mark was also concerned about Superintendent Banister, who simply looked a bit flushed and unhealthy at 7am. While the man did have a long history of chopping wood for fitness, in the tradition of President Ronald Reagan, his appearance was not very reassuring. He may have been able to chop wood for 15 minutes at a stretch, but did not appear prepared for hiking a total of 11 miles of steep terrain in one day.

Coming along to document the auspicious occasion was a camera crew of three. Then there were two additional dignitaries whom Mark was totally unfamiliar with. One was a man from the EPA, the other a woman from the Sierra Club, both invited at the last minute by Banister. It was assumed this was another move for him to assuage criticism that he was a traitor to environmentalists everywhere. The two additions were both in their 30's and appeared to be in good shape, but sometimes a person's condition is unable to be ascertained just by looking at their exterior. What if they were diabetic? Did they have asthma? Allergies? What about a bad knee? All of this created uncertainty in Mark's mind, but for now these concerns were out of his control. He and his team would do their best to keep the hike uneventful.

Talia looked about anxiously. It was a big day. She glanced about for Banister, finding him, and then moving close to him. There was an affinity between them, and staying with him helped assuage her anxiety.

With the prospect of a long hike ahead of them, everyone was surprised to find horses waiting for them. Belle had heard Mark's reservations about this hike, and decided to bring in horses to assist during the first three miles up the mountain. This put a smile on Mark's face, as this was not the first time Belle had performed amazing feats of brilliance. He was not the only one who was happy, as all but one of the other members of their party were excited to eliminate three miles of foot travel.

Once assembled at the Anthony Creek Trailhead, most of the hikers mounted up for a ride. Belle's team remained on foot, and consisted of herself, Mark Powers, Talia Manaia, and Dan Lawson. They were seasoned rangers, with only Mark and Dan representing law enforcement.

There was one other party member who did not ride: Isabella Lopez. She would not tell anyone why she refused to ride, allowing others to assume Isabella had a fear of horses. Later she mentioned she thought it was barbaric to enslave animals to do the bidding of humans.

The dignitaries brought with them a change of clothes that would be used during the video shoot if they were to have gotten their hiking clothes too dirty or sweaty on the trip up the mountain. This had been Isabella's idea, always keeping her boss's PR considerations in mind, despite forgetting the fact there were no changing rooms on the mountain. Lopez opted to carry the extra attire in her own backpack which she also carried instead of burdening the animals.

The four key dignitaries dressed in cool looking, and high priced, outdoor apparel from expensive outfitters. The governor's apparel appeared never to have been worn before, with Mark giving her notice that she still had a tag dangling from her brand new hiking boots.

"Isn't this an exciting day," said Janet, who was not only happy for the project to officially begin, but because she would not be spending another day in video conferences.

"Let's hope the coolness of the trees brings a little comfort throughout the day," said Banister, "but don't count on it, governor."

"That would be great, but why wouldn't that be the case?" asked Janet.

"It all depends, governor. Sometimes you might feel a nice breeze before heading up, but once you get in there, the trees cut down on airflow, holds onto moisture that raises the humidity, and it feels hotter than when you started. But that's all a moot point, dear governor, since the Anthony Creek trail follows Anthony Creek. It will be like our own private air conditioning unit to keep us comfortable. We'll cross back and forth over that creek numerous times along the way."

"Well, I'm glad to hear that," replied the governor, with a tinge of relief in her voice. "I don't want to have to redo my mascara over and over again before they take the photos."

"Folks," said Mark, speaking loudly enough for the other 13 to hear. "The more moving parts you have in a machine, the more likely something will go wrong. We have 14 of us here, plus nine horses, so that's 23 possible living things that can experience problems. I just encourage you all to be focused on this hike, especially once you are on foot. We don't want to have someone get a sprained ankle along the way, for example. Please keep an eye on the trail, looking for roots or rocks that can trip you up. We'll also be stopping often for hydration and rest."

While Mark continued, Shane Goodwyn decided to joke with his wife and those around him. "If you folks should happen to see any large boulders blocking the trail, just let me know. I'll move them out of the way for ya," he said, following his remarks with a flex of one of his biceps.

"It looks like someone ate his spinach for breakfast," commented Craig Banister. Banister was saddened that his remark was lost on everyone who could not see the reference to Popeye the Sailor Man.

Mark closed his preparatory remarks with a few words about horse safety and first aid, and then the group began to move out. Belle and Dan led the way on foot, followed by the others now mounted on horses. Following on foot at the rear were Mark and Isabella.

There were only a few of the law enforcement officers in the park service that Mark thought had the right stuff to become a special agent, and Dan Lawson was one of them. Mark thought he was smart as a whip, and had a good, keen sense for investigation. He had been raised in Chattanooga, and been a rower in high school. He stood 6'2" and had a long wingspan, plus a 'never say die' attitude, which was a perfect combination for rowing.

The trail they followed was actually a combination of other trails, causing some confusion as to what all the different nomenclature meant on the signposts. This was precisely why Belle was in front; as long as the group followed her, it would not matter what the signs said.

The horseback portion of the hike was both useful and entertaining for all, but ended all too soon. They had travelled three miles, and would need to cover the rest of the way on foot. The horses were tethered to nearby trees and handlers had been waiting for them there with oats and water. Unfortunately, they could not be available later in the day, meaning the party would descend the full five-plus miles on foot.

Everyone drank water and consumed power bars. Shortly after resuming their move up the mountain on foot, they encountered an amazing thicket of rhododendron plants which were so large they formed a tunnel for the hikers to walk through. All commented on how beautiful they were, and how unique a feature it was. Belle commented that had they been passing through one month later, they would have been treated to beautifully scented blooms, as well.

Nearing the five mile mark, the trail T-boned directly into Bote Mountain Trail. They would follow that for just a short distance before following a new trail blazed by the park service to take the travelers directly to the bald on the side of Thunderhead Mountain. That is where Echo Ridge would become a reality. An additional trail could also access the site from the Appalachian Trail atop the mountain, but for this occasion, the shortest path possible would be this newer path branching off Bote Mountain Trail.

The new trail required them to walk single file. They descended an embankment that crossed a little stream, and then headed back up again toward the bald. This would be their final uphill and for many, the most difficult part of the trail.

Craig Banister would not be with the others to see the beautiful spring flowers and spectacular views from the bald. He had slowed noticeably and was far behind the lead. Mark Powers and Shane Goodwyn had elected to stay behind to accompany the elder statesman at a slower pace. This could have appeared a kind gesture from Shane, but it was obvious his offer was rooted in a need to save face. He was struggling with the cardiovascular challenge the trail presented a man of his build, and was looking for a good excuse to ascend at a slower pace.

Talia came back from the main group. "Marky Mark, I can help Mr. Banister. Why don't you go stay with the others," she offered.

"Ah, yes, I enjoy Talia's company," said Banister.

Mark thought on it for a moment. "Thanks for the offer, Talia, but we don't need three people taking care of Mr. Banister. I need to remain in the rear anyway, as part of our security arrangement. You can just rejoin the others, and help Belle and take care of the rest of the group."

Talia froze for a moment, not wanting to leave Banister behind. Mark's logic seemed hard to combat, and he was, after all, in charge of the security details of the journey.

Banister spoke after an awkward silence. "It's okay, young lady, thanks for your kindness. Go on ahead, I'll be okay. You stay out of trouble up there, okay?"

"Okay, sir, if you are sure."

"I'll be alright."

Later, along the walk, Shane and Craig struck up an instant friendship as they recognized a common interest in Civil War history. Mark listened as the two men compared and contrasted the valor of Stonewall Jackson versus Joshua Chamberlain. At times, Banister became so winded he could not even continue his conversation.

"I'm sure I'll be alright," said Banister, "I'm just not as young as I used to be. My brain thinks I'm 27, but by lungs tell me I'm 72."

"You're 72 years old?" asked Mark, amazed that this information was not shared earlier.

"Ah, that's nothing. I chop wood to stay in shape. I think this is just the heat, gettin' to me. I just need a few more rests than the others, but I'll be fine."

Shane grabbed the light backpack worn by Banister who showed his appreciation with a pat on Shane's back. He was delighted to allow the larger man to carry his pack the rest of the way. Mark, however, was not so sure they should even continue. He caught a glimpse of Banister rubbing his forearm and hand.

"Are you experiencing any physical sensations you are not used to?" he asked the chief forester.

"I said I'll be alright, young man. I do feel a little tingling in my arm, but I'm sure that's just the backpack cutting off my circulation."

"Well, sir, with all due respect, we need to consider if something more troubling might be going on here."

"You're going to say a heart attack, aren't you?"

"Yes, sir."

"Well, like I said, I'm in great shape. And I don't have any heart disease in my family. My daddy lived to be 98, and his pappy before him lived to 106. We Banisters don't have heart attacks." The man wiped sweat off of his neck and forehead, and looked up the trail, sighing as if he knew darned well they were getting farther and farther behind the others as a result of this stoppage.

"Mr. Banister, there's aspirin in the first aid kit. You should take a couple of those," added Shane. "I've heard that's really important if you are having a heart attack."

"Now that sounds reasonable, as a precaution, Shane... thank you, young man," said Banister.

Mark also complimented Shane for the quick thinking and motioned for the first aid kit. Even if Banister was not having a heart attack, the aspirin would be a good preventative measure.

"When I played football," said Shane, "we had this wide receiver. Lean and mean, not an ounce of fat on him. Dropped dead during practice one day. No trace of heart disease in his family, either, and so you have to be careful."

Banister did not appear to be encouraged by Shane's trip down memory lane. Mark, too, paused to question the wisdom in Shane's story delivered to a man in his 70's. "Yes, well, that player must have had an undetected heart defect. I don't think we need to be worrying about that here today," said Mark. "We all would have found that out long ago if any of us had such a condition."

After Banister took the aspirin, Mark suggested they wait a bit longer and see if the tingling sensation went away. Soon he reported feeling perfectly fine and insisted they continue. Mark was not convinced it was the right thing to do, but his superior was growing tired of Mark's constant worry, and it appeared they would continue despite Powers' reservations. Mark radioed ahead to let Belle know their position and likelihood they would be arriving at the peak long after everyone else. He suggested the preparations be made to conduct the ceremony so Banister could show up, rest a bit, get captured on film, and then retreat casually back down the mountain. Lingering in the sunshine would not be good for the elder statesman. Banister overheard Mark's request, and thought to later thank him, if everything turned out okay.

Taking the new trail that split away from the traditional path allowed the group to bypass Rocky Top, the mountain known far and wide because of a song of that title, written by Felice and Boudleaux Bryant. The tune was the official song of the state of Tennessee and its lyrics served as the fight song for the University of Tennessee.

They also bypassed Second Rocky Top, which led to the summit of Thunderhead Mountain. Their path would lead them directly to the Echo Ridge. That name was just a marketing term. There was no existing place on the mountain with that name, but it was speculated the name would certainly find its way onto the map once the resort had been built.

As they neared the bald, they emerged from a thick tree line with a large open space ahead. It sloped to their left, westward, on the Tennessee side of the mountain. A gentle breeze was detected by the travelers, and was as equally welcoming as the sunshine that warmed them. The area appeared to be just a large grassy meadow, with a few outcroppings of rock, fallen trees, thickets, brambles, and colorful flowers everywhere. Numerous species of birds were flying about, and bees were gathering abundant pollen from the wildflowers. With the breeze stirring, the hikers were soothed tremendously after such a strenuous trek.

The bald provided a spectacular view of other mountains to the west, including the Cades Cove area. This would provide a remarkable view for visitors of the future Echo Ridge Resort.

Talia stepped beside Belle to comment on the location. "So they want to bull-doze this little paradise? And why is that necessary again?"

"Don't start now, Talia," replied Belle as she dropped two shovels she'd been carrying since they left the horses behind.

"It's just greed. Plain and simple," said Talia, getting the last word.

The bald sat in somewhat of a basin on the hillside, relative to the ridge to the north and east. This geography would be important for a rifleman who would figure into the day's drama, who was present just a few hundred yards away. He sat at a higher elevation and had a clear view of the Echo Ridge bald below him.

Lunch was taken, as many were ravenously hungry. Janet Goodwyn made certain five sandwiches and waters were set aside; one each for Powers and Banister, and three for her husband. All three men had yet to reach the bald.

As soon as the lead group was finished eating, Belle Whittle spoke with the camera crew to make sure they were ready to begin shooting as soon as Craig Banister arrived. In the next few minutes the dignitaries would practice holding their shovels at various angles, attempting to discover the optimal photo op.

"Governor," said Isabella, now coming up close to her boss, "I really think you need to remove your ball cap before they begin shooting."

"And why is that my dear?" asked Janet.

"Because, that woman over there is also wearing a ball cap, and you both are wearing the same color jacket." Isabella was referring to Belle Whittle. In fact, Belle and Janet were dressed similarly, from head to toe.

"But she's not going to be in the photo shoot. I'll be the only one with the ball cap, so no worries."

"But..."

"But what? If I don't wear this ball cap, my dear, my hair is going to look like a bird's nest flapping in this wind."

"I could pull your hair back, I have some scrunchies in my backpack. And, do you want to change into..."

"Isabella, it's not a big deal. I am perfectly presentable. Now let's just drop it." The governor was short with her assistant, knowing the young woman had a penchant for worrying about every little detail. Isabella, on the other hand, was growing more and more resentful of her boss's stubbornness.

"Where's my husband," asked Janet, aloud. "Oh, that's right, he's helping the old man get up the hill. Sheesh. When are they going to get here?"

"Everyone," said the director of the camera crew, "we're going to line you up and allow the camera team to get some light readings, and then we'll be ready to shoot as soon as Mr. Banister arrives."

"Ah, that won't be necessary. Mr. Banister isn't feeling well. They just radioed in saying to do the shoot without him." announced Belle, who'd just gotten word over the walkie-talkies of Banister's situation.

Minutes earlier, Mark, Craig and Shane were approaching the bald along the tree-lined trail. They reached a point where they had just a slight uphill section to go before reaching the spot where the trees ended, opening up to the future Echo Ridge location. Mark received a call on the walkie-talkie radio, asking how much longer before Banister would arrive. She also informed them that they had already eaten and wanted to start the photo shoot. Despite being so close, Banister once more complained he was not feeling well, and told Mark he needed to just stop, and forgo the photo shoot. Mark, still thinking Banister may have been experiencing heart problems, informed Belle to go on with the ceremony and photo shoot.

"I'm holding everyone up, Mr. Powers. I'm terribly sorry but I can't go on at the moment. I need to stop once more."

"Are you feeling that sensation in your arm again?" asked Shane, now with renewed concerns of a heart attack. Shane hoped his question would show he was a caring man, but in reality, was just one more good reason for him to stop and catch his breath.

"No, son, it's not a heart attack. Really. Unfortunately, I have to take a massive shit, and it's not going to wait."

Mark and Shane looked at each other in amusement as Banister shuffled deeper into the wooded area, looking for a spot to do his business.

"Always remember to poop on a slope so it can roll downhill behind you," said the old woodsman, his voice growing quieter with distance. Mark could hardly believe this was happening. They were almost there, but then again, perhaps Banister had it right. He would not want to participate in a video shoot if he was holding back a massive bowel movement either. Mark knew something had to happen. There were 14 in their party, so something had to go wrong with at least one of them.

"Will you be needing some wet wipes, sir?" yelled Mark, prepared to retrieve a package from his backpack.

"Those are for sissies. I'm looking for leaves," came the distant reply.

"How about a shovel?" asked Mark. "You know what they say, sir... leave no trace!"

From Banister's direction, Mark heard laughter. "I hear you. But that's only for young people. I'm tired and you're not going to get me expending more calories digging a hole for my poop."

Shane Goodwyn looked at Mark with an amused smirk. "Hey, it looks like you've got this covered. I'm gonna go join my wife, if you don't mind, before he asks one of us to go dig his latrine."

"Sure, go right ahead," said Mark. With that, Shane moved further along the trail, still at a snail's pace for the last uphill portion of the trail before he reached the Echo Ridge bald.

"Let's all get into a line," said the director after hearing Banister was not participating. "Somebody distribute the shovels, please."

Goodwyn, the EPA Director, and the woman from the Sierra Club, all lined up. Belle stepped in for the missing Banister. She stood at the far right of the line, next to the governor. Janet adjusted her ball cap, now self-conscious that perhaps the rim might hide too much of her face. She removed her makeup compact with a tiny mirror, and applied a dash of powder to fight the shine. She did a mental double take that perhaps she should have listened to Isabella about the ball cap, but decided to stick to her guns anyway. The ball cap would remain.

The camera and video crew had already checked the light settings, and were just about ready to shoot. Belle felt a tug at her left leg, as if someone had snagged her thigh muscle with a fishing hook and took a hearty tug on the fishing line. In an instant after feeling the sensation, she heard a cracking noise floating on the breeze, but in a state of disorientation, it remained foreign to her. She looked down. A portion of the fabric of her pants had ripped, midway up her thigh. There was something about the visual that her brain could not compute. Then it made sense as she saw blood begin rolling down her leg.

A second bullet smashed into an outcropping of rock next to where the dignitaries were posing, quickly followed by another cracking noise from the distance. Only after the second shot did Belle realize the bullets were coming in before the sound of the rifle that sent them. Again and again, more bullets came whizzing into the group, and for the first time, they found human targets. One of the camera team fell to the ground, soon followed by the dignitaries from the EPA and the Sierra Club. Talia saw them go down, and she was frozen in her tracks. Before she could get her feet moving, another bullet sliced into her body. She twisted around, now looking at the tree line from which they'd recently emerged, and collapsed to the ground.

It didn't take long for everyone else to find cover, which was in short supply. Some dove behind small clusters of rock, others behind a fallen tree, which still left portions of their bodies exposed and vulnerable to harm.

Belle saw the governor leave her side and run up the slight incline, heading for the protection of the tree line along the ridge. It was a risky move, as she was in the wide open for a moment until she reached safety. Three bullets, delivered in rapid succession, tossed up dirt as they missed the governor during her sprint. Belle spied Isabella also running for the trees. She was not targeted, as it seemed the sniper was more interested in the governor. Within ten seconds, everyone had moved behind some form of cover.

Belle maintained her position behind a rock formation. She began scanning the terrain in front of her to identify where the shots were coming from. Straight ahead of them there was nothing but wide open spaces, facing the mountains to the west. She realized the sounds were coming from the North, She noticed how the ridge they'd been walking on continued past the bald before making a slight north-westerly curve. Still more bullets were flying in, hitting wood and rock, and she determined the shots had to be coming from farther up along that ridgeline, where the curve presented the shooter with a better shot at the bald.

Looking into that curve, she saw a small flash of light amid the trees. It was followed by another bullet clipping a fallen tree nearby. That was it. The flash was an indication of gunfire and her guess had been right as to where the shooter was positioned.

"Shooter to the far right!" yelled Belle.

"Got it!" responded Dan, now wielding his own gun.

Both Dan and Belle estimated the gunfire was coming from about 200 yards away, which was far beyond the range of their pistols, but their natural reaction was to shoot anyway. After a few rounds, both knew pistols were futile.

"Hold your fire!" shouted Dan. "We can't reach him. Plus we might need our rounds in case there's more than one shooter who's closer to us!"

Belle thought about it, and agreed with Dan's strategy. No more rounds were dispensed from the pistols.

When Mark Powers heard the gunshots in the distance, he knew he could not stay out of the action. "Stay where you are, chief, there's trouble ahead," he said, and with that Banister was left squatting in the woods, alone. Mark sprinted up the trail, still feeling he had fresh legs after such a slow ascent. As Mark reached the bald, he saw Shane Goodwyn with his back to a tree, breathing heavily, and looking as if he'd seen a ghost.

Mark knew the look, as he'd seen it before with young rangers. For being a well-known gun advocate, Shane appeared unwilling and unprepared to step into a real gunfight. "Shane, let's go... we could use your help!" said Mark, breathing heavily, as he sprinted past the ex-football player. Shane did not follow as he was helplessly frozen in his anxiety.

Coming to the spot where the trail yielded to the bald, Mark saw mayhem unfolding before him. He used the protection of a large tree as he looked out upon the bald sloping down and away from him to his left. He saw several bodies lying in the open, with others hiding behind rocks and trees. The woman from the EPA, and the man from the Sierra Club appeared on the ground, completely motionless, blood upon their apparel. His search and rescue team member was down as well. Then he saw what appeared to be the body of Talia Manaia. Luckily, he saw motion from her thick crop of hair, indicating she was still alive. He also saw the governor hiding behind a tree to his left, and the governor's assistant doing the same to his right, on the other side of the trail.

Belle and Dan were in the open, sheltered only by small outcroppings of rock, with their pistols drawn and pointing to a location beyond the bald where the trail curved to the left. Mark shimmied downward, now running with his rifle balanced in his right hand instead of being carried upon his back. Unlike the governor, he was not fired upon as he crossed this portion of the bald on his way down to where Belle and Dan were located.

Mark took up a position next to Belle and asked her for an update while he readied his weapon. He also peeked over the rock, scanning the trees for the shooter. Mark propped his rifle upon the rock in front of him and used his scope for a closer look. Belle did her best to explain where to look in the sea of green. Through the scope, Mark caught a brief glimpse of what appeared to be movement amongst the trees, and with a little patience, his suspicions were confirmed that there was a man visible through a branchless gap in the curve of the ridge.

Just as Mark was in position, and ready to shoot, the incoming fire ceased. Mark lost sight of the sniper. Seconds passed, with no one willing to test their luck by stepping out from behind their shelter. The noise of the wind, blowing trees and grasses, was all that remained audible as the birds had flown elsewhere, their songs understandably missing from the moment.

Then there was a shriek, followed by three simple words: "Oh my God!" It came from behind Mark and Belle. It was a female voice in great distress, coming from the tree line behind them. Belle and Mark turned to see Isabella, kneeling down beside the governor at the tree line.

Mark scrambled back up the embankment to where Isabella was kneeling. The assistant appeared to have been grazed by a bullet in her right arm, but that was not the reason for her shriek. The governor was laying on her back next to a kneeling Isabella, the former with blood running profusely out of her chest. Janet struggled to say something to Mark as he approached. Suffocating from the blood filling her lungs, she managed to verbalize, 'shhh...' followed by a cough. That was quickly followed by 'did...it' before closing her eyes in death.

Mark stared at the woman's face, having just seen her life escape her. It was particularly painful for him to witness, as it conjured up memories from his own past, when his parents were killed. This was not the first time he gazed into a woman's face as she took her final breath. He felt the same panicky sensation come over his body and mind as he had before. He struggled against it, and succeeded in handling the situation rationally. He knew he had nothing more he could do for the governor, and yet, the current situation was not fully resolved. He had a responsibility to assume control of this chaotic scene of this crime.

Mark stood and faced back down the trail, and saw Shane Goodwyn now taking his final steps to where his spouse lay lifeless upon the ground.

Moments later, Banister appeared behind Shane.

"What's going on over here? Is everyone okay?" asked Banister.

"Sir, we've been attacked by a sniper, several are dead, some wounded I think," reported Mark.

Mark sensed Shane wanted to say something, although it was apparent he did not yet realize his wife was on the ground. Mark turned to let the man speak.

"Sorry about that, Ranger Powers," said Shane, "I, uh, I don't know. I just couldn't, uh," he said, unable to produce a credible excuse for cowering behind a tree during the outbreak of gunfire. "I guess I wussed out."

Mark stepped closer to Mr. Goodwyn. "Shane, I hate to be the one to tell you this, but your wife has been killed by sniper fire." Mark stood aside, revealing a small crowd of others who were still kneeling around the governor as Shane's eyes captured a glimpse of his wife. He lunged forward and crouched down by her side, speechless, before weeping like a baby. He then scooped his arms around her and pulled her up from the ground a bit, just enough to hold her one last time.

This was all too familiar to Mark, having gone through the same experience. He felt a need to reach out to Shane, to sympathize with him. Mark knew Shane would not have made a difference in fighting the shooter, just as he had not himself. However, he might have been able to protect his wife, averting this tragedy in the process. It may have been an old fashioned notion, but Mark believed that a man should do everything in his power to protect his wife, even at the expense of his own life. Shane had failed in that regard. Still, he felt bad for the man. Shane was one of many who knew how to operate a gun, and hunted regularly, but did not know how to react when bullets were coming in his direction. Mark tried not to judge him in his moment of grief. Many expert gun owners would also freeze-up in a similar situation. It was a natural, but unfortunate, human reaction.

Mark was aware he had other urgent matters to attend to, like tending to the wounded. He turned and left Shane in his grief.

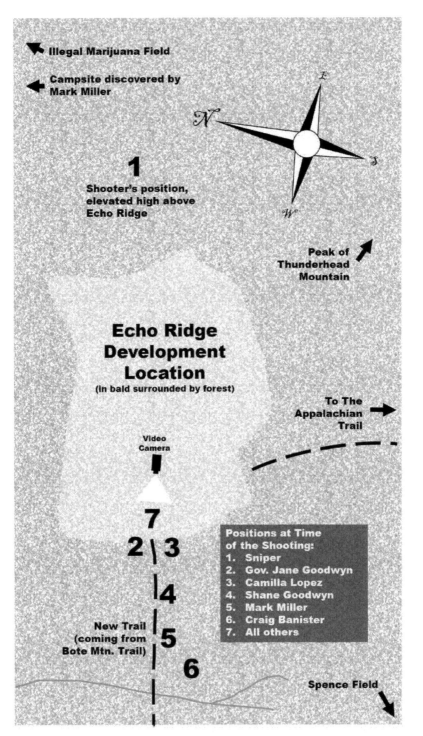

Illegal Marijuana Field

Campsite discovered by
Mark Miller

E

N

S

1

Shooter's position,
elevated high above
Echo Ridge

W

Peak of
Thunderhead
Mountain

Echo Ridge
Development
Location
(in bald surrounded by forest)

To The
Appalachian
Trail

Video
Camera

7

2 \ 3

Positions at Time
of the Shooting:
1. Sniper
2. Gov. Jane Goodwyn
3. Camilla Lopez
4. Shane Goodwyn
5. Mark Miller
6. Craig Banister
7. All others

4

New Trail
(coming from
Bote Mtn. Trail)

5

6

Spence Field

Chapter 7

Ten years before Laurie's Murder

Many of Mark's friends had already established themselves as family men, so by their reckoning, he was getting married late. But that is not how Mark saw it. He'd had many grand adventures in his twenties, and started dating seriously at 30, which all felt perfectly natural to him. He had been a park ranger for a decade, which was his dream job, and the timing felt perfect to settle down and possibly have children.

Being his wedding day, he naturally thought of his parents and siblings. None were present, but he longed for them to be there. His parents were no longer living, and his siblings were geographically dispersed, holding down careers that did not afford them time off to attend the wedding. But he was in a reflective mood, and found himself retracing his footsteps on the trail of his life.

After two years of geology at Northwestern, his parent's deaths inspired Mark to drop out and pursue a career similar to his father's. He moved south and attended the Tennessee Law Enforcement Academy with the end goal of becoming a ranger in the Smokies.

It was while studying in Nashville that he happened to meet Laurie Pendleton on Honky-Tonk Row at 4:30 a.m. Mark had been told by a friend that one could see some of the world's best musicians on Nashville's main strip, even in the middle of the night. When insomnia struck him on one occasion, he decided to put that statement to the test. He put on an old pair of torn up jeans and an old Coca-Cola T-shirt. He wasn't too concerned about his unkempt appearance since he assumed most establishments would be close to empty at that time of the night.

There was generally no cover charge in those places, and if the bands were to make any money at all, it would be through donations. Keeping a tip jar at the edge of the stage was not enough to pry cash out of visitor's wallets, and so beautiful women roamed the room asking politely for patrons to put cash in the jar. This is exactly how Mark met Laurie.

While watching a world class country boy play a Fender Telecaster like he'd never seen before, Mark's view was blocked by a gorgeous woman holding the tip jar. Her smile was generous, her body voluptuous, and her attire a nod to Daisy Duke.

"Hey there, good lookin'," she said, loudly, "how about a few bucks for the band?" She was leaning over the table, allowing him to see how her tank-top was failing miserably at keeping her breasts covered. Both of them knew it was not accidental.

If ever there was an investment worth making, Mark determined a tip was it. He quickly retrieved his wallet, and fumbled for cash. Then, his credit cards spilled onto the floor. Feeling the fool, he squatted below the table and gathered the cards together, realizing he still hadn't put cash in the jar. When he resurfaced above the table, the dazzling beauty had moved on to another table.

"Missed your chance," said someone next to him. Mark looked over and there, sitting at the next table was a modestly dressed woman with a look of amusement upon her face.

"I'm sure she'll be back," said Mark.

"Or maybe not," said the woman. "Sometimes you miss your chance if you wait too long."

"Let's just see about that," said Mark.

The air in this establishment was filled with cigarette smoke, and the colorful lights used to illuminate the stage leaked throughout the bar, giving the smoky haze a pinkish hue. Mark hadn't noticed at first, but this woman to his right was also beautiful, but in a different way. She had the face and hair of Farrah Fawcett, but an air of modesty that was miles apart from the tip jar woman. She wore a cowboy hat that caused her feathered hair to flow down upon her country-blinged-out blouse that looked something like a pink and white picnic tablecloth.

Mark was now out of ideas for what to say next, but there was some expectation that hung between them, like an unspoken invitation to connect. Her words echoed in his mind. He had better not wait too long to speak next, and he did not. By the night's end, he had her hard-won telephone number. She proved to be a tough woman to get in touch with, and it took several days before he got through to her. In their first phone conversation, she brought up the tip jar woman.

"You were prayin' hard that she'd come over and talk to you again, I could see it in your face."

"Yeah, I guess I kind of blew it when I spilled my cards all over the floor. Funny how things happen."

"Yup. Just like Garth Brooks says... thank God for unanswered prayers."

By the end of the century Mark found himself ready to jump into marriage with that woman, quite literally. As he held her hand, their bare feet were firmly planted upon the rock at the edge of the cliff, nearly ready to jump.

"Do you have the ring?" said the minister, terrified and barely audible above the background noise of the waterfall.

"What?" asked Mark.

"I said, DO YOU HAVE THE RING?" shouted the pastor, this time perhaps a little too loudly.

"Oh, yes. Yes, I do." The groom had no best man for this occasion. It was just his fiancé, the pastor, and himself on the edge of the cliff. Space was tight, and the pastor was terrified of heights. How he'd been talked into this was anyone's guess.

On a ledge behind them was a long line of vacationers, most of them children, waiting for their turn to move out onto the point of the cliff and jump. Most of them looked impatient. They didn't understand how these people in front of them could hold up the works at The Sinks just for a wedding. Who in their right mind would do such a thing?

This Sinks was quite an attraction, where visitors gathered throughout the summer months to plunge 25 feet into the icy waters below them. It was a popular tourist spot, with its own parking lot off of Old State Hwy 73. Not only was there the cliff, but coming from under a bridge was a glorious waterfall that produced remarkably deep waters at its base, the waters into which the bride and groom would jump momentarily.

The couple said their vows to one another, and the pastor prayed over them. All that remained was the ring, the kiss, and pronouncement of marriage. Mark carefully untied the strings that held his bathing suit tight at his waist, to retrieve the ring that had been secured there. He knew if he dropped the ring, it would fall to the water below, never to grace his lovely wife's finger. Steadily, he produced the ring and placed it on her finger.

"Then it is my honor, in the eyes of God and those gathered before us, to pronounce you man and wife. You may now kiss the bride, and take the plunge!"

The pastor's words had barely passed his lips before the couple embraced with a passionate kiss. Dozens of onlookers began clapping and whooping it up, their voices competing inadequately with the sound of the waterfall.

With the kiss finished, both Mark and Laurie turned and looked below them. It seemed like such a great distance. They stood side by side and screamed their prearranged signal to the crowd that they were jumping: "Cannonball!!!"

Both stepped over the cliff's edge, hurled toward the water, and wrapped their arms around their knees to produce a big splash for the onlookers. Once they resurfaced, they swam to each other for one more kiss and laughter. Then they allowed the current to carry them to shallower waters. Once their feet could touch the bottom, they embraced for another kiss. This was followed by a moment where they gazed into each other's eyes.

"So, Mrs. Powers, it's official," said Mark.

"Yes it is!" replied his bride.

"How long before you'll be accustomed to the new last name?"

"Who knows, but it will be fun. Besides, at least I'll still have the same initials. That should make it easier." Mark hadn't realized that to be true, with her last name changing from Pendleton to Powers.

"I hope so," he said with a quick kiss.

"Honey," she said, "I want to ask you for a favor."

"Okay, what's that?"

"Will you come here with me on our 50th wedding anniversary?"

"Of course I will!"

"And will you jump off that cliff with me, then?"

"Hmmm. Let' see, I'll be 84 by then. I might break a hip jumping from up there," said Mark, eliciting a giggle from his bride.

"Or maybe we can pull over along the road somewhere, still in this same river, and we could wade into the shallow water with our walkers." Her comment got them both laughing.

"Let's come here for our 25th anniversary, and see how that goes," said Mark, and his comment was received with yet another kiss. Mark could not believe how cute and funny she was, and how lucky he'd been to spill his credit cards all over the floor in that honky tonk bar.

Above them they glanced at the pastor as he was nervously led back to safer ground by someone more sure-footed. There were a couple of moments there when they thought he might topple over the edge and join them.

It had been rather simple to arrange things at The Sinks, far easier than a traditional wedding in a church. After obtaining the proper permit from the park service, the couple discovered the most difficult arrangement was in finding a southern pastor who would marry them on a cliff. Some pastors thought it was too dangerous, some thought it was too far of a drive, and others found it to be too irreverent and disrespectful, being married in bathing suits. But to Laurie's way of thinking, Jesus had been baptized in a river, so why shouldn't they be married in one as well?

And Mark believed there was no greater place to enter into marriage than in one of the most beautiful cathedrals in this part of the country... at the base of that beautiful waterfall near Gatlinburg, Tennessee.

Chapter 8

The sniper was disgusted with how things had gone down. He only had one opportunity and luck had given him a cold shoulder. He'd been shooting since he was seven years old. He knew how to handle a high powered rifle, and had brought down some rather large game on several trips to Africa. Yet, he had never struggled this much to hit his mark. There were a number of difficulties that ate at him.

First, when he'd arrived on the mountain a day earlier to clear branches, he discovered the angle was going to be very difficult. Given the curvature of the ridge, he needed to set up farther away to see more of the bald. But the further away he was, the more drop he would experience with his AR10 shooting .308 rounds. Eventually he settled on a slightly difficult angle, at a distance of 200 yards. This would mean he'd have to aim about 4" above his targets, knowing the bullet would drop that much in flight. This compromise was a difficult one, but he knew any other arrangement would make him fully ineffective.

And then there was the fashion fail. He'd gotten a good look at the governor days earlier in the parking lot near the

Gatlinburg Trail posing as the hiker. But through his scope, he found it difficult to identify her when it really counted. He saw two middle-aged women in similar outfits. Both wore ball caps with blond ponytails pulled through the hole in the back. Compounded by the sway of the tree in which he was sitting, he simply could not tell which one was the governor. If he had waited moments longer, he would have seen the governor holding a shovel while being photographed. The other woman would have stepped to the side. But he did not wait. He decided to target both of the similarly dressed women, alternating shots back and forth. His payment for this job would be cut in half if he missed the governor, and he was only concerned with getting the full payment. Unfortunately for him, shooting both women would not be done so easily because of another challenge he faced: the wind.

He had shot many long range rifles in some pretty lousy conditions over the years, and had a good feel for shooting in heavy rain. But the wind currents atop Thunderhead Mountain created a disturbance that made his job much more difficult. He was not in a steady position laying upon the ground; in order for his shots to clear the trees, he had found it necessary to be elevated in a deer stand. Even the slightest sway of the tree was making it that much more difficult to take a steady shot. At the time he had agreed to this job, he had no idea the deer stand would be necessary, nor the task of clearing so many branches. But this was his fate and he had no choice but to cope with the challenges.

Once he began firing and could see his bullets finding rock and wood rather than flesh, he decided to go with quantity over quality. He shot rapidly and hoped he could learn from the wind how to compensate.

He knew his misses just might hit other people because they were huddled closely together in preparation for a photo shoot. He recalled the meeting where he had been given conflicting orders. They told him not to hit anyone but the governor, yes, but they'd also said if he could not achieve that goal, to create chaos by shooting many rounds for as long as he could. He decided not worry about collateral damage. His pay would be double if Goodwyn died, but there was nothing in the arrangement that negatively affected his pay if he shot others as well. And so, the bullets flew indiscriminately.

He was also frustrated at not seeing Mark Powers amongst the targets. His team had told him Mark would be there, but Mark was missing. He could not have known the ranger would still be making his way up the trail with a couple of slow-pokes.

His final problem was a jam. After he replaced his first magazine and prepared to continue his assault, his AR10 refused to fire. In total disgust, he settled for having created a great deal of chaos. It had been some time ago that the terms of his hiring had been discussed, but he hoped he would still get paid for what he'd done, in the full amount. If not, his employer might face unplanned trouble.

He decided it was time to run. Before leaving, he remembered to do something rather important, and devious. While still wearing his shooting gloves, he hid a small ultra-light tent and a boom box (rolled up within the tent) into the bushes near his firing site. Then he evacuated, and travelled down from the mountain to a nearby stream which he would follow until meeting his team by a gravel service road. But after hiking about 50 yards, he discovered a very small gap in the trees where a few skeleton hemlock trees were leaning at an angle. This allowed him to scan most of the crime scene. While he could no longer shoot, this would now provide him with an excellent means of viewing the aftermath with his scope.

He surveyed the chaotic scene below him. It appeared one of the two women with the ball cap was now looking in his direction using a rifle scope. He decided that woman was not the governor because he could tell the woman wielding the rifle was very comfortable with a gun in her hands. This meant the other similarly dressed woman was the governor.

He scanned about, looking for Janet Goodwyn, and initially could not find her crouching behind any trees or rocks. Then he saw several people milling about at the edge of the bald, where a trail emerged from the tree line. There he saw a huge man, Shane Goodwyn, cradling a body in his arms. The killer watched for a prolonged period of time, and eventually Shane stood upright as the body remained motionless on the ground. That clarified things for the sniper. He was now reasonably confident that the governor was either severely injured or dead. He presumed the latter, because her husband would not just allow his injured wife to lay on the ground like that. A reasonably loving husband would continue to cradle his injured wife until she could be moved to a more comfortable location.

Next he wondered how the governor was no longer where he'd seen her when he tried to shoot her. He assumed he must have shot her out in the open, after which time her husband carried her to the edge of the bald where she then died. That made sense to him, and that was the story he would tell the others.

It was time to move on, and he would hike for several hours to reach his rendezvous point with his team. There he hoped to get media reports of whether the governor had perished or had just been wounded. The size of his paycheck would depend upon that outcome.

Belle and Mark were kneeling down and looking at their friend and fellow ranger, Talia Manaia. She had been shot once in the sternum and was not responding to them. Occasionally she would moan and appear to be coming to, but then she would return to a catatonic state. Belle had stopped the bleeding with a bandana, and they knew Talia's survival was hanging in the balance. She needed medical assistance, and fast.

Mark left Belle as she attended to Talia. He stood and looked around. *Somewhere out there is a killer who could still be watching us at this very moment,* thought Mark. He knew the next steps their team took would determine if the rest of his party would make it down the mountain alive. *Safety First!* It was such a trite little saying, but quite true. It popped into his head as he wondered how to attend to the injured. His immediate concern was to get the living members of his party back down the hill, but that would not be possible for Talia. He used his radio to call for a helicopter.

"I've got a 10-35. Repeat, a 10-35. Operation Honey Badger...3 injured, conscious and not terminal. Add several dead, including MockingbirdOne. Request two birds and four medics for transport. Out."

"Roger that. Medics on the way," said the dispatcher.

"Also, put in a 10-05 for the State Troopers and the FBI. We need ECU assistance ASAP."

"Roger that. Can't say which bird they'll be in but you'll know it when they get there."

"Do what you can, but hurry. We've got one of our own in a lot of pain," said Mark.

His next priority was to get everyone else off that mountainside. He spoke loudly and addressed the survivors to get further into the tree line. There they would make immediate plans to descend the mountain.

As far as the dead, Mark knew what would happen with the bodies. They would remain on that mountain, exactly where they lay, throughout the night. While he wished to afford them respect, he understood they were people no more; now they were evidence, and had to be treated as such. They would not be removed until the crime scene could be fully evaluated.

Next he would need to ensure the dead would not be disturbed by wildlife, be it a wolf or turkey vulture, or even a bear. He considered posting Dan at the scene for the duration of the night. But at the same time he wanted another law enforcement ranger with him to protect the party as they descended the mountain. He decided to ask Belle if she could remain behind with plenty of ammunition to guard the bodies.

"Of course I will," she said without hesitation. "I spent half my childhood keeping critters out of the garden from my bedroom window, with a 4-10 in my hands. Plus if you're leaving now, I can keep watch over Talia till the choppers get here."

"Great. Let's do that. It might be a little rough for you hopping down the mountain with that injury to your quadricep muscle anyway."

"Agreed. Can you call back in to the dispatcher and have them bring me a jacket? It's already starting to get cold. Get some blankets for Talia, too."

"Sure thing," said Mark.

Mark knew Belle had EMT training, whereas Dan did not, and thus it made sense that Belle remain behind. She might have had the softer job of PR for the park service these days, but he knew she could stand her own with his rifle by her side.

Before evacuating the site, Mark asked the survivor of the video crew to use their camera equipment to record as much of the attack site as they could to take advantage of the light of day. He knew the Troopers and FBI would want a totally undisturbed crime scene for evidence collection. Since they would not arrive until after dark, photos from earlier in the day would be very helpful to them.

One of the media personnel called to Mark. "Excuse me, Ranger Powers," said the woman. "There's only one video camera, and it's partly laying under... our fallen co-worker, Greg. I'm guessing you don't want us to remove that?"

"Good call. No, don't disturb his body. Just leave the video camera where it is. If all you have are still photos for the investigators that will be better than nothing."

Once a number of photos were taken, the group made their way down to the valley. Mark asked Dan to lead at the front of the column. Mark would pull up the rear.

Shane Goodwyn was not happy at all about leaving his wife's body up on that mountain, yet he understood it was important for the party and his own wellbeing to get to safety in case other gunmen were nearby. Mark explained Belle would remain behind so the body would be safe.

Besides Talia's and Belle's injuries, there was one other injury in the party, and that was the right arm of Isabella Lopez. It seemed much more serious than the grazing to Belle's quad muscle, but Isabella was so traumatized by her boss's death she did not want to stay behind for the airlift. She said as long as her legs were working, she did not want to stay on that mountain another minute. She received some quick field measures to apply pressure to the wound and stop the bleeding, and she was ready to go. Mark was impressed by her, having walked up the mountain the full distance without a horse, and now she was prepared to hike another five miles in a significant amount of pain.

Craig Banister was not injured, but had recently made his way to the bald, and decided he'd take his chances staying with Belle rather than slow down the group on their descent. That would allow Mark and Dan to keep the others in a tight group for the entire trip, all the way down to Cades Cove. It also gave Mark comfort knowing someone was with Belle.

The trip down the mountainside was much easier than the ascent. At about the half-way point, Isabella made her way to the back to ask Mark an important question.

"Mr. Powers, I for one would like to know how much longer before we find a restroom!" Mark nodded to her that it was a good question, although others in the party had been sneaking off into the woods all day to do their business, and he wondered why that had not occurred to Lopez. He spoke loudly as he addressed the others.

"Everyone... if you have not yet noticed, we're far from a bathroom. We won't have one for our use for more than another hour, so I suggest you find a spot in the woods and do your business. We do have some sanitary wipes if you want a little creature comfort, those are in Dan's backpack, I believe." Nearly everyone complied.

Mark noticed Shane appeared the only one with no need to relieve himself. Instead, he was tossing his pocket knife at a tree, hoping to get it to stick. Mark noted Shane was repeatedly able to get the blade into the tree successfully.

"Uh, Shane," said Mark, coming up behind him.

"Yes, Sir," Shane said.

"Could you please not do that? It's technically against the law." Mark did not think his request was unreasonable.

Shane turned to look at the ranger, towering over the much shorter man and with a menacing look upon his face.

"You're kidding right?"

"No I'm not. You might think that's an innocent way to pass the time, but as I see it, that's vandalism."

"Holy shit man, I just lost my wife, and this is just me working that out. Can't you make an exception?"

Mark had heard that so many times before. *Can you make an exception? Can you just give me a warning?* And after two decades of hearing those pleas, he had given up on leniency. Mark had a flashback, a flickering memory of his father, the police officer. When asked something similar, his father would always recite a little rhyme,

> *"I'm not the judge,*
> *I'm not the lawmaker,*
> *I'm just the enforcer,*
> *who stops the lawbreaker."*

Or sometimes he'd say,

> *"You want me to do my job AND the job of the judge? I should get paid double!"*

"Shane," said Mark, sternly, "let's cut the crap. There's no need to damage the trees because of your grief. I hope you'll find some other way to work that out, but c'mon, it's time to go." By now, Shane could feel the eyes of everyone else upon him, and he also recognized Mark's plea for expediency as legitimate. Begrudgingly, he placed his knife back into his pocket, muttered "dick" as he turned, then resumed the downhill march with the rest of his party.

Chapter 9

With just about a mile to go along the trail, and darkness closing in, Mark and the others heard the helicopter fly overhead. Everyone heard it long before they could see it, and caught a slight glimpse of its running lights through the canopy of leaves overhead. Mark, as well as Dan, took a sigh of relief that the helicopter was about to arrive. This would mean a greater likelihood of Talia's survival, and to a lesser extent, would bring comfort to Belle Whittle and Craig Banister knowing they would no longer be alone upon Thunderhead Mountain with the night closing in.

That's not to say things would go easily. The helicopter had nowhere to land, so medical personnel would use a rope ladder, which was no small feat. Then, if Talia needed transport, they would lower a basket, pull her up with a hoist, and fly her off to the LeConte Medical Center in Sevierville. There was no margin for error in any of those activities, especially in the light of dusk.

As they continued leading the party over a log bridge spanning Anthony's Creek, Mark and Dan chatted about what they would find when they reached Cades Cove. Hopefully there would already be an FBI presence that would initiate the investigation. As it worked out, they reached the camp ground to find no FBI, but they did not need to wait very long. Minutes later, another helicopter was heard approaching from the north. Once close enough to land, everyone in their group stood quietly, with their hair and clothing fluttering wildly in the gusts of wind generated by the helicopter.

Quickly exiting the helicopter, in a semi-prostrate position, a woman moved to where Mark Powers stood, as he waited to speak to her.

"I'm Special Agent Mark Powers. I'm glad to see you," said Mark, loudly.

"Nice to meet you, Agent Powers, only I wish it were under different circumstances," she replied. "I'm Agent Sandra Toney, but just call me Sandy," replied the woman, sporting her backcountry clothing instead of the usual professional business attire. The high-tech fabric of her jacket was adorned with large, yellow letters on the back: FBI. I've got two evidence analysts with me, and Agent Tom Luken, FBI, who is out of Knoxville, and Agent Jeannine Gallenstein who is from the Tennessee State Troopers and will work with us in a joint investigation. Both lead their respective evidence collection teams. Others will be here shortly."

Mark noticed the latter two agents as they emerged from the helicopter and walked in his direction. Mark had a funny habit of thinking just about every stranger he met looked like someone famous. In this group of agents, he saw Sandy as Halle Berry, Luken as a young Burt Reynolds, and Gallenstein as forever-young-version of Morgan Fairchild.

"Can you join us to go back up to the crime scene?" asked Agent Toney.

"Of course," replied Mark, "we have a critically injured member of my team being airlifted right now. We may need to have your pilot get word when there's room for us up there. It may take some time to get Talia into a basket. Sadly, we also have four dead up there, including Governor Janet Goodwyn."

They waited for clearance to go to the bald while Mark started his long story, including every detail as best as he could piece it all together. Once airborne, he described the trails leading up the mountain, which he could no longer show them in the darkness. He wanted the FBI to get all the details about how there was a horse trail during one segment of the climb, in case that might shed light later on how the sniper may have travelled up and down the mountain. It seemed like overkill, but he knew some cases like this could be solved from strands of such minutia.

Flying above the bald, Mark looked down upon Belle Whittle as she stood alone. Talia Manaia and Craig Banister had been whisked away by the previous helicopter just moments before the second helicopter arrived.

The helicopter's propellers thrusted circular patterns into the grasses and wildflowers in the bald as they hovered. They, too, would need to use a rope ladder as landing on the hillside was out of the question. Agent Toney commented the lack of a landing spot was going to make it very difficult to retrieve the dead.

Mark climbed down first, with the beating of the propellers and the stirring winds consuming all of his hearing ability. Once on terra firma, he immediately went to get a status update on Talia from Belle Whittle.

"She doing okay?"

"Same as when you left, but she's still alive."

"Any trouble while we were gone?"

"None. Mr. Banister cleaned and dressed my wound. He was also very helpful in keeping me company. It's been a little... uh... strange up here." Belle grew emotional while looking around at the dead, and feared the worst for Talia Manaia. Aside from Talia, Belle did not know any of them except for the limited time she had spoken with them on the hike up the mountain.

After the remaining two agents had followed Mark and Sandy to the ground, it was time for Belle to ascend the rope ladder. Each step she took on her wounded leg generated searing pain that nearly caused her leg to collapse before it could be extended. After just two instances of this, she began going up like a child learning to take steps for the first time, using only her good leg for extensions between steps. It was slow going, but she made it into the helicopter just fine.

Once the helicopter's chopping noises had faded into the distance, Mark finally continued his conversation with Agent Toney, relieved by the relative silence all around him. Her associates were already busy examining evidence. Agent Gallenstein removed a roll of crime scene tape and sat it on a nearby rock. Agent Toney looked at her with a piercing glare. "Tape, up here? Really?" she said.

"Standard procedure, right?" countered the other woman.

"Don't worry about it, unless you think the bears up here can read."

"Well, we are sitting a little bit down from the Appalachian Trail," injected Mark, "and hikers sometimes come down to this bald to camp. Maybe it's not a bad idea to put up crime scene tape because there could be hikers coming through here at any time."

Agent Toney conceded to his advice and begrudgingly motioned for the other agent to proceed with the tape. "I'm not in Quantico anymore. I suppose I'll need to defer to your judgement when it comes to this wilderness. Why don't you continue telling us what happened here."

"As I said before, when the shooting started, I was still further back in those woods, along the approaching trail, with Craig Banister and Shane Goodwyn. The first I saw of anything up here in this clearing was when I ran ahead of the other two gentlemen, into the bald, and made it right up here to this rock, looking down and around the sloping meadow," he said, using his finger to point at key locations as he spoke.

"Was the sniper visible at that time?"

"No, but Belle pointed up and to the right, and I used my rifle's scope to see flickers of light amongst the trees, signaling gunfire. That's a slightly higher elevation, and I think the shooter had a great shot at us here, down in this sunken meadow."

"How far away, do you think?"

"Too far for our pistols to return fire, that's for sure, or even my rifle. Maybe a couple-hundred yards. But I was willing to try. Only thing is, by the time I was in position, the shooting stopped. Then I couldn't get a fix on where to aim."

"What do you think made the sniper stop," asked Toney.

"Good question. I don't know. I'd like to think he used his scope and saw me with a rifle. Maybe he thought there was a chance I could take him out, but you know, that's not very likely."

"The M.O. for these kinds of things is that a sniper would be well stocked with additional rounds of ammo, although sometimes that's just for insurance. From what you described, I'm surprised the sniper didn't shoot longer, and that there were not more casualties. How many people were up here at the time?

"Fourteen."

"Maybe the sniper was after just one of them. Maybe the governor. High profile."

"You may be right about that. You know, Belle says the first shot grazed her in the leg, but she was standing right next to the governor. I think that bullet might have had Janet Goodwyn's name on it. And, just right after the shooting stopped is when we heard the governor's assistant shout out that Goodwyn had been shot. Seems to me the sniper got who he wanted to get, and stopped shooting."

"So let me get this straight... something you told me earlier. Everyone else was down in the clearing, taking cover, but the governor decided to run for it, back up to the tree line?"

"Yes. Belle can tell you more about what she saw, because I was not up here at the time the governor made a run for it. But Belle told me the assistant, Isabella Lopez, also ran up to the tree line at about the same time as the governor. However, she was on the other side of the trail, across from the governor. The two of them were on each side of me as I passed into the clearing, and after that point they were out of my view, behind me."

"I can see how the assistant, feeling a sense of loyalty, might think her boss's decision to run for the woods might have been a good idea for herself, as well."

"Yeah, I suppose."

"Why do you think the governor didn't just duck behind a rock like everyone else?" said the FBI agent, now writing everything down in a notepad.

"Another good question. I would assume it's because there wasn't much cover to be had. We had 14 people in our party, and very few fallen trees or boulders to hide behind. Maybe she panicked, and just thought she could make it. Oh, and you know, her husband was still just back along the trail, somewhat. Maybe she wanted to run to him. She had commented he was going to be her personal security for the day, but apparently not a very good security guy because he couldn't keep up with his wife on the steep incline of the trail.

"So he was behind the others because he was slow?"

"Well, up to a point he was. Toward the end, he could have made it into the clearing but he froze at the sound of the gunfire. He appeared to have a bit of a panic attack and was sort of MIA while all the shooting was going on. I mentioned to you on the way up that Craig and Shane were with me prior to the shooting; we were pulling up the rear. We were almost to the bald when all hell broke loose here in the clearing."

"That's plausible that she wanted to be with him. Too bad we can't just ask her," mused Sandy. "What about the others? Do you know details about when they were shot? In what order?"

"That's another good question for Belle," said Mark, now thinking it's a shame Belle was not with them to field these questions. He might be the special agent, but Belle had been in the center of the attack, from the beginning.

Toney must have thought the same thing as she asked "And that woman who just struggled to get up that rope ladder... that was Belle?"

"Yes. I'm sorry, I wanted her to get better medical attention for her leg, but we'll just have to talk with her to get most of these questions answered."

"Sandy," said Agent Tom Luken, who was inspecting the crime scene, "I found a digital video camera, and it's still recording!"

"Well say amen and hallelujah to that," said Mark, thinking that could never have happened back in the day of analog video tape. That digital camera must have had a great battery life and plenty of storage.

Sandy joined Mark in running over to see the discovery.

Agent Luken, now wearing latex gloves, carefully removed the camera and its strap from around the neck of the dead videographer. It was attached to a long monopod used for steadying the camera during a shoot.

"I need to stop it," commented the agent.

"Yes," responded his boss. "But whatever you do, do not accidentally erase anything. Be very careful. Let's try to preserve the batteries for playback once we get back to town. Look in the equipment bag. See if there are any other battery packs or chargers to go along with it."

"It was laying on the ground, with the deceased laying on top of the monopod. Let's hope it's not just one long shot of the grass," said Luken.

"Sounds like one of my early video shoots" said Mark.

"Okay," Sandy said, "on to other things. What I want to know is where the shooter was located. I'd like to take a little hike and look around. Will you join me?'

"Yes, I am very curious about that too."

"Well, I brought a laser pointer," said Sandy.

"Which is for what?" asked Mark, now interested in her use of technology, which he was always in the mood to discuss.

"We're going to set this up on a tripod and point it up to where you think the sniper fire came from, high along that tree line. Then we're going to take a little hike and see if we can locate where the laser is making contact with the landscape. That will be the shooter's position."

"Sounds like a plan. But wouldn't it be easier to investigate in the morning?"

"Evidence might expire overnight, with moisture, wind, critters. We need to get there tonight."

"Okay. I'm on board," said Mark.

"Agent Gallenstein, keep identifying bullet strikes, see if you can dig a few slugs out of a tree or the dirt. We'll have the rest of our team coming up on the next helicopter run. Agent Luken, you can come with us."

Mark could feel the cold of night settling over the mountain, and he stared at the laser as Luken attached it to a tripod he had brought with him.

"This works very well at night. The laser is about as thin as a strand of spaghetti at the source. Once we get farther away, it will fan out. You said maybe 200 yards? I have that set so we'll have a big red spot to look for where you pointed to as the shooter's location," she said, confident the technique would bear fruit.

Mark led the others due south, as they followed a small access trail further up the mountain where it connected with the Appalachian Trail. They would have the luxury of a wide, well-trodden path to follow in the dark, heading east. Shortly thereafter, they would stray from the AT and move northward to the laser pointer illuminated the supposed shooter location. There would be more undergrowth for them to contend with at this point, but they were lucky to find a deer trail leading them to where they wanted to go. It had been used by the shooter as well.

It did not take them long to hike to the sniper's location. Luken reached into his backpack and withdrew slip-over foot coverings and latex gloves, intended to keep them from infecting the scene with their own shoe-prints and fingerprints. Mark knew this was a trend in high-tech evidence collection, but he was cynical that all those precautions were necessary in the mountains.

They approached carefully, with their weapons drawn, and fanned out, with Luken providing cover from behind a tree as the other two moved ahead. They did this until they approached the general area where the red laser spot was penetrating an opening in the trees and illuminating pine needles upon the forest floor.

"Let's comb the area," whispered Agent Toney, motioning with her hand. Ten minutes later, their cautious surveillance of the surrounding area was complete, and they reassembled where the laser glowed red upon the trees and the ground. With the aid of their flashlights, they spied a few shiny objects on the ground, presumed to belong to the shooter.

"Mark, can you remain on guard while we inspect?" asked Toney.

"Certainly."

With that, the two FBI agents quickly located a number of brass shells that were scattered amongst the pine needles and undergrowth. But there was something not right about the location of the shells.

"The opening in the trees is far above the spent shells. He was not standing here when he shot, he was elevated, up in the tree, and the shells fell all the way down here" said Luken. They looked up with their flashlights, and while difficult to see at first, they noticed a portable deer stand attached to the trunk of the tree, about 12 feet up.

"Looks like somebody took a little time to get everything set up the way they like." said Toney.

Mark looked up at the deer stand, and around at nearby trees. He saw plenty of cuttings laying in shrubbery and upon the ground. The killer had been rather enterprising, for sure. "You're right. He showed up well in advance of the shooting, did all this cutting to make sure he had a clear shot."

"That means he didn't just follow your party up the trail, then find a place to shoot. He knew they were going to be there well in advance," added Sandy.

"That's what I'm thinking," said Mark. "That's interesting because we kept the date and time of this groundbreaking ceremony a close secret. Somebody on the inside must have tipped him off about the when and where, in order for him to be this prepared."

Agents Toney and Luken continued to explore the site with the aid of a flashlight, when Luken found something else of interest. It appeared orange in color, and was sticking out from nearby undergrowth. Slowly he approached, examining carefully with his light. He tugged on the orange object until it pulled clear of the bush.

"Well, lookie there," said Luken. "This appears to be an ultralight tent." He held it up in the air as it unfolded, discovering something heavy was inside. It made the tent heavier than it should have been. He looked inside to discover a small Bluetooth music speaker system. "And the sniper also looks like he was a music lover. Maybe he was listening to a little Mariah Carey as he was gunning people down, what do you think boss?"

Sandy smiled, knowing Luken was making fun of her musical tastes.

"Interesting observation. But I think we lack evidence to prove that Mariah Carey would drive someone to go on a killing spree."

"Just listen to her greatest hits record a few times," added Mark. "That might change your mind about that." The three all smiled at the joke, but quickly returned their minds to the seriousness of their current situation.

"But you're right, the tent and the boom box is very curious," said Sandy. "This suggests he spent the night out here during his preparations. Not sure why he didn't take it with him, though, unless he departed so quickly he didn't have time. Kind of careless to leave something like this behind, it just might have a lot of good DNA evidence for us, or maybe some prints. You'd think he would have considered that as a risky move."

"And it seems to me like he shoved it into the bushes, intentionally," added Tom. "It was in there pretty good, not like the wind blew it in there. Plus, with the boom box inside the tent, there's no way the wind could have blown it snuggly into the bush like that. If he was in such a hurry that he wouldn't take it with him, why did he then take extra time to shove it into the bush? Did he really think we would just walk right past it? Seems like this guy isn't too bright."

"Tom, that's great observation," said Sandy. "Capture that part about how it felt tucked. And make sure to get the tent and boom box into an evidence collection bag as soon as the team arrives." As she spoke, Mark noticed some rope ties attached to the tent, with yellow stakes still attached and dangling below.

"I have a hunch you're going to find that some of those stakes are missing," said Mark. Luken inspected the corners and sides of the tent, and sure enough some eyelets had thin ropes attached, and others did not.

"And how did you know that, Agent Powers?" asked Sandy.

"Because the missing ropes and stakes are already in my possession at the Little River Station. And I have the charging cable that goes to the boom box as well."

"And how is that?" asked Sandy.

"This guy is really sloppy. He left some of his gear in another camp site further down the mountain, which I found last evening. I think I may have chased him off when I came upon the site. Looks like he left in such a hurry that he grabbed the tent that was already set up on the ground and just ran away with it. The boom box must have been inside at the time."

"Imagine that," said Luken. "A killer running through the woods carrying an uprooted tent with Mariah Carey music coming from the inside."

Chapter 10

Two decades before the Echo Ridge shooting.

He arrived at the Sevier County courthouse at 7:00 a.m. to have a consult with his law team and the DA. They were to outline their response to the media on the courthouse steps following the sentencing. Mark felt like it had been years since giving his testimony, but it had only been a few weeks. He had made a good impression, using video footage on his laptop and a portable projection system for the jury to see. He had also been the first ranger in the park to employ motion sensitive cameras for surveillance, and it was this footage that helped find and apprehend the ringleader of a local, but dangerous, band of pot growers. Franco Hufnagel had used federal lands to grow illegal crops, and used troubled teenage boys for his harvesting operations. If that wasn't bad enough, he armed them all with handguns to protect their crops, using guns brought into Tennessee illegally from North Carolina. In the end, it was Mark's use of motion sensitive cameras that led to Hufnagel's arrest.

Now the jury had completed their deliberations and announced their findings: Hufnagel was found guilty on all counts. All that remained was sentencing. On this day, Franco Hufnagel would learn his fate on charges of drug trafficking, transporting guns across state lines, child endangerment, and a long list of other offenses. The prosecuting attorneys were hoping Hufnagel would get 20+ years in prison.

"You did a fantastic job, Mark," said the lead attorney. "You produced a mountain of evidence. The jury took only 12 minutes to reach a verdict. Thank God he was found guilty. I'd like to see what happens to him once he's in the brink. I hope someone on the inside teaches him a lesson."

Soon it was time for the judge to announce the sentence. Mark looked around the room. All the seats for spectators were filled, and the press flooded the isles around the sides and back. Mark glanced over and saw a young man, just 15 years old, Jebidiah Fields, who'd testified against Hufnagel, sitting nearby. He was one of Franco's under-aged field workers whom he'd armed with handguns. In fact, it was Jebidiah's impassioned testimony that had likely sealed the deal for the jury to convict Hufnagel on all counts.

Powers admired Jeb for what he was doing, mainly because the boy didn't have to testify if he didn't want to. Yet, he was eager to, and his family permitted him to do so. His life had been threatened by Hufnagel on several occasions, and he believed if Hufnagel did not go to jail, his tyranny would continue. Long after the trial was over, Mark would continue to keep in touch with Fields, and in some ways, came to think of him like the son he would never have.

Once the judge entered the courtroom, and some announcements were made by the bailiff, the judge wasted no time in announcing the sentence. Franco would see just eight years in prison.

The district attorney objected to the light sentence but his protestations were ineffective. Mark Powers sat there, wondering how the justice system could have let Hufnagel off with such a mild sentence. It occurred to Mark that in eight years — or less if he was released on good behavior — they'd have to contend with Franco Hufnagel walking amongst them as a free man. It just didn't seem long enough.

Dressed in his orange jumpsuit, Franco was led from the courtroom by two of the sheriff's deputies, his hands cuffed in front of him. Before he left the courtroom, however, Hufnagel turned to say a few words to Mark Powers.

"This is not over, Powers! Eight years. The clock is ticking until you're a dead man!"

Juror's gasped, mouths dropped, and deputy's head's swiveled toward the judge at the front of the room.

"Hold on there, deputies" said the judge, now looking over his reading glasses and his eyebrows seriously arced. "Mr. Hufnagel, did you just threaten a federal agent in my courtroom?"

"Claro que sí, madre folladora," mumbled the soon-to-be prisoner in a hushed tone. One of the deputies motioned for another to take his place, then walked to the front of the courtroom where he whispered to the judge.

Now speaking loudly for the whole courtroom to hear, the judge clarified what he'd been told. "Thank you, Officer Quinones. I'm delighted you speak Español. Please let the record show I am adding two additional charges to Mr. Hufnagel's record. One is terroristic threatening against a federal agent, the other is contempt of court for suggesting yours truly enjoys carnal pleasures with my mother. Mr. Hufnagel, that kind of talk may be a part of your normal vernacular, but I find it reprehensible. Your remarks just bought you another four years in the Mountain City Hilton. Would you like to say anything else that might earn you an even longer sentence?"

"You can't do that!" shouted Hufnagel, struggling against the grip of the deputies.

"I certainly can, and I just did. Bye-bye now, Mr. Hufnagel. I suggest you quickly learn to play well with others before you end up in a prison cell with someone who can do you physical harm."

A smattering of applause erupted by those in attendance, but the judge asked for order in the court. The drama of the judge's response met the approval of the public, including the jury and Mark Powers. An additional four years made him feel a little better, but he was still thinking about the threat. As a young law enforcement officer, it bothered him. He was not hardened against such threats. This was a first for him, and he did not yet have the thick skin of a veteran. This would eat at him for quite some time.

The proceedings were over by 9 am and Mark's legal team congregated in the lobby of the courthouse. Suddenly, from behind him, someone grabbed his elbow as if to suggest they wished to speak with him. He turned to discover it was Craig Banister, the Assistant Superintendent of the park at that time.

"Congratulations, Ranger Powers. I'd like you to call me next week. Your work on this case was exemplary. I'd like to speak to you."

"Why thank you sir. I'd be happy to talk with you. But can you tell me what about, sir?"

"Your investigative skills. I think it's plain as day that you should consider being a special agent, not just a ranger. But let's talk about the pros and cons, and see if you would be interested in taking that career path. Good job, but I've got to run."

"Thank you, sir. I'll be in touch next week, for sure."

Banister winked at the young ranger as he walked away, smiling.

"Well, congratulations, Mark. Looks like this case has gotten you a promotion!" said one of Mark's lawyers.

Mark was ecstatic about the brief conversation, and it made him forget all about the threat from Franco Hufnagel, at least temporarily. He had only been a ranger for a few years, and was already on his way up the ladder. It seemed this had turned into one of the best days of his life.

Chapter 11

Mark Powers, Agent Toney and her team returned to the Little River station at about 2 a.m. They were replaced on the mountain by a much larger ECU (Evidence Collection Unit) who flew in to begin a more exhaustive site analysis which would leave no stone, or twig, untouched. Once at the station, they went to consolidate evidence found where the shooter had been positioned with that which Mark had confiscated from the abandoned campsite lower on the mountain. Sure enough, the tent stakes were identical. They now had a connection between that campsite and the shooter.

"What were your first impressions at the site," asked Sandy.

"You mean the campsite from the night before, or the site of the shooting?"

"The night before."

Mark replayed how he had stumbled upon the site after smelling smoke, and every other detail. His final comments were about how uncanny it was that he'd found that site which might have a connection with the Echo Ridge case.

"I think it's safe to say those backpacker's chainsaws you found were used to cut down those branches to give him a clear shot of the bald," said Sandy.

Agent Toney turned to agent Luken. "Let's start fresh in the morning with some metrics on who sells that brand of gear in this part of the country, 100 mile range. Get a data dump from Amazon and Cabela's for online buyers. I'm talking about sales of that brand of tent, the boom box, and the coffee pot. We can cross reference all of that and look for a common buyer."

"On it," said Luken.

"Great. Jeannine, I'd like to put you on the .308 caliber shells you dug up from the dirt on the bald. Look for any purchase histories, online or local shops, get 'em both. Let's see if anyone on that list matches the purchase histories for the other gear. Get the name and model of that deer stand, too, I almost forgot about that."

"Yes ma'am," said Jeannine.

Sandy knew they would not have footprint impressions back from the site until later the next day, so she didn't mention follow up on those items.

"Special Agent Powers," she said, "thanks for calling us into this investigation so quickly. Some locals wouldn't be so quick to do that, hoping to make a name for themselves."

"I'm not a local, I'm a federal law enforcement officer. I don't have a problem calling in other agencies, in fact, I welcome the help."

Mark grew silent, as did the other two. They were all churning over what they'd found, and how best to test their evidence for ways to identify the killer. Mark had been so convinced that the campsite had belonged to potheads, and yet now appeared to be wrong. And boy was he glad he was wrong... to think he'd actually stumbled onto a campsite being used by an assassin. Now he just hoped that the find could contribute something fruitful to the investigation.

"Agent Luken, I'd like you to send an evidence team up to the campsite Mark told us about. Comb over it. See if you can find anything that Mark didn't see. It was dusk when he was there, you might find more in the light of day. Mark, do you have directions for how to locate that encampment?"

"Will GPS coordinates work?"

"Ah, that's just the ticket. Excellent," said Luken.

"I'm still curious about the timing," said Sandy, going back to her own train of thought. "The shooter would have needed to know the exact location and time of the groundbreaking ceremony, so he could arrive early to saw off the branches like he did, AND, so he'd be in the perfect spot to have a shot at the right angle. This was all premeditated. He must have had inside information about where to be and when. We need to know how he got that information. We're going to need to question anyone who had access to that itinerary."

"I can get that for you," said Mark. "There was only a small inner circle of people who knew the exact date, time, and location. Belle and I were the only two who knew the specifics. Not even Banister knew until the last minute. Now, with respect to the media company, they were told they needed to be flexible enough to go on a moment's notice, so I think Belle notified them at like 7 pm the night before. That gave them 12 hours' notice. That was about the time when I discovered the empty campsite. Obviously, the shooter was already there, and already clearing branches, so he would not have gotten his info from the media company. The two vics from the EPA and the Sierra Club were notified days in advance and their attendance was optional. They were among the victims, so I think we can rule out that they tipped off a killer to go up there and start shooting."

"Another thought," said Agent Toney. "What if there were some architects or surveyors doing work up there on a deadline that could have used that drop-dead date to estimate a date for the ceremony?"

"But for all we know," added Gallenstein, "the gunman could have been staying at that campsite for days or weeks in advance, waiting to get word when the time was right. Maybe it wasn't critical to know the date up front."

"That's true," said Sandy. "You're right. Tom, when you go back up to that makeshift campsite, see if you can get an idea of how long it had been in use."

"Well, I can tell you," said Mark, "that there were practically no supplies up there. Unless the killer took the supplies with him when he fled the campsite. But I did not get the feeling that the site had been in use for more than a couple of days. But I guess there is still a chance he could have been up there for a while. No guarantee he wasn't moving around, camping in different spots until the time is right. Kind of hard to tell."

Sandy turned the conversation back to the information leak. "I am willing to bet we did have a leak that allowed that gunman to take the time to get ready for the shooting. It could be an inadvertent leak, or perhaps the shooter obtained the information covertly, via theft, or surveillance. Maybe the leaker didn't know their info was being compromised for this purpose. So when we begin questioning, let's remember the leaker may not have done this with intentionality."

"Sure," agreed Mark, "no problem there. But really, the only two people who could have leaked were Belle and myself."

"Well then we will need to conduct interviews with the two of you," agreed Sandy. This was not exactly the response Mark wanted to hear, but he knew if there was a leak, it was because the information was taken in a covert manner, not because he or Belle had loose lips.

"Whatever works," said Mark.

"Uh, I totally forgot to bring this up earlier, but I have something important to share while it's fresh in my mind, if you don't mind," said Mark. Sandy blinked a sleepy blink back at him and nodded for him to continue.

"I think there's a possibility that the governor knew who was responsible for the attack."

"Really? And why do you say that?" Sandy asked.

"Once I got to where she was lying, and while she was still alive, I heard her last words. Keep in mind, she was coughing and having a hard time using her breath to form words, but she said 'Shhhh....' at first, and then she had a little coughing spell. When she finished coughing, she said 'did...it.' And that was it. She took her last breath and died right then."

"And what do you think she meant by that, Mark?"

"First impression? Well, I thought she was trying to say something that started with the s sound, or the sh sound, like maybe she wanted to speak to her husband, Shane. Seemed logical. But then she coughed and said 'did... it.' I have to tell you, once she said that, it kind of made me think Shane might have had some connection to the shooter. I doubt he could have shot her from where he was because someone would have heard that shot. At least, I think they would. At one point Belle was shooting back at where she thought the sniper was located, and using a pistol, so if Shane did take a shot, it might have gone unnoticed."

"Could he have used a silencer?" asked Luken.

"No, I saw his weapon. No silencer," replied Mark, "although he could have had the suppressor attachment hidden in his bag or on his body, but because of the timing of things, I really doubt that was the case."

"Special Agent Powers, why didn't you share this earlier, this mention of her last words?" asked Agent Toney.

"I meant to say something, but we were so entrenched in the physical evidence up there, I never got around to telling you. But there it is. Right now. I should also tell you this is what I think she said. Isabella was closer than I was, and might have heard differently. But that's what I recall."

"It's obviously something we will focus on. I think once we do some interviews with others we might gain clarity. You said Shane was not present when she spoke those last words?"

"He was behind us, in the woods. Once she'd died, and he approached from behind, I don't believe he was aware that she'd said anything to Isabella and me. He wasn't even aware she'd died until he saw her lying on the ground, with blood on her torso. He had an instant reaction."

"Was she looking in his direction when she uttered those last words?"

"No, she was making pretty solid eye contact with Isabella and I. Janet was kind of looking back and forth between the two of us, almost in a panic. She knew she was dying and was looking at each of us desperately, like either of us had a chance to help her, or hear what she had to say. That's my take."

"When she said 'did... it,' is there any way you may have mistaken those words?"

"Like I said, Isabella was leaning forward, more than me, so maybe she heard things differently. But I've told you what I thought she said, and I'm sticking to it. What else could it have been?"

"I don't know. Maybe she was trying to say 'Shane, did it get Shane?' meaning 'did the bullet get Shane?' Could it be she was concerned about him, since she could not see him?"

"That's interesting, but no, I was positive at that moment she was trying to tell us who killed her. That's just how it came across."

"Okay. In the morning, our first visit will be to this assistant, Isabella, and we'll see if her thoughts match up with yours. And we'll pay Mr. Goodwyn a visit as well."

"Definitely. But there's one more thing," said Mark. "It's so remote up there on the mountain top. I know your collection team is up there right now, but how long do you think this is going to last? We have contractors who are supposed to begin work up there in a few days. I need to know if we will keep this designated as a crime scene long enough to delay their work."

"Logistics, logistics. Yes, we need to talk about all that, as well as our use of helicopters to get up and down that mountain. But Mark, I'm about to fall asleep standing here, so we're going to have to save that conversation for the morning. Which is just a couple of hours away. Is there anywhere I can close my eyes here? And maybe for Tom and Jeannine as well?"

"There's a sofa in the break room, and a couple of cots in the closet. Or you're a few minutes' drive to a hotel."

"I'll go with the sofa," said Sandy. "If I lay down on a comfortable bed, I'll sleep for 12 hours, and I can't afford to do that!"

With the dawn came the media tidal-wave of inquiry surrounding the shooting on top of the mountain. Mobile news vans from Knoxville, Nashville, Chattanooga, Atlanta and Charlotte were all finding prime locations in Cades Cove so their reporters could have a view of Thunderhead Mountain in the background. Hours later, national outlets arrived to have their own reporter talent captured by their cameras instead of leaving that to the local affiliates. In just the span of a morning, hundreds of hotel rooms in Townsend and Gatlinburg were booked solid with reporters and their crews.

Not satisfied with the short, bulleted list of facts offered up by the GSMNP, some news crews began to work their way up the mountain, only to be turned away by its brutal pitch and crime scene tape. Then there was an appearance of privately chartered helicopters that formed a swarm in the skies above Thunderhead Mountain. They attempted to capture video footage of the crime scene, even if there were few other facts about what happened to relay to their viewers.

Belle Whittle became the voice of the park, fielding questions, and offering insight at a noon-time press conference from the Sugarland Visitor Center. She covered the same talking points that were offered earlier over the Associated Press, but she did elaborate on some of the finer points as many reporters proactively questioned her for more details.

By day's end, the entire nation knew that the governor of Tennessee and several others were killed on the side of a mountain near Gatlinburg, although some outlets erroneously reported the mountain was actually in Gatlinburg. It had also been reported that this had been the work of a solitary shooter, working alone and from a great distance.

The cable news networks were cranking up their hype machines by interviewing supposed gun experts who speculated the shooter used an automatic weapon to kill the victims. There were renewed calls by new program hosts to ban assault-style weapons. Then a clip of Governor

Goodwyn stating she was in favor of more gun control legislation was unearthed and replayed every 15 minutes. The NRA would produce a swift and strong rebuttal to the gun control sentiment flooding the airwaves once their leadership had a complete and consistent understanding of the facts. As for Shane himself, he was barricaded in his hotel room, trying to cope with not only the media in the lobby, but also his feelings for the loss of his wife.

At about the same time as Belle's press conference, Isabella Lopez was resting in her hotel room with a sore and bandaged arm. She had spent the night in the hospital, and had been released early in the morning. The bullet had not been lodged in her arm, but instead passed through muscle only. She cursed the wound, which now was patched up by stitches, right where she'd had a rose tattoo applied a few years earlier.

She ensured the adjoining door was fully closed and locked. She felt quite awkward that her boss's husband was just on the other side of that door, and yet, her boss was dead. Isabella never liked Shane, especially with his recurring racial slurs, and she wanted nothing to do with him at the moment, nor ever again. Yet, she felt sorry for him now, having lost his wife. She shook her head, wondering how she ever got involved in such a soap opera.

Isabella had other concerns. She did not want to be harassed by the media; she was uncomfortable being in the spotlight. She had worked hard to get a governor elected, but was always behind the scenes. She would not allow Janet to bring her out onto any stage, or in front of any audience. That was not her style. She was also terrified at the idea of being interviewed by the FBI. That was pressure she simply wanted to avoid at all costs.

She heard a knock on the door, but then realized it was not *her* door. It was Shane's. Just as she heard him open his door, there was another knock, somewhat louder, on *her* door. The timing was odd. She opened her door to find Agent Toney to greet her. Quickly a badge was displayed while Sandy introduced herself.

"Good morning Ms. Lopez. I'm Agent Toney with the Federal Bureau of Investigation. I would like to ask you a few questions. Is now a good time?"

As the agent spoke, Isabella could hear the familiar voice of Mark Powers saying something similar in the hallway, but to Shane Goodwyn. It appeared Powers and Toney had arrived together. How convenient for them that both of the people they wanted to talk to were in adjoining rooms.

"Do I have a choice?" asked Isabella.

"Of course you do," said the agent. "You can talk to me now or you can talk to me later. I'm flexible that way."

"How late is later?" asked Isabella.

"Oh, I don't know. I could give you 15 minutes to freshen up, if you need the time."

"Yes, I can see that's very flexible," said Isabella. "Come in."

As Sandy entered, she asked, "How are the walls in this hotel. Thick enough?"

"Not bad. I could hear Janet and her husband over there sometimes."

"Well then, let's go have an espresso, and get away from those two in the other room. My treat," said the agent, with a big, inviting smile. It appeared genuine, not manipulative.

"But the press. They are everywhere outside the hotel."

"We can leave through the kitchen, and go out by the dock. We'll get you into a car with tinted windows. And then… perhaps we'll visit some quaint little Gatlinburg coffee shop, or pancake house. Have you eaten today?"

Isabella felt as though something was not right. From everything she had ever seen in the movies or on television, this was not how the FBI rolled.

"It's okay. Isabella. Some of us FBI agents can be serious, and casual, all at the same time. It's an art, really."

"Well then, okay."

Minutes later the two were sitting at the Pancake Pantry sipping on coffee drinks. A waitress wearing a traditional apron over a knee-length skirt brought a pile of chocolate covered pancakes topped with powdered sugar and sat it on the table in front of Isabella. With one arm in a sling, Isabella was going to have to get to work with just one hand. The pancakes did a lot to help her relax, although she was still worried about what they were going to discuss. Sandy asked about Isabella's injury prior to diving into the questions. With the pleasantries aside, they got down to business.

"So, Isabella, tell me everything you remember about what happened up on the mountain."

"You must surely already know, right?" asked Isabella, wondering why she would need to rehash everything.

"We know the story as it's been told to us by others. We don't know your story, yet. So tell me."

Much of Isabella's story matched what Mark Powers had told Sandy as they helicoptered up to the scene for the first time, but Mark had not been in the bald when the gunfire erupted, so his account was limited. In addition to using a notebook, Sandy was also using a voice recorder app on her phone to capture this discussion. She began taking more copious notes once Isabella got to the point where they were under fire.

"I took cover behind a rock, but it was not very big and I was afraid I was going to get shot," said Isabella. "I looked over and Janet was in a similar situation. I could see panic on her face."

"How far apart were you?"

"Maybe 15 feet."

"Had you been standing next to her when the assault started?"

"I was with her most of the time. Side by side. I loved working for her. I can't imagine why anyone would want to kill her?" Isabella shed tears, and the agent waited. She knew the emotional scars of the event ran deep, and time was needed to steady the witness if they were going to get through this conversation without an emotional breakdown. Once Isabella returned to her pancakes, Sandy took that as a sign she could resume.

"It sounds like the two of you sought cover apart from one another. Why was that?"

"We did. I had been by her side before the shooting, but then, well, this is going to sound silly, but the outfit she was wearing was ridiculous. I suggested she remove her ball cap, but she refused. I think she was trying to go for that sporty look like the other ranger had going for her, but it wasn't working for Janet. Anyway, I went to get my backpack to get a hairpiece I wanted to suggest to her and then the shooting started. At that point forward, we were separated."

"What happened next?"

"A few people were shot, and fell over. It looked like we were all going to die. I... I thought I was going to die too.

And that's when Janet started looking around in a panic. I could see her looking behind us, back to where the trail was. Then she ran up the hill, back to the woods. At first I thought she was crazy, but she made it, and I made a decision that maybe she did the right thing, and so I ran up there too. I ended up behind a tree across the trail from her. We looked at each other at one point, glad that we were both safe. Or at least we thought we were."

"So she had not been shot, yet, when you both found cover in the tree line, right?" asked Sandy.

"That's right. We were both standing behind these big trees, and I felt safe there."

"So tell me when and how she was shot."

"I did not see that. I saw Shane coming up the trail behind us and then he ducked behind a tree, farther back, behind us. And then maybe a minute after that, Mark Powers came running along from behind us, too. He passed me and Janet, out into the open, and he was carrying his rifle, I know that, but I didn't see what happened with him after that. Honestly, I was so afraid I just crouched down and had my eyes closed. I'm ashamed to admit that I was crying, too. Not exactly what you'd expect from a strong woman, but I'm just being truthful. I just wanted it to be over. Then, just like that, the shooting stopped. I looked over at Janet, and that's when I saw her on the ground. I called to her, but she did not answer. Then I saw... a, um..."

"It's okay, Isabella. Take your time," assured the agent, seeing Isabella was growing upset.

"A, um, blood stain on her jacket. She must have been hit by one of the last bullets fired."

The agent had previously considered it was the governor that was the primary target in the shooting, and this piece of testimony supported that idea.

"But you didn't actually see her fall?"

"No."

"Did you see any gunfire from the distance, while the attack was still underway?"

"No. Like I said, once I got to the tree, I was terrified and didn't dare stick my head out to get hit in the head with a bullet."

Sandy paused and gathered her thoughts, followed by additional note taking.

"Did you notice anything peculiar at any other point during the day, leading up to the shooting?" asked the agent.

"Not really, other than I was surprised to see they had horses for part of the hike. I love horses, but I don't like them being slaves, working for the amusement or convenience of humans. In fact I hate that. I'm a PETA member. That's why I declined riding a horse, and chose to walk."

"But nothing else that might be suspicious, like strange comments or looks from the people handling the horses... or weird behavior from the media company... anything like that?"

"No. The people taking care of the horses were all very nice. Once we finished riding, they were gone. They should set the horses free, though. Please put that in your records. I want people to know my stance on that."

Silence grew between them, until Lopez brought up something entirely different to talk about.

"Agent Toney, there's something else that I have to tell you." Isabella was now perking up, filled with energy, with her sadness about her boss and the horses suddenly gone. "Janet's last words were that Shane did it."

"Really? You're absolutely sure about that?"

"Yes, she said his name, then she coughed, and then she said 'did it.'"

"You're telling me you heard her clearly articulate his full name. Is that what you are saying?"

"Yes. She said Shane, for sure. Now, how he did it, I have no idea. After all, she was shot by the sniper who was in front of us, and Shane was behind us. Maybe she meant that he was responsible, and hired someone to do it. I want to help this investigation as much as I can, and I believe to the bottom of my heart that Shane Goodwyn killed his wife, somehow. He was involved, for sure."

"That's very important insight, Isabella. I'm glad you thought to share this with me. Why did you not tell me this right away?"

"I don't know. I'm nervous, I guess. But look, I've watched a lot of CSI episodes in my day, enough to know that the husband is one of the first persons suspected when a wife is killed. That's because men are generally evil. There might be a few good ones out there, but the rest are like Shane Goodwyn. You should take a good, hard look at him. He's shady. I've known Janet for a few years, and can tell you that he is not a good husband. He yells, or... yelled, at her all the time. I never saw him hit her, but sometimes when he'd get really mad, she'd cower like she was about to get punched or slapped. It was kind of like she'd been conditioned to expect it. And I could see the fear in her eyes. I don't think she knew he was going to try to kill her up on that mountain, but once she was shot, I think she knew it was him behind it. That's why she said he did it."

"How long have you known Shane?"

"For as long as I have known Janet. They have always been married for as long as I worked for her. And he has always said racist things to me, and treated me like I did not matter. Of course he'd later say he was only joking. Janet was always apologizing for him. What she saw in that man I do not know. I mean, yes, many women probably find him to be good looking, but his personality is severely lacking. He is an abuser and an oppressor of women. He's also the reason I'll never get married, which is a worthless institution anyway, born of a ritual where women were traded from fathers to suitors like cattle."

Sandy was getting quite a hefty dose of Isabella's politics in this exchange, but she tried to remain focused on gathering details relevant to the case.

"So you are saying Shane and Janet had serious marital issues, to the best of your knowledge?"

"Yes."

"You were sharing an adjoining room at the hotel. Could you hear if they were fighting then?"

"No. In fact, it was weird. He was being a jerk to me, as usual, but he was being really nice to her all of a sudden. It was not normal. Almost like he was pretending. You might think I'm crazy for thinking like this, but in planning her death, suddenly he knew she was going to be out of his life, once and for all, and he was happy about it, so it was a 'it won't be long and I'll be done with you forever' kind of thing, so he was being nice."

Agent Toney paused and considered the accusation. "Isabella, do you *really* think Shane Goodwyn hired someone to kill the governor? We have another account that she did not fully say Shane's first name, but it was more like a 'shhh' sound."

Isabella realized that testimony had to have come from Agent Powers. She knew there was a chance he might disagree with her recollection of exactly what Janet had said, but she was going to move ahead with her assertion that Shane's name was upon her lips, regardless of what Mark might have said.

"I can't say for sure if he was involved, but it would make sense to me if he did, especially because of her last words, that he did it."

"Okay, thank you. We will look into this closely, for sure," said the agent.

Toney was not in a position to discuss alternative scenarios with witnesses. She needed to gather, not distribute, details of the case. She regretted having let it slip that someone else had heard Janet say something different than what Isabella had heard. It was too late, she couldn't take it back, but she was compelled to find out if perhaps Mark was in the wrong about Janet's last words.

As Sandy sat there, fending off the temptation of pancakes, she considered the possibilities surrounding Isabella's theory. This killing had all the marks of an assassination of a political figure, not the work of a husband looking to get rid of his wife. But what if that's what Shane Goodwyn wanted it to look like? That would also explain why, per Mark's recounting of events, Shane did not proceed into the bald area to be with his wife. He may have wanted to stay out of harm's way as the bullets were flying. Yet, three others were killed too, and another critically wounded. If a sniper were brought on for this attack, surely they would be capable enough to not hit four of the wrong people before the intended target. If this attack was an attempt at killing a spouse, it was definitely *overkill,* the word being a bit punny, but terribly accurate.

Before they finished their interview, agent Toney spent some time getting the backstory of how Isabella became involved in politics, and more specifically, with Janet Goodwyn. Nothing there seemed surprising, or remarkable, except that Isabella was politically to the far left and working for a conservative republican. Isabella was a graduate student in Poli Sci and had volunteered for a number of political action groups before getting on board with Goodwyn, just in time for her run for governor.

After more questions were asked, and the waitress refilled Isabella's coffee several times, the interview was over. Additional measures were required to get Isabella back to her hotel room without the media discovering her. As Isabella entered her room, Sandy placed her ear to the door of the adjoining room and could tell Mark was no longer interviewing Shane Goodwyn. She then returned to her vehicle, eager to speak to Mark to learn about his impressions of Shane Goodwyn.

Mark had been greeted at the door by a smile-less face. Goodwyn did not appear to be sad or somber the morning after his wife was killed, rather, he seemed angry. Mark considered this could be due to his interaction with Shane during their retreat down the trail when Mark scolded him for tossing his knife into a tree. Having grown up with three brothers, Mark was not accustomed to this kind of grudge holding. He knew star athletes could sometimes be narcissistic and egotistical, and thought perhaps that was where Shane's vibe was coming from.

Reluctantly, Shane invited Powers into his room, the latter walking quite stiffly. Not only had the previous day been a life changer, it had also left the big man aching all over his body. Mark took a spindled chair near the room's desk, while Shane was seated on the edge of the bed.

Mark decided to lead with some light banter before diving into the questions. "We did about 15 miles on those trails yesterday. Quite a workout, eh?"

"Are you saying I couldn't handle it?"

Mark was shocked at the combative reply. "Well, no, I didn't mean that at all. I'm just saying, that's a lot of miles in one day. I'm even a little sore from it, too."

"I'm not sore. Maybe just a little tight, that's all," said Shane, wanting the record to show he had no long term discomfort from the workout.

Mark looked around, and noticed all of Janet's belongings had been placed in a pile on the floor near the door. "Again, Mr. Goodwyn, let me say how sorry I am for the loss of your wife. I'm sure it must have been difficult to return to this room and deal with her belongings," he said, glancing at the stacked items.

"Yeah. What am I supposed to do with the stuff? I don't know. Get rid of it, I guess."

"Everybody handles it differently, there's no manual on how to become a widower. I had the same thing happen to me 10 years ago."

"Really?" said Shane, eyebrows raised in surprise, his demeanor now less defensive. "I did not know that. I'm sorry."

"Thanks. I still think about her every day. Probably always will."

"What did you do with all her stuff? Get rid of it?"

Mark felt suddenly uneasy to reveal his answer. "No... I still have it all. Just like she left it. But... you know, that's just me. So Shane, let's get down to business here. We're talking to everyone who was at the scene of the attack to get their recollections of exactly what happened. We're hoping there might be something in the details that will lead us to the killer.

"Everyone... right. I know what you're doing, Powers. You're mostly interested in me because I'm the husband, aren't you? The world always thinks the evil husband killed his innocent wife. Well that's bullshit. There's no way I could have killed her myself, and I didn't have anything to do with this at all. So maybe I need to have my lawyer present. Isn't that like part of my Miranda rights?"

"I have not read you the Mirandas because you're not under arrest. You are not even a suspect. All we are doing right now is gathering facts, which you can do cooperatively, or not."

"But you're targeting me just because I'm the husband."

"That's not true. Everyone who was in our party going up that mountain will be interviewed. Even the horse handlers will be paid a visit. In fact, the FBI are talking to Isabella Lopez as we speak."

"About me, right? They are asking her all about me, I'm sure, because that's how it works these days."

"Look, Shane, I hate to be the bearer of bad news, but the world doesn't revolve around you. And even if I was here to talk to you, and only you, all about you, it's not because we have a conspiracy theory about you."

Shane rose from the bed, with his head nearly touching the ceiling of the hotel room. His size was double that of Mark who was still seated. He pointed a finger at Mark and delivered a threat. "You better be careful, little man. You don't know who you are talking to. You mess with me, and I can break you."

Mark retained his composure and calmly replied, as if Shane's threat had never been mentioned. "Sit down Mr. Goodwyn. We can do this your way, or we can do this my way. Your way is that of resistance. That just might make you an official suspect. And if that happens, the media will have a field day with you. And then once you are in the media spotlight, the court of public opinion will sway against you. And lastly, of course, your gig with the NRA will be terminated because you'll be useless to them. You're in PR, and they are surely a little sensitive to negative press. They will drop you like a hot potato. But I'm sure you'll find more work. Ripley's is just down the street. You could be in their display case as the 'guy who lost the best job ever, believe it or not.' So I suggest we do this my way, and you politely answer my questions without all this animosity. So how's it going to be? Your way, or my way?"

Shane stood motionless, mentally processing what Mark had said with a surprisingly cheery demeanor. Then Mark continued.

"Oh, and by the way, I'm a special agent of the National Parks, a federal organization, so you've just threatened a federal agent. Maybe you could take that finger you just pointed at me, tap it on your phone, and Google how long you could end up in jail for threatening a federal agent."

Shane stared at the happy-go-lucky ranger who was not fazed by the threat at all.

"Go ahead. I have time to wait," added Mark.

Shane didn't take much longer before he nodded, a gesture which clearly meant he would behave. He finally resumed his sitting position on the corner of the bed, facing Powers.

"What I want to know," said Mark, acting as if the threat had never been levied, "is exactly what happened when you went ahead of me and Mr. Banister on the trail that day."

"Well, it's pretty simple. I went ahead, and was maybe just a little down from where the trail opens up into that field up there. That's when I heard everyone yelling about something. I really couldn't see anything going on there because it kind of sloped down and away from the trail. I could not hear gunfire at first, but I heard people yelling that there was a shooter."

"So you didn't see any bullets hitting rocks or trees, or sadly, some of our party, is that correct?"

"No. I was too far away, still. When I heard 'Shooter on the right!', that's about when I leaned up against the tree and began to ready my weapon and think of a plan for how to help out."

"And that's when I came running along, towards the bald. But Shane, I didn't see you readying your weapon. It looked like you were just frozen with fear. I'm just telling you that was my impression, and I've already spoken to the FBI about what I saw. I've seen that look, many, many times before."

Shane's temper appeared to be building but he kept a lid on it.

"Well then you saw wrong, mister forest ranger. I was just thinking about what I should do next when you passed me. THEN I readied my weapon. But I heard someone shout "Hold your fire." Then I kind of figured, like, *what's the point*? The only reason I should have gone up would have been because I had a gun, and could help out that way, but then they said to stop shooting. THAT's why I wasn't budging, Ranger Powers. I'm no pussy."

"I never said you were, Shane. But you're a married man, and your wife was up there. Didn't you want to go up to at least check on her?"

"Of course I did. And I did do that, as you know. That's when you were crouched down there with Snowflake and the two of you were looking at poor Janet, dead on the ground."

Mark gave the moment its due and continued.

"Now. Let me go back to what happened when you were still in front of me on the trail. I'd like to know if you saw your wife or Isabella Lopez once they ran up the bald and hid behind a couple of trees."

"I only peeked that way once. I saw somebody on the left of the trail, and someone else to the right. There were some bushes blocking my view of the person on the left and now I guess we know that was my honey, but I didn't know it at the time. And I also know the person on the right of the trail ended up being Snowflake, the one who worked for Janet, but I didn't recognize her at that time either."

"You didn't recognize her..." said Mark, with his head down, repeating Shane's comments while he wrote them in his notebook.

"Not really. I couldn't see her face, but I could tell it was a woman because she had long hair and I knew a few of the women who were up there that day had long hair. None of the dudes did."

"When you decided to come up behind me, what was happening then?" Mark asked.

"I didn't walk up to where you were until I heard 'Oh My God!' That's when I saw Snowflake kneeling next to a body, and you were kneeling there too. And, uh... then I walked a little closer and I kind of realized that was my honey lying there on the ground. I was in shock."

"Shane, you keep referring to Isabella Lopez as 'Snowflake.' Do you have a problem with calling her by her real name?"

"Sort of. I don't like that chick. She would always whisper bad things about me to my wife. She'd land me in the doghouse, all because she was sticking her nose in where it didn't belong. I call her Snowflake just to piss her off. You know, that's what they call the college-aged lefties these days. The same thing with calling her a chick. I know women don't like that term these days, but I use it intentionally with her to piss her off. She's so damned sensitive, it doesn't take much to tick her off, like calling her Snowflake."

Mark figured there was a lot of personal history there that probably did not figure into his investigation, so for the time being he dodged Shane's strange comments once more. His apparent chauvinism and political bullying would be noted in his report, however.

"Did you see any of the people who were leading the horses come further up the trail, behind us?"

"Nope. Once we headed up on foot, that's the last I saw of them folks."

"What about Banister? Did you see him at any time between when you walked away from him, when I was still with him, until the time when Janet was shot?"

"Nope. I just assumed he was still taking a shit. Old men, you know, need lots of fiber to get their bowels in order, do you know what I mean?"

"Yes, I think. Okie-dokie then. Is there anything else you can think of that ran through your mind during the whole episode? Anything that you thought was curious, or weird? Anything we have not talked about, that I have not thought to ask?"

"Well, there is one thing that I kind of already mentioned, but I think it might just have been my imagination. Maybe."

"What's that?"

"When I was readying myself to jump into action, listening to everything going on, I thought it was kind of interesting that I could not hear any of the gunfire from the sniper. He was too far away, for sure. But it reminded me of something. Or somebody. Do you know of Chris Kyle?"

"I sure do. The American Sniper. They made a movie about him. A true patriot."

"Yeah. Well I've met him. He could take someone out from a mile away. In those cases, he said, the target's not going to hear the shot. All they're going to hear, if anything, is the hiss of that incoming bullet before it takes them out. So you know, since I could not see what was going on, I was listening closely. There was obviously a shooter out there, but I could not hear his rifle. But then our folks were shooting back with their pistols, and I heard those loud and clear. Then I heard one pistol go off that sounded like it was pretty close to me. Like... it was in the woods, not out there in the bald, as you call it. Then I had this idea that maybe whoever was attacking us had more than one gunman. It seemed so much closer, like this other person was maybe within twenty or thirty yards of where I stood."

"So you are saying the sniper did not act alone?"

"Yeah, because that one gunshot sounded so much louder than the rest coming from your people on the bald. I'm thinking they might have been working together, somehow."

"What do you mean by that?"

"Well, as I think about it now, like what if the sniper was just trying to get everyone to run away from the grassy bald area, and back down the trail. Think about it. Everyone would be more in single file. Then you would just need one other shooter within the woods to have an easier shot at closer range as my wife ran by. Maybe there really was someone else there, and I just never saw them, although, like I said already, I might have been hearing things. I mean, look, Janet did not get shot until she got back to the woods, you know? That jives with what I'm saying. Or maybe I'm just bat shit crazy. I don't know."

"It is possible you heard someone shooting in a different direction, just for that one shot. It could have been a misfire, maybe from someone on my team, even. For example, Talia Manaia was critically injured by the sniper, and maybe as she was shot, she pulled the trigger of her gun while falling backwards. That shot might have sounded different to you back in the woods because it was the only round shot in your direction."

"Maybe. But I was so focused on running up that hill and jumping into the fight that my adrenaline was pumping big time. Maybe it was just my imagination, blowing that sound out of proportion."

"I'm not going to discount anything at this point," said Mark. "You could be right about a second shooter. That's a common tactic used by terrorists. They attack a group of innocents, and when the first responders show up, there's another wave of attacks just for them. They use the first attack to lure more victims."

"Something like that, yeah."

"But you're the only one who has any evidence of a second shooter, at least that I know of, and it wasn't visual evidence, just something you heard. I think we'd need more than that to go on if we can use that to find a second shooter, but we will definitely examine this as a possibility."

While Agent Toney had been cautious not to discuss alternate theories during her interview of Isabella Lopez, that was not Mark's style. He believed insight could come from anywhere and was always willing to expound upon possibilities, even while conducting interviews with a witness.

"And Shane," continued Mark, "why didn't you bring this up on the mountain? If you thought there could have seriously been a second shooter, it would have been good to hear this as we headed back down the mountain with the whole group. And when we stopped for a bathroom break, you were just casually tossing your knife into the tree. That doesn't sound like a man who's worried of being shot at any moment."

"Honestly, well, this might sound like I'm an asshole, but you know..."

"Go on. What is it?"

"Well... to me it was obvious they had already gotten what they came for already. Everything seemed to settle down after Janet was shot. She was dead and those bastards probably hightailed it. My gut told me that once they got her, it was over. That's kind of when I figured what I heard must have been my imagination. Plus, you know, you were pretty high strung about getting everyone down the mountain, so it didn't seem like a good time to go into what I might, or might not have, heard up there."

"Okay, so I just have to get you to settle on one of these two ideas. As you sit here now, what do you believe the most? That there was a second gunman, or not?"

"I really can't say. I'd say it's a 50/50 tossup. I just don't know. All that stuff that happened up there was like happening so fast. I really can't say anything for sure."

"Shane," said Mark with a pause. "I have one more question, and it's a doozie. I have to ask this to get your response on record, and if I were you, I'd see this as a way to state your case. And I have to ask because you did have a weapon with you. Shane Goodwyn, did you use the gun you were carrying that day to kill your wife?"

"There it is. See, that's what I'm talking about. What took you so long? Always blaming the husband."

"Shane, keep your composure. If you expected me to ask that, then you should not be surprised. I can't just NOT ask that question. It's my job. So answer me, did you kill the governor?"

"Absolutely not. I did not fire my weapon at all that day, or since. I loved my wife and still do. To suggest I'd harm her like that is disgusting." The big guy moved to a suitcase and removed his CCW holster and the gun nestled inside. He handed it to Mark, handle first, but Mark quickly retrieved a plastic bag from his pocket and had the gun placed inside.

The weapon was a Houston H9, an elegant, cutting-edge pistol that had only recently been introduced to the market. It was state-of-the-art and yet practical, fitted for a 9mm round, the most common round available for handguns. It featured a 1911-style trigger and a low bore axis which would produce minimal recoil when discharged. It was a futuristic-looking weapon, to be sure, and perfectly in line with what would be expected of a spokesperson for the NRA.

"Do all the damned testing you want on that thing," continued Shane. "It's still got all 15 bullets in the mag, one in the chamber, the safety is on. I dare you to find any proof it was used to shoot my poor honey."

"Thank you. This will be helpful. And Shane Goodwyn, did you have any involvement with another individual or individuals in the planning, funding, or execution of the attack against Janet, your wife?"

"Hell no. But whoever did better hope you find them before I do."

"Thank You, Shane. I'll take good care of this handgun. It is a real trophy weapon, isn't it?" Mark was once more trying to diffuse Shane's temper, and it was working.

"You're damn right. My price was goose eggs because it was a gift from Houston. Your price would be $1500. It's a beauty. If there's a damned mark on it when you return it, the forestry service can buy me a new one."

"We're not the US Forest Service. We're the National Park Service. Two different things. Smoky Bear's not one of us."

"No kidding. Never knew that."

To Mark, it seemed talking about guns put Shane in a more manageable mood.

"What exactly do you do for the NRA, Shane?" asked Mark.

"I'm a spokesperson, of sorts. Part of the job is for me to maintain a good relationship with manufacturers and gun outlets, like firing ranges. On the high end, I get to meet dignitaries from other countries. I can wine and dine them, take them hunting... it's a pretty sweet deal."

"International politicians? Really. The NRA has an international presence? I just thought they were an American organization."

"Mostly."

"You take them hunting around here?"

"Anywhere we can legally hunt. Been to Canada a lot. Africa. Wherever."

Mark's phone buzzed, so he glanced at it. Belle was texting him. "Let's chat when u have a chance." He ignored it for the time being, and resumed working in his notebook, feverishly trying to catch up with everything Shane had told him. The feeling between the two men was that the interview had just ended. While Mark wrote, Shane got up from the bed and walked over to the pile of Janet's belongings. He stared at them for a moment before speaking.

"You left all your wife's possessions just like she'd left them?" asked Shane.

"Yes, I did. All her photos and awards are still on the walls of our house. I kept her trinkets. Her favorite coffee mug. Even a letter she wrote to me which I didn't open before she was killed. One of these days I might just have to open that letter, but for now, I like to think there's something she still has to tell me, like she's not really gone yet."

"Killed, huh?"

"Murdered. Yes. But I'd rather not talk about that, if you don't mind."

"Yup. Sorry to hear about that, man. I'm going to do the same thing with Janet's stuff. Once I get back home, you know. I guess I'll try to put these things back where she would have kept them. Can't exactly leave everything like she left it in a hotel room... they're expecting me to check out sooner or later."

Mark could detect a slight thread of humor in Shane's remark, although still tinged with sadness.

"Do what you got to do. That's all I can tell you," said Mark. "But if you don't mind me giving you some advice, well, if you need to take off work for a month, do it. Or if you need to work overtime to keep from getting depressed, well then you do that instead. Everybody's different. Just do what you think feels right. I went back to work right away, and people were whispering that I must not have loved her very much because I wasn't grieving or some other bullshit like that. People just don't understand. I advise that you do what you got to do. Don't listen to anybody else, except maybe a therapist, a pastor, or a really good friend."

Mark stood and shook Shane's hand, immediately wishing he hadn't. While not a sign of aggression, Shane's handshake was slightly painful, evident that the man didn't exactly know his own strength.

Shane managed a slight smile. "Thanks, man. Sorry about being an asshole earlier." Mark recalled some of Shane's comments throughout the interview, and considered the sentence would be more accurate without the adverb at the end. He was quite certain Shane was most likely an asshole all of the time.

With that, he bid Shane farewell and left the hotel room in search of his new partner from the FBI. He could not wait to share his thoughts on Shane Goodwyn.

Chapter 12

Late the same evening, several hospital patients in wheelchairs were sitting under a car port at the LeConte Medical Center in Sevierville. They were waiting for their rides to circle around and pick them up and were being treated to a down-home jamboree of music. A pickup truck had entered the lot while blazing bluegrass music from its stereo system. It was none other than Mark Powers, driving his own truck for a change, instead of his cruiser.

Generally, Mark was quick to draw a distinction between traditional bluegrass and what he called 'Newgrass.' The later was his favorite, with artists like Bela Fleck, Sam Bush, or Alison Kraus & Union Station being top tier. Only rarely did he dive into the traditional catalog of Flatt & Scruggs, Ralph Stanley or Bill Monroe. In this instance, he was taking a hybrid approach, listening to a young band with a traditional style, called *Blue Highway*. Loudly, for all to hear, they were crooning a song called *It's a Long, Long Road*:

"It's a long long road to wander all alone
It's a cold cold wind hear it moan
Crying like a lost child out in the night
Searching for the way and looking for the light

Back in the days when we were happy
Our love was the warmth and the light
But now the dark shadows are falling
And day is quickly fading into night

When the sun goes down behind the mountain
And the chilly wind is blowing through the pines
How often do I think about my darling
And the sunny garden where the roses twine."

After parking, Mark entered the extra wide sliding doors at the main entrance. "Go tell it on the mountain!" said an old-timer in his wheelchair as Mark passed. Mark smiled and tipped his hat the old man who was happy to have had some reason to tap his toe.

Expressly, Mark received directions to the ICU where he could find Talia. His badge helped him get in to see her, whereas normally non-relatives would not have access.

When he entered the room, there were two nurses who greeted him. Seeing Mark's uniform, the nurses correctly surmised he was a coworker of the woman lying in the bed. Mark also clarified that he was an investigator, and flipped his badge for good measure. The male nurse gave Mark an update on Talia's condition while the female nurse continued recording data into a computer tablet. After shifting where they stood to give Mark bedside access, he looked at Talia. Her closed eyes were all he could see of her face, as a respirator mouth-piece covered her nose and mouth.

"What's the prognosis? Is she expected to pull through?" asked Mark.

"You'll have to talk to the 'attending' about that," said the male nurse, not wanting to overstep his bounds.

Once the nurses left the room, Mark pulled up a chair and sat down next to his coworker.

"If you can hear me, Talia, I just want you to know it's Mark. I'm here."

There was no response, no reaction whatsoever.

"I should have come earlier, but you know, there's an investigation going on. Look, uh, I know I given you a hard time about stuff lately...like all the flirting."

A smile came to Mark's face as he imagined what her response would be if she were awake: *you can give me a hard time anytime you want, Marky-Mark. The harder the better!*

"Funny thing is, I'd give anything right now to hear one of your raunchy flirtations. Political correctness stinks. Those flirts of yours add a little spice to my day, truth be known. I understand it's just your style. I just give you the warnings because I don't want someone else to take you too seriously and get you fired. I like you, Talia, and I think you are a great asset to the park service."

Mark thought about how odd it was to be talking to someone who was unconscious, in an empty room. Yet, he'd read about how sometimes they still understand what someone says to them, and so he was playing the odds that just maybe she did too.

"And Talia, I know about that incident that happened when you were first hired. I know it was classified as confidential, at your request, but I overheard a couple of rangers talking about it. That's the only way I know. I'm just so sorry for what you went through. I admire you for being such a strong woman. If you could get through that, you can get through this, Talia. That's why I'm bringing it up. Not trying to ambush you with bad memories when you're in this state, just wanting you to know you can do it, because you've already done it before. I'm your biggest fan, right about now, and I'm going to be here for you, as often as I can be, until you get better. And when you come back to the office, it will make my day to hear you call me Marky-Mark. I still don't get that, by the way, but it's a funny thing you do. We will have those laughs again, I'm sure. Just keep fighting Talia."

There was still no reaction from his co-worker. Mark sat for a few more minutes, thinking about many of the laughs they'd had together, but now finding his mind drifting toward the evidence and the unanswered questions. He wanted to fix this, and since he was not a doctor, finding the perps was the only way he knew to help.

Eventually he caught himself feeling sleepy. He was accustomed to knowing how to work through drowsiness, but this was the kind of sleepiness that would start to close his eyes without permission. Still, he knew when he finally rested at home, he might get four hours of sleep before his mind would jolt him back into consciousness. This case would seep into his dreams and keep him awake for the rest of the night. He came to recognize this pattern during the months following Laurie's murder.

He patted the blanket covering his coworker, and rose to leave. He slid the chair back from the bedside, and departed. As he walked slowly back to his car, he talked to Laurie in his mind, asking her to put in a good word for Talia. He did not feel worthy to come before the Creator and ask for much of anything, as he'd spent much of his life dismissing the afterlife, and any form of deity. But with his parents and Laurie departed, he began working toward a day when he could commune with his Creator, knowing his loved ones were in his presence.

Just minutes later, Talia had another visitor. Unlike Mark, this person did not go through the proper clearance, but managed to slide into the ICU undetected. He didn't want to be on record as having been there, and figured asking for forgiveness would be easier than gaining permission. He looked terrified at what he saw as he entered the room. Terrible feelings of guilt welled up inside him, with his hands beginning to tremble while holding his hat, clasped tightly by his fingers. He could stay but just a moment. He simply had to check on her to see for himself how she was doing. He grabbed the chair near the bed, and scooted it closer, just as Mark had done moments earlier. Upon sitting, he observed the seat was oddly warm. He stared at the woman in front of him for a few seconds before he whispered to her, pleadingly.

"Talia, my dear. Young, brave Talia. I never meant for any of this to happen to you. You should have been with me. I should never have gotten you involved in all of this. I'm so terribly, terribly sorry."

Chapter 13

The Little River Station was just a short walk from the Sugarlands Visitor Center, so Mark decided to arrive early and visit Belle. They'd talked a few times via phone since the shooting, but he wanted to see her in person. Then he'd be able to meet at the station with Agent Toney to discuss the latest on the investigation which was now being referred to simply as Echo Ridge.

Mark found her at the coffee pot, appearing to be in no particular hurry to do any work.

"There she is," he said, reaching for his own paper cup to her left.

"Hey, Mark, how are you doing?"

"Great, all things considered. But the real question is how are YOU doing? How's the leg?"

"Sore. Mostly when I'm using the stairs. But it's okay. I can get around."

"And what about the media? Feeling like a lion tamer right about now?"

"You know that's right! Luckily, what with the timing of all this and my injury, they have brought in the Marines. I was supposed to have two interns this summer, but both of them finished their finals early and started already. I'm calling them Thing One and Thing Two."

"Dang," said Mark. "Sounds familiar, but just can't place it."

"Dr. Seuss. Cat in the Hat stuff."

"Oh, yeah. Now I get it. Just don't call them that to their faces."

"Too late. It was their idea, so no biggie. The good news is that they are both top notch. I have them handling most of my other duties so I can focus on Echo Ridge."

"Yeah, about that. Look, I wanted to tell you that was pretty special what you did up there. I've since come to find out there is the possibility there was another shooter on the mountain. Luckily nothing more happened, but it could have. For you to take care of Talia, along with Banister, well, that was pretty awesome."

"What else was I going to do? Hobble down the mountain for five miles, this time with no horse support?"

"Yeah, and about that too… it was very cool how you arranged those horses for the trip up. I really don't think some of those folks would have made it the whole way otherwise."

"That was a no brainer. I guess we were on the same wavelength, then."

"Good teamwork, Belle. Glad you are up and getting around."

"Thanks, hey Mark, I need to share something with you."

"Sure. Can we talk here, in the break room?"

"It's not hyper confidential or anything, but nobody else is in here, so let me just tell you. This is what I texted you about, even though you never responded."

"Oh, sorry about that. You are not the only one who's been a little busy. Whatcha got?"

"When I was up there on the mountain, waiting for chopper support, while you took the group back down to Cades Cove, something kind of odd happened up there. I just thought maybe since you're investigating, you should know."

"Really? Okay, so spill the beans."

"It was Banister. I told you he did a good job of dressing Talia's wounds, and mine too, and yeah, that was all good, but then later he was sobbing over her. I mean, in a weird way. He was like pleading with her not to die. For some top brass like him, who didn't even know her, I thought he was overdoing it a little, you know?"

"Well, we are all employees of his, so to speak. Maybe he's just taking it personally."

"But Mark, there's more. At one point I moved around to double check that the dead folks were actually dead. I wanted to just double check, you know. I was freaking out thinking that maybe they might still be alive or something. But that's when it happened. I had my back turned, but when I turned around, I kind of caught a look at Banister leaning over and whispering to her in her ear."

"Could you hear what he said?"

"Barely, and this is the weird part. I'd swear I heard him say, 'I'm so sorry.'"

"I don't think that's too odd. He was just saying how sorry he was that she'd been shot, right?"

"Well, I think if you'd have been there, and seen how he was sobbing, you might have gotten a different vibe. To me, it was more like he had personally done something to her."

"Okay, so let me get this straight. You think he was apologizing for her getting shot?"

"That's the vibe I got. It was that kind of context, but then again, I'm not 100% sure that's what he whispered to her. That's just what it sounded like to me."

"Why didn't you tell me this before now?"

"I did try to text you, while I had a moment. In case you hadn't noticed, Public Relations is like bizarro-world right now."

"I know, and you're right. It's just, well, I think we're going to have to address this with Banister."

"And I'm going to lose my job because of it."

"Really? You think so?"

"Stranger things have happened. Think about it. I'm the only one who would have known what he whispered to Talia. So... I'm tattling on him, and he might not like that."

"There is a little sensitivity about this, for sure, but I'm sure we can handle this correctly. Plus, you know, that would be wrongful termination and all, so I don't see that happening. On the other hand, you may never get another pay raise for the rest of your career, but that's different."

"Ha ha, Powers, very funny."

"No, look, we'll bring HR into this before we talk to him, and I'll make sure Agent Toney conducts that session with Banister. That will give all of us a little bit of insulation from the big boss. Maybe that will help. But yeah, I see what you mean that his could be a little awkward. I'm supposed to have an evidence review with the FBI team here in a few minutes, and then you're joining us for a media response update at the end of that meeting, right? Maybe you could bring this up then, and we'll see what Agent Toney thinks about this."

Mark was about finished with that part of the discussion, another detail popped into his head.

"Oh, and you know what? I just remembered when Banister was slowing down, on the trail that morning, there was this moment when Talia came down and said she would take care of him so I could join the group. I told her I would stay back, and thanked her for the offer, but you know, Banister said something then about how he loved Talia's personality or something like that. I'm thinking maybe he and her might be pretty familiar with each other."

"What, like you mean maybe they were getting it on?"

"C'mon, Belle, this is the workplace, you're starting to sound like Talia."

"Ok, let me try again. Do you mean maybe they were sharing carnal knowledge?"

"Ah, yeah, more scientific. I don't mean this in a gossipy kind of way, but yes, I do think that's possible. Talia loves men like bees love honey. So maybe they are involved, who knows."

"Sounds like you have a salacious secondary investigation to conduct, now."

"No, not unless it has something directly to do with Echo Ridge."

"So how's all of that going, anyway?"

"Just starting, really. There's a lot of people to talk to, and notes to compare. That's where we're at right now... lots of interviews. How about you? I'm guessing the media is in a real frenzy, probably wanting to know if the resort will still be built, right? Like now that the governor has been killed, will the project be cancelled? I can't imagine anything would stop it now, but who knows."

"That's one of the questions I'm getting a lot of. Banister promised me an answer any day on that, but it's still up in the air. I keep pestering him via email, but nothing's come back yet. The media will just keep asking until we get an answer on that one."

"Motive. That's what I keep thinking about. Even with several dead, it kind of feels to me like the Governor was the main target of the shooting. Once she was down, the shooting stopped. The question is, was this a political statement, since she was pushing for the resort? Or was it personal? Did someone just want her dead, because of who she is, not for political reasons?"

"Are you thinking Shane killed her?" asked Belle.

"Well, it's a little early to call him a suspect. And technically, it's probably best that you don't know anything about our investigation, Belle. I know you're a professional, but, if you let something slip in one of your press conferences, you know, during a Q&A session... some of those reporters have a way of phrasing things to get that kind of info out of you."

"You are right, no offense taken. I was just curious. Don't tell me what I don't need to know, until I need to know it."

"But I will say, there's a chance it was a personal attack, not a political one. And, with that, Ms. Belle Whittle, I must be off. I have a meeting with the FBI. Got to run."

When Mark stepped into the meeting room with Agent Toney he had expected a larger group to be waiting for him.

It was only Agent Sandy Toney and Agent Tom Luken sitting at the table.

"I know," said Sandy, judging his expression, "It's a small group today. The rest of the team are still doing research. I've compiled their findings for your review."

Mark was not prepared for the onslaught of data they had prepared for him. They started with every conceivable forensic metric he'd ever heard of with amazing mathematical analysis taken from the bald and the shooter's location. There were hairs found within the tent, skin samples as well, and fingerprints from the boom box and coffee pot. They even found a small, spent marijuana joint that had some DNA evidence on it. They also mentioned they had processed the video footage that was captured by the videographer's gear after he was killed. They would wait until the end of the meeting to discuss that footage. Analysis of Shane Goodwyn's Houston H9 handgun was not included, as he'd only turned that over for analysis the night before.

Most compellingly, Sandy mentioned they were running all the data through the national crime database looking for matches. The output would be a list of known criminals that had partial fingerprint matches and who could have been in the area at the time of the shootings. They did not yet have the results of the analysis, but they were expected at any time.

Both Mark Powers and Agent Toney had sent each other their complete notes from their respective interviews, but neither report had yet been discussed. That was next on the agenda. The FBI team leader started with a summary of her discussions with Lopez, followed by Mark's key thoughts on the discussions with Shane Goodwyn. Other interviews had also been conducted by Agents Luken and Gallenstein with the media team, Dan Lawson, and Craig Banister but much of those accounts revealed no details warranting discussion.

"So, basically," said Sandy, "it appears Isabella thinks we need to take a hard look at Shane, because he and the governor had a long history of domestic strife," said Sandy. "We're dealing mostly with Isabella's observations of mental cruelty as well as suspected physical abuse. I think it is important to consider these charges as credible since she had the unique vantage point of someone who was frequently in the Goodwyn's home, as evidenced by how she was occupying an adjoining room at the hotel during the days surrounding the attack. Her testimony is credible enough to warrant additional talks with, and perhaps surveillance of, Shane Goodwyn."

"And," replied Mark, "regarding Shane, he surrendered the weapon he carried that day of the shootings, and we'll get a ballistics report on that within two days. He also stated clearly that he did not kill his wife, or have any involvement with her death."

"And for Agent Luken's sake, can you summarize a few more key points from your meeting with Mr. Goodwyn? I did not forward your report to him, so he's not read your report like I have."

"Sure. Goodwyn pretty much recounted much of what we already knew, and he added a few new points about how he could see Isabella hiding behind a tree, and at one point she had curled up into a fetal position, crying like a baby. Other than that, most of the timeline, positions of others in the area, etc., all that stuff jived with what we already know. But... there was one part of the conversation that I found particularly interesting. Shane speculated there could have been another shooter within the woods, someone working in concert with the sniper. He thinks he might have heard the crack of a handgun at close range, and that occurred seconds before Lopez shouted at finding Janet Goodwyn shot on the ground. His theory was that the sniper attack may have just been a way to send everyone back into the woods where a second shooter could take out the governor at close range."

"But why," started Toney, "would a second shooter in the woods not just kill the governor as she was coming up the mountain, since everyone was in single file? Why the need of anything more elaborate, incorporating a sniper?"

"That's a great question. Maybe in the chaos of everyone running away, that second gunman's shot would not have been witnessed by anyone. Maybe. I really don't know. I don't have an answer for that. Keep in mind, this is just Shane's speculation at this point. I'm not sure I buy it either. You have a sniper out there who's left four people dead, including the governor who we all believe to be the primary target, so you know the shooter's got skills. I don't know why on earth he would need an additional gunman. And, to your point, Sandy, if he wanted to shoot at close range, he could have taken out a lot of us quite easily on the way up the mountain, if he'd been using a semi-automatic, or automatic."

"I think Shane might be onto something. Maybe he knew they had one chance at getting this right," added Luken. "A second gunman might have given them a little extra insurance. Like, let's say the sniper ran into a gun problem, or fell off a cliff or encountered a bear or snake, something, anything like that, you know, then they'd have their plan B ready to cover for him."

"I can see that, maybe," said Mark, "but I'm inclined to think they'd choose simplicity over complexity. Get in, get it done, get out. The more moving parts, the more there is that could go wrong."

"Mark," said Sandy, "did Shane try to suggest it could have been Isabella Lopez who was the second shooter? I didn't see anything like that in your report."

"No, he didn't suggest that, and I didn't think to mention it, honestly. But he did say he spent very little time looking out from behind his tree. He did so only once, and he didn't have a good view of his wife or Isabella, in fact, he didn't even recognize them for who they were until later when he got closer. So I would speculate it's possible that Isabella could have shot the governor, but I'm not sure there's any clear motive as to why she would do that. It sounds like the governor was her gravy train, her paycheck. Seems like a stretch to me."

"I only ask," replied Sandy, "because of what Agent Luken has to show you here in just a few minutes. Plus we'll soon find out more about the bullet that killed the governor, once the autopsy results are delivered."

"And between the two of them, we do know," added Mark, "Shane was clearly carrying a handgun, so he'd be the leading suspect if we did find the bullet was from a pistol."

"That's right. We're minutes or hours away from getting the autopsy report, and I'm pretty confident that it will match some of Agent Luken's findings."

"But there's one more thing, can I just finish before moving on to what Agent Luken has?" asked Mark.

"Of course. We're not trying to rush you along, Mark, but we just think Agent Luken's presentation will be very compelling." said Sandy.

"I'll be quick. We might have one more potential suspect, or person of interest."

"And who might that be?"

"Craig Banister," responded Mark

"Agent Gallenstein interviewed Banister yesterday, and there was nothing revelatory about that meeting in her notes. I'm curious what you may have to offer that she didn't find out," said Sandy.

Mark then proceeded to relate what Belle had told him earlier, about how Banister had an emotional moment with Talia at the top of the mountain once the larger group had gone back down the mountain.

"That doesn't sound incriminating or suspicious to me," said Sandy. "That just sounds like a man who was emotionally distraught regarding one of his own."

"That's what I said to Belle, but she told me there was a special context to what he whispered to Talia. Apparently, the way he said it was as important as what he said. His apology for having involved her was more like an admission that he was responsible, not just empathetic that she'd been injured. Belle seemed pretty convinced that it was suspect. It sounds like we need to revisit Banister as well as Goodwyn. And, by the way, if we do, we'll need to consider how we can protect our security team from backlash from Banister."

"Backlash?"

"Yes, well, Belle's the only one who heard him whisper to Talia, and she's afraid she might get fired if we start asking about that moment. Obviously, he'll connect the dots. I'd request one of your agents talk to him and we see if an HR representative from the park service can be present at the time."

"We can do several things. Does the park service have an internal affairs department?"

"Not locally."

"Okay. We'll find out exactly what to do, there. I believe Belle is to join us at the end of our meeting. Can we just bring her in early?"

"Sure, let me buzz her," said Mark. Moments later, Belle walked in and took a spot at the table.

"Hello Belle, it's good seeing you again. How is your leg?"

"Healing up just fine, thanks for asking."

"So Mark says you think Mr. Banister was overwrought with some kind of guilt?"

"Yes. I thought I heard him whisper to her that he was sorry, and it sounded to me, anyway, like he felt he was to blame. That's just how I took it. Maybe I'm just imagining it."

"I don't know," said Sandy, "sometimes our intuition can be a powerful tool, and we should not ignore it. I think we can schedule another session with Banister, and frame it as a follow-up from Gallenstein. I'm not inclined to think this is a top priority, however. We've got a lot of other interviews to conduct, but we'll come back around to this one later. When it does happen, I'll ask Jeannine to craft her interview in such a way as to take the heat off of you for having brought this to us. We can also learn a lot more in seeing if he purposely avoids telling us that he was sobbing over Talia. If he does not willingly divulge those details, that would mean he has something to hide. He didn't mention anything about Talia in the conversation he had with Gallenstein, so if he dodges that topic in a second interview, there might be something there. And, we'll also report this to your HR team and internal affairs group prior to the next interview, so that if any on-the-job difficulties arise, you'll have a leg to stand on with a dispute. "

Belle didn't really think anything would happen to her career over this; Banister was a professional and should know that it was her civic responsibility to divulge this kind of info to the investigators. With Toney's extra steps of caution in place, she was fine with how it would be handled.

Agent Toney now turned to Mark Powers. "Mark, can you get a few Sevierville uniformed officers to stand outside Talia's room at the hospital?"

"Why, do you think she's in danger?"

"No, but if Talia regains consciousness, I'd rather Banister not have contact with her. If Belle's hunch is right, that there is more between those two than meets the eye, it could be useful to question them apart from each other, to see if their stories match. If they don't, we could find out valuable information about the case. This all assumes, of course, that Talia regains consciousness."

"Sure," said Mark. "We'll get a detail out there."

There was a short lull in the discussions as Toney looked back to her agenda. "Now, Mark, you heard us say a few minutes ago that Agent Luken has some compelling evidence to consider, and Belle, I think it's a plus that you are here early because you may have input on this as well. Tom, do you want to share what you have?"

"I do," said Luken. "That video camera we found lying on the ground had hours of footage showing nothing but the grass blowing in the breeze and the tree line in the background. I've edited it down to just the part where the camera fell to the ground and the moments that followed. We found something very interesting, a lucky find in my opinion." Luken then activated the display at the end of the meeting room to receive the video from his laptop.

The footage started with a good deal of shaky camera work, as the videographer appeared to be seeking shelter like everyone else. At one point, the camera was pointed toward the mountainside to the right of the bald where the shots were coming from. There was audio as well, but it was marred by jostling and wind noises. The videographer could also be heard breathing heavily, and mumbling about trying to see where the shots were coming from. But then, the audio revealed the sound of the man's grunt. This was the moment he was shot. The footage once more became chaotic but resolved quickly as the camera came to rest on the ground, pointing back up the bald toward the trail, in the opposite direction of where the sniper's shots were coming from. Background noise continued to capture the panic that ensued across the bald during the attack.

"So, watch this... the footage is a little out of focus now, but we're lucky that autofocus was turned on and it started focusing on the tree line. I'm going to show you the moment the governor was shot in normal speed, then we're going to look at it in slow motion. Now, what I want you to see in the next few frames is going to be visible right here," he said as he paused the video, rose from his seat, and pointed to a place along the tree line. "Keep your eyes here," he said. He returned to his laptop, resumed playing the video, and the others saw what he had queued up for them. They saw the governor fall to the ground from behind a tree. It did not look to be very revealing at all.

"Let me replay that once more, in super slow motion, with a slight zoom. Let's see if anything about this strikes you as interesting," said Luken.

Once more the footage was played, but this time creeping along at a snail's pace. Luken rose from his chair once more, and began pointing his finger at specific locations of the video being displayed on the display screen.

"Note, at the start, we do not see her at all. She's fully protected by the tree she's hiding behind. But watch here... we're going to see her right foot appear first. She's taking a step backwards, and as we see the foot we can also see her shoulders coming into view as well, turned slightly. Now, she's taken a full step backwards, and we see some of her back, the shoulder blades, and then the left arm. This means she's coming out from behind the tree, turned slightly, and fully vertical. As she continues to back up, notice she's holding her arms directly out in front of her. We can't see her hands yet, but as she continues to backup, you can clearly see her arms are straight out. Now watch this. All of a sudden, you'll see her upper body accelerate much faster than we've seen up to this point."

Luken let the super slow motion footage continue to play, and at that rate of speed, it was quite noticeable that it did appear that the woman took some kind of a jolt to the upper body.

"My friends, what you are seeing here is the moment the bullet hit the governor in the chest. The bullet has jolted her into an accelerated backwards motion and she's no longer walking backwards; this is where the fall begins, through to the point where she crashed to the ground. Notice she did not collapse downward, rather her legs and midsection remained unbent, and she fell like a tree." Everything he mentioned was plainly visible to Mark and Belle, both seeing this footage for the first time.

Tom Luken replayed the footage in slow motion one more time, allowing the rangers to really let it sink into their visual memory.

"So the big learning here is what?" asked Luken.

"She's being shot from within the woods, not by the sniper," said Mark.

"Bingo!" said Tom. "You are absolutely right, sir. While it's a bit difficult to say exactly where she was shot from, I think it's safe to say it was from within the woods. That's because she was turned slightly behind her position, just before taking the jolt from the shot."

"I think it's also safe to say that if the sniper had gotten her, the bullet would have hit her in the arm or skimmed along her back while she was in that position, but would not have entered the chest," added Mark.

"Exactly," added Sandy. "And notice how she's holding her arms out in front of her. The victim raised her hands in a defensive posture as she was about to be shot. That's an instinctual reaction for gunshot victims when they see the shooter point the gun at them. They hold up their hands in front of them like it might stop the bullet. That's quite Illogical and ineffective, but it is very common. Everything we're seeing here suggests a second shooter within the woods, and most likely from somewhere on the other side of the trail running through those woods."

"From Isabella's interview, she admitted she was on the other side of the trail, directly across from the governor," said Mark. "In my mind, that would put her in exactly the right location to take that shot."

"Ah, true, but again, the governor was turned slightly as she came out from behind the tree. At the moment of impact, when that bullet hit her chest, it's my contention that she was not facing directly across the trail to where Isabella was hiding, but rather somewhat further into the woods, behind her to some degree. Does that suggest she was NOT shot by Isabella? No. It does not rule that out, but it does open the possibility that it could have been Shane Goodwyn as well. Or even Craig Banister, or some unknown shooter in hiding."

"Yeah. Shane was not at the tree line," said Mark. "At least not at the last moment that I saw him. It's possible that after I ran past him, and commented to him that I could use a little help up ahead, he just might have crossed the trail, closer to where Isabella was hiding behind her tree. After all, he did say he could tell she was a woman, although he didn't have a clear view from where he was, at that time. So maybe he crossed the trail, into the woods on

Isabella's side of the trail, and got close enough to see she was not his wife. Then he looked at the other person across from Isabella and saw it was Janet. From where he was at that time, this might explain why Janet raised her arms slightly behind her, as we saw in the video."

"I think if we are going to treat this footage as the game changer that I believe it truly is," added Sandy, "I think we're going to have to accept four possible shooters. By everyone's accounts, Isabella, Shane, and even Craig Banister, were all in the woods behind you, Mark, once you mobilized into the clearing at the top. According to several accounts, you had already come out of the woods while Janet was still alive, so you are not on that list of possible shooters."

"Thank goodness for that," said Mark. "That's interesting you've considered Banister, because I hadn't really considered him. I never actually saw Banister relieving himself. I suppose it's possible he could have changed position and come closer toward the bald. But you said four possible shooters," said Mark.

"An unknown shooter, in league with the sniper," said Sandy. "But at this very moment, these are our interpretations of the data. I'll take hard evidence any day of the week over subjective inferences. Let's see what we get from the autopsy. I'll put good money on the bullet being a handgun round, but until we know that for sure, there's no reason to speculate further about these four possible shooters from within the woods. I do think it's safe to say our main focus, now, is to remove anyone in the bald as possible suspects. We'll get the autopsy and move forward looking at these key suspects."

"There is a very remote chance," added Luken, "that the governor was struck in the chest with the sniper's .308 round just before the camera fell to the ground. In that scenario, she'd already been shot by the time this footage caught a glimpse of her. This would also mean after getting shot, she returned to hiding behind the tree, and that's when the camera fell to the ground. Then, with the camera pointed in her direction and recording, it would have captured her falling backwards. However, I'm not buying any of that. There's too long of a pause from the moment the camera settles on the ground to when we see her fall backwards. The ballistics team members I spoke to at Quantico said that even the long distance shots with the .308 round are so lethal, the bullet would go right through her body and she'd drop in a second. On this video, however, she would have had 4 or 5 seconds of remaining upright after being shot by the .308 round, and then walk backwards before falling. Just doesn't add up for me."

"Ballistics also confirmed our suspicions that a standard pistol shot within 25 feet would most likely have enough force to knock her off balance, or knock her over completely. And that jives with what we saw in the slow-motion video." added Sandy.

"Wow," said Mark, now in agreement that this video footage was, indeed, a very lucky find. Agent Toney also appeared to be reveling in this treasure trove of evidence. There was silence in the room, momentarily, while everyone mulled over the details in their minds.

"Has anyone yet asked themselves the basic question of why the governor was not wearing a protective vest?" mumbled Sandy. "That's remarkably common these days, when a governor goes out in public."

"I know," said Mark. "She mentioned at one point, after we started hiking and no longer had the use of the horses, that she was glad she did not wear her bullet-proof vest or else, in her own words, 'it would have killed me.' A little dark irony, there, eh? Plus, she didn't want a full security force from the State Troopers, who would normally handle her detail. She thought the park service and her husband would be all the security she would need. Unfortunately we let her down."

Mark's cell buzzed in his shirt pocket. He reached and checked the screen to see if he wanted to answer. "Speaking of irony, it's the coroner!" said Mark to the others as he proceeded to answer the call.

As he digested the information coming across the phone, the others watched on, all interested in knowing the results of the autopsy. There was some back and forth between Mark and the coroner, but the pivotal question was finally asked by Mark: "Did you find a bullet that killed her?"

There was a dramatic pause before the coroner replied. "And what caliber?" asked Mark. He waited until the coroner provided the answer. Mark looked up from the phone and made eye contact with those in the room as he replied, "It was an 8mm handgun round, you say?"

That was enough for Whittle, Toney and Luken to know the video footage had been correct in the suggestion that a handgun had killed the governor, not a long-range rifle. Once the call ended, the four nodded in agreement that the investigation had just taken an important leap forward.

Mark retrieved his phone and picked a number from his contacts list. Seconds later he said, "Dan, gather a team of a few rangers with good tracking skills. I have a job for you."

Chapter 14

It was not a Barbie Doll. It was not a Sit-n-Spin. It was a Pentax K-1000 that had been her favorite toy. Growing up on a farm, Laurie Pendleton was an only child, and struggled to find things to do each summer while school was out of session. Her mother had purchased the Pentax for her own use, thinking she would become a famous photographer one day. That dream died quickly when she was lost in the terminology of F-stops and apertures. The camera purchase, however, proved beneficial in another way, as Laurie took to it with a passion after finding it tucked away in a closet. She didn't let the technical details get in the way of pure experimentation. Mr. and Mrs. Pendleton were proud to watch their daughter develop into a truly gifted photographer. Her parents were not ones to spend a lot on their daughter, but when they did, it was with an endless supply of film and the creation of a dark room in the barn. With that kind of support, there was no stopping Laurie Pendleton from becoming a world class photographer.

After going to the Ohio Institute of Photography and Technology in Dayton, Ohio, Laurie returned to Nashville to begin her photographic career. It proved to be less glamorous than she had bargained for. Her first job was taking photos of roasted turkeys, paper towels, canned goods and other sundry items for grocery circulars. She had become a pretty good cook in the process, as she was required to produce a good looking turkey before taking its photos. That job paid the bills for a while, but barely. She also had a knack for capturing the lights of Honky-Tonk Row and the characters who frequented there. But her true love was nature photography.

When Laurie married Mark Powers, they got a place in Townsend, to the west of the GSMNP. It was during this time she blossomed as a photographer, earning a reputation as a real pro. This was, in part, thanks to a long cable to hold open the shutter, and a great knack for lighting. Laurie soon learned how to produce time-lapse images. In particular, it helped her produce amazing pictures of waterfalls. While she thought it was impossible to improve upon what God had created, many complimented Laurie saying her waterfall photos looked better on film than in real life. Before long, she landed many of her shots in magazines such as Nature, Southern Living, and National Geographic.

Although The Sinks was personally significant to Laurie, she was finding it more and more difficult to take photos there due to tourists climbing about on the rocks by the falls. Armed with some new filters, Laurie planned to experiment with night photography under a harvest moon. Perhaps then she could capture nature without a tourist in view.

One night she pulled into the nearly empty parking lot just off of The Little River Gorge Road. Her Honda Civic was slowly becoming inadequate to support her career. She loved her little car, and its zippy responsiveness, but as she accumulated more photo gear, it was feeling a bit cramped. She removed a large duffle bag from the back seat, and then headed to the trunk to retrieve her monopod and tripod. Therein were blankets, ponchos, jackets, extra socks, and other items she might need while forcing mother nature to squeeze herself through one of many lenses.

It was just after dark and there were only two tourists remaining to ruin her shots. In time they moved elsewhere which gave Laurie the impression she had The Sinks all to herself.

Laurie had also brought with her a head-mounted flashlight often used by serious backpackers, giving her the slight appearance of a coal miner. She moved along Meigs Creek Trail to where she'd been married ten years earlier. Everything looked much different cloaked in darkness. Moments later she was far from her Honda, and unaware that someone on a gently rumbling motorcycle had pulled onto the bridge above the falls. The motorbike's purr was masked by the roar of the water below.

She was conscious of the sounds of the water, and of insects deep in the surrounding woods, all pushing for a grand finale in their mating life before winter set in. Somewhere beyond the scope of her headlamp were two or more owls trading hoots at frequent intervals. She also heard the sound of her boots crunching the gravel along the trail and the rush of water that continued to flow even when the tourists were tucked away in their tents, cabins or hotel rooms.

She found a terrific spot near the foot of the falls and set up her equipment. She realized, that night, she would have more than one subject for her photography. While the falls were eagerly awaiting, a beautiful moon was rising above the tree line behind the nearby bridge that vied for her attention. She pointed her camera toward the beautiful orb but found it more difficult to dial in the appropriate settings in the dark, even with the head lamp. In short order she began taking shots skyward.

Several shots were taken and she previewed them digitally in her viewfinder. She had finally gotten an expensive digital camera, and was thrilled with the ability to preview her work without the need of developing film. She was very pleased. She was so engrossed with the new technology she did not notice the man upon the bridge, looking down upon her. Click-Click-Click went her camera. Pop-Pop-Pop went the gun, each shot missing her in the darkness. The fourth shot, however, was a direct hit to Laurie's stomach. The hit bent her over at the waist, and with her balance compromised, she tumbled into the rush of the waters. The beam of her headlamp alternated between submersion and illumination of the nearby cliff. After mere seconds, the light shone only into the depths of the river, her body floating face-down. The swift currents carried her down river until she was stopped by rocks in the shallows.

Immediately after the last shot was fired, the man placed his handgun back into the inner pocket of his jacket as he mounted his motorcycle. He sped off, continuing for several miles before turning onto a service road. There he loaded the motorcycle into the bed of a pickup truck and covered it with a tarp. Once driving, he returned in the opposite direction on Little River Gorge Road, heading south. He approached the scene of his crime, the sound of the falls still roaring its eternal song which he heard through an opened window. He did not pause, he just drove on by, as if nothing had happened. He only cared about his drive to Bryson City, North Carolina.

The next day, when Laurie's body was found by tourists, rangers identified her car in the parking lot. At the time, they were puzzled at the large marijuana leaf pinned below her Honda's windshield wiper. Only one of the rangers knew what it meant, and that ranger was Mark Powers.

Chapter 15

**Video Transcript:
Wandering Ranger #25
(YouTube Channel)**

Visual Description:

START VIDEO: Mark, talking to the camera while sitting on a large boulder next to a hiker's backpack.

Audio Script:

Greetings. Thanks for watching another one of my Wandering Ranger videos where I share my day-in-the-life perspectives of a Ranger. Maybe I should say week-in-the-life, because it's been just about a week since I posted anything. You may have read about the assassination of Governor Janet Goodwyn in the news. Unfortunately, I was present at the time of the shooting, and I'm involved with the investigation. So you see, I've not had much time at all to post any of these videos. But I decided this might just help me relax a little bit, and give me something else to think about for about an hour, now here I am. I cannot make any comments about the investigation, but instead I would like to discuss something I'd planned to talk to you about before the shooting. So here it goes.

As usual, we're getting lots of visitors to the park. Last year we had about 12 million people visit us, and we love the company. Some of those visitors are backpackers. If that includes you, I'd like to talk about preparation for the trail.

When I was a kid, we'd visit Gatlinburg and hit the souvenir shops. My parents were not made of money, a fact my dad reminded me of all the time. My brothers, my sister and I were allowed to get one cheap souvenir per trip, and nothing more. One year, dad let me splurge, and I got a deluxe, hand crafted, varnished hiking stick. It was a beauty. It had a leather strap to go around my wrist, you know, in case I might drop it in the middle of a grueling hike. That strap just might keep me from facing a hazardous trail without my stick, so I could not take a single step unless I had that strap around my wrist. Somebody was really thinking when they put that strap on there, I'm tellin' ya.

As a kid, that's all I thought was necessary to get out on the trails. Have stick, will travel. I look back on that age of simplicity, and I really wish it was just that simple. But if you're going on remote trails, or you plan to deviate from the trails in this park, you better have a good plan for what to take with you. This is especially true of young hikers.

First, I should say, before you make plans of camping deep in the woods, far from the designated campgrounds, please know that's against the law unless you first get a permit. If something were to happen to you, we need to know where you were planning to be so we can rescue you, so this is not only a legal requirement, it's a damned good idea.

So, how do you know what to take deep into the woods? Experts talk about the 5 C's when packing for a long hike. These are: Cutters, Cover, Combustion, Containers and Cords. That means things like knives, tents or lean-tos, matches or flint, something to store water in, and ropes for tying things down. That's all good, but I think there are a couple more C's we can add to that list. Obviously, Consumables. Having a container for your water is good, but you're going to need the water to put into it. It's not advisable to drink from the streams out here unless you know how to filter the water to get rid of bacteria and other nasties. And, Consumables includes food, too, unless you are so awesome as to live off of roots and berries while you're out here.

And one more C to know about: Communications. I'm not talking about a smartphone, but at minimum you should have a dependable GPS device. I know, phones have GPS built into them, but they are not a good choice because you are at the mercy of very limited battery life.

Visual Description:

Mark pulls out a small GPS device from the backpack and zooms in to see it better.

Audio Script:

But all self-respecting outdoor shops sell GPS devices that will last for weeks, even months, and can send out a distress signal with your coordinates if something happens to you. Remember that guy out west who had to cut his arm off to survive? I bet he sure wishes he had one of these things. These babies weigh next to nothing, and most people would find them to be affordable, so there's little reason to go into the back country without one. The trails in the outback are riddled with roots, loose dirt, and rocks that can shift under your feet in a heartbeat. What are you going to do when you break your leg 12 miles out, especially if you are alone? Definitely, never hike alone without a GPS, and for that matter, leave your hiking plan with someone back home. And even if you are not alone, your partner or trail mates probably can't

lug you back to civilization with a bad leg, so you
still need a GPS.

So, that's about it, hikers. Get a GPS and it might
just save your life. As I just recently learned with
the shooting, just about anything can happen when you
least expect it out here. I guess that about does it.
Oh, and remember, you need a permit to camp in the
outback. With that, I'm finished. Peace.

Visual Description:

END VIDEO: Fade to black

Mark's time with the FBI was consuming most of his waking
hours, as well as a few hours when he should have been
sleeping. He'd found it necessary to hand off his involvement,
in other local affairs, to Dan Lawson who had designs on
becoming a Special Agent in his career development plan.
Mainly, this meant Dan was in charge of investigating the pot
growing activities elsewhere on Thunderhead Mountain. His
involvement was characterized by high energy levels typical of
young detectives with something to prove. That energy was
evident when Dan grabbed Mark Powers by the arm just
outside of the Little River Station.

"Mark, I know it's getting late, but you have to see what I
have on my computer!"

Mark was, indeed, ready for a hot dinner and soft bed, but
knew he could not pass up Dan's offer. Since Belle was with
him, she followed as well. Once inside, the three of them
gathered around the PC Dan had been working on, and he
pulled up a video clip for the others to see.

"I retrieved the footage from your motion sensitive cameras
in that seized pot field."

"Great. Did we get something other than wayward deer?" asked Mark.

"There's a few of them in there, including a 14 pointer, but that's not what I want to show you. Check this out."

For the second time in a matter of hours, Mark began observing, and analyzing, film footage that would have significance in an investigation.

"In just a second, you'll see the man come into view on the left." As promised, the hidden cameras kicked on just in in time to record a man in his mid-thirties marching through the empty field where his pot crop had once grown. He walked with a slight limp. He was of a build similar to Mark's. He wore a baseball cap sporting the Red Man Chewing Tobacco logo, jeans and muddy, steel-tipped boots. With every third step or so, the man kicked at the dirt, in obvious anger at having discovered his crop was gone. Not far behind him came into view a much larger and hairier individual who showed little emotion.

"Amateurs," said Mark. "But I think I've seen that tall guy before, in town. Eating, somewhere. Pancake house or something."

"I've seen him around, too," said Dan. "Out by Cades Cove, I'm sure of it. What do you think he is, about 6'5"?"

"Thereabouts," replied Mark.

"How do you know they are amateurs?" asked Belle. "That field of plants looked well cared for before we had them seized. That doesn't sound like an amateur job to me."

"I think what we have here is someone who knows the horticultural side of the business, but not the details for how to actually run the business without getting caught."

"But they weren't caught, we just took their crop," countered Dan.

"Sort of. What I mean is this: there were no boobie traps surrounding the field. Or at least none that I could find. A true professional would have known the instant Belle, and Talia, had found the field because they would have had it wired and hooked up to a communications device. But here we are more than a week out and they are only now surveying the damage."

"Well, to be fair, check out the date stamp," said Dan. "This particular footage was two days after the find."

"Still, that's two whole days we're talking about. Plus, I really doubt a pro would have risked going back to survey the loss. Pros would be using cameras of their own, the kind with satellite feeds. They would have been watching you the minute you found the crops. When I put those cameras out, I honestly didn't expect the culprits would come back around, not if they were professionals. But what do you know. Looks like we got lucky!"

"So why did they come back?" asked Belle.

"They've never been caught, or had a close call. That's my guess. Look at him. He could almost taste the money he was going to make, and here he's seeing those dreams of a big harvest go up in smoke. No pun intended."

"Yes it was," said Belle. "You make puns all the time."

"Okay, so you got me. But yeah, if this guy was just running this like a business that he's been running for years, he would not be exhibiting such an emotional response. He's pissed. Just look at him, kicking at the dirt. Watch his mouth, too. Do either of you read lips? This could be a training reel for people who want to read lips for curse words. Hufnagel... he would never have come back to his plot after it was seized. He'd cut his losses and move on to another location immediately, assuming it was early in the growing season. That's the only way to survive in that business."

"Now check this out. Here's where we get real lucky," said Dan, excitedly.

In the footage, the man wearing the hat, the apparent leader, was unaware of the camera's existence.

"Well lookie there. He's coming right up to the camera!" said Mark, now quite delighted. "Why don't you do us a real favor and take off your hat?" he added, speaking to the man in the video. The criminal removed his Red Man hat and wiped his sweaty forehead with the sleeve of his forearm. Just as quickly, he returned the hat to his head.

"Oh my God," said Belle, "It's like he heard you!"

"Can you rewind that, and then freeze it to right after he wipes his forehead?" asked Mark of Dan.

"Sure. And I'll zoom in, too." Seconds later, Dan delivered.

"I'll be damned," said Mark Powers. "Grasshopper." He recognized the man, despite his thick sideburns and goatee. Mark had known the man since he was 15 years old.

"Hmmm?" asked Belle.

"Grasshopper. Did you guys ever see the old TV show called *Kung Fu*?"

"Heard of it, never seen it," replied Dan.

"The main character was this student of the martial arts. He learned to fight, and live the way of a kind of ninja from this old man who was a Shaolin monk. The old guy always called his student by the name of Grasshopper. Exactly why, I do not know."

"And... why is that relevant?" asked Belle.

"Because you are looking at none other than Jebidiah Fields, who learned all he knows about growing pot from the original marijuana master of Tennessee, Franco Hufnagel."

Both Belle and Dan knew that name all too well. Anyone who knew Mark, and many who didn't, had heard the legendary story of the enterprising pot grower who Mark sent to jail after an extensive investigation. While the court case at the time received a lot of media coverage, the story really heated months after Hufnagel was released from prison nine years later. The man had threatened to come after Mark once released, and many believed he was responsible for the killing of Mark's wife. A Marijuana leaf had been left on her car's windshield, enough of a hint to let Powers know who was responsible. However, it was not enough evidence to even keep Hufnagel detained for questioning. He claimed to have started a new life as a butcher in Bryson City, NC, and the owner of Steve's Steaks had provided an airtight alibi for Franco on the night Laurie was murdered. Hufnagel never saw justice for Laurie's murder. In fact, Mark was still highly agitated that the man had gone free, explaining why Mark was always so eager to be involved in any pot growing cases in hopes he could once more prosecute Hufnagel.

"How do you know Jebidiah?" asked Dan.

"I'm positive that's him, although, I'm curious about his limp. He didn't have that when I saw him last. Other than that, I believe that's Jeb. We'll see if our FBI friends can run this through their facial recognition software to confirm. But I can see that boyish face of his even though he's now got facial hair. Hufnagel employed a lot of under-aged teens to save money. Jeb was one of them. Hufnagel was an arrogant kind of guy, and fancied himself a gun expert. He outfitted all of those boys with guns he'd purchased in North Carolina, and well, you know, the state line is just over the hill, and these teens were sporting the guns on the Tennessee side. That's how we added a few years to his sentence. Jeb was a big help to our case. He testified to avoid prolonged juvenile detention or being tried as an adult. Putting himself on the stand at the age of 15, going up against his murderous boss, man I'm tellin' ya that kid had nerves of steel. I've always respected Jeb for what he did there."

"When was the last time you saw him?"

"Honestly, only about a year ago. We ran into each other in town every now and again. I look back on all that and feel kind of sorry for him. He was in the wrong place at the wrong time, manipulated by Hufnagel. I know in his heart he's a good man. BUT, lookie here, turns out he's a parasite now, back into the drug trade."

"Looks like he's taken up his boss' old business," said Belle.

"And that's a recent thing, I'm betting," replied Mark. "When Hufnagel went to jail, word on the street was that Jeb took over the business, but it didn't work out. He might have been too young to run that operation at that time. I know he's had a lot of jobs in town, working at a few of those miniature golf places, and other tourist jobs. But those were always low paying jobs. Now that he's older, and he has a family of his own, he might have gravitated back to something he knew would generate better money. Kind of breaks my heart, in a way. Damnit, Jeb, what the hell are you doing?"

"So now what?" asked Dan. "Should we get a warrant?"

"Absolutely," replied Mark, "but we're not going to use it unless we have to. I have a history with Jeb. I'd like to see what I can get out of him first before the full court press. If he doesn't cooperate, we'll hit him with the warrant. Above all, though, I need to be the one to talk to him. It will go smoother that way."

"But Mark, when will you have time? This other investiga..."

"...don't worry," he interrupted, "I'll make time for this."

Franco Hufnagel, and his assistant, who went by the solitary name of Haus, were driving in a drizzle, with mud-streaked windshield wipers barely doing their job. The men bounced along in Franco's truck, carefully navigating some back roads near Fontana Dam that most locals didn't even know existed. They were checking the traps they'd laid out the previous night. They could not afford to wait very long if they'd succeeded in snaring a black bear. Certain organs needed to be processed immediately if they were to survive a trip to China in a cold-pack.

Franco originally got into the poaching game while hunting illegally in the park. But he knew he could make bigger money if he resorted to trapping techniques. While he would miss the sport of shooting, the traps would allow for more catches, especially in the summer months.

Haus was a quiet, woodsy kind of guy, living an indigent life in the woods. He had no immediate family, had grown up in foster homes, and was happier with nobody around. Standing 6'5", he was the brawn of the operation, helping Franco field-clean the bears, and load their carcasses into the bed of his beat-up Ford F-350. Once loaded, the bear was covered with a tarp, and the men parted ways.

Haus was not only working for Franco, but he was also working with Jeb Fields growing pot. At least until they were busted.

Neither Franco nor Haus were aware they would soon be sought for questioning by the FBI. It would not be an easy task to apprehend either of them. Franco had a lot of enemies, and knew what he was doing would send him back to prison, if caught. He kept a very low profile, moving from one hotel to another every few months, just to keep the world from getting too close to him.

Haus would also be hard to find, simply because of a lack of address. His old '75 Yamaha xs650 Scrambler motorcycle was registered using an address of one of his Foster-dads in Oak Ridge, so it wasn't likely anyone would easily track him down via that registration.

One evening, after Franco had heard through the grapevine that Jeb's pot business had been busted by the feds, he longed to learn more details, and pushed Haus into sharing.

"So I heard you and Jeb got busted growin'. Did they catch you in the act?"

"No, we weren't there when they found it. They just came 'n took our shit."

"All of it? Was it the DEA?"

"I guess. The feds are all just sittin' back smokin' our doobies', I'm tellin' ya."

"Do they know you or Jeb were responsible?"

"Shit, I hope not. I might just lay low down here for a while. I was hopin' to see if maybe there was any other work down here for me."

"I know a guy who has a meat shop. I'll see if he needs some help. You'd be good at handling those sides of beef, I'm sure."

"I'd appreciate it."

"I guess what you're doing for me isn't paying enough?"

"Nah, it ain't that. It's just I'm startin' to think I'm not gonna want to live like this in 20 years. Who wants to be livin' on the land when you can't even outrun a hog no more?"

"You got that right." said Franco. "I was like you, livin' off the land when I was in my 20's. Got tired of keepin' my shit dry all the damned time. It's like some freaking Seattle around here."

"So you got a house somewhere, don't you Mr. Hufnagel. Where's that at?"

"You ask too many damned questions, boy. Let's just say in Georgia somewhere. My EX is livin' there right now, no good reason to get down there much. If you do go and get yourself a place, watch the trail your' leavin'. In our line of work, you can't afford to have a deep footprint. You don't want nobody knowin' where you are, as much as possible."

"That's what I was tellin' Jeb. I told him, like, I need to lay low like you 'cause if I get caught, I don't wanna spend no time behind bars. He kind of laughed when I told him how you always park behind the hotel buil..."

"Were you talking about me to Jeb?" asked Franco, interrupting.

"Well, not really, I just said how you were good at layin' low, like you just said for yourself."

Franco hit the brakes, halting the truck abruptly along a sketchy stretch of road. He jumped out of the cab, slammed his door, and moved quickly around the back of the truck. From the bed, he retrieved a rifle and checked to make sure the magazine was loaded. He stopped at Haus' passenger side door. With little warning, Haus was staring down the wrong end of a rifle, with Franco ready to shoot at the other end.

"I oughta drop you right now. Get out of that truck and pick your spot to die!"

Haus had not seen this coming and was terrified. He had a pistol tucked into the waistband of his jeans, but by now it was too late to use it... unless Hufnagel made the mistake of giving Haus the chance.

"Are you serious? I, I, uh... I'm sorry, Mr. Hufnagel, I didn't mean to..."

"Shut your mouth. Get out of the truck."

Haus thought the man had gone insane, and it appeared Franco was serious about carrying out his threat. Trembling, Haus ducked his head and clumsily got out of the truck. He moved toward the rear of the vehicle per Franco's direction.

Franco was furious that Haus had mentioned him to Jeb Fields, but he knew he had himself to blame as well. Only, he would not admit that. It had been his idea for Haus to work with Jeb, so Franco could keep up on what was happening in Jeb's world. Franco was not happy that Jeb had rebooted the pot business while Franco served time, and had ideas of taking it back some day.

"I told ya once not to say a damned thing about me to Jebidiah, or anybody else. I even said...'you don't know me', and you agreed. Do you remember that?"

"Hey man, I'm sorry, I..."

"Sorry ain't good enough. Now... I'm tellin' you as plain as the moon is full, if you EVER mention me to ANYONE else, I will hunt you down like a lame hog and shoot you dead. Maybe even sell your balls to the damned Chinese. Get your ass walkin'. You don't work for me no more."

Haus was relieved that his life was not in immediate danger, but distressed at knowing his Yamaha was a good 15 miles away. The drizzle was turning to rain, and he would be walking all through the night just to get to his bike. He had no protection from the elements, and dreaded what now awaited him down the dark mountain road.

Franco was not bluffing. He did, in fact, leave Haus on his own, in the middle of the mountains, deep in wild hog country, and bear country at that — without a gun or flashlight. As Haus saw the tail lights disappear around a corner, he cursed the name of Franco Hufnagel and swore he would one day repay the man for this act of brutality.

Chapter 16

Agent Toney was in a rental car on her way to a morning visit with Isabella Lopez, followed by an afternoon meeting with Shane Goodwyn. These interviews were to be held in Nashville, and Toney was glad of having Agent Gallenstein along for conversation as they drove westward across the state.

Isabella had returned to the state capital to move on with her career, despite the loss of her employer. She would continue transitioning Janet's work to the lieutenant governor who had been sworn in as the new governor within 24 hours of the Janet's death. Perhaps more out of pity than necessity, the new governor took Isabella on as a second personal assistant.

Shane was in Nashville only for a few days while he visited local shooting ranges and giving speeches at gun clubs. He had since conducted a funeral which had garnered a great deal of media coverage within Tennessee and beyond.

It was within the confines of a statehouse meeting room that Agent Toney re-acquainted herself with Isabella Lopez, and Agent Gallenstein served the role of witness and audio recording technician.

"I'm not lucky enough to be treated to breakfast this time, eh?" asked Isabella, as the three of them sat at a boardroom table next to the governor's office.

"Sorry, not this time," said Sandy. "There's no media hiding in the lobby, so I don't think we need that diversion."

"That's not exactly true," countered Lopez, light-heartedly. "There's always some reporter lurking at every door when I arrive, and leave."

"And I suppose you're just giving them the 'no comment' cold shoulder, right?"

"Yes. That was good advice, but they still won't go away. They followed me to the mall the other day. I had to get the mall cop to kick them all out. They kept saying they had every right to be there because it's a public place. The cop said 'the public does not own this mall, they just shop here, now get off our property!' I suppose it's nice, every once in a while, for the male patriarchy to flex their Neanderthal muscle."

"Well, for what it's worth, I'm sorry you're having to go through all of that. But let's get started, shall we?"

"Yes, well, I'm a bit worried about why we have to do this a second time. Was there something I said last time that's not accurate?"

"It's normal procedure, Ms. Lopez. As additional evidence comes in, we sometimes need to clarify things we talked about last time. And sometimes the new evidence requires us to ask new questions that we did not ask last time."

"Like what?"

"Well, first, I want to handle this a bit more officially. As the investigation continues, we need to cross our T's and dot our

I's, as they say." Sandy looked at Gallenstein, giving her a moment to do her thing.

Jeannine spoke into the mobile recorder's microphone. "Agents Toney and Gallenstein are present for an interview with Isabella Lopez, April 13th, 2019, 11:00 a.m. The interview is being conducted at the statehouse in Nashville, Tennessee."

Once the recorder was activated, Agent Toney Mirandized Lopez.

"Am I under arrest?" asked Isabella with grave concern.

"No, just informing you of your rights. That's all," replied Sandy. "If you want to stop and get legal representation for this, we can come back."

The formality appeared to have Lopez worried, judging from the expression on her face.

"Well, let's just see how it goes. If I think I need a lawyer, can I stop at any time?"

"You may."

"Okay, let's try to get this over with."

"Let me start by asking you, Isabella, if you have ever borrowed a handgun from anyone."

"Me? A handgun? Seriously? Even though Janet was a Republican, I'm not. I oppose the gun lobby. Which is why Shane Goodwyn makes my skin crawl. We've had our share of arguments about gun control. Honestly, if Janet had not been married to him, I just might have convinced her that gun reform is desperately needed in this country. But with him around, that effort was always like taking one step forward and five steps back."

"Thank you for letting me know how you feel, Ms. Lopez," said Sandy, "but you did not answer my question."

"No. I do not own a gun. Nor will I ever own a gun. Guns are the reason children are being mowed down..."

"...Ms. Lopez," interrupted Sandy, "I appreciate your passion for your politics, but I did not ask you if you owned a gun. We already know you have never registered a weapon. That is low hanging fruit for the FBI. I want to know if you have ever borrowed a gun from someone else."

Isabella stalled. "Oh," she said, as if she were mentally trying to arrive at some clarity in her own mind prior to answering. Toney was unsure if this was a tactic to generate an answer that might evade this line of inquiry, or if Lopez was genuinely confused by what she was being asked.

"I know if I don't answer you that might make me look guilty, so I want to be careful how I form my sentences. To be clear, I have fired handguns before at a shooting range, just to educate myself so I could effectively argue my position about gun control with rednecks like Shane. Would that count as 'borrowing' a handgun? The gun belonged to the shooting range. I wouldn't want that to come back on me later if you ever made me take a polygraph, or something like that. "

"No. Let me get right down to it, Ms. Lopez. Did you have possession of a handgun concealed on your person, or within your backpack, or concealed in any other way on the day Governor Janet Goodwyn was killed?"

"I don't understand why you would even ask that question. Everyone knows Janet was killed by the sniper. And snipers don't shoot handguns, right? At least I don't think they do. They use those big long ones, the rifles. Surely your gun experts have figured that out by now."

"Autopsy results revealed three of the victims were shot with a .308 caliber slug, indicating a rifle of some sort. Lots of long range rifles use that caliber. On the other hand, the governor was shot with an 8mm slug, indicating a handgun. We know for a fact that the sniper's rounds killed three people, and someone closer to the governor killed her with a rare handgun. You seem like a smart woman, Ms. Lopez, so I'm sure you can see why we would want to ask you these questions given this new information. So I'll ask again. Did you have a handgun on you that day? A Yes or No answer would be appropriate at this juncture."

"I still can't believe you're even asking me that. Like I said, guns make me sick to my stomach even talking about them. I took one shot at that shooting range and swore I'd never touch another one again in my life. So to answer you as clearly as you've asked, Agent Toney, no, I did not have a handgun with me on that day."

"A direct answer this time. How refreshing," replied Sandy.

"Look," said Lopez, now leaning forward so her face was closer to the FBI agent, "The last time we spoke, you asked me questions about what happened up there that day. And I was happy to help the investigation by telling you everything I knew. But now it appears you are possibly thinking I could be a suspect in that shooting. Maybe I should have a lawyer present after all."

"And that would certainly be your right. Or you could help us resolve this case faster by having an honest and unobstructed conversation with us right now. "

""If a speedy investigation is what you're after, you should be talking to Shane Goodwyn instead of me."

"He's next. But right now, I'm talking to you. Shall we continue?"

"Go ahead," said Isabella, with a tone in her voice like that of a teenager being lectured by a parent.

"During the attack, as you stood behind the tree, across the trail from the governor, did you see her at the moment she was shot?"

"I did not. Well, once the shooting stopped, I think I was the first one to notice her laying on the ground, which is why I ran over to her to see if she was okay."

"Did you look at the governor at all between the times that you took your position behind the tree and the time you saw her laying on the ground?"

"Only at the first moment we took cover. We both looked at each other."

"Why didn't you look at her again, during the rest of the attack?"

"Why should I have? What, do you think we were going to strike up a conversation about politics or something? We were under attack! I was fearing for my life! The best I could do was to crouch down and cover my head with my arms. I was trying to minimize my profile, give the shooter less to shoot at."

"And you were crying."

"Yes, I was, but Agent Toney, why do you feel it's necessary to bring that up?" said Isabella, sternly.

"Because it's one more recollection that you freely offered the last time we met."

"So if you know it, and I know it, why do you need to rub my nose in it? I am a strong woman, and so are you, so I deserve your respect."

"I'm not rubbing your nose in it, I'm merely recounting your previous statement. That's part of what we are doing here today. We're revisiting the events of that day, in an attempt to gather more information and clarify your previous comments. That's all, Ms. Lopez."

"I'm beginning to feel like you don't like me, Agent Toney. Reminding me of a character flaw is not going to ingratiate me to you, you know."

"I'm not here to make friends, Ms. Lopez."

"Then why did you take me out for pancakes?"

"Because I felt that would be a pleasant setting in which to talk after all you had been through, and to get you out of that hotel room, away from the men in the other room, so you'd be more comfortable answering my questions. Do you have a problem with that?"

"It's just that you are so different this time. You are hurting my feelings."

The agent could hardly believe what she was hearing. She glanced over at Agent Gallenstein who was taking notes, and it appeared she was struggling to hold in laughter. Sandy did not find this funny at all, however. Did this 'strong woman' in front of her just admit that her feelings had been hurt from merely recounting details of the events on Echo Ridge? Isabella was sounding like a confident woman one moment, and a spoiled child the next.

"Again," said Sandy. "I'm not here to make friends. Like it or not, feelings may get hurt in an FBI investigation. That's just how it works, I'm afraid."

"You are mean spirited. You're a hate-filled conservative, aren't you? I thought you FBI agents were supposed to be on our side."

"Pardon me? I don't follow."

"You know, with the Mueller investigation on Trump? The Russian collusion probe? Apparently you didn't get the memo. Go on, say what you need to say. I want to get this over with."

A small burst of breath slipped past Gallenstein's lips. She nearly broke out in full-blown laughter but managed to retain her composure as Sandy continued.

"I suggest we remove politics from the conversation and stick to the facts of this case. I want to know, while you were in your crouching position behind the tree, if you caught sight of Shane Goodwyn, or Craig Banister, who were somewhere deeper in the woods behind you. Did you catch sight of them during the shooting?"

"No. I only saw them after Janet had been shot. Actually, the first person who I saw was the park ranger. Mark was his name, I think. We were both with Janet at the moment she died. I'm sure he'll tell you that she said that Shane did it, too. Did he tell you that?"

"We do have his statements about the events of the day, but let's move on. Next, let me ask, did you hear any gunfire from your position behind the tree? The sound of a pistol, for example?"

Isabella brewed on the question. After a long pause, she answered, "Yes, now that you mention it. There was one loud cracking noise I heard. It didn't really strike me as a gun noise, but I guess it could have been."

"You said earlier you had once shot a handgun at a shooting range. Did it sound similar to that?"

"Now that you mention it, yes. It did. But that shot at the shooting range was really loud, even with ear muff thingies on."

"From what direction did the sound come from? From behind you? From the bald in front of you? Or from your left or right?"

"I can't say."

"You can't say because you are compelled not to, or because you don't recall?"

"Because I don't recall. See, there you go again, you are being mean spirited. You are hurting my feelings."

Sandy prided herself on conducting herself calmly in all circumstances, but she had her limits. She did not appreciate someone challenging her professionalism.

"I assure you, Ms. Lopez, that if I intended to be mean spirited, you would have known it long before now. Perhaps it's just that you are overly sensitive? I would have thought this room, being so quiet, would qualify as a safe space for you."

"Not with you in it," quipped Lopez, sending a laser-like stare at the FBI agent.

"I'm sure as a strong woman, you can handle the adversity. But if you feel threatened by hard questions, perhaps I could acquire some crayons so you can draw some nice pictures of unicorns and rainbows to alleviate the stress of being questioned by the FBI."

"See, now you are mocking me."

"If I'm to be accused of being mean spirited, then I may as well deliver the goods."

After this, the women grew silent, unsure how to proceed. Sandy sighed, and continued with her questioning, having vented her frustration with Lopez. The questioning went on for another thirty minutes, and both agents were weary of their interviewee's belligerence and glad to escape that room. Sandy and Jeannine left that interview with one goal in mind: to find the nearest honky-tonk to grab a drink and have a good laugh at Isabella's expense.

Chapter 17

While Agents Toney and Gallenstein were in Nashville, the results came back from forensics regarding the evidence found in the tent retrieved from the attack site. Luken had called Powers to let him know the results. There were fingerprints on the boom box that belonged to one individual in their national database: Jebidiah Fields. This news saddened Mark since Jeb was now going to be the target of the pot growing investigation *and* was now implicated in the shooting of the governor of Tennessee.

Mark Powers had originally planned to go with Agent Toney to Nashville but changed his mind when he learned about the evidence about Jebidiah Fields. Dan had planned on visiting Jeb at his home in Pigeon Forge, but after Mark received news of the fingerprints, he informed Dan that he would be the one to make first contact with Jeb.

Mark thought deeply about the fingerprint evidence. On the surface it would appear that Jeb himself had been the sniper, but Mark found that hard to believe. Yes, it was possible, but Jeb's personality didn't fit the profile of a blood-thirsty gun for hire, especially on the level of political assassin. This was based on Jeb's testimony as a 15 year old that he really didn't like guns, but was forced to carry one by Hufnagel. That was 20 years ago. Mark considered a lot could have changed in that time, and perhaps Jeb had grown into a marksman, but he still wasn't buying it. The impression he'd gotten from Jeb the few times' he'd seen him in recent years was that he was a slacker. He simply did not seem to be motivated enough to become a well-trained marksman, capable of pulling off such a hit on the governor.

Mark's intuition spawned a theory. Jeb might have been an accomplice, or an assistant, to the sniper. For example, Jeb might have assisted in clearing branches and erecting the deer stand at the shooting site. Or, perhaps Jeb was the second shooter, assuming he'd shed his dislike of guns at some point. Jeb's DNA showed he was at the attack site, but when it came time for the close-range attack, Jeb could have relocated to a position in the woods where he could shoot the governor. He would base his questions on this theory for when he finally talked to Jeb. He only hoped his hunch was not born of an affection he had for Jeb two decades earlier. He could not let his personal feelings get in the way of doing his job.

Mark had updated Agent Toney that he planned to locate and visit Jeb to conduct a one-on-one conversation. Given the high profile nature of the case, she did not want to take any chances and insisted her staff serve as backup for that visit.

Before Mark could talk with the young man, he was first going to have to figure out where Jeb was living. Mark had an older address for Jebidiah, from when he lived with his parents. That's where Mark went first, but Jeb's father was not interested in saying anything to get his son into trouble. Mark tried to downplay the need to speak to Jeb, but the father suspected his son was up to no good, and refused to answer any questions from Mark. All he offered was that his boy was now a man, and had his own life; he claimed to have 'nothin' to do with that boy's mischief no more.'

Then Mark visited several of the places where Jeb had once worked, and a fruitful lead was gathered. His most recent manager at Dollywood told Mark he could probably locate Jeb at the River Rapids Mobile Home Park just outside of Pigeon Forge. After conferring with the trailer park manager, Mark found Jeb's trailer.

It was a sunny spring day, warmer than most, and Mark noticed windows open on Jeb's trailer as he approached. There were no cars to be seen, and he wondered if anyone was even home. He looked around to see if he could spy any of his FBI support team in the neighborhood. Although unseen, he knew they were there and monitoring his conversation by way of a wire Mark was wearing.

There was a badly damaged screen door on which Mark knocked, but the main door was wide open. Mark glanced in and spied a number of toys and laundry lying about the trailer. Outside, too, were an assembly of plastic baseball and basketball toys, and a beat up old BMX bicycle. Nobody answered Mark's knock, and he decided to walk around the trailer to take a visual inventory.

A motorcycle was heard starting up, its sound coming from the other side of the trailer. Mark ran around to that side, and saw curtains from a side window blowing in the breeze. More importantly, there was Jebidiah on a dirt bike, with his Red Man Chewing Tobacco hat on backwards, fleeing the scene. Down the street, an unmarked FBI car came skidding into Jeb's path, clipping the assailant on the right quarter-panel and knocking Jeb off of his bike. The hit was unintentional, and minor, but ended what could have been a high speed chase. Jeb, now sitting in the street, did not attempt to escape on foot. Soon he was surrounded by a half-dozen agents, with Mark Powers trotting down the street to join them. He pushed his way through the other agents to ensure he was the first contact with Jeb.

"Jeb... put your hands in the air," said Mark, sternly. Jeb glanced at him in recognition.

"Shit, Ranger Mark, what the hell is going on here?"

"Are you armed, Jeb?"

"Hell no. I was just going out for a ride, and you coppers just come and run me over!"

Mark moved forward, now sure that Jeb recognized him, and offered the man a hand to get up from the street. As Jeb rose, he hobbled on one leg.

"Are you injured?" asked Mark. "We can get you an ambulance?"

"Shit, I'll be alright. Dale Earnhardt over here got mostly my bike, but is someone going to pay for that?"

"Do you have a street license for that dirt bike?"

"Uh, no."

"So what do you think?"

"I'm shit out of luck?"

"SOL, Jeb, that's right."

"Damn. Probably ain't nothin' I can't fix myself, though."

"Where were you running off to, Jeb?" said Mark, agitated.

"I wasn't runnin', Ranger Mark. I was just goin' to head for the woods on the other side of the trailer park and do a little joy ridin'. The wife's out with the boy, gittin' some jeans."

"Do you normally exit through a window of your trailer when you want to go riding?" asked one of the other FBI agents who had seen him do just that.

"Damn. I guess you got me in a fib." Jeb sported thick sideburns which did not connect to a diminutive goatee, pinkish cheeks filling that void. He had straight, greasy hair down to his shoulders, the top half contained by his dirty ball cap. He wore a stained, wife-beater T-shirt under a plaid, long sleeve shirt. On his lower half were tattered and oil-stained jeans. His pointed-toe boots were not well designed for a footrace with the police, but would have served him well to shift gears on his dirt-bike.

Mark turned to the other officers and agents, some still in their cars, others on foot. "Folks," Mark said, "can I get some time alone with Jeb?" The others obliged and backed off while still remaining in eyesight. Mark read Jeb his Miranda rights, and informed him that he was not under arrest, but that could change at any minute.

"Damn," said Jeb who had since placed his bike in an upright position, with it resting on its kickstand. "What's goin' on with all this, Ranger Mark? Why's there so many cops here anyhow?"

"I think we both know the answer to that," replied Mark.

"I ain't got no idea what you're talkin' about."

"Let's just get one thing clear," said Mark, now standing face-to-face with the younger man. "You and me, we go back a long way. I've looked out for you, from time to time, and you know that's true. I'd even consider you my friend, Jeb, and you damned well understand that. But dammit, what the hell are you doing growing pot in the park again?"

"So that's it... this is a bust?"

"No, I'm not. That's not why we are here. In fact, that's the least of your worries at the moment. These are FBI personnel here, Jeb. They want to take you in for questioning about the death of the governor up on Thunderhead Mountain. We found your DNA at the scene of the crime."

Jeb's blood turned icy at hearing those words.

"Oh, no, Ranger Mark, there must be a mistake, I didn't do nothin' like that, I'm tellin' ya."

"I told them you and me have a history, and got them to agree that you might tell me what we need to know without spending a few days in the tank. So you can talk to me here, man to man, or you can talk to them in custody. If you talk to me, every word you say better be the truth. Like I said, we know about your pot farming, and we know a great deal more about you than you might think, so I'd suggest you tell me the truth or else things are going to get a lot more difficult for you, Jeb. What's it going to be, me or them?"

It didn't take the young man long to respond. "You, I guess."

"Just what I wanted to hear. But if you lead me down a trail of lies, Jeb, it's going to get real ugly, real fast."

"I figured you was here about the pot field. But now you're sayin' somethin' about killin' the gov'nor. I don't get that, Ranger Mark. I just might fill my drawers here any second... hopin' you can tell me what the hell you're talkin' about."

"First, let me say we do know all about the pot field."

"What d'ya mean?"

"We have clear video footage of you at the pot field. That same spot you worked with Franco all those years ago. We placed cameras out there. You were wearing the same hat you have on right now. You took it off for a moment in that video, and we had a clear look at your face. That's when I recognized you."

"That wasn't me, I'm sure. Lots of dudes look like me, man. I didn't do nothin'."

"Strike one. There are others in my station who know you, and they recognized you in the video as well as me. Keep in mind we know you used to work on that very spot of land for Franco Hufnagel."

"Like I said," said Jeb, still not quite willing to give it up, "I'm not the only one on the planet with this kind o' hat. They got 'em for sale at the Trader's Market up in Pigeon Forge."

"Strike two, and Jeb, if you strike out here, I'm not helping you at all... I'm going to turn you over to these other fellas. According to the FBI facial recognition software, it was you. And the computer was 97.4% sure. We've got footprints from up there, and I'll bet they match those boots you have on right now. And then... dirt samples. And, we have a warrant to search your trailer. I'm sure we'll find something to link you to the pot business there, don't you think? You will not be able to fool a jury with that kind of evidence working against you. There's more going on here than you even know, Jeb, so I suggest you stop messing around. You need to start talking the truth, and now's the time to do it."

Jeb looked over Mark's shoulder, spying the FBI agents, milling about like a pack of wolves ready to tear into an injured doe. "I guess I don't have much of a choice."

"No you don't. Let's have a seat," said Mark, as both men took a few steps to lean against an electrical transformer. Mark noticed Jeb had a slight limp as he walked.

"I'm serious, Jeb, if you've been injured, we can get an ambulance out here to give you a look."

"Nope. That ain't from today. I got Franco to thank for that limp."

"Seriously? How so?"

"He's just a total bastard asshole. You know that's right, don't you Ranger Mark?"

"Of course he is, but tell me about the limp." This was not what Mark wanted to talk about. His main objective was to find out more about why Jeb's DNA was found on the tent. However, having stumbled onto this surprising revelation, he wanted to find out more about what Franco Hufnagel might have done to Jebidiah Fields.

"Not a lot to tell. When Franco got out of the pen he was mad as hell that I had testified against him all those years ago. Plus he weren't too happy I took over his gig, and let me tell you, we were growing some good shit, too. A whole lot better than his."

"When was that?"

"Oh, I don't know. What… eight, nine years ago, maybe. But you know, I didn't really have a crew, just me and one other dude. Franco didn't like me carryin' on what he started. He followed me up into the woods one day when I was alone and smashed my leg up with a baseball bat."

"Wait, was this before or after he killed my wife?"

"Just right after, I think. He musta found out I gave you some tips I heard about him, you know, about where he might be stayin' and stuff like that. So you know, that on top of me testifying to send him to the pen, he wasn't too happy with me. He damn near ruined my leg for good, that's for sure. The bastard just wanted to cripple me, ya know. He had every opportunity to crack me in the head, but he didn't. Just wanted to ruin my leg. Anyway, I had to quit growin' then. I couldn't do that job no more because of all the back n' forth on that mountain.

"What did you do after that?" asked Mark.

"I started workin' the tourist jobs. Souvenir shops, restaurants, and miniature golf. Ranger Mark, I'm here to tell ya, If I'd a had to look at another parent in the eye and tell them there's no freakin' way their big-ass kid was under 12 years old just to save a few bucks on the price of admission, well I think I might'a killed somebody. Anyhow, I finally got a good job at Dollywood, runnin' some rides, had benefits, and I got me a surgery. The leg's a lot better now, but shit if that don't hurt like a son-of-a-bitch gettin' hit by that cop car like that. How the hell did he ever get a driver's license, anyhow?"

"Back to Franco. You said he attacked you on the mountain. It sounds like that was within the national park?"

"Sure was."

"This is odd, because I'm pretty good at remembering those kinds of things, but I don't remember seeing a police report about something like that. Did you file a report at the ranger station?"

"Nope. He told me he'd get the other leg if I mentioned it to anybody."

"Sounds like both of us have good reason for wanting our man Franco back in prison."

"You got that right, Ranger Mark. Actually, I'd prefer dead."

"Ah, Jeb... don't go threatening anyone in front of a law enforcement officer. I know you're just venting, but you got to watch what you say. It could come back on you in the future."

Jeb kept it to himself that he was not just venting. He meant every word of it.

"Have you seen him since?" asked Mark.

"Nope. But I keep tabs on him. My partner was workin' for Franco for a bit."

"Who's that? Haus?"

"How'd you know that?"

"I'm an investigator. After I saw him in the video of you and your crew discovering we'd taken your crop, I started poking my nose around. He looked familiar to me. Found out people know him as Haus. I'm going to want to talk to him, eventually, too."

"He might be hard to find, Ranger Mark. He's homeless, sort of."

"What do you mean, sort of?"

"No address. He couch surfs when it gets cold, but now that it's warmin' up, he's got a hammock and a tent, a few cooking things too. That's all he needs. He lives in the woods. Moves around a lot."

"Well I'm hoping you're going to help me find old Haus, shortly. But Jeb, we're way off topic. Your pot business is not why I came to talk to you, although that's serious business for another day. We've got bigger fish to fry, at least for now."

Jeb grew quiet, knowing the FBI suspected he had something to do with the governor's murder.

"The real reason I'm here is to talk to you about a little campsite I found near Thunderhead," said Mark. "It was not far from the pot field. Was that yours?"

"Yup, sure was. Or at least I think so. Got a real big pine by the campfire?"

"That's the one. Tell me all about it."

"What do you wanna know about it?" asked Jeb, seeking clarity.

"What were you doing up there? Was that some kind of basecamp?"

"Shouldn't I get a lawyer or somethin'?"

"Of course you can get a lawyer if you want one. I just thought you'd want to talk to me instead of the FBI. If you talk to them, yes, you're going to need a lawyer. But then, you won't be talking to me anymore. Things will get a little more serious for you, then."

Jeb remembered it was time to come clean, and with Mark's help, maybe they'd go light on him.

"Well, after gettin' my leg fixed, I started growin' again. I know, not very smart. That's what you're gonna tell me, right?"

"No comment. Keep going, I'm not interested in your mistakes right now, Jeb."

"Okay, well then, Haus and me got in touch again, got a pretty good crop growing until your people came n' took it from us. Left us with nothin'. We started lookin' for another spot, something smaller maybe. It was easier to stay up on the mountain for a few days while we looked around, instead of comin' and goin' every day. Even though I can walk pretty good now, I don't like doin' more than I have to."

"Okay, so now I know why you were up there camping, without a permit I might add. But on the night of May 22nd, one night before the governor was shot, you appear to have had a tent, a campfire, and some tools you left behind when I came upon the site at about sundown. You left a fire burning. It looked loaded up with firewood, like you were planning on being there through the night, but nobody was around. I'm just curious if you saw me coming and fled the scene, or if you just happened to be stupid enough to leave with a campfire still burning."

"Hold on there, what do you mean, when you got there?"

"Just what I said," clarified Mark. "I got there at about sundown, you weren't there. Why did you..."

"...Hold on, Ranger Mark. Sundown? I know the night you're talkin' about, but I didn't see you comin' like you say. And we took off long before sundown."

Mark sensed both of them could be talking about two different things. "Explain," he said, allowing Jeb to provide clarity.

"I remember that day pretty good. Me and Haus was at that site at like five o'clock or so, when Franco showed up, not you."

"You saw Franco?"

"Sure as hell did. I had just put the wood on the fire, and we made some coffee, and was ready to have some jerky. Then I heard a noise, caught sight o' Franco comin' our way, carryin' a rifle. He might have seen the smoke and came to look around, cuz I'm sure he had no idea I was there. Then again, Haus was workin' for him every now and again, too, so who knows, Haus could have mentioned we was there. I really don't know. If he did, well, that would suck because I told him not to say anything about my business to Franco."

"Why didn't you ask him about that, if he'd said anything to Franco?"

"I did later, but Haus won't talk about Franco no more. He's all clammed up. I wish he'd tell me why, but he won't."

"So maybe he did say something about you to Franco, and now he's gone silent about all that? Do you trust him, Jeb?"

"No, we're good, but you know, he could have let somethin' slip by accident. I wouldn't be happy about that, if he did, but I don't think he'd ever double cross me on purpose."

"Okay, fine, but go back the story. What happened next when you saw Franco coming?"

"I kinda whisper-shouted over to Haus and said we should get the hell out of there. We grabbed our backpacks and ran like hell. I wasn't about to get my other leg smashed, ya know?! Our timin' really sucked because Haus was cleanin' his gun at the time, and he couldn't 'o used it if he wanted to. I'm tellin' ya, I was not about to fight Franco without a gun, even though it was two to one."

"Did Franco see you, or Haus?"

"I can't rightly say. If he did, it was just the backs of our heads, because we were hightailin' it pretty good."

"Did you get a good look at the rifle he was carrying... before you 'hightailed it'?"

"Nope. But he's always been a gun lovin' kinda dude, that's for sure. Back in the day, he'd bring his big game guns up on the mountain and let us kids give 'em a shot or two. He kind of thought it was a funny thing to see us get knocked on our asses. You know he's been to Africa, shootin' over there? And I should'a told you, too, I saw in the news about that Shane fella bein' married to the governor. Shit, you might wanna give him a good look too, Ranger Mark, because I can tell you for a fact that him and Franco have been on hunting trips to Africa together. At least that's what Haus told me."

"I did not know that," said Powers, jotting that down in his notepad. "If true, this would shed a very suspicious light on

Shane Goodwyn." Mark made note to convey this to Agent Toney as soon as possible.

"So what did you do when you saw him coming?" asked Mark, attempting to keep Jeb talking.

"I told you, we up and hightailed it. We didn't have time to take nothin' but our backpacks. Haus tossed all the gun stuff into his backpack and we just made a bee-line back down the mountain to the parking lot, plowin' through sticker bushes 'n all. That messed up my leg pretty good, too. I ain't in that good a' shape no more. It nearly killed me, huffin' and puffin' like that."

"Why did Haus run? You said he was working for Hufnagel. Doesn't seem to me he had much of a reason to run."

"You know, I think he just ran because I did. Or maybe something happened between those two cuz Haus won't talk about him no more."

"I find this interesting. Why would two of you young men in your 20's be so afraid of Franco? He's my age."

"There's somethin' about him, Ranger Mark. You should know. He's like got this thing about him. He's like Darth Vader or something. Nobody messes with Franco."

"Oh, don't get me wrong, I do know how cunning he can be, but in terms of physicality, your buddy Haus is apparently an intimidating fella."

"He is big, but I'd put my money on Franco anyways."

"Alright, so, did you go back to the site to get your stuff later?"

"Two days later Haus did. You know, now that I think about it, Franco must 'o gotten a look at us runnin' away, because that asshole took our tent and some other stuff of ours. He must 'o taken it thinkin' he was gonna put us in a bind because it was supposed to rain that night. I'm tellin' ya, I hate that son-of-a-bitch Hufnagel. I think he knew it was me 'n Haus up there, and takin' the damned tent was just another way o' him messin' with me. He might have thought it was funny, but I don't find any humor there at all. Do me a favor and put him away for poachin' the bears if you get a chance, will ya?"

"Hold on a second, Jeb, did you say he's poaching bears?"

"Oh, well I figured you knew. Well you will be interested in this for sure. Franco's not growin' anymore, he's poachin' him some black bears. Apparently he's livin' just outside the park now, down past Fontana Dam or maybe over toward Carolina, somewheres like that. But that's what Haus was doin' working for Franco, helpin' him with the bears. Franco's selling parts to China usin' FedEx 'n UPS. And he does poachin' in Africa, too, when the bears here are hibernatin'. That's the big time, right there, brotha. But don't it figure? He's a freakin' asshole, so of course he's killin' those elephants and rhinos over there. What else would you expect from a grade A asshole?"

"I could believe every word, but coming from you, Jeb, it's just hearsay. Sounds like Haus knows a lot about Franco, and I'm going to want to talk to him about all this. Why haven't you shared this with us before now?"

"For the same damned reason I didn't file a police report when he took battin' practice on my knee. I still got one good leg 'n I intend to keep it that way. But I was about to tell you the same thing a few minutes ago, but you said you didn't want to talk about Franco no more and just wanted to know about my campsite up on the mountain."

"This changes things, though." Mark had read internal memos that Banister was forming a task force to look into poaching in the southeast corner of the park. Mark had wanted merely to speak to Jeb about why his tent was found at the shooting site, but never bargained on getting all of this info.

"I'm a tellin' ya, Ranger Mark, I'm sick n' tired of runnin' away from that bastard-ass prick. Maybe if you can do something about him. That just might keep me from filling his lungs with lead using my daddy's shotg…"

"…Uh, Jeb, don't finish that sentence."

"Oh, right. Well, maybe I wasn't really thinkin' of killin' him. Maybe just give him a few more holes to breathe through."

"I know your anger, Jebidiah. He took my Laurie, as you know, even though we could not prove it. Believe me, I've had thoughts of revenge for the last ten years. Maybe if I wasn't a law man I might have made the wrong choice by now. Thinking it and doing it are two different things, I know, but you can't let an evil man make you evil too."

"I get what you're sayin', Ranger Mark. And I know if I ever got caught gettin' my revenge, that'd be bad for my family, so every day I give those thoughts their due and put 'em away. But that sure would be gratifyin' to know he's feedin' the worms, man o' man."

"OK, Jeb, let's get back on topic. Just to clarify about the tent, you never saw him take the tent, right? Or your boom box, or coffee pot."

"Nope."

"Would Haus say the same thing?"

"Yup."

"How can you say for sure Franco took the tent, if you or Haus didn't see him do it?"

"You know as good as me when you are off trail, you can sit up there for weeks on end before you see another human bein'. There's no way somebody else just happened along, and decided to take our stuff. He's got to be the one who took it, because he knew where the pot field was, and he might-a seen smoke while he was over there seein' what we was up to."

Mark wished Jeb had answered differently; if this was ever used against Franco in a court of law, it would be more powerful testimony if Jeb had actually seen Franco with the tent in his possession. For now, it was merely speculation that Franco was the one who had stolen the tent and transported it to the shooting site. Yet, at the same time, Mark was now invigorated to hear there was a chance the shooter was not Jeb, but instead, Franco.

Powers considered the whole conversation. He believed that what Jeb was telling him was the truth, although, he had reached a different conclusion than Jeb about Franco's motivations. Mark did not believe Franco stole the tent so Jeb and Haus would get rained upon. No, Mark believe Franco had stolen Jeb's tent to seed the shooting sight with someone else's DNA or fingerprints, intending to throw investigators off of his own scent.

"Jeb, I thank you for what you've told me here, today. I'm going to have to ask you to make this all official, though. We need you to come into the station and give an official testimony on everything you've told me here."

Jeb grew angry. "You told me I wouldn't have to do that if I told you everything I knew right here!"

"I'm not asking you to go in for three days of interrogation. Some of what you told me tonight is very important, and we will want to have it recorded. But we are not going to keep you for three days."

"Thank the Lord in high heaven for that."

"At least not now. I can't make any promises for what might happen later in the case. You need to be prepared for anything.

Now… we'll also need to collect a DNA sample and someone's going to want to talk to Haus, too, so we're going to need you to tell us where to find him."

"Oh shit, he's going to be pissed at me for ropin' him into all this."

"Jeb, he's chosen to work with you, growing pot on federal lands, and with Franco to poach bears on federal lands. Doesn't sound to me like you roped him into anything… he's a willing participant in multiple crimes. He should not be surprised to see us."

Jeb grew silent, processing the complicated mess in which he was now embroiled.

"Ranger Mark, one question. You said you found the tent at the spot where the governor was killed. How did you come up with my finger prints, anyway?"

"Mainly on the boom box that was tucked inside the tent."

"But how did you know that was *MY* DNA?"

"Remember when you were 16. That DUI?"

"Oh, yeah. Forgot about that. So you still got my prints on file from that?"

"We sure do. But if what you are telling me is true, and Franco really did steal your tent, I'm thinking we'll probably find other clues to point us toward Franco. But don't get me wrong, for now, you are a still a suspect in the governor's death. Along with Franco. Anything you can tell us to implicate him further will be good for you, but you need to make sure everything you tell is completely factual. If you lie, you can go to prison for impeding a federal investigation. Now, last bit of digging I did on Franco shows that he's been in Bryson City, NC. Does that sound familiar to you?" asked Mark.

"Sounds about right. Haus will know for sure."

"Believe me, when we find Haus, we're going to have a long talk. Again, do you know where we can find him?"

"Any time we work together, we just agree when and where we're going to meet next. But, we ain't been back there since that run in with Franco. Last we talked, we's gonna meet at the Chimneys Picnic Grounds early next week. But I wouldn't have no idea where to find him before that."

Mark and Jeb continued talking about a few minor details, and eventually it was time for Mark to put an end to this visit. He called a few of the FBI members to give them a summary of what he and Jeb had talked about and informed them that they would need an APB on Franco Hufnagel. He informed them about finding Haus as well. And to end with, they agreed to take Jeb into headquarters for a recorded interview before the day was over.

As Mark gave them instructions, he handed over his notebook. The agent he spoke with found it curious. Before he could ask why, Mark remembered a few more things to say to Jeb.

"Jeb, by the way, Franco doesn't have your gear any more, I do. It's all in the evidence room. You'll get it all back one day, after the investigation is over. Assuming you're not the killer and you're going to jail."

"Real funny, Ranger Mark. That ain't gonna happen cuz I didn't do nothin' wrong," said Jeb.

Mark walked closer to Jeb once more, and spoke with a lower voice.

"Jeb, you're going to need a good lawyer, like you said. You can have one appointed, if you'd like."

With that, Jeb's friendly little talk with Mark was over. Mark returned to the FBI agent to whom he'd given his personal notebook.

"Are you sure you want me to have your notes? Aren't you going to type them up in your report?" asked the agent.

"Nope," said Mark. "I'm off the case. Somebody else will get the pleasure of completing the forms."

"What?" said the agent, incredulously.

"The man whom I tried to prosecute for the murder of my wife ten years ago is now a new lead suspect, along with Jeb Fields. I have a conflict of interest based on my history with Hufnagel, as well as a bias in favor of Jeb Fields. I'm sure you'll agree I need to step down immediately. Looks like you'll get to make sense of my chicken scratch. Call me if you want some clarification, but I'm no longer on the case."

Driving back to Gatlinburg via the bypass, Mark called Sandy. He gave her a summary of his conversation with Jeb. This included the long history of how Jeb had testified against Franco Hufnagel twenty years ago. He also told her about how Franco was the leading suspect in his wife's murder.

Regarding the interview with Jeb, he told Toney that he found Jeb's story to be credible, especially Jeb's assertion that it was Franco Hufnagel who'd stole the tent, and the next place the tent was found was at the shooting site. This made Franco Hufnagel a prime suspect. He told Sandy to make sure they processed Jeb's testimony properly, because this could be the testimony that would ultimately find and convict their sniper.

"I've got one more little surprise for you," said Mark. "It's a little something for you to explore with Shane Goodwyn when you see him next. Do you recall from my first interview with him how he'd briefly mentioned he'd gone on hunting trips with international dignitaries?"

"I do recall seeing something about that, but go on."

"Yes, so today I also learned from Jeb that Shane has been hunting in Africa before, on a safari of some sorts, with none other than Franco Hufnagel."

"You don't say?"

"If true, I would find it very suspicious that they know each other, especially now that we have reason to believe Hufnagel is the sniper. What are the odds they would know each other and Shane not have some involvement with the death of his wife?"

"IF... what Jeb Fields says is true," countered Sandy. "It sounds to me Jeb could be pinning the blame on Hufnagel, trying to take the heat off of himself. After all, the only biological evidence we have at the shooting site belongs to Jeb. He's feeling the heat."

"I have known Jeb for most of my life, and even though he's a pot growing parasite, I don't believe he's a sniper who would be involved with this high level crime. What he told me about Hufnagel, well, I believe every word."

"Because you want to, given your history with that man? Or because you really think Jeb is being truthful?"

"Both. Just being honest."

"I appreciate that. But that's why you're taking yourself off of the case, remember? Because you are biased."

"Absolutely. It's up to you to follow his leads and build your own case against Hufnagel. Or against Jeb, if that's what the facts tell you. Don't take my word for it."

"I thank you, Mark. I'm glad you see your own bias, and thought to remove yourself. You've done excellent work. I'm going to miss you on this investigation."

"Yeah, it sucks to bow out. But do me a favor and solve this case. I'd be real happy if Franco Hufnagel is the sniper when all is said and done. The world would be a better place with that man behind bars."

"I'll follow the evidence, Mark, wherever that may lead," said Sandy. "Next thing, we'll see what our friendly NRA spokesperson has to say about his hunting trips with Franco Hufnagel. I'll let you know how that goes."

Chapter 18

Hours after meeting with Isabella Lopez, and then speaking with Mark Powers on the phone, Agent Sandy Toney found herself in a wholly different environment, prepared to speak with Shane Goodwyn. Not only was the meeting location a total departure from the statehouse where she and Agent Gallenstein had visited earlier, but so too was the character of her next interviewee much different than that of Isabella Lopez.

Shane was currently making his rounds to Nashville gun shops to meet with store owners about a new National Rifle Association membership drive. As such, Shane had agreed to be interviewed at Buckshot Bev's firing range. Toney had spent plenty of time at firing ranges at Quantico, Virginia, and regularly had to log hours to satisfy her FBI firearms competency requirements. What she did not expect, however, was how this firing range projected an Appalachian flavor, complete with buxom women dressed in their best 'Daisy Dukes' working behind the counter. The professionally clad duo of Sandy Toney and Jeannine Gallenstein were greeted by copious quantities of cleavage as they asked a female clerk if Shane Goodwyn had arrived.

"Yup, He's back in the stockroom I think," said the woman behind the counter, who wore a checkerboard shirt with its tails tied in a knot over her ample chest. "You here to shoot?" she added.

"No," said Sandy, "We're just here for a meeting with Mr. Goodwyn."

"You can go on back. I'll buzz you through the security gate to get ya back there," replied the clerk.

Moments later the two agents were in another world. The stock room was filled to the brim with shelving that was packed with a wide variety of ammunition, ear-protection devices, shooting glasses and other safety gear. There was also a wide variety of stuffed animals, including one upright bear, two raccoons and one bobcat, posed aggressively.

"Excuse me," said Sandy, loudly, "Is Shane Goodwyn back here?"

"Who wants to know, baby cakes?" said a cartoonish voice coming from behind one of the bears. Shane Goodwyn began rocking the bear side to side as if it had suddenly come to life.

"FBI," said Sandy. Shane stepped out from behind the trophy animal looking slightly embarrassed.

"Mr. Goodwyn, good afternoon. Are we meeting... here?"

"Sorry about that, I, uh, thought you were one of the ladies from the front counter. And I'm sorry about the location. This is the best I can do given my schedule. I'm a busy man, lots of travel this week. Welcome to my world, ladies. You got questions, well, take your best shot."

Sandy asked, "Yes, well, may we sit somewhere..."

"... Did you get that? Take your best shot?" said Shane, totally ignoring the woman's question about seating arrangements. "We're at a firing range. Do you get the joke?"

"Oh, I hadn't noticed it was a joke," chimed in Gallenstein, "But now that you've pointed it out, I get it."

"I do my best to entertain. Especially the ladies," said the ex-football player, with a devilish grin. Sandy thought it was a strange comment coming from a man whose wife had been murdered weeks ago. Coupled with his 'baby cakes' comment, it appeared that he had quickly reverted back to a bachelor lifestyle.

"We won't need entertaining today, Mr. Goodwyn, we're here on business," said Sandy. Shane looked at her face, and that of Agent Gallenstein, and could tell they were uncomfortable with his male bravado.

"Listen, if you gals have a problem with my so-called toxic masculinity, you should have brought hazmat suits, because I'm the epicenter of masculinity around here," he said proudly. "I'm afraid I can't turn it on and off, it's just a part of who I am."

This time, his remarks were met with stifled laughter, but neither woman gave him eye contact. Both were totally confused as to whether he was joking or serious. Sandy asked where they might be able to sit for the interview. The group walked a few paces, with Shane accidentally knocking things off of the shelves as he went, unable to maneuver easily because of his large shoulders. Momentarily they found an old poker table in a dimly-lit corner of the store room. It was to be their meeting table.

"Want any pop from the vending machine out front? They just got some Ale-8 and Mr. Pibb. You want some?" asked Shane.

"No thanks," said Sandy, as Jeannine echoed the sentiment with a shake of her head.

After getting situated, the proceedings began with Jeannine's activation of her recording app on her phone and the reading of Shane's Miranda rights. He seemed unfazed by the formality of it all and waited silently for the first question from Sandy. He was in far brighter spirits than he had been when Mark had visited him the first time.

"The taxidermy is very interesting," said Sandy.

"Yeah, they usually put those out for Christmas, and put Santa hats on them. They have some crazy people working here."

"I hear you're a hunter. Have you had any of your own kills stuffed and mounted?"

"A few grizzly from up in Canada. A moose, although only the head was taxidermized. Same with more deer than I can count. Elk. Turkeys, too."

"Anything from Africa? I saw in Ranger Powers' report that you occasionally take dignitaries on safari trips. Have you ever 'bagged' a big animal over there?"

"Of course I have. I won't shoot endangered species, though, but I've taken down a number of wildebeests. Completely above board, nothing illegal, if that's what you're digging for."

"No, of course not. I'm just interested in people who hunt the big game. Believe it or not, I hunted rabbit and squirrel with my father through most of my childhood."

"Really, you look so... sophisticated. Wouldn't peg you as a hunter."

"I just had a little 410 shotgun, but those were great days with my dad while he was still alive. I do want to ask, though, about the people you've been hunting with. Just political dignitaries?"

"Mostly."

"Have you ever been hunting with someone named Franco Hufnagel?"

"No, I don't think so. I mean... sometimes the dignitaries have a few tag-alongs... usually their security detail people, so maybe it could have been... wait... was he by any chance a Latino?"

"I don't know," replied Sandy. "I can certainly find out, thought."

"It's been about five years ago, but there was a guy I thought was named Marco, but could have been Franco, something like that. He was on a trip with some folks from around here. A group of Tennessee people. They were UT fans, and they knew me from when I was a player, and when they found out I did trips to Africa, they all signed up for a trip with me as their host. We had African locals as guides, or Sherpas, you know, everybody does that, but I was the gun guy. I'd present a number of manufacturer's latest pieces, and build good rapport in the gun community while doing what I love to do. It's a sweet deal if you can get it. I believe I'm well suited for the job, being a highly recognizable football celebrity and all. And terribly good looking, as well. That never hurts, right?"

Sandy moved ahead without recognizing his last comment. "Have you remained in contact with Franco since that trip? Have you ever seen him locally?"

"No. Why do you ask?"

"Just curious. I'd think a fan might try to keep in touch once they'd gone hunting with a legendary UT football celebrity. Has Franco Hufnagel ever attempted to contact you? Or have you had any written, electronic or telephone contact with him since that trip to Africa?"

"No. Nothing. Zilch. Nada."

"Do you remember what he looks like?"

"No. Most of them look alike, you know."

Sandy had never had such a bizarre interview. It was all she could to do stop herself from getting angry with the man in front of her, but she knew she had to ignore his rhetoric and stick to the task at hand.

"What did you talk about that time you were on the trip together?"

"No real conversation that I can remember. I do seem to recall he was a bit of an egomaniac, always trying to compete with me over our shooting prowess. So I didn't really like hanging with that guy. I tend to be more of a modest man myself, and don't mix well with those guys who think they are all that."

There was a noticeable moment of silence between the two women upon Shane's comment, but after that, Sandy felt she'd asked enough about his trip with Franco and decided to move on to other matters.

Let me ask you about your relationship with Janet. Would you say the two of you were happily married?"

Shane knew he'd get more of these kinds of questions, as he had when interviewed by Mark Powers. But this time, Shane had prepared himself, and was doing his best to keep his temper under control.

"Yes. We were. Very happy."

"No disagreements... arguments... any kind of marital discord?"

"We did argue, but so do all married couples. There were times I was mad at her, and times when she was mad at me. Usually both at the same time. But we really enjoyed making up, if you know what I mean."

Focus, thought Sandy. "What were your arguments about? Generally speaking."

Now Shane was starting to lose his calm demeanor. "Nothing unusual. But that's not what you want to hear, is it, lady. Why are you asking me *that* kind of question??"

"Just doing my job," replied Sandy.

"No, no, there's something about how you asked that question. I know what you're doing. You are looking for a way to make me look bad so you can pin the murder on me. You don't really want to find out the truth, you want to make it the way you want it to be. 'Let's make the white male take the fall. He's a gun advocate, let's take him down!'."

"That's not the case, Mr. Goodwyn. I'm merely expounding upon what we know and hoping to learn more about what we don't know. It's standard procedure, and nothing personal."

"I already talked with Powers. Don't know why I have to go through this a second time. He's an ass, by the way. He thinks he's such a big shot with his Wandering Ranger videos on YouTube, like he thinks everyone in the world gives a shit about his job."

Agent Gallenstein could not allow that comment to go unchallenged. "Well, his videos have actually been watched by hundreds of thousands of viewers all over the world, so I don't see how he could be wrong if he truly believes that. But I don't believe he's ever claimed that *everyone* likes his videos. Maybe you should try building a following of your own, sometime. I'm sure you'd be loved as much as Ranger Powers. Especially by the ladies."

Toney gave a sideways glance to Gallenstein, a very subtle look of approval for Jeannine's brilliant sarcasm.

"But, getting back to business," said Sandy, "What did you argue about with Janet?" It was a question that was left unanswered minutes earlier, and she would not forget to get an answer.

Shane reluctantly continued. "She got elected governor. I never expected her to win, but I supported her anyway. I even got the NRA behind her, and then she nearly went and blew it all to hell by saying in an interview that she might be open to gun reform legislation. What the hell was that? I'm her husband, and I work for the NRA!! We went round and round about that. For the record, Snowflake is a hyper-commie-liberal, and I know she was putting all those thoughts into Janet's head about gun control. That's a good part of the reason I don't trust her more than I could throw her... which would be a good 40 yards, by the way. So yeah, Janet and I argued a lot about that. But all of our other argument were over stupid stuff."

"Like what?"

"You know. She wanted me to do the dishes, all the time. Even cook, too. But I sucked at all that. I'd put in a load of laundry, then forget to put it in the dryer so it would get all smelly and had to be rewashed. Or I'd run the dishwasher and forget to put in one of those soap pods. Once I put in dishwashing liquid and it overflowed with suds. I'm not the housewife... how am I supposed to know that soap isn't just soap. Got to have a special kind of soap for the dishwasher, apparently. Stupid stuff like that. Somehow she thought I should become the woman of the house once she was the almighty governor. I did the best I could, but I was not happy about it. We did argue about those things, but they were mostly just disagreements, nothing serious."

"Mr. Goodwyn, this next question may help set the record straight about rumors we've heard in the media, but I want to be clear we have no evidence of this. But Shane, did you ever abuse your wife, mentally or physically?"

"No. Never. Her father did, though. And when I'd get angry, I could tell she thought I was going to hit her. I'm one of those guys who talks with his hands, and when we argued, if I did that she would run away from me like she thought I was going to whap her upside the head or something. I can't help the thing with my hands, though. My mother is full-blooded Italian, we always raise our hands when we're arguing. Hell, we raise our hands when we're NOT arguing. We just use our hands a lot, like a lot of Italian people do. After a few years of marriage, when Janet's dad died, she finally told me all about how he would hit her all the time. It all made sense then. I tried to stop using my hands like that, but it's something I've done since I was a little kid, kind of hard-wired into my brain, you know."

"I'm sorry to hear about that. That's very useful information. Is Janet's mother still alive?"

"Yes, she is."

"And she can validate that Janet's father abused her?"

"Yes, I'm sure she can, and will, if you do."

"We'll do that."

"Go ahead. I never touched Janie. She was my wife, why would I hurt her?"

"Unfortunately, spousal abuse is a real thing, Mr. Goodwyn. Now, here's another sensitive question. Did you have more than one gun on you the day your wife was shot? You had the one gun in your holster, the Houston H9, but was there any other pistol concealed on your person? Or did you have access to any other handgun, that might have been located somewhere in the woods of Thunderhead Mountain, where it could be retrieved by you?"

"Nope. You guys are really desperate or something. Where do you come up with these questions? You really think I had more than one pistol up there?"

"That's for you to answer, not us."

"And look, I had a holster on, how could I have carried another gun, even if it was concealed? In my butt crack or something?"

"I suppose that could be possible, or there could be other possibilities. Wearing a football jersey, you could have merely had a small pistol tucked into the waistband of your shorts."

"Could have, but I didn't. I was wearing breathable fabric, exercise shorts, stretchable. If I had a gun tucked in there, it would have slid down during the hike. I already have enough firepower down there, a gun would not be necessary."

Again, Gallenstein nearly lost it, and struggled to keep from laughing at Shane's hilariously egotistical comments.

"Noted, but I don't think that will be necessary," said Sandy. She glanced at Agent Gallenstein, who was taking elaborate notes, and she began drawing a cartoon snake on her notepad. Its comical appearance brought a smile to Agent Toney, who then struggled to retain her composure.

"So do you deny having a gun hidden somewhere on the mountain, Mr. Goodwyn."

"I did not have a gun hidden up on that mountain."

"Shane, did you kill your wife, or have any knowledge of plans executed by others to kill your wife?"

"Plain and simple, NO! You're really pissing me off with these questions, you know."

"Shane, we have testimony from someone else who was there that Janet's last words were 'Shane … did it."

"Who told you that?"

"I cannot say."

"It had to be Powers or Snowflake. They were the two who were crouched down beside Janet when she died. I want to know who told you that. Which one of them?"

"I can understand you want to know that, but I am not at liberty to share that information. Please just respond to those last words. Why would your wife, with her final words, say that you did it?"

Shane grew angry once more, and this time he did unleash a rant, with intimidating volume.

"I don't believe that! She did not say that. I did nothing wrong. I loved my wife, and I had nothing to do with her death. That's all bullshit. Total crap. Janet did not say that, I know she didn't."

"Please settle down, Mr. Goodwyn. That's all we need is your response. Is there anything else you want to tell us?"

Shane was now fuming mad, and had a bead of sweat forming on his forehead, which he promptly wiped away with the sleeve of his shirt. He appeared to be searching his mind for his response, as if sifting through memories to find something worthwhile to mention. "You didn't bring up the gunshot noise I heard."

"Is there something you want to add about that?"

"I'm damned sure that has something to do with whoever killed my honey. I suggest you start looking into that instead of continuing to insult a dead woman's loving husband with all these stupid questions."

"I read Ranger Powers' report, it seemed thoroughly detailed with respect to your recollections of the sounds during the shooting episode. I will tell you this, Shane. The autopsy report has revealed that Janet was killed by an 8mm round most likely fired from a small pistol. That means your theory of a second shooter is accurate."

"And my gun shoots 9mm, so now you know I could not have been that shooter, so why are you hounding me? I told you I heard that gun go off, and so you need to be looking at someone else, not me!"

"Please realize we're asking similar questions of not only you, but everyone else who was up on that mountain that day, Mr. Goodwyn. Now, I believe we have all we need, and if you have no further questions for us, we will be going."

"I do have a question. When do I get my H9 back?"

"You can pick it up at park headquarters anytime you'd like," Sandy said.

Moments later the interview was finished and the recording device terminated. Shane was no longer hospitable, and did not walk the investigators to the door. The ladies walked out on their own, and stopped at the counter for a recommendation for someplace to get dinner. Shortly thereafter, they were gone. Shane had finally emerged from the stockroom, and watched at the front window of the firing range as the agents drove away. Over the sound of gunfire in another part of the building, Shane whispered to himself, "Snowflake. That bitch is going' to get hers."

Chapter 19

Craig Banister was a busy man. His calendar was chock-full of seminars, banquets, hearings, investigations, visits, round-tables, support calls, commencements and other time consuming events. Not being one to keep up with ever-changing technologies, Craig reluctantly tolerated the internet. While he had an email account that worked just fine, he had his receptionist print hard-copies of every email message he received and leave the stack on his desk. He would answer them in his own handwriting, return the pages to his receptionist, and she would reply to the senders via email. It was highly inefficient, but exceptionally comfortable for the man in charge.

If there was one form of technology he did love, it was the smartphone. Granted, its functionality was very underutilized by the older man, but he was dazzled that he could have conversations anywhere he pleased. Or at least *nearly* anywhere, as service was very limited within the park. While he loved that freedom, he did not like talking while he drove. He'd heard too many stories of accidents involving phones. As he was driving through North Carolina, he received an incoming call. He looked at the phone sitting next to him, and was perturbed. *How dare someone call me while I'm driving! I can't look at the damned thing, my eyes belong on the road!* He cheated and felt guilty about it, by glancing at who was calling. When he saw that name, he immediately looked for a place along the road to pull over.

"Hang on a gall-darned second," he said aloud, as if the caller could hear him. Once he pulled over, he answered the phone and began speaking.

"I'm driving. And why are you calling me?"

Now with the phone firmly planted against his ear, he listened to the reply from the caller. Then he replied.

"I told you, I'm busy. I will get down there soon enough."

Again he paused and listened.

"Damnation, don't you go getting pissy with me. We had an agreement and I'm a man of my word. Just hold your horses and I'll deliver when I get down there."

He paused.

"I have every penny that's coming to you. A deal's a deal."

He paused again.

"I'll shuffle things around on my calendar to fit you in the best I can."

He paused once more.

"The next time we talk it will be me calling you from a safe phone, like we agreed. Now I'm hanging up.... I've got a good distance to go. Goodbye!"

With that he pressed the little red button on the glassy surface of his phone and tossed the device onto the passenger seat.

"Where did all the gentlemen go?" he whispered to himself. "Now all we got are assholes!"

He jammed the gear shift back into drive and sprayed gravel behind him as he pulled his BMW Alpina B6 back onto the twisty roadway ahead. He was glad to have it back again after being out of commission for a few days, for new paint, glass, trim, etc. He was not happy at having the black spray paint applied by apparent vandals, but it helped with perceptions. It was a perfect opportunity to lock in belief that the protesters were angry at him for siding with the developers. Who could possibly think he was one of them? But he still was not happy about including his own Beemer into the equation.

It had been several weeks since the attack on Thunderhead Mountain. Mark and Belle started their day sitting near one another at the Little River Ranger Station. Coincidentally, they were using the same two desks where they'd sat when Talia Manaia had last been with them, and had flirted so energetically with Mark. There was a cloud hanging over their heads, as there was no change in her condition. She remained in a coma and had been moved out of the ICU into a long-term care monitoring room.

"I still can't believe all of this. A coma. How horrible," said Belle, sipping on her coffee. "And here I sit, with a mocha latte. How can I enjoy this while I know she's on death's door?"

"Don't feel guilty. You and Mr. Banister probably saved her life. She could have easily bled to death if you hadn't attended to her."

"Mostly Banister," replied Belle. "I did my best, but he really knew what he was doing."

The two sat silently for a moment, lost in their own thoughts on the subject, set against the busy sounds of the Ranger Station. Finally, Mark broke the silence.

"I'm still churning my brain on that whole thing you said about how Banister was crying over Talia. Seems so odd. He barely knew her."

"For all we know. Not to speak badly of her while she's not here, but that woman did get around, by her own account. Maybe her and Banister had a fling," said Belle.

Mark's eyes, previously staring into space, darted in Belle's direction, making contact with hers.

"Seriously? He's like 70 years old! That's twice her age!"

"Come on now, Mark, I'm just saying. I mean... she has a thing for you, right? You're twenty years older than her."

"But I'm not like... OLD, am I?"

"No comment," said Belle. She tried to conceal a smile, but failed.

"Look, I know what you mean, but I just don't see her with someone who's 70," said Mark.

"Stranger things have happened. And listen, I've had girl talk with Talia and I'm here to tell you, I can see her jumping his bones no matter how old he is. When she hit a dry spell, I honestly wondered if she wouldn't do it with ANYBODY who gave her attention."

"Maybe we should look into this idea a little further. Find out if she was ever in a meeting, or seminar, with Banister. Anything like that. She's quite the environmentalist, and so is he. Maybe they met somewhere along the line, struck up a friendship."

"Talia does not have friendships with men. She has flings with them."

"I'm trying to be polite," finished Mark.

"How do we look into it? Seems like HR might want to know we're digging into their pasts, especially Banister's."

"Let's get their approval to check out Talia's online calendar, first. Maybe we can search for Banister's name and find any occasions where they were at the same event, or had dinner together... anything like that."

"You're going to have to do that, Mark. I'm not a special agent like you are."

"But that doesn't mean you're not special," replied Mark, playfully.

"You better watch out, you're starting to sound like Talia."

"Okay, good point."

"And... if you are no longer on the case, isn't this going to look like you are still involved?"

"Well, I'm not investigating anything related to Jeb Fields, which is where my conflict of interest was, so I'll consider this within the bounds of acceptability."

Mark reached for his mouse and was about to send a meeting request to the HR department, when he was interrupted by someone from behind.

"Mark Powers?" said a younger man, mildly obese and sporting greasy, black hair.

"Oh, hello," said Mark, "Can I help you?"

"Sort of, sir. I'm the IT guy. Did you get an email that we'd be stopping by?"

'No, I sure didn't."

"Figures. The email server is showing its age. I'm Gary."

"Mark."

Mark shook the young man's hand, still awaiting an explanation.

"So... Gary... you mentioned 'we', like 'we'd be stopping by', so is there someone else coming besides just you?"

"Uh, the HR lady."

"What's this about, Gary? Am I about to be led to the door for doing too much shopping online?" joked Mark, though he'd never done such a thing while in the station.

"I've been sworn to secrecy under the penalty of death or extreme torture," said Gary. Mark laughed, although the young man did not crack a smile.

"Ok, then we'll wait for the HR lady," said Mark, a little annoyed by all the ambiguity. Minutes later, a woman in her twenties named Tiffany Bradshaw, from HR, entered the station. She quickly found Mark and Gary, then petitioned them to move to the meeting room. She was not dressed in a typical ranger uniform, instead more of a corporate-looking woman's dress suit. Her long blonde hair was contained in a large cinnamon-roll-looking bun on the top of her head. Moments later they were all in a meeting room.

"Mark, Gary, I see you've met. I'm Tiffany Bradshaw, HR."

"Will I need a box to pack up my belongings?" joked Mark.

"That's no joking matter, Ranger Powers. I dish out brown boxes far more often than I care to. Not the best part of my job. I have something else to discuss with you."

Now Mark was truly curious what the matter could be. The first thing to enter his mind was all of the salacious banter with Talia. He worried someone had complained that there was far too much of that between the two.

"We have a problem with one of our other rangers, and it involves you, Mark," said Tiffany.

There it was. Mark had been validated in his concern. Yet, something didn't seem right. If there was a sexual harassment issue going on, then why was the IT guy, Gary, sitting in the room?

"I realize Talia is still in the hospital, and for all we know, she may never return to her job. However, I want to address something that involves the two of you that happened shortly before the attack."

"Look," said Mark, "I just have to say, I'm not the initiator of all the flirtations. In fact, if you ask Belle Whittle, she will back me up, and tell you that I was the one who was constantly trying to keep Talia from going a little too far."

"How so?" asked Tiffany.

"Well, you know, with her flirtations."

"Really? Did she do this often?"

"Just about every time I was here. Lots of sexually suggestive innuendos, if you know what I mean."

Tiffany took out a blank sheet of paper and asked Gary to step out of the room for a few moments. Then she asked Mark to give examples. He did as she asked, and their exchange went on for another ten minutes. Mark grew increasingly uncomfortable with the passage of time, knowing he should never have participated in those conversations with Talia. Why hadn't he shut them down? He knew the answer was that his masculine ego was flattered that another woman still found him attractive at his age, and after all he'd been through. He actually liked it, despite his protestations.

"Thanks for all that information, Mark. I'll be speaking with Talia upon her return, should she rejoin us. Now, let's talk about why I came here today." With that she called to Gary, just outside the room, and he returned.

Mark was now more confused than ever. "Wait... you're here for something else?"

"I am, but I'm glad you shared those details which I'll file away for a rainy day. But for now, we have a much more serious issue to discuss. And I must tell you this is highly confidential, and should not be discussed with anyone else. Gary, here, is a contractor in our IT InfoSec group. He runs analytics reports on a monthly basis to look for any kind of high risk behaviors for all park employees. It appears Talia has gained access to our offices in the middle of the night."

"I'm sorry," interrupted Mark, "but would you not want to discuss this with Talia once she's out of the hospital. I'm not sure why you need me here... she does not report to me."

"I'm getting to that, Ranger Powers. You see, after entering the offices, Talia spent time on one of the office computers. Gary, do you want to fill in the rest?"

"Yes, ma'am. Our reports have no record of her logging into the computer network with her ID and password. I thought that was kind of strange, because security cameras show her sitting at a computer and typing away like crazy."

"Sounds odd," said Mark, "you know, her job duties would not really require her to be in here at night at all. I mean, I can't remember the last time I even saw her use one of those computers. That was months ago when she worked on the environmental impact study. But how is it she was using a computer without having logged in?"

"The key here is that she didn't log in AS HERSELF. When I researched our computer logs a little closer, I found out she was logging in as you, Ranger Powers."

"What?!" asked Mark. "Seriously? How could that be? She would need to know my password to do that."

"That is correct," agreed Gary. He slid a computer print-out across the table for Mark's inspection. "Your log-in took place just minutes after she swiped her badge to get into the station. And, your login took place at exactly the same time we see her sitting down to the computer on the video footage, comparing the encoded time stamp."

Mark could hardly believe what he was hearing. Then he thought back to all those times Talia sat upon his desk when he'd come into the office, giving the appearance she was interested in a friendly chat. She loved taking short little 'selfie vids', as she called them, videos of the two of them. Those little videos would have captured his keystrokes as he logged in, which could have been analyzed later to determine his password. He informed Tiffany and Gary about those videos and they agreed they were the most likely way she'd compromised his credentials.

"You know, I always think of computer hackers as these young men sitting in a room somewhere in China or Russia, using high-tech hacking skills to get into our computers. Here it was a flirtatious co-worker taking selfie vides. Embarrassing. So the big questions now, is: do we know what she was looking at?"

"We have logs that track USB port and internet activity. During those times when she was logged in as you, she did not use the internet. But she did copy a few files from your hard drive to her USB drive. She probably didn't realize we could track that, and thought she would not be found out."

"But all of my classified info is stored on the cloud. That's protected by a second layer of authentication. Whatever she got from my hard drive was probably useless."

"No, that's not true, Ranger Powers," said Gary, "because the default cloud settings are to synchronize your cloud content with your hard drive. So whatever you put in the cloud is also on your hard drive. She could have gotten anything she wanted."

"Normally," added Tiffany, "We'd send officers to her home and see if any of the files she'd taken were on her home computer. That would become evidence of her intentions to distribute classified information to others outside of the park service. But of course, she's in a coma. We need you to look over the list of files she copied to the USB drive and let us know if they were classified or not. If so, we will figure out a legal way to gain access to her home and check things out."

Mark glanced at a piece of paper provided by Gary. There were hundreds of files listed there, some of them typed documents, many of them photos. All of them had to do with his investigation into EarthForce1 with the exception of one. That was a profile history of Franco Hufnagel, including his past criminal exploits and recent sightings and interactions with other known criminals.

"Yes, all of those are classified." said Mark, dejectedly. He now wrestled with the knowledge that Talia was up to no good, and her flirtations were merely an act to gain his confidence as a friendly coworker. He knew she was politically opposed to the Echo Ridge project, also the clear mantra of EarthForce1. It seemed a reasonable conclusion that she was feeding that info to EarthForce1. But what could she have wanted with the info about Hufnagel?

"Thank you, Mark," said Tiffany. "In your estimation, could the information contained in these files be linked, in any way, to the attack on Thunderhead Mountain?"

"That is distinctly possible."

"Well then, you may keep these copies of the log files, and we'll electronically forward this information to Agent Toney of the FBI. Unless, of course, you'd rather be the one to share with her?" asked Tiffany.

"I'll do it," said Mark. "I'll call her today. And I'll be seeing her tomorrow. I'll give her your number because I'm sure she's going to want to hear it from the horse's mouth."

Tiffany stared at Mark, and there was silence.

"Oh, not that you are a horse or anything. You know what I mean. I hope you do, anyway. I know I should never call a woman a horse, and mean it, you know. And... not that it only applies to women, because, well... is that sexist? I don't mean for it to be. I hate political correctness. I just have to go on record. We have to be really careful about what we say in this day and age, don't we?"

Tiffany smiled. "I know what you mean. Thanks for clarifying."

"And Ranger Mark," said Gary, "It might go without saying, but you should probably walk right back out there and change your password, right away."

"Absolutely. You got it."

Mark was deeply saddened by this conversation. It now appeared Talia's flirtatiousness was born of a hidden agenda, and one that was likely nefarious. How could he have fallen for letting her sit next to him and taking videos while he logged in? He began processing all of their conversations, replaying them in his head like they were recordings. This non-stop evaluation played out for days. Now, Talia was no longer the upbeat and perky personality he had known her to be. She was a deceitful, underhanded criminal. And, given the possible ties she now had with EarthForce1, and their public objections to Echo Ridge, he felt Talia was now a person of interest in the governor's assassination.

Chapter 20

After the HR meeting, Mark considered how he needed to carry on with his day, despite the news he'd just learned about Talia. It was nearing lunch time, and Belle could tell something was bothering Mark.

"Yo, Marky Mark, what's eating at you?"

Belle was trying to greet him in a friendly, upbeat fashion, but inadvertently used the nickname that Talia had always used for Mark. He immediately looked up at her, frozen in his stance.

"Ah, yes. The old Marky Mark nickname," he said, once more realizing Talia's friendship with him was a facade.

"Sorry, I didn't really think..." said Belle, assuming the nickname had reminded Mark of their fallen coworker who was clinging to life. Belle had no idea his sadness was linked more to disappointment in Talia's behaviors than her medical status.

"There's now another level of investigation to conduct," said Mark.

"Really? About what?"

"You busy for lunch?" he asked.

"No. You got something in mind?"

"What do you say we head up to the hospital and check in on Talia? We can see if there's any progress. And along the way I'll fill you in on this new wrinkle."

"Sure, that sounds interesting," said Belle.

"Although, I'm not sure why I said there might be progress." said Mark. "How can there really be any progress with someone who's in a coma? Either they are, or they aren't, right? Seems kind of binary."

"Oh, Lord in heaven above, please come rescue me from these geeks who throw computer words into everything they say! Binary?"

"Sure. That's not just a computer word, you know. Its origins are ancient. A term in astronomy is a binary star which means there are two..."

"... STOP, please. Sometimes your geek comes out and I can't take it. You got a little too close to that geeky guy, Gary, didn't you? I bet it rubbed off on you."

"Okay, I'll spare you the etymology."

"THERE... even that. What on earth is etymology?"

"Word origins."

"Can't you just call it word origins? Who talks like that?"

"I do."

"Not all the time, only when you spend time with fellow geeks."

On the drive to the hospital, Mark filled Belle in on all the details about Talia. She could hardly believe it. Talia's flirtations suddenly made sense.

"You know," she said, "I'm going to contact that Gary fella, too. If Talia wanted into your system because of her opposition to Echo Ridge, there's a good chance she hacked me, too."

"I'm not so sure about that. They said she came in after hours, just once, and hacked my password. Look, I'm telling you this because I'm hoping you can think back in your mind about times Talia may have said or done something that seemed peculiar. I can't tell you what files she took off of my computer. I hope you understand. I've got to keep this between me and Sandy for now."

"And HR. And IT."

"Yeah, you make a good point. Lots of folks know about this now, but even still, I'm going to keep this information close to me and Sandy. As much as possible."

"That's fine, but you know, can I say I told you so? How many times did I tell you to stop going along with her flirtatious fun and games? I told you it would get you into trouble."

"You are right," conceded Mark. "I mean, I considered her a friend, didn't want to get her in trouble by reporting it to HR, so I just thought I could police that myself. I should have been a little more... aware."

When Mark and Belle arrived at the hospital, they inquired about Talia at the front desk and were informed she was no longer in the ICU, but still in a coma. They found their way to the room she now shared with three other patients. As they approached the room, Mark happened to glance down a hallway and spied someone who looked familiar. There, far down the hall, and speaking with a nurse, was a man who looks quite like Craig Banister. Mark tapped Belle on the arm.

"Is that Banister? Or just someone who looks like him?"

Belle turned and looked. "I think you may be right. That sure looks like him."

"C'mon. Let's take a little walk."

"What are you going to say to him?" asked Belle.

"I don't know yet, but I want to see if that's him. This is our chance to dig in and maybe find out why Banister is so emotionally invested in Talia."

They began to walk briskly down the long hallway.

"Are you sure you want to do this? He's kind of like our boss, you know."

"That's alright, as long as we keep it friendly, we'll be okay. Don't mention anything about the case or Talia, just play it like we're surprised to see him here."

As Mark spoke, the man down the hallway glanced in their direction incredibly briefly, and immediately cut short his conversation with the nurse. He quickly departed down another hallway which ran perpendicular to the one now occupied by Mark and Belle. He was no longer in view.

Mark picked up the pace, turning it into a trot.

"Hold on, are we actually going to chase him?" asked Belle, keeping pace.

"Why not?" asked Mark. "I have a case to solve."

Their trot turned into a full blown run as they reached the intersection of hallways. They looked both ways and did not see Banister. Along the hallway were a number of other doors. One of them had an Exit sign overhead, and Mark decided that was the one to take. The two quickly entered a stairwell, with just two flights to go to the first floor. Mark peered down the middle of the stairwell, and while he could not see Banister. He heard a door close loudly. Mark and Belle darted down the steps, thinking they should have narrowed the distance between themselves and Craig by then. Mark noted that the only way they had not caught him by then was if Banister, too, was running. Once on the first floor, they could have exited the building, or entered a set of double doors that would have led to additional hallways within the hospital. Mark figured if Banister was truly evading them, he would have left the building, so Mark and Belle took the exit.

They were greeted by an explosive bounty of sunshine as they left the building. Off in the distance they could see a car disappearing down a nearby road, leaving Mark to wonder if that was Craig Banister or not. Unfortunately, he could not see the make or model.

"Damn, he's fast for an old man! If that's him, at all. I'm betting it is."

"How do you know?" asked Belle.

"That day at the restaurant when the cars were vandalized, I got a pretty good look at his car. It was the same color, same style, but too bad I could not get a better look. Just another hunch, nothing definitive."

"So if that's him, why do you think he avoided us?"

"You know, I'm not sure I want to accuse him of anything just yet. If he's hiding something, he could easily say it was just his time to leave, and pretend he hadn't tried to ditch us. But I'm damned sure he was running. He had to be to stay that far ahead of us. I think it's time to speed things up with Banister. He's long overdue for an interview. And when we get back, let's check with HR about getting access to Talia's computer. I'm even more curious now as to whether her path has crossed with his, before the attack."

Mark picked up his phone and called Agent Toney. After their talk, she dispatched Agent Tom Luken to locate, and visit, Craig Banister, even if they had to walk up a treacherous mountain pass to do it.

Video Transcript: Wandering Ranger #26 (YouTube Channel)

Visual Description:

START VIDEO: Mark sitting on the hood of his cruiser, with an RV park visible over his shoulder.

Audio Script:

Hello everyone, and welcome to another of my Wandering Ranger videos. I'd like to offer you a cautionary tale of stupidity from my youth. As you may know by now, I came to the Smokies every year with my family. One year many of my brothers and sisters, the ones older than me, had summer jobs and didn't want to come down here anymore. So it looked like it was going to be just me and my folks until they said I could bring my buddy, John. He was the pitcher on my baseball team, Tom Gross Auto Body Bandits. Now let me tell you, John loved a good adventure and got me into some crazy predicaments over the years. But in this story, John learned a lesson about being a rebel, all by himself.

Behind me used to be a quiet little campground that I believe used to be called the River's Edge Campground, which is now the River's Edge RV Park. We're just on the eastern side of where the parkway disappears into the woods leading towards Gatlinburg. So anyway, for those of you old enough to remember what this used to look like, they had a giant water slide built into the hillside up there.

Visual Description:

Mark pans the view of the camera to show where the waterslide once existed.

Today we live in the era of plastic tubes in massive waterparks, but back then, all we had were these big, hillside waterslides made of concrete. They ran a little water down the trench, and kids would sit on rubber mats and slide their way down the twisty-turny hillside until splashing into a pool of water at the bottom.

Now John, he didn't like the mats. He knew that if you arched your back, and only your heels and shoulders were touching the smooth painted surface of the slide, you could go a lot faster and make a huge splash at the bottom. He did that all day long, but it seems John got tired of even that, and was looking for a bigger thrill.

I think we need to mention there was a big sign with rules on it, which clearly said you had to use a mat, and you had to go down in a sitting position. We were already breaking the rule about the mat, and then John decided to break the rules even more and go down on his stomach, feet first. Can you picture this? This meant he could not see where he was going. I told him it was not a good idea, but he was not listening to me that day.

So there's my buddy, John, a big smile on his face, hoping to impress these girls we met in our campsite, pretending to be some kind of Evel Knievel. He gets me to push him off and send him on his way, feet first. He sure looked happy before he disappeared around the first turn, but that didn't last long. You see, John hadn't trimmed his toenails, and at some point, while he was zipping along at a pretty good speed, a piece of paint chipped off of the concrete and went right up under his big toenail on his right foot. We're talking   ALL — THE — WAY — IN. Now, just imagine that for a minute. I know it's painful to think

Page 246

about, but yes, it actually happened. I could hear him screaming in pain starting about halfway down the run. By the time I got to the bottom, the lifeguards were all kind of running around, looking for their first aid kits, wondering how to get that paint out from under his toenail. My dad eventually got there and used a pair of pliers to yank it out, kind of like how you pull a Band-Aid off real fast. I never heard somebody howl at the mountains like John did on that day.

Yes, John was a rebel. He loved testing the rules all the time. But that was one case where he learned the hard way that rules are usually in place for a pretty good reason. You've heard me say it before, and I'll say it again, far too many people see the law as dispensable when it's in conflict with their own beliefs or desires. John desired to impress those Missouri girls so bad he disregarded the rules, and he paid a price. I've spent my whole career in law enforcement and I see this every day with grown adults, who simply cannot follow the rules. So let me remind you to obey the rules of the park. Stop by the Sugarlands Visitor Center and make sure you know what those rules are. Some key rules are:

- Don't approach wildlife any closer than 50 yards.
- Don't feed the wildlife.
- Dogs and other pets are prohibited on the trails.
- Drones… nope. The park is not an airport for toys.
- Picking plants, and removing objects from the park, can't do that either.

These are just a few of the rules, and I'd suggest you NOT be a rebel like John. Make sure you know the rules, and stick to them. That's it for now. Peace.

Visual Description:

END VIDEO: Fade to black

Chapter 21

Agents with the FBI generally tried to be amenable to the schedules of high profile individuals they wished to interview, unless, of course, the person was a viable suspect. In Banister's case, he was not exactly a suspect, although the question about his relationship with Talia Manaia was certainly a curiosity. Banister had been exceptionally hard to pin down. Agent Tom Luken threw politeness out the window and forced Banister to meet in a location where he would be passing through on business. It was in Bryson City at the local Sheriff's station.

Luken wore a smart, but sterile, gray business suit for the visit. He had come up through the ranks of evidence analysis, and had a keen eye for detail, but had only conducted a few interviews like this one, earlier in his career. While interviews were not his forte, Luken was confident he could get answers out of anyone. When Luken arrived, the superintendent of the GSMNP sat in a small room with a large mirrored window, often used for observed interviews.

"So I'm going to be in one of THOSE rooms, eh?" asked Banister. "You're treating me like a common criminal?"

"No, Mr. Banister. We could move to another room, but it would have bars on it, so I decided this was our best option." Tom wanted to quickly establish that he was in charge, despite Banister's formidable standing within the park service. Tom followed the normal protocol of engaging a recording device and reading Banister his Miranda Rights. Then they began to talk.

"I'm afraid I don't have much time for this," said Banister, "but I'll do my best to answer all your questions."

"I appreciate that, sir."

"I must confess, I can't imagine what you would want to ask me. I told your other agent, Miss Gallenstein, everything I had to say right after the incident."

"We don't consider that an interview, Sir, more like a chat. Everyone else in the party has already been interviewed, in a formal setting. I'd like to start by asking you more about what happened later that day. Agent Gallenstein's report shows the two of you only talked about the first part of the day, including the hike up the mountain and the attack. But please tell me what happened once the other members of the party descended the mountain, and you remained with Talia Manaia and Belle Whittle."

"Well, there's not much to tell, really. I have had extensive field training for treating injuries, so I took measures to stop the bleeding for Ms. Manaia, which was no small feat, I must add. She was injured pretty badly. Then I bandaged up Ms. Whittle's injury on her leg. She and I talked a bit, and then that was about it, if I recall properly."

"Did Agent Whittle leave you at any point?"

"Ah, yes, I believe she did."

"And why did she do that?"

"She explained to me that she wanted to double check to see if there were other survivors amongst those we had assumed were dead. She didn't want to take someone else's word for it, so she went checking each body for a pulse. I was quite impressed with that young woman."

"And what did you do while she was inspecting the others?"

"Now let me think. I must say I became a bit emotional for a brief moment or two. I was quite upset, you see. Both Talia and Belle are employees of the park, and thus my responsibility, you might say."

"How emotional would you say you were?" asked Tom, writing everything down in notes as well as recording the conversation on his phone.

"I know, everyone expects a man to be a stone wall in times of adversity, but I must admit I had a moment of weakness. I believe at one point I was bawling my eyes out, if you must know."

"So, from your description, it sounds like you think you may have overreacted. Is that safe to say?"

"By some people's standards, yes, but most people were not in Vietnam. That's what else got to me. As the helicopter was leaving us, my mind was back in the rice fields. A real flashback, I'm tellin' ya. I just went to pieces. That hasn't happened in a very, very long time. It's so strange how the mind can work."

"Thank you for your service, sir."

"Why thank you, young man. But I really expected Talia to die. I did not even think she'd survive to see the arrival of the next helicopter, to be honest. I suppose I was grieving her loss a bit prematurely. That was part of it, too."

"Mr. Banister, you do realize that any attempt to mislead the FBI in this investigation is a crime. And..."

"Oh, I'm not lying. I'm telling the truth!"

Luken regretted his words had come out in a way he had not intended. "Please let me finish, sir. I am not suggesting that you have lied, but I want you to know this applies to everyone we've interviewed. Including Ranger Whittle. When we interviewed her, she was pressed to share every detail of her experience on that mountain just as you are right now. So it should not come as a surprise to you that she was bound by duty to tell us everything."

"Yes... go on..."

"Sir, Agent Whittle told us that she overheard you whisper something in Talia Manaia's ear. To Ranger Whittle's recollection you said 'I'm so sorry.' She said you were crying quite heavily at that moment, which gave her the impression that maybe you were somehow feeling responsible for Talia's injuries. Possibly... you felt *primarily* responsible."

"Well, I can see why she might think that, but it was in a general sense of the expression, I assure you. I was, and still am, unapologetically sorry that such a vibrant, young woman was about to die. At least I thought so at the time. And, I suppose, there is more to the story as well. If you must know, Talia Manaia was once attacked by a wild hog during her first year here in the park. If you are not familiar, these are indigenous hogs that were interbred with Russian wild boars, so they are very dangerous. Many of the locals call them 'Rooshins' because of how the Appalachian accent once pronounced Russians. But yes, she almost died. I was aware of her story because I was more localized back then, not spending as much time out of the park as I am now. Her struggle to live moved me back then, and honestly, I simply could not bear to see her go through another fight for life after being shot on Thunderhead Mountain. Nobody should ever have to go through something like that twice in a lifetime, if ever. This also got me a bit emotional, I suppose. It was a perfect storm, I suppose you could say: Talia's past struggles, my feelings of responsibility for these people, and of course there's Vietnam coming back to haunt me once again."

Luken continued writing. As he did so, he felt a tinge of disappointment at not having known any of this prior to their meeting. As he would learn much later, this was all true, yet he wondered why Belle Whittle or Mark Powers would not have revealed this piece of Talia's history to the FBI prior to his interview with Banister. Perhaps they did not connect the dots between Talia's past to her present in the same way Banister had. But given all this, it seemed perfectly logical to Tom that Banister would react as he had. Tom continued to ask additional questions, but was merely going through the motions. His goal had been to probe why Banister might have whispered to Talia and Tom felt the man's explanation was logical enough to move on. He was so moved by Craig's responses, in fact, that he did not press with additional possibilities that Craig and Talia might have been involved romantically. It seemed going that route would be unnecessary, and disrespectful.

Minutes later, Banister reminded Luken that he had a prior commitment and needed to leave. Tom's main line of inquiry was sufficiently addressed, and he had no reason to continue. They exchanged more pleasantries before they both departed.

Banister watched from his BMW as Agent Luken departed in his own car. He brewed on what they'd talked about. He was left with a bitter taste in his mouth, a taste of betrayal. He resented how Belle Whittle had told the FBI of his emotional moment with Talia, even if she was bound by duty to say so. If Belle were ever up for a promotion,

Banister vowed he would piss it away, remembering how she once brought a critical eye toward him during this FBI investigation.

He drove across town for his next meeting, pulling into a freshly black-topped parking lot next to a brightly colored building. It was a boxy structure which might have served as a garage in a previous life, but had been renovated with a high-class sign out front announcing it was the home of Steve's Steaks. It prominently displayed an SS logo, designed to look more like a custom hot-rod body shop than a butcher shop, playing on the well-known Super Sport car logo.

Craig, carrying a briefcase, entered through the front door, causing an antique bell above him to ring, letting the employees know they had a customer. Craig sized up the establishment and considered it was, perhaps, the cleanest looking, hipster-era butcher shop he had ever seen. The interior featured a shiny chrome meat counter, plush furniture in a waiting area, LED lighting fixtures, and an old-school, molded tin ceiling that resembled what one might have been found in a bank during the late 1800's. The owner, Steve Blair, had apparently spared no expense to let the community know he planned on serving them for a long time to come, after paying for such elaborate features.

Steve peeked around a corner from the back room and spied Banister. Steve turned behind him, and speaking to someone in the back room, said "It's for you!" Seconds passed before Franco Hufnagel came walking out into the customer area.

"Well, look what the cat drug in," was Franco's response at seeing Banister. He immediately walked to a sink behind the counter and washed his hands. "Pardon me while I clean up first."

"Certainly," replied Banister. "Take your time."

"We can talk better in the back. Follow me," said Franco, returning to where he'd just come from, with Craig and Steve in tow.

"This is quite a nice place you have here," said Banister, who held out his hand in greeting toward the owner. They shook.

"We like it," said Steve. "I kind of figure if you got to drag your ass into work every day, you might as well make it a cool place to be."

"A good outlook," agreed Banister. Steve Blair turned his head in response to another jingle of the antique bell, indicating another customer required his attention, and he left Franco and Banister to discuss their business. Franco walked over to a stainless steel cutting table, turned, and leaned against it as an indication it was time to talk.

"So where's my cash?" said Franco, coldly, with his arms crossed across his torso.

"I have it here," said Banister. He reached into his briefcase and withdrew several stacks of cash. He tossed them on the cutting table, within Franco's reach. The younger man glanced at the cash and performed some mental mathematics. His tabulation revealed it was a lesser amount than what he had expected.

"Looks like you're a little short, there partner," said Franco.

"Not per our agreement. It's precisely the amount we agreed upon."

"Not by my reckoning, it ain't. Maybe you need to explain what you mean, old man."

"You were paid to kill the governor. You did not kill her."

"That's bullshit. You're just trying to short me what I got coming."

"It was in the autopsy report, which is now publicly available, if you don't believe me. It looks like our backup shooter was the one to get the job done correctly. So you get only half."

"It was fucking windy up there, man. Nobody could have hit shit up there."

"You did hit something. Several somethings, in fact. One of them was Talia Manaia... Remember her? And others who were never supposed to die that day. You were reckless, and don't deserve the full amount."

"You told me to create chaos, if nothing else worked, and that's exactly what I did. There was nothing in our agreement about collateral damage costing me cash, man." By now, both men were speaking in heated tones. A tap on the swinging door, from the other side, reminded them that Steve could hear them in the front of the butcher shop where customers were present.

Banister, still angry with Franco's performance, had more to say. "So why didn't you just napalm their asses? You might as well have because you sprayed that mountaintop with bullets all over the place. Hell, I could have shot just as well and I have cataracts! I can understand if they were all in the vicinity of the target, but it looked to me like you were just firing at random, hoping you'd get the governor. You were explicitly instructed not to hit our own people. You are lucky you're getting this much."

Steve walked through the swinging door and approached the two, his customer now gone. "Gentlemen, need I remind you this is my establishment, and a legitimate place of business. I'd suggest you keep your voices down and be careful about what you are talking about. Sounds carry in this room."

Banister and Hufnagel heeded the warning, but still looked at one another with anger in their eyes. Craig meandered about, cooling off and gathering his thoughts for what to say next.

"Well, I've said my piece, and I'm holding firm. Not one penny more."

Franco looked miserable, but in reality, he knew Banister was right. He was merely arguing to see if he could intimidate Banister to cave. He now arrived at the conclusion he was not going to see any more cash come out of that brief case. Its lightness appeared to indicate it was empty, anyway.

"But now onto another problem, gentlemen," said Banister, hoping to smooth things over by changing topics. "I have another important topic to discuss with you both. It seems we have a growing problem with bear poaching in the area. We need to talk." Banister was merely interested in probing these two men, who might have been approached by local poachers to have the bears cleaned in their butcher shop. Banister had not yet learned that the poacher in question might be standing right in front of him.

Even though Hufnagel had been a hired gun for Banister, he was now concerned that Banister was about to accuse him of the poaching. For all he knew, Banister was bugged with a microphone and agents were in a van outside, ready to storm the facility. Steve and Franco exchanged glances, and both men knew what they had to do.

"Uh, Mr. Banister," said Steve. "I just have to ask you... did you tell anyone you were coming here today? I don't want anyone to trace you to us, you know. I had nothing to do with that Echo Mountain shit, I've got a legitimate business to run here." As Steve took over the conversation, Franco went out the back door for some unexplained reason, which was to look for any sign of agents. It was all clear, so he returned to standing at the metal carving table.

"No, I assure you, you are safe in that regard," replied Craig. "Do you think I'd risk someone finding out I know Mr. Hufnagel? I'm the top dog in the park, and I would never jeopardize my standing like that."

Again, Steve and Franco carried on an elaborate conversation between them with just their eyes, no words needed saying.

Franco reached under a cutting table and retrieved an automatic weapon. He it at Banister. Steve grew visibly upset at what was transpiring.

"Ok, old man. Take off your clothes."

"What?" asked Banister.

"It's time to make sure you're not wired. Get going."

Banister had not expected any of this, he was only interested in knowing if the butcher had any leads for finding the unknown poachers. He had not expected that he'd be speaking directly to the source of the problem.

Craig protested disrobing, but it was futile. While he undressed, Steve retreated to the office to watch their security camera footage. He needed to see if any new vehicles were about to approach the building. During the next few minutes, he saw no activity. He ran to the front, placed a "Closed" sign in the front window, and locked the doors.

Steve returned to the back room where Franco instructed him to look through the clothing, in Banister's ears, etc. to find a microphone.

"Why do I have to touch his wrinkly old ass?" protested Steve.

"Because I'm the one holding the gun," replied Franco, irritated.

Steve looked thoroughly and found no wires. He then positioned himself in front of Banister, with Franco standing behind Banister. Craig began shivering before complaining, "It's cold in here. You've seen no microphones, so can I please get dressed?"

"Mr. Banister, I have a trivia question for you," said Steve, ignoring Craig's request.

"This is humiliating. Why are you doing this, and what does trivia have to do with anything?" stammered Banister. Panic could be heard in his voice as he spoke.

"Trust me. It's important. What was the last name of the family on the old *Leave It to Beaver* show, back in the fifties?"

"Ah, 'Cleaver', of course. But what the hell does that have to do with anything?"

"Good night, sir," said Steve, as Franco swung a six-pound meat cleaver which sliced through the top of Banister's skull with ease. One hit was all it took to deliver his body to the floor, lifelessly.

Minutes later, Banister was hanging from a hook in a freezer where Franco Hufnagel had been processing black bear parts for shipment to Shenzhen, China. Later that night, once it was dark outside, Franco took care of the bloody cleanup while Steve took Banister's car to a nearby salvage yard where a buddy of his took care of hiding it forever. On his walk back to the butcher shop in the deep of the night, Steve fretted.

When he entered the back of his shop, Steve needed a few reassurances from his old friend, Franco. He'd known Hufnagel since they were in prison together, and they had bonded like brothers. When he got out, Steve had an inheritance waiting for him, and that's when he decided to open a butcher shop. Now he had a legitimate business going, and had spent every red cent of the inheritance to succeed as a butcher. So when Franco came knocking with an idea for how to make some extra cash, Steve was all in, letting Franco use the place for his poaching exploits, and taking a slice of the cash for himself to build his savings. Both men agreed their success would depend upon how quiet they could keep their operation.

"Shit, Franco, what the hell? How did he know about the poaching?" said Steve. Both men had misinterpreted Craig's inquiry about poaching. The elder statesman was not on to them at all, only asking for their help to catch the poachers.

"I think I have a pretty good idea. When I hired Haus, I hand picked him not just because he's as strong as an ox, but because he was growing weed with Jebidiah Fields. That's the little shit who testified against me. I thought it would be a bonus if Haus could give me updates on ol' Jeb, so I could keep up with his business. I was thinking about rubbing Jeb out and taking my business back again. But I didn't want Jeb to know that Haus was working for me, too. I warned Haus not to say a damned word about me. I was pretty sure he wouldn't. You see, I thought I had Haus by the balls... he deals meth around here, so I thought I had that hanging over him. I even warned him, like 'you say shit about me to Jeb and you'll be in jail for selling meth.' But I'll be damned if he didn't double cross me anyway. I guess now I'm going to have to teach both of those boys who they are dealing with."

"But I still don't get it... how did Banister..."

"...Oh yeah... Our boy Haus must have told Jeb about how I'd hired him to do the field cleaning and transport of the bears. Then Jeb got busted for growing — I know that's true, by the way — and just like he did 20 years ago, Jeb started singing to Powers like a songbird to save his own ass, to cop a plea. Then, of course, Powers reported it to Banister, and then here he is, confronting me about it."

"Damn," said Steve. You should not have trusted Haus, he's too young."

"I know that now. Loose lips sink ships, and gets morons killed."

"But why did you want to kill the old man? Wouldn't he have looked the other way for the poaching, because otherwise you could have burned him about orchestrating the shooting, right? You had that on him, why kill him?"

"I don't know man. He paid me in cash. If I burned him, he could have always denied any connection to me, said I was lying just to tarnish his rep. He could have even said I was making it all up just because he busted me for poaching. I'm an ex-con, he's this big hot shot. Who do you think they would have believed?"

Steve let it all sink in.

"So, I'm going to disappear for a while," said Franco, with confidence. "You're going to carry on with your business like nothing ever happened. If they show up asking about Banister or poaching, you just play dumb. If they ask you about me, you can just say I am your old friend and that I have a key to the place in case I want to clean my own game... legal game. That's it... you let me use the place as a favor to an old friend. You can be totally honest about how we met in prison. Sounds legit, you know? Nothing more needs to be said. Just play dumb, blame everything on me, and you're off the hook."

"Yeah, man. I'm chill with that. But when are you leaving? You gonna leave me with this mess?"

"I'll clean it all up right now. I'll be done by the morning, and then I'll go."

"And the body will be gone? And everything will be clean? Right?"

"Absolutely. The FedEx guy should be here shortly for my last package of bear goodies, so there will be no poaching evidence. Before sunrise, Banister and the rest of the bear remains are going to be slop in a barrel and headed for the pig farm," said Franco.

"Where are you going to go?" asked Steve.

"I'll be at my hotel until I can figure out what to do next. I'll let you know if go someplace else to stay. But don't call me. Don't visit me. We need to make a clean break from one another for now. And hey, man, I'm really sorry for all this shit going down. I appreciate you letting me use the place."

"Nah, no worries, man... bear balls are great money, and I never knew it! Maybe in a few months we can pick up where we left off if this all blows over."

"Yeah. Maybe. But man, tomorrow I'm going to relax by making a couple of Molotov cocktails. Then I'm going to take a little trip up north and share one of them with my old friend, Jebidiah Fields."

Chapter 22

Mark had been going non-stop since the attack on Thunderhead, but once he removed himself from the case, he found his hours were dramatically reduced. He hoped to join Dan in handling of the Jeb Fields' pot growing investigation, but since Jeb and Haus were embroiled in the Echo Ridge case, there was no movement on the pot growing charges.

With Franco Hufnagel once more weighing heavily on Mark's mind, he found himself thinking about Laurie more frequently. Unfortunately, it was the horrible memories of her murder that came to the forefront initially. It required a feat of emotional strength to sift through the pain in search of the positive memories of his wife. But once he intentionally started thinking about her, and the good times he'd had with her, every trouble in the world would go on hiatus.

While remembering how she cut heart shapes out of the pie dough and put them on his nose, something important came to mind. It would require his immediate. He spent most evening watching Netflix until he fell asleep from exhaustion. But he would not settle for this mundane existence on this occasion. He would go home, get dressed as if it was a date night, and hit Gatlinburg.

In Townsend, he drove up the red-dirt road past the old barn that sat on the edge of his neighbor's property. The structure had seen better days, but it had a rustic appeal that eased Mark's soul every time he saw it. It was a red, metal roof which provided a pleasing contrast to the green foothills behind it and the blue skies above. And more importantly, he could not drive past the barn without seeing the ghost of his wife, feeding the neighbor's cows through the electric fence as she had done many times when they walked the road on beautiful summer evenings. Tonight, he would celebrate such moments.

After a short drive down the dirt road, it turned into a driveway which straddled a white picket fence. The wooden structure enclosed a large front yard, the house, and the large pines growing in a small back yard. This was home to Mark Powers.

As he stepped out of the cruiser, Mark approached the gate, placed his hand upon it, and paused. He'd built the fence by hand, including the gate. He'd done so at Laurie's request. Then she had painted most of it white. On the gate, she painted every spindle alternating pastels of green and yellow, finishing the job with miniature sunflowers painted in an arc across the top and down the sides. After a decade without her, the paint was beginning to chip. Not only did he regularly struggle to preserve her memories, but the same was true of her artwork. He'd applied polyurethane a few years back, hoping to preserve it a while longer, but now the ravages of time were once more stealing her from him.

He spied the flowerbed running along the inside of the fence. That was more of her work, although now ravaged with weeds. The flowers painted on the mailbox, again, hers. Inside the house, all of the decorations were frozen in time. He continued to dust the trinkets and photos every few weeks, never letting the place show signs that a widower was in charge. He even used the same feather duster Laurie had bought and used. So many of her things still existed, a desperate attempt to never let her go. But on this particular day, some additional fanfare was necessary to remember Laurie.

He changed out of his uniform, first thing. He put on an old pair of jeans that once offered generous room in the legs, but were now tight on him. For the shirt, he picked one she'd given him for Christmas just prior to her murder. It was one of their best Christmases together, although he struggled to remember it as *great*, instead of *last*. It was a wonderful time for them as Laurie would learn she was pregnant shortly after the holidays. Then it all came crashing down.

He never thought about the baby. Or at least, only for a few seconds. After ten years, when the thought of their unborn child came to mind, it would just as quickly be ejected, as if too much for his soul to take.

Once on the road, the negative thoughts had been banished, and he was well into the positive zone. He thought of how beautiful Laurie looked on her wedding day despite the rain nearly ruining the outdoor ceremony. He remembered the cute little garden hats she'd imposed upon her bride's maids; none of the women were thrilled about them, but it turned out the hats proved useful keeping raindrops from ruining their hair. He recalled how in the middle of saying their vows, a driver sped past on a nearby road and yelled "Don't Do It!" out his window, which elicited laughter from everyone present. He remembered even simpler memories, every day reminders that he'd picked the right woman. He recalled how she loved her little white dog, Sydney. How she spent hours decorating the Christmas tree and threaded popcorn and cranberries into long chains to wrap around the tree. He recalled how she only had two meals she knew how to cook in the early days: quesadillas and fajitas (which she admitted were basically the same meal but in different forms). He recalled how they spooned on cold nights until they fell asleep. How she had named her car Rhonda, because it was a Honda. Rhonda the Honda... she was quite proud of that bit of silliness. He also remembered how she loved to listen to Patsy Cline when she was doing her makeup on date night. And the list just went on and on.

He followed Route 321 into Pigeon Forge, and then followed the Parkway south toward Gatlinburg. He'd find a parking spot near intersection #3. From there he would begin ambling about on foot, hoping some sight or sound would trigger hidden memories of her.

He remembered the Greystone Hotel, one of the earliest and largest hotels in town. He and Laurie had stayed there for their honeymoon. It held a special place in his heart. The Greystone was now crowded by a Jimmy Buffet-themed hotel, and an Aquarium attraction. His favorite little town in the mountains was growing up fast.

He found himself walking along a sidewalk, flanked by a stream populated by dozens of ducks. They looked no different than the ones he remembered from his childhood nor the ones he and Laurie would feed their leftover French fries. He revisited some of the same little gift stores she had loved so much. There was the Mountain Mall, The Village, the old Ski Lift which now featured a glass-bottomed SkyBridge at the top of the mountain. There was Ripley's Believe It or Not, and the Space Needle... all of them had been Laurie's favorites. She loved those touristy spots whereas many of the locals did not. After eating at the Cherokee Grill and Steakhouse, he bought salt water taffy from The Ole Smoky Candy Kitchen where they made taffy with a mesmerizing machine in the front window. All that remained was his final and most important stop.

A Christian giftshop within The Village had been Laurie's favorite store of all. It was called *God's Corner*. Mark walked in, still feeling like he didn't fit in, knowing she was more of a believer in God than he ever would be. Their conversations over the years had instilled a respect for faith, but he still struggled with apparent conflicts between faith and science. Before he started thinking about those issues again, he walked into the store and found the small section of Christian books. There he found the Laurie Teremi coffee table books. He laughed at how the Powers name wasn't good enough for her photography identity, and how she chose to write under the last name of a Cincinnati photographer she admired.

Usually there would be six of her books for sale, but on this occasion he noticed one was missing. He asked a clerk if they still carried it, and was informed their copy had sold recently, and had not yet been restocked. That put a smile on Mark's face. People were still finding value in her work after all these years. He was unsure of how much money was being generated by the books since he'd donated all future profits to Laurie's beloved Roaring Fork Baptist Church, located on the appropriately named Church Street.

He pulled down one of the books from the shelf. He had all six installments at home as well, but he wanted to crack one open in the gift store and take in that *new book smell*. Page after page featured amazing nature photos from within the Great Smoky Mountains National Park. Below each photo was one of her favorite passages from the Bible that spoke of God's love.

As his arm reached up to the shelf to return that first book, he glanced at the tattoo on his forearm. The numbers on each arm were meaningful, and moving. Then he thought of The Sinks, where he and Laurie had been married.

He glanced at one of her other books, and retrieved it from the shelf. It was her last book. He marveled at the front cover photo of a beautiful waterfall. That was the last one she had ever taken. That shot, along with others from that night, were included in this last book, along with her "greatest hits" from the first five books. They were all dazzling, but the cover shot had a tendency to move people the most. Mark had been the one to work with her publisher to produce her final book, posthumously.

As he placed the book back on the shelf, he was ambushed by the rage he felt for her loss. He'd been holding back the hate all evening, focusing on the love, but his defenses finally wore thin. He gave himself a pep talk, coached himself inside his head, and willfully pushed the bitterness to the back recesses of his mind. He was determined that they could not, and would not, ruin Laurie's birthday.

Chapter 23

Visual Description:

START VIDEO: Mark, talking to camera, at Grotto Falls.

Audio Script:

Hello everyone, welcome to the latest Wandering Ranger video. Today I'm on one of the most popular trails in the park, Grotto Falls. What makes this such a nice trail is the waterfall at the top of the trail, which you can actually walk behind. Yesterday we had a report of a bear sighting here early in the morning, while foot traffic was limited. Seems an older man and his wife were up here, and found themselves alone by the falls.

Visual Description:

Mark begins pointing to several places around the falls as part of his explanation.

So here's their story. The man went behind the falls while his wife remained on the trail to take his picture. While the man was behind the falls, a black bear came out of the woods across the stream from where the woman was standing. She tried to warn her husband, but he could not hear her from behind the falls. When the man emerged on the far side of the stream, he found himself about 10 feet from the bear.

If this happened to you, what would you do? Walk away? Run away? Stand your ground? Span your arms to make yourself look bigger? Lots of people give lots of advice about what to do when you encounter a bear, but how do you know what advice is the best advice? Well, it all kind of depends upon how far you are from the bear, and whether it's a mother with cubs or not. If you have cubs in the mix, and you find yourself within 20 yards of the cubs, the mama might get more irritated by your presence than if it's a male, or a female without cubs. In these cases where there's a mama and cubs, you should slowly back away from the cubs, and away from the mother. Don't run, just do it quietly, like you are tiptoeing.

Now, if you just came upon an adult bear at close range, you still want to back away, but once you get about 20 yards away, or more, you want to gently raise your arms and make yourself look bigger, maybe even pick up a stick and hold it above your head with both of your hands. And here's why. Bears have bad eyesight. You are blurry to them at that range, and so putting your arms up, maybe holding a stick or waving a stick, just might make them think you are bigger than they are.

Also, some people think it helps if you talk to the bear, telling it to go away, kind of like you are scolding a dog. Some credible sources say that works.

Page 269

And, if you have food laying around, like at a campsite, relocate yourself away from that site so you disassociate yourself from a food source. Bears have an amazing sense of smell, and would be more interested in your meal than they will be of you.

In this incident at Grotto Falls, the man, woman, and bear managed to escape unharmed. They were kind of lucky in how this worked out. It seems another elderly couple came upon the scene, and saw what was happening. The man had a jar of honey in his backpack, which he removed and poured on a rock near the stream. The bear crossed over quickly to have a little snack, providing a diversion for all four humans to escape back down the trail.

People… let me tell you, this may have worked this time, and I'm not sure where the older man had ever gotten the advice to carry honey with him in case of a bear encounter, but this is NOT a good idea. First of all, when bears have repeated interactions with humans and they receive food in that exchange, they will learn to associate humans with food. With that comes future expectations. And then, somewhere down the line, if a bear is really hungry, he or she may attack humans to get food, and in very, very rare cases, the human becomes the food. I hate to think of what could have happened if that bear was unwilling to wait for that man to get the honey poured out onto the rock, and decided to go for fast food. Honey Man might have lost an arm, or worse, in that exchange, I'm tellin' you. Many people do not understand the power of a black bear. An adult bear's claws can slice right through a chain link fence. Try not to think of them as lovable. Dangerous is a better adjective.

Lastly, please just never feed bears or leave food unattended near human recreational areas. The more they associate food with humans, the more dangerous they will become to other hikers in the future. That's all I've got this time. Peace.

Mark was drinking coffee from a mug he'd gotten from Laurie for a birthday present. He had a pair of earbuds in, plugged into his phone to stream music from his favorite band, *The Infamous Stringdusters*. He'd been stuck on that band for a few months, finding them to possess a solid grasp of traditional bluegrass chops, but with a youthful energy and vitality. They were presently singing a tune of particular poignancy in his life. It was a song called *Gravity*:

> *"I saw you from a distance*
> *Swinging from the high line*
> *All that was before you*
> *Vanished in a moment's time*
>
> *We thought the race was a long war*
> *We didn't know that we'd win it*
> *We thought the good times were yet to come*
> *We didn't know we were in it."*

Indeed, ten years with Laurie was far too short, especially since they'd spent much of that time planning for the years to come. Too bad, he thought, that they did not spend more time living in the moment, in case their future did not arrive as planned.

He was staring out a window and contemplating a drive back to Cosby to check on the motion sensitive cameras. He was in a foul mood because he would no longer be involved with the Echo Ridge case. However, he did recognize there were pros and cons to that development. On one hand, Mark's recusal from the case would reduce the odds that a judge or jury might side with the defendant because of perceived bias from Mark due to Franco Hufnagel's alleged, but never proven, murder of Laurie Powers. But on the other hand, Mark hated that he could not be directly involved with putting Franco behind bars for the rest of his miserable life. Not only did Laurie and Mark deserve that justice, but so did Jebidiah Fields, and other unknown victims of Hufnagel's. Those victims also included the black bear population of the Smoky Mountains (assuming Franco's poaching activities were not just a baseless rumor). All that mattered to Mark now was to see Franco pay a stiff price for his deeds, and if that was more likely with Mark on the sidelines of the Echo Ridge case, he was fine with that.

Mark's thoughts were interrupted when his name was called, the voice belonging to Dan Lawson. He was now in charge of the pot growing investigation, although it was temporarily stalled. He had led a team up to Thunderhead Mountain per Mark's recent request, and was now coming to report what his team had uncovered. Dan followed a circuitous route between desks until he approached Mark at the window.

"Hey, Mark. Looks like we scored big time."

"What... did you put money down on the Vols again?"

"Funny, but no. We have a game changer here. It's about our trip out to Thunderhead." Dan did not want to endure small-talk, and handed Mark a transparent evidence bag. Inside it was a gun.

"And what, pray tell, is this?" asked Mark.

"It's a gun, duh," quipped Dan.

"Now tell me something I don't know."

"I can tell you about this, right, even though you're off the case, right?"

"I'm not dead, just dormant. The way I see it, I just can't DO anything with the case, but that doesn't mean I can't KNOW anything about the case. Go on then, tell me."

"Like you asked, I took a team out there to scour the five mile route up and down the mountain, looking for any other evidence we could possibly find, anything that might be related to the shooting. We couldn't sweep too far off trail or it would have taken us years to do the search. We kept it tight, but when we got a couple of miles up the trail, one of our scouts pointed out that a lot of the ground vegetation had been disrupted, and not in a way that you'd expect from wildlife. It all looked kind of familiar to me, and I believe it's where we stopped on the way back down on the day of the shooting to relieve ourselves. Thinking we had folks moving farther off trail, we looked off trail a little deeper. And thank goodness we did. Somebody stepped on something, looked down, and saw this tiny little gun sticking out from under his boot."

"And this is that gun?" confirmed Mark, in a question.

"Very smart, Mark. That's why you're a Special Agent."

"Luck be a lady," said Mark, now nodding his approval. "Or as my wife would say, this is a minor miracle."

"I'd have to agree with her. What are the odds, right? But get this. It's a gun nobody can buy. This was released by the Houston Company as a prototype. There were only 12 of them made, and given to prominent gun owners to get feedback. And guess who it's registered to?"

"Please tell me this is good news."

"Yup. It belongs to one Shane Goodwyn."

"How do you like that?!" said Mark, excitedly. "You be sure to share that with the FBI right away. Sandy didn't share with me the results of her most recent interview with Shane, because I'm off the case. But I do know she planned to ask

Shane, Isabella and Banister if any of them were carrying a concealed weapon that day. Granted, we knew Shane had the H9 in his holster, but he could have been carrying this little H4 to shoot his wife."

"Yup, he could have carried it where the sun don't shine," said Dan.

"I'd rather not conjure up that image. But anyway... later, he'd offer up the H9 for testing to show how cooperative he was. Kind of like a decoy. He might have used the smaller gun for the murder, and then offered up the bigger gun to throw us off."

"But wait, there's more," said Dan. "We haven't done a full ballistics run up on this one yet, but the bullets from this little thing are 8mm rounds. That matches the bullets documented in the governor's autopsy report. That caliber is pretty rare. Seems like proof positive this was the gun that killed her. We'll do some striation testing to make sure."

"But why would Shane have made such a stupid mistake as to leave the gun up on that mountain? And why would he wait until we were halfway down the trail? If I were the killer, I'd want to get rid of the gun as soon as possible."

"True," said Dan, "but there were an awful lot of people around up on top. If you think about it, once everyone stopped to use the bathroom, maybe that was the first chance he had to ditch it while nobody was looking."

"Maybe," confirmed Mark. "But I could have sworn he didn't bother with the bathroom break. He was just tossing a utility knife into the side of a tree. So now you got me thinking. I know at about that time I mentioned the FBI were coming, he might have wanted to ditch it quickly. Maybe he did scamper off into the woods after I told him to stop with the knife. Or I supposed he could have given it the old heave-ho and tossed it as far as he could into the woods when I wasn't looking. I just wasn't focused on keeping track of anyone, I was more interested in getting us off of that mountain."

"However he did it, he dropped this out in the woods and boy were we lucky to stumble upon it," said Dan.

"I wasn't the only one who could have seen Shane ditch the gun. Why don't you follow up with everyone else who was there..."

"Uh, Mark, stop right there buddy. Sounds like you are consulting with me on the case. Can't have that, you know, because you can't get involved, remember? But I did want to at least show you what we got. And I think I get the idea of what you were about to say."

Mark hated the fact that he could not participate in the case any longer, but was happy to see the investigation creeping closer to being resolved. As long as they were collecting more crucial evidence, he believed it would be only a matter of time before the case would be solved.

Just because Mark was not actively working the case, it did not keep him from evaluating the new evidence in his mind. Mark thought Dan's assessment was spot on, that a Houston pistol generated significant suspicion of Shane Goodwyn with respect to the second shooter. If no prints could be retrieved from the new pistol, it would be important if anyone else had witnessed Shane stepping off trail, especially if they could recall Shane's location as being near where the gun was discovered.

More than anything, Mark wanted to tell Dan how to further this part of the investigation, yet he could not. He was off the case. He contemplated leaving suggestions in an anonymous note to Dan, but he knew going that far was just getting a little ridiculous. He opted to trust that Dan would handle matters appropriately.

It was then he decided to drive to Cosby to check on the cameras. He simply had to get out of the station, get some fresh air, and work a case. Perhaps that would help him get his mind off of Echo Ridge.

The next morning there was a staff meeting at the station with Agents Toney, Luken, Gallenstein, as well as Lawson, Whittle and other rangers who were also involved in the case. The only one missing, was Mark Powers.

Chapter 24

Two days later, Belle Whittle was pulled into an emergency meeting by the head of Human Resources, Tiffany Bradshaw, to discuss Craig Banister. The meeting lasted nearly two hours, and the information discussed required Belle to develop an emergency communication plan. There would be email announcements delivered in multiple phases, the first of which would target all park GSMNP personnel. That memo would include detailed instructions for how employees should react if reporters attempted to ask them questions about the news that would soon be announced. Other phases would target the media and outside law enforcement agencies. It would be an announcement that would surely take many by surprise: GSMNP Superintendent Craig Banister had just been added to the national Missing Persons Registry.

Such news would be of significant importance even if the Echo Ridge shootings had never happened, but they did, and his mysterious disappearance promised to fan the flames of gossip and speculation. Belle's job as the voice of the park had just gotten significantly busier.

Toney's team grew larger, now, with additional resources to investigate Banister's disappearance. She also urged Belle to craft a message to the public that would not make direct connections between his disappearance and the Echo Ridge case. Left unto their own devices, the news media and the public would probably link the two, suggesting Banister had something to do with the shootings.

"At this point in time," said Sandy to Belle, "the only question we have about Banister is his emotionally overwrought apology to the injured Talia Manaia which you witnessed. That and the fact he was in the woods at the moment the governor was shot, make him a person of interest, yes, but at this time we're not going to release this to the public. We have no solid evidence, or motive, for why Banister would kill the governor. Some might say they were political adversaries, but if you're going to include political opposition as a motive for murder, then one half of this country's citizens have motive to kill the other half. We're so divided right now, it's crazy."

"I hear that," said Belle. "I still think there's some funny business going on with Mr. Banister, though. Maybe it's just intuition, but the day Mark and I saw him at the hospital, it really seemed like he was avoiding us. I really think he ran from us. Mark is not so sure, but that's how I feel about it."

"But according to what you told me, you can't be certain Banister saw you and Mark, and thus you can't be certain he wasn't just leaving the hospital as anyone else would, with no intentions of losing you in a chase. And maybe he was in a hurry, and you could not catch him. Just playing devil's advocate."

"He glanced in our direction, then he quickly turned and left. It felt like he was leaving *because* he saw us."

"But you told me he was separated down a long hallway. So long, in fact, that you and Mark were not certain it was him at first. If the hallway was that long, how do you know he even recognized the two of you when he glanced in your direction?"

"I know," said Belle. "Just a feeling, I guess."

"And remember, Agent Luken's follow up revealed he became emotional because of his Vietnam service and Talia's prior brush with death. Both seemed like perfectly reasonable explanations for why he grew so emotional with her on the mountain that day. I do not see Banister as a suspect. After meeting with Isabella and Shane, I think we have more important lines of inquiry to pursue for the secondary shooter, along with several suspects for the primary shooter. That's not to say we won't keep Banister in the mix, and examine any new evidence that might implicate him, but I'm not interested in any further interviews at this time."

"Okay. I'll do everything I can to keep the Echo Ridge case and his disappearance as two distinct events," said Belle, referring to her communication plan.

"With all that said," replied Sandy, "while I don't see Banister as our focus, I do fear someone may have tried to silence him. He may have known something that the real killers were afraid of. Anytime someone disappears like this, in a case like this, it wreaks of foul play."

"If we're looking at Isabella Lopez and Shane Goodwyn as suspects, do you think it's possible one of them may have reason to fear Banister would rat them out? Do you think one of them could be responsible for his disappearance as well as responsible for the death of the governor?"

"That's a very reasonable question," said Sandy. "I do not believe Isabella would have had the opportunity to directly harm or abduct Banister because I've spoken with her periodically over the past three days using her office phone at the state house in Nashville. Banister would have had to be in

Nashville for Isabella to have done something to him. His secretary did not find anything in his calendar that would require him to be in Nashville. She could have hired someone to abduct or harm Banister, but now we're just guessing. I'm less inclined to suspect her than I am Shane. He's been on the road, within the past couple of days and had every opportunity to come back this way and do something devious.

"We also have new physical evidence in the form of a new pistol found along the trail most likely belonged to Shane, which escalates our interest in him as the second shooter. But for that matter, we also know Banister travels a lot, so Shane would have had to track him down. To be honest, all of this is just pure conjecture, we have no evidence demonstrating either of the two harmed Banister. And, I must tell you, we have a third primary now. Franco Hufnagel may have been the shooter from a distance, responsible for three deaths, while it's Shane and Isabella who are primaries in the death of the Governor. For the record, this Hufnagel character could have had a reason to silence Banister as well."

"Although," said Belle, attempting to inventory all possibilities along with Sandy, "we should keep in mind that if he's been traveling, a man at his age could have had a heart attack and run his car off the road. His disappearance might be a lot simpler than we're making it out to be."

"Yes, Belle, those of us in our profession may be jaded to look for sinister causes, for sure. My first hope is that Banister just wanted to get off the grid for some hiking or fishing."

Mark had packed a lot of work gear into the trunk of his cruiser prior to leaving for Cosby. He had been distracted with bigger things and had not followed up on the motion sensors he'd left to look for those responsible for stealing lumber from the edge of the national park. If nothing panned out there, he decided to make good use of the personal time he'd recouped now that he was no longer on the Echo Ridge case. He hoped to do some hardcore hiking on Gabes Mountain trail which would lead to a beautiful cascading waterfall over rocks and moss. It was one of Laurie's favorite photo ops. He hoped taking in some of the park's most beautiful spots would conjure some positive memories of his beautiful wife.

He was cruising along Highway 321. As he drove he pondered on the big questions of life, such as whether man had a purpose on the planet, or if we are just winners in some amazingly improbable cosmic lottery, lucky that life had evolved, incomprehensibly, out of nothing. Laurie found it impossible to look at the beauty of nature without seeing the fingerprints of God. Mark was not so sure, because he felt those same fingerprints could be found on the less beautiful things in life as well. He preferred blaming God for the bad, never wanting to buy into the possibility of a little red man with a pitchfork being part of the equation. They had argued over these theological beliefs many times, but Laurie was adamant that a loving God was not the author of evil, and it was every man's enemy, fueled by freedom of choice, who was responsible for all the darkness. One thing was sure, though: that Mark Powers wanted to believe in God, a God of love, mercy and forgiveness. He wasn't sure how to believe just yet. He hoped it would happen someday, but with 10 years behind him since Laurie's death, he was doubtful it ever would.

These thoughts lingered as he moved through his day. He collected the cameras he'd previously set up in Cosby. He would wait until he was back at the station to analyze them, which would be time consuming. After that, he headed for Gabe's Mountain and spent the rest of the day on a glorious hike, enjoying the remarkably beautiful fall foliage.

It was just getting dark when he started back home in his cruiser. He then received a call from Dan on his cell phone.

"Mark, did you hear on the scanner about a fire burning right now at the River Rapids Mobile Home Park?"

Mark had not, as he'd been away from his cruiser during the hike. It took little time for Mark to recognize the location Dan had mentioned. It was the trailer park where Jebidiah Fields was currently living.

"Did you get an address?"

"Negative. I heard it, but didn't write it down."

"Was it 435 Rising Water Way?" asked Mark, now anxious. There was a small pause before Dan replied.

"Yes, that sounds familiar, I think that was it," replied Dan. Mark activated the siren and lights. Just a few miles down the road, he swerved aggressively onto Butler Branch Road, northbound, toward the trailer park.

He wondered if showing up at Jeb's was going to stir up trouble since he was no longer on the Echo Ridge case, but his emotions had gotten the best of him. Just because he wanted to check on Jeb and make sure he was alright didn't mean he was getting back into the case. At least that's how he saw it. He decided to throw caution to the wind and make sure Jeb and his family were unharmed by the fire. He was close enough to do this in person, rather than wait for reports later.

Mark showed up to a scene of chaos in the trailer park with several fire engines present and dozens of trailer park residents drawn to the danger like moths to a porch light. Most of Jeb's neighbors were milling about, chatting with one another, speculating what had happened. It was now well after dark, and the place was lit up like Christmas with the police, EMT and fire presence. Mark parked far out of the way, and approached on foot.

He could not visually spot Jeb, and took in the billowing black smoke that was still rising from a fire-less shell of a trailer. The smoke was easy to see, illuminated by spotlights from the emergency vehicles, but it turned invisible as it rose into the night sky.

Mark talked to a fireman, who gave some details. It had not taken long to put out the fire, but by that same measure, it also hadn't taken long for the trailer to transform into a total loss. It was over before emergency crews could even get to it.

"What are you doing here?" asked one of the Sevierville police who knew Mark fairly well. "There ain't no bears here that need to be darted. You best be gettin' back to your picnic grounds, park boy." There was no real animosity in the man's comments, it was purely for humorous effect.

"That may be true, but let's face it, the fires you boys deal with are kind of like campfires compared to the forest fires we deal with! I figured I'd stop and lend a hand in case you fellas couldn't handle this one on your own." That made the officer smile, and even chuckle a bit, despite the tragedy before them.

"This place belongs to Jeb Fields. Did everybody get out okay?" asked Mark.

"Mostly. They're in the chief's cruiser back over there, behind the ambulance. The boy's burned up pretty bad, I bet he's gonna have some 3rd degree burns."

Mark hated to hear Jeb's child had been harmed, especially by fire. It was too much pain for a child to endure.

"When did the fire start?"

"'Bout a half hour ago."

"So it was already dark?"

Page 283

"Yup. Heard 'em say it looks like arson. Some coward waited until it was dark, probably so he wouldn't be seen."

Soon Mark located Jeb who was giving a statement to the chief in the back of a cruiser while his wife sat in the back of the ambulance with their son and two other EMTs.

Jeb's eyes were red, as if he'd been crying. Later Mark would learn it was from chemical burns to Jeb's face, the result of toxic smoke from the fire. When Jeb saw Mark, he left the back seat of the cruiser and rushed over to Mark for a firm handshake. Mark turned it into a man hug, shoulder to shoulder. There was no trace of their last meeting, where Mark had to deliver some hard truths to the young man about his involvement in the Echo Ridge case, or his pot growing activities. All that was shared now was the longstanding connection between the two men that was formed back when Jeb was only 15 years old.

"Thanks for coming, Ranger Mark." His voice was trembling as if he was holding back a tsunami of emotion.

"No problem. How's your boy?" His son was the reason for Jeb's emotive state, and Fields broke down, nearly bawling.

"They don't know if he's gonna make it. He's burned up pretty bad," muttered Jeb.

Mark froze at the thought. He glanced over at the ambulance, wondering why they hadn't departed for the burns unit at the hospital by now.

"Looks like they are treating him in the ambulance. Maybe it's not bad enough to take him to the hospital. It might just be minor..."

Mark was cut off by the sound of a shriek, followed by screaming from within the ambulance. "No, No! Oh my God, NO!" shrieked a woman's voice. Moments later, EMT personnel emerged from the ambulance to tell Jeb his son had just died. Jeb rushed to the ambulance, disbelieving what they'd told him, and needing to see for himself. There he joined his wife, the two of them revolting against their new reality and violently grieving.

Mark had seen some pretty nasty things during his career. He'd pulled charred bodies out of wrecked vehicles which had caught on fire. He had also discovered the skeleton of an unidentified hiker whose flesh had been eaten by Russian half-breed hogs. Standing outside that ambulance left Mark with a heavy ache deep within his chest. He'd never had a child of his own, but detected the depth of a parent's anguish, if only as an observer. An innocent being subjected to such horror was one of many reasons that kept him from trusting in the Lord, as faithfully as Laurie had. He also knew if she were still with him, she would be quick to tell him such tragedy was not the work of a loving God, but rather, His enemy.

Mark knew he should leave, satisfied he had had the chance to give Jeb some moral support. He wandered away to observe the devastation. He decided to look at the burned-out trailer, the way he would, if he were the lead investigator.

He examined the trailer from the road, with the emptiest part of the remains being in the back, farthest from the road. That would indicate the fire started in a bedroom and might be the result of falling asleep while smoking. At least that would be his default assumption. But now that he'd already heard speculation of arson, he was curious what other evidence there may be to support that notion.

He did his best to stay out of the way of fire personnel, and to keep from stepping on the fire hoses on the ground. He made his way from the road toward the rear of the trailer. He glimpsed at the neighbor's trailer, next to Jeb's. He noticed their cheap Polymer siding had bubbled and melted from the fire being so near to their home. He walked to the rear and noticed the fire detectives were already on the scene and making a detailed inspection. He didn't want to intrude, but listened closely.

"That's what the owner said, a Molotov cocktail," said a woman with a clipboard.

"Did he mention if the bottle broke when it entered the window?" asked another man.

"He said he was not in the bedroom at the time. He heard broken glass and thought someone was breaking in. By the time he got to the bedroom, it was engulfed in flames. He had to enter those flames to get to his screaming son. That's what he told the chief, anyway."

Mark now felt that ache in his stomach growing more prominent. *Who would toss a Molotov cocktail into Jeb's trailer to begin with, let alone into the bedroom where a child was sleeping?* Granted, Mark did not know all of what Jeb could have gotten himself into, or who else might want him dead, but one man came to mind immediately: Franco Hufnagel.

Mark continued to the other side of the burned out structure, where there were no emergency personnel. He produced his flashlight and clicked it on. He noted how much it seemed like a Star Wars light saber, its light illuminating the smoky air as if it were some kind of laser. Using it, he peered into the darkened space between the two trailers where he saw Jeb's motorcycle laying on the ground next to a pickup truck. One side of the truck was damaged from the flames, and Mark continued walking past it on the far side. The driver's side seemed unscathed, although it was littered with debris and ash all across the hood and roof of the vehicle.

As he found himself walking past the hood, his eyes were drawn to something which subconsciously caused him to grow sick. He felt cold and nauseous as if he were about to vomit. There, partially obscured by ash and other debris, pinned below a windshield wiper blade, was a fully grown marijuana leaf.

Now there was no doubt in Mark's mind. Franco Hufnagel had destroyed the Fields family home, and killed Jeb's only son. He grew emotional, and wondered how he would deliver this news to others. Slowly he walked to find the chief of police, and he would deliver what he'd just learned. But then he changed his mind. That would mean he was getting involved in the case, and he prayed the other investigators there would see the leaf on the windshield. Even if they did, he knew it would have no significance to them, other than being surprised that someone had left a pot leaf on the windshield. It would be no value to them in the fire investigation. It would be ignored. And even if they did know what it meant, Franco's calling card had not been enough to convict him of Laurie's murder, nor would it likely be enough to convict him of this atrocity, either. Mark would, however, reserve this information for Sandy Toney, and let her communicate it to the appropriate personnel in Sevierville.

Once Mark was back at the Little River station, he located Sandy Toney and asked if they could talk. They met privately in the same meeting room where they discovered that the governor had been shot with a pistol, not by a sniper with a long-range rifle. Both had some catching up to do, as Sandy shared her details from her trip to Nashville, as well as the details from Agent Luken's meeting with Banister. Mark also hoped to get an update from Sandy about the Echo Ridge case, as well as tell her about what happened at the trailer park.

"First," said Mark, "I'm curious if anyone tracked down that guy named Haus."

"That's a status update I cannot give you, Mark. It's related to the case."

"Well, I thought it would be okay for me to know what's going on with the case, just so long as I'm not actually working the case."

"That's a matter of interpretation, Mark. For me, I ask myself if there is there a need for you to know. Obviously, since you recused yourself from the case, the answer is no. Therefore, I'm not going to share updates with you.

"By recusing myself, I am mitigating the risk of influencing the case with bias. But that's going to still be the case if you give me an update... I'm still not in a position to influence anyone, right?"

"Mark, you're making this more difficult than it needs to be. I just think the more I keep you in the loop, the more prone you might be to get involved again, especially since you have an emotional investment with some of the suspects."

"Okay, I get it, you don't have to tell me anything, as long as someone's trying to get to that Haus guy. He's going to lead you to your man, I'm sure, but not if he's dead. Something happened last night to Jeb. It worries me that Franco Hufnagel might be after Haus as well."

"It's an active investigation Mark," was all she would say. What she might have told him was that Agents Luken and Gallenstein were actively working to find Haus. They had learned his real name was Hugh Schoborg, but had little luck in locating him. It seemed Haus never used credit cards or ATMs (a habit he picked up from his work acquaintance, Franco Hufnagel), and could not be traced to an address from any recent transaction history. Department of Motor Vehicles and Medical records drew blanks as well.

It was as if they were trying to find a modern-day Grizzly Adams.

"I guess you should know I interacted with Jeb Fields yesterday," continued Mark. "We did not talk about the Echo Ridge case. This was a personal matter, as I've known Jeb since he was 15 years old. There was a tragedy at his place, which I need to tell you about."

Sandy's facial expression turned sour but she allowed Mark to continue.

"It appears someone set his trailer on fire, and his son died in the blaze, after suffering terribly I might add. This was a personal tragedy for Jeb, and I felt compelled to make sure he was alright."

Mark appeared to be filled with a degree of frustration as he spoke, but if Sandy perceived this, she was wrong. He was actually simmering with hatred for Franco Hufnagel, but knew he needed to suppress his feelings if he was going to get through to Sandy.

"I can understand your personal desires to look after Mr. Fields, Mark," replied Sandy, "but your involvement with someone in this case is out of bounds. Given that you once charged Hufnagel with murdering your wife, we cannot have you involved in this case, directly or indirectly. And you know this, Mark. You pulled yourself off the case, for crying out loud. So why must I be the one to remind you of this?"

Mark sighed. He knew this was coming. He was getting scolded by the FBI, and yes, he should have known better. His emotions had gotten the best of him. He gave himself another pep talk to mask his anger toward Hufnagel, and try again.

"That was before I knew the kid was going to have his life destroyed by an arsonist..."

"None of that matters, Mark, you can't get sucked in emotionally. If I need to spell it out, you are not going to speak to, or be involved with, any person or persons who have any connection to this case until I say otherwise. Do you understand me? That would include the people who handled the horses that day. Or even the helicopter pilots. You'll not communicate with *ANY* of them. And if you do, Agent Powers, I'll charge you with interfering with a federal investigation, and oh do I mean it! Is that clear?"

"Yes," said Mark, feeling ashamed that he'd not handled the situation more professionally.

"What about my coworkers? Are you saying I can't speak to Dan or Belle, just because they were on the trail that day?"

"I would say that's okay, as long as you are not discussing the case."

'What about Talia?" asked Mark.

"What do you mean?" asked Sandy.

"Well, can I go see her at the hospital?"

"What do you think?"

"I guess she's out of bounds too, since she broke into my computer."

"Correct. She's not just your coworker, she's a person of interest."

"But if I'm not working the case, and I just want to go check on her, you're telling me I can't do that."

"You just said for yourself, no. You already know why, Mark, so why are you even asking?"

"I guess it's because I've never taken myself off of a case before, and even though I did, I wasn't thinking it would mean total banishment from people I care about."

"Why don't you check with your boss, Lt. Henderson, see what he says. He'll tell you the same thing, I'm sure of it."

Mark knew that would be fruitless, as the man was never around, and hardly ever checked up on Mark or any of the other law enforcement rangers, until they'd done something wrong. He was pretty much hands off. Yet, Mark knew the man well enough to know he'd agree with Toney's total hands-off approach.

"Okay, you win," he said. "But there's something I saw at the scene of the fire that will be critical for you to know, and I want to tell you about it as my last and final word on the matter" added Mark.

"I'll see it in the Sevierville report," she said.

"No you won't," said Mark.

"And why is that?" asked Sandy.

"Because I am not really sure the investigators saw what I saw."

"Mark, you are driving me crazy."

"I believe it will turn the tide in your investigation for Echo Ridge, but I'm the only one with this information. Do you want to know or not?"

Sandy rubbed her forehead with the palm of her right hand, as if combating a headache. "Of course I do... but..."

She wanted to know more than anything, but she knew she should not be talking to Mark about the case. Her eyes looked at him with a burning intensity, a glance designed to punish him for putting her in this situation.

"If you saw something important you should have pointed that out to the detective on the scene."

"Ahhh, but then I would have been involving myself in the case, which is now forbidden."

Sandy stared at him like she was at a crossroads. She needed to know what he'd seen at that trailer park, and was now going to have to cave on her stern warnings to Mark in order to get to that information.

Mark took off his badge and placed it on the table. "Civilian Mark Powers would like to tell you something he saw while at Jeb Smith's trailer fire, ma'am. I was not working at the time, it was in the evening. Does that help?"

"It doesn't work that way, Mark. But look... you tell me what you have and it better be good, and this conversation does not leave this room!"

Mark was now excited at the green light he'd been given.

"Have you heard much about when my wife was killed?" asked Mark, taking Sandy on a surprise U-turn.

"I know some of it. If I recall, you accused Hufnagel, but the DA would not prosecute for a lack of evidence."

"Correct. But did you read about the pot leaf?"

"I don't recall anything about marijuana. Explain. But only if this is relevant to the trailer fire."

"Well, of course it is. Where my wife was killed, in a secluded location, a marijuana leaf was found on her windshield early the next morning after she was killed."

"With what significance?"

"Ten years earlier, I helped get Hufnagel prosecuted for growing pot on federal lands. So once he got out of jail, he killed Laurie as payback to me. He left that pot leaf on her windshield as a calling card. It was left for me. There's no doubt in my mind what it meant and who had put it on her windshield."

"Interesting, for sure, and I can see why you'd think that, but was that the only thing to link Hufnagel to your wife's murder?"

"Nope. Just the bullet that was in her body. Unfortunately, nothing else linked directly to Franco."

Sandy sat and took in Mark's story, and found it tragic that the killer was not prosecuted, but it was not a unique story. She'd seen hundreds of cases go south for a lack of evidence.

"Last night," continued Mark, "I saw another pot leaf on a windshield... right next to Jeb's trailer. And while I'm not exactly sure, I think it was Jeb's truck. I recognized his motorcycle, which was right next to the truck, so that's why I'm guessing it was his too."

"And now you think that also means Franco Hufnagel is responsible for the trailer fire? Another pot leaf, after a decade or more?"

"Absolutely."

"What would Franco's motive be for setting Jeb's trailer on fire?"

"Well, mostly just that there's a history between Franco and Jeb. Much of it's just Jeb's side of the story, but he claims Franco assaulted him with a baseball bat some years ago, and Jeb was nearly left permanently disabled from the attack. Only problem is, he didn't file a police report."

"Then that's just a big nothingburger, now isn't it? One man's word against another's. Even if there was a motive for the fire, Mark, how does this help us in the Echo Ridge case?"

"Because Jeb has officially stated it was Franco who stole his tent the night before the attack. If that's true, and Franco was the last person we know to be in possession of that tent, this puts Franco at the scene of the shooting. Agent Luken found it shoved in a bush. I believe Franco may have put that tent there knowing the boom box inside of it most likely had Jeb's fingerprints all over it. It was a setup. My gut tells me that's what happened. I know how this Franco guy thinks. Plus, we already know Shane and Franco were on a safari together. Seriously, that can't be a coincidence, and is definitely worthy of further investigation, don't you think? And 20 years ago, when he was busted selling pot on federal lands, we seized a dozen long range rifles of his. Hufnagel is our sniper, I just know it. And once you get Hufnagel, my gut tells me that's going to lead you to the second shooter, and right now it seems like that is Shane Goodwyn."

"And what might Franco's motivation be for his part in the shootings, even though he apparently missed his main target, the governor?"

"I'd have to guess he was just a gun for hire. Or maybe he is unhinged, politically. Although, it was all so well planned, and coordinated, it seems, and there was a second shooter, so that lessens the likelihood this was done out of anger. But there's tons of connections to this guy."

"Connections do not guarantee guilt," said Sandy. "They help us find other people so we can ask more questions, but connections are not evidence, in and of themselves. We need physical evidence. Just like the case with your wife, we have no physical evidence for him being her assailant. But we do have physical evidence that puts Jeb at the scene of the sniper fire. I do not see Hufnagel as a primary suspect, at least not yet, for the sniper fire. It's looking more like Jeb Fields."

"You know, Sandy, it almost sounds like you are trying to look the other way on this. There's plenty of reasons you should now be looking for Franco, and you know I'm right about that. You FBI guys are the best in the world, right? Don't just go after Jeb because you know where to find him. Yes, Franco will be harder to find, but once you do find him, I know you can build a solid case against him. I know it's just a gut feel, but I'm telling you, it's Hufnagel, not Fields."

"We will examine all possibilities, Mark. I'm only challenging you to generate a little debate. That's always healthy for police work. Now, I'll admit, what you've brought to the table with this pot leaf is intriguing, and could be important. We'd be negligent and unprofessional not to look at that. Many times I've seen cases get cracked wide upon because of a seemingly insignificant detail. Although, I will say this: from where I sit, there's a stronger case against Jeb than against Franco at this moment in time. Jeb's fingerprints are the ones found at the scene of the shooting, not Franco's. For all we know, Jeb could be telling you Franco stole the tent just to make it look like it was Franco who was the shooter. I'm afraid your history with Jeb may have biased you against considering that scenario. We have not yet found this Haus fellow, to corroborate Jeb's story that it was Franco who stole their tent. Maybe that never happened. Jeb could have set fire to his own trailer and placed the pot leaf on his own truck windshield just to make it look like Hufnagel as well. Jeb is not out of the woods just yet. We'll be bringing him in for questioning."

"Jeb would not set fire to his own trailer with his kid sleeping in bed. That's not logical."

"There could be a simple explanation for that. We simply can't ignore other possibilities, Mark. Yes, we will look for Franco, but until we find him, we're going to bring in Jeb for more questioning."

"You asked me for Franco's motive for killing the governor. Well then let me ask you the same about Jeb? Why on earth would he be a hired gun? He only owns a 12 gauge for Pete's sake."

"That's what he told you. And you believed him. And why? Because you want to believe Hufnagel is the killer. You are biased, Mark. In your mind this is how you're going to repay Franco Hufnagel for killing your wife, and if you were honest, maybe you'd just admit that here and now. So Mark... I'm reaching the end of my patience with you. This is not your case any longer. It's time to drop it."

Mark wanted to scream. He was terribly frustrated that Sandy could not see it the way he did. He knew Franco would be hard to find. Of course he would be, because he's the guilty man, and guilty men are the ones to hide.

"Fine. Do what you need to do," said Mark. "I believe if you do some digging on both of those men, the truth will come out in the end. And that's the important thing."

"Our conversation is at an end. And, I believe we both know this chat... right now... it never happened, right?"

"Correct."

"This will be the last time I find you have any connection to the case. Direct or indirect. Are we in agreement on that point?"

"We are."

From that point forward, Mark owned those words, but he wondered if he'd be able to live up to them.

Chapter 25

The Infamous Stringdusters seemed omnipresent on Mark's list of current favorite groups. Several of their songs on their *Laws of Gravity* album seemed to have been authored about his life with Laurie, and he latched on to every word. As he drove down the road, they played through a Bluetooth connection to his stereo. Its blue LED lighting up the cabin of his truck as he navigated through the darkness on the highway. He was listening to a song called *Soul Searching*:

> *"I'm just a man making my way*
> *Sometimes a sinner, sometimes a saint*
> *I carry on, do the best I can*
> *But still I struggle with who I am*
>
> *Soul Searching*
>
> *Once was a girl that held me tight*
> *And I took her love like a thief in the night*
> *After all this time, I'd never dream*
> *That I'd be holding on to her memory."*

In time, he reached the parking lot and found all spaces available. If the moon had been full, it might have been just like the moon which shone the night Laurie had been killed. But it was not full, rather a thin sliver of a crescent. The night sky was overcast, leaving very little of the moon's light to help Mark find his way from the parking lot to the cliff.

Mark's night vision had grown less effective over the years, and once he entered the woods, he decided to use a flashlight. He recalled a fellow ranger from back in the old days who swore never to use a flashlight at night, especially on horseback, as it would ruin the night vision of the horse and the rider. No horses were present on this occasion, and Mark opted to use the flashlight, despite the sage advice of that old timer.

After he reached the ledge of the cliff, Mark crouched down, tossed his lower legs over the edge, and was seated. This was the very spot where he and Laurie were married. It was the epicenter of his memories of his wife, and replays of their wedding vows played through his mind.

Downstream, the river was filtered by rocks both large and small, and that is where Laurie's lifeless body had settled just after she was murdered. Here he began thinking about how his older, more treasured memories were forever tainted by newer, less desirable ones. Many times he had considered doing one of his videos on that topic, but always kept it in his back pocket as an idea he could use when nothing better came to mind. Perhaps once this case was over, he would revisit that topic.

He really missed her. Although, amid the good memories lay one minor regret. They had argued, just one day before her murder. He wished it had never happened. He'd been assisting search and rescue teams for days on end, trying to locate an older man who'd vanished from the Appalachian Trail near Clingmans Dome. When it was over, he had been invited to join the others for a beer, which he did. It had slipped his mind that Laurie might want to see him, especially since it was their anniversary. He returned home late, and let it slip he'd been out for celebratory pilsners. An argument ensued. He was angry with himself, but at the same time, could not muster an apology, as Laurie did not understand the depths of the bonds that existed amongst his fellow rangers, especially during trying circumstances.

Before Laurie left for her photo shoot of The Sinks, the night after their argument, she penned a letter to Mark on her favorite stationary and tucked it in her bible next to a verse she had quoted in the letter. Because of the murder, it was never delivered.

The sound of the river seemed to completely ignore the darkness; it was just as loud as if it were mid-day. Looking up, he could see the moonlight illuminating a few gaps in the clouds, showing promise the clouds might clear soon. Within minutes, the clouds grew thin and the slender crescent moon shone impotently upon the scene below him. It was not much light, but it was better than nothing.

He chose not to look downstream, where her body had been found. He set his mind to thinking about her in a positive way, as his drive to The Sinks was dominated by negative thoughts and downright anger toward Franco Hufnagel.

As he sat upon the cliff, his hands upon his knees, he twisted his arms slightly so he could see the tattoos on the insides of his forearms. On the left arm was the number 40.1276. On the right arm, -78.0628. Latitude and Longitude for the very spot he now sat upon. He was not a tattoo kind of guy, but once Laurie was gone, he wanted to memorialize her in some way, and he chose to add the coordinates of where they'd been married. With the passage of time, he seldom looked at those tattoos with love, as he more often was reminded of her murder.

He glanced straight across the river at the bridge. It was the spot where Mark believed Franco Hufnagel stood and shot Laurie to death. It would have been either there or the parking lot, but Mark guessed the bridge since Franco would have had a faster getaway. Mark tried to push away the memory of a shooter standing on that bridge, dominant foot forward, leaning forward slightly, arms straight in front of him, with a beautiful woman in the guns' sights. He did not want to think about that, but there were times when the negative thoughts would consume him. Even now, Mark felt as if some ghost of Franco was standing there with his gun, ready to shoot again, only this time to take out the husband as well.

His hatred for Franco took his mind to more current events, as he thought of Jeb's son, burned alive in a fire he knew was set by Franco. That boy had suffered from third-degree burns, until it was too much to endure any longer. Anyone who could do that to a child was deserving of similar treatment, or worse, as far as Mark was concerned. But he knew the justice system was not perfect and had seen many cases on television where the system went light on the perps, while the victims suffered. His father would say *the system isn't perfect, but it's the only one we have and it's the best damned system in the world.* Mark knew his father was right, but he didn't want to settle for less than perfect. He wanted to ensure Franco Hufnagel would feel the same pain he'd cause others.

What must it be like to lose a child? thought Mark. He knew what it was like to lose a father, a mother, and a wife, but not a child. He'd heard that losing a child was far worse. Granted, that was a life experience he would never want to have, but he could not help himself pondering how Jeb was coping with that reality.

A son. It was a foreign concept. He had always wanted a boy. Or a daughter would have been just fine, too, but he had hoped mostly for a son. It just did not happen. He and Laurie tried for a few years, but repeatedly came up short. Nearly a decade passed before she was with child. Having waited so long made it that much more difficult to accept the murder. It was two murders, really. But he'd never seen the child, and had never bonded with it. He had buried his feelings about the baby for all these years. Finally, at the cliff, he wept for the life that was never given a chance to be lived.

Ranger Powers began thinking of alternative justice. His father was always quick to point out that it was not the job of a police officer to make the rules, nor to be the judge. The police officer was merely there to protect the public as best as they could from crimes that were yet conducted, and also to bring criminals into the justice system, to be evaluated by judge or jury. His father had many great sayings and quotes about justice, two of which came to mind:

"Injustice anywhere is a threat to justice everywhere."
— Martin Luther King Jr.

"Punishment is justice for the unjust."
— St. Augustine

He also recalled a quote while reading a book about vigilantism. It was a quote his father would not have approved of.

"Sometimes justice is better served by those who have experienced the pain."
— Mark W. Boye

How long would Franco Hufnagel's tyranny go on? He knew the answer: as long as Franco Hufnagel roamed the earth. Or... until someone did something to stop him... permanently. As he sat on his perch above the roaring waterfalls, he resolved to do something. He could not murder another man, not even Franco, but he could not sit by idly and tally the victims as they continued to add up over time.

He tried praying, as if he could open up some portal to the heavens, now more visible with the clouds gone, so he could speak to Laurie. He'd tried to speak to God before, but was hesitant. He preferred speaking to those he'd lost: Laurie, and both of his parents. He asked for guidance, most often. Tonight, however, he turned his thoughts to them for forgiveness. *Please put in a good word for me up there. I'm going to need forgiveness for what I'm about to do.*

Mark stayed for over an hour. But once he was finished concocting a plan, he returned to his cruiser, exited the parking lot, and turned left onto the highway. He headed south, away from his home in Townsend. The next morning, Mark was in Bryson City, North Carolina.

Driving and looking. That was the most basic means of finding someone. All he had to go on was the year, make, model, and plates of Franco's truck from his last speeding ticket. He had dug up a report from a fellow wildlife ranger who found bear traps in the high country near Fontana Dam. Mark figured Franco was likely living somewhere in that vicinity. This report was not included in the data he'd handed over to Sandy, as it had caught his eye just days after he'd pulled himself off the Echo Ridge case. He also had a lifetime of keeping track of Franco, and felt he had an intuition about the man, something the FBI did not have. If he had some kind advantage over the FBI, he knew it would not last for long. He had to get out there and look before some super computer at Quantico produced new data that would lead them to Franco first.

The profile he'd kept on Franco showed he owned a home in southern Georgia but was making his money in Tennessee and North Carolina. It was likely he was bunking in makeshift situations, by staying with friends, in a remote cabin, or a hotel. If it was a cabin, he'd never find Franco. He knew Franco loved a good restaurant, and this alone gave him hope the man would choose to bunk closer to civilization, and so he continued driving and looking for that familiar truck.

Digging deep into Franco's past, Mark recalled the first place Franco had been required to report his residence to his parole officer. It was a roadside motel called The Bismarck. Granted, a decade had passed, and The Bismarck had closed, but Mark figured Franco might still be calling a roadside motel his home all these years later, especially since he was actively poaching in the park. The motel scene gave criminals a way of moving around, not having to leave traces of apartment leases. Franco could use whatever name he wanted and the motel manager couldn't care less.

He also considered the trips to Africa as a reason Franco would not have settled into any kind of long-term housing arrangement. Mark had done his homework, searching the area for apartment complexes that would offer a 6 month lease. Those he found, he called, and inquired about tenants driving a black F-350. That turned up nothing.

The Bismarck had been located northeast of Bryson City and Mark hoped perhaps Franco had migrated to another cheap motel in the same area. Little did he know, Franco had moved between a half dozen motels over the years, for a change of scenery, as well as, a means of remaining invisible. With this in mind, Mark drove back and forth between Cherokee and Fontana Dam over a three day weekend, keeping an eye out for a black, 2006, Ford F-350, per the state registration records. It was late afternoon on a Sunday, just an hour before he planned to return to Townsend, when he spotted the truck.

He had passed a little roadside motel on his right as he drove north-east on Route 19, just past Bryson City. It was called the Sleeping Bear Motel, and it looked like it had seen better days. It featured a clean-looking swimming pool off to the side of the parking lot, with some beautiful pines framing the property in an arc. From his angle, he happened to notice such a truck pulling around to the back of the building. Mark wondered if that would be the truck he was looking for, and decided he needed to see the license plate.

He turned around, pulled off to the side of the road, across the street from the motel, and removed a pair of binoculars. Squirming in his seat, he leaned out his window and used the binoculars to see if the truck was still in view. Unfortunately, it was not. He would have to go look for sure.

Mark wondered if there was any way to look at the license plate without being seen. Driving the cruiser had been a mistake. He should have brought his own Chevy S-10. He drove further south and spied a used car dealership. He pulled in and asked the man if he could leave his cruiser on their lot for a while and was met with open arms.

Mark grabbed a hoodie from the back seat, hoping to look less official, and put it on. He grabbed his hiking bag and crossed the street. The forest's southern pines came directly up to the road. Mark detected the sounds of the Oconaluftee River nearby. He stepped about 50 feet into the confines of the woods and headed toward the motel. Soon he could see the establishment through the trees, and saw the truck had, in fact, parked behind the building. He did not see the person who had been driving, as he had already gone to a room. He had a direct line of sight to inspect the pickup truck with his binoculars. He dialed them into the right magnification and spied the license plate. It was Franco's truck. He could not believe his luck.

Now his game plan moved to the next phase. The laborious looking was over, it was now time to jump into action and execute the critical part of his plan. The pickup was very close, and he knew he could do his business immediately and get away quickly. After watching and thinking for nearly 10 minutes, he opted to go for it. He knew that poachers were often active at night, and if Franco was actively in hunting mode, he might actually be settling down for a nap in one of the motel's rooms at that very moment. But Franco Hufnagel was not asleep. After switching to traps, Franco found he no longer needed to spend his nights in the mountains, hunting his prey, and had returned to a more normal sleeping cycle.

Inside room 2112, Franco was talking to his buddy, Steve, on the phone while he looked out his window at an inviting swimming pool. For being such a ruthless man who barely valued human life any more than animal life, he loved to pamper himself by chilling poolside. As he finished his conversation, he told Steve he was about to take a dip in the pool, which garnered laughter from his business partner.

By now, Mark had gotten to the truck. He removed something from his bag, inspected it, and made sure it was in working order. Quickly he was on his back, under the truck. He made haste with his mission, but cursed himself for taking longer than he had wanted to take.

Franco, wearing little more than a pair of cutoff jeans, was rounding the bottom of the outdoor stairwell with his flip-flops smacking rhythmically upon his ugly and calloused feet. He was in the shade, but looked forward to the sunshine. He'd learned to appreciate these moments after he left prison. Basking in sunbeams only happened there while wearing a ridiculously hot jumpsuit instead of a bathing suit. As he was about to walk out into the sunlight when something caught his attention and turned his mood sour.

Mark had succeeded in his mission, and pulled himself out from under the truck. He was startled to see someone there, staring at him. It was a seven-year-old boy, unattended, and bored. Mark had no idea where he'd come from, but didn't care at this moment in time. Some other law enforcement personnel could deal with locating a parent, but not him. He heard some ungodly smashing noise from around the corner, accompanied by cursing, and did not want to encounter the child's parent, so he hustled quickly back to the woods.

Two more kicks proved fruitless, and with the last kick, Franco's flip flop came off and required him to retrieve it. He was totally pissed off. The ice machine was out of order, and the Margarita supplies he carried in his bag would need to wait for another day as he would not drink them if they were warm. He then returned to his room to retrieve a cold 6-pack of Busch Beer, from his room's tiny refrigerator, before finally making it to the pool.

Ten minutes later, Mark was back to the cruiser, speeding down Route 19. He drove quickly, hoping to get back home before dark, and feeling a rush of excitement at what would happen next. He stopped for a moment, and considered if he really wanted this to play out. He could easily deliver Franco's location to Sandy and be done with it, although he'd be in significant danger of losing his job or going to jail if she knew he was trailing Franco Hufnagel. No, he'd chosen this path the night he'd visited The Sinks. Now he was in too deep to turn back. That night he'd contemplated the concept of justice, and decided personal justice was just as good as federal justice. He knew his father would be rolling over in his grave, but it was time to stop Franco Hufnagel before the man killed anyone else.

Mark had left his cell phone in his car while traipsing through the woods. It was during this time that he'd gotten a call from Sandy Toney which had gone to voicemail. He did not notice the message until he was approaching the Tennessee state line while driving on Route 441. He glanced at his phone and saw the red indicator. He pulled over to the side of the road and listened to the message.

The message was from Sandy, calling to notify him that Talia had woken from her coma. She mentioned she did not want Mark to visit, even though he had a personal friendship with Talia. This was not a surprise. When he pulled himself off of the case, he had no idea he would encounter these difficulties. He wanted nothing more than to visit Talia, especially having learned she had broken into his computer and taken files. How could he not want to satisfy his curiosity, to question her and find out what her motivations were, and what she did with the information gained from his files. If he had a chance to talk to Talia, it might turn unpleasant, for sure. Perhaps it was best he did not go, after all.

Talia had gone through several hours of tests and evaluations from the doctors at the hospital before they would consider allowing any visitors. Once the doctors gave their clearance, Sandy and Jeannine Gallenstein entered the room and introduced themselves. They read Talia her Miranda rights and began to record the conversation. There would be no concessions for her medical trauma, Sandy was more concerned with getting to the bottom of Talia's mysterious involvement with the Echo Ridge Case.

Talia had looked surprisingly well prior to the introductions, and had been smiling to learn her injuries had healed significantly during her extended unconsciousness and that the doctors had given her a positive prognosis. But the smile left once she realized she was speaking with the FBI. In fact, she was terrified.

"I guess you know why we are here," said Sandy. "We want to talk to you about the shooting."

Talia was in a tough spot. She felt as if she'd just woken up immediately after the shooting, as if it had happened just minutes earlier. When the doctors told her she'd been out for over a month, she could hardly believe it. Now there were FBI agents in her room and she was terrified of what they may have learned in those unconscious weeks. Were they now aware of her relationship with Banister? Had they found out about how she had hacked Mark's user account at headquarters? If not, why else would the FBI be interested in her? She felt ambushed. She had not had any time to prepare herself for their questioning. She considered asking for a lawyer, when another idea came to mind.

"Excuse me," she said, directing her question to both Sandy and Jeannine, "But before you ask any questions, I would like to know something. Have you found whoever shot us?"

"That's why we are here," said Sandy, "We hope the answers you provide to us might help make that happen." This was good news and bad news for Talia. It was good news that a month had gone by and none of her co-conspirators had been caught. It was bad news, because with nobody caught, she might face some heat, still.

"Did you see any of the others get shot?" asked Sandy.

"I did. First it was the guy with the camera. Then the man and woman from the EPA and the Sierra Club, they were shot too." She grew quiet, now reluctant to include herself to the list of victims.

"And that's when you were shot?" asked Sandy.

"Yes. And then the governor," added Talia.

The two agents looked at each other in surprise. "You were still conscious when the governor was shot? And you saw it happen?" asked Sandy.

"Yes," said Talia. "Yes to both of your questions."

Her panic was irrational. Had she been thinking more clearly, and less emotionally, she might just have asked for the lawyer. But she knew in time they would likely know the whole story, but her frantic mind chose to give them something that might take the heat off of herself, if not just for a little while. And if that meant she needed to throw someone else under the bus, so be it.

Jeannine double checked to make sure the recorder was still capturing the conversation. Sandy could hardly believe what Talia had said and felt it necessary to repeat the question.

"Let me get this straight, Talia. You saw the governor get shot, but are you also saying you know who shot her?"

Talia prayed giving up this information would not come back to harm her, but she was scared for her own future, and it seemed the best way out.

"I certainly am," she said, and proceeded to tell Jezelle what she had seen.

Chapter 26

The Chimneys Picnic Area #1, along Route 441, is a very popular family attraction in the Great Smoky Mountains National Park. Just seven miles from Gatlinburg, it is an easy excursion for vacationing families who can grab some fast food and get to the picnic area before the food gets cold.

Sometimes confused with another popular hiking attraction called the Chimney Tops, The Chimneys also have a longstanding reputation as being a good place to catch sight of a black bear. It seems the bears frequently catch wind of the picnic food, or leftover garbage, and risk getting darted by a ranger in order to get a little human food in their bellies.

This had been an epidemic problem in the 70's before rangers conducted an educational campaign to inform the public that they should not feed the bears or leave food behind. After decades of driving that message, they were experiencing some success. The park service had also employed the practice of darting bears with sedatives and relocating them deeper into the forest, many miles away, if they showed they were habitually foraging for human food in areas frequented by tourists.

Mark drove his cruiser past the entrance to the Chimneys, heading south on Route 441. That picnic area had been where Jeb and Haus had recently met, along with Mark, and where they agreed to meet nearby once Mark had succeeded in locating Hufnagel. The time for this meeting had finally come.

After negotiating a number of twists in the road, and reaching the midway point between The Chimneys and Newfound Gap, Mark approached a gravel road used only by park personnel. He pulled over and exited his vehicle while it sat idling. He removed a padlock holding a chain between two posts, one on each side of the gravel road. This allowed him entry. Shortly after he pulled the cruiser up the service road, he exited once more and reattached the chain. No cars would be following him, but that did not mean he wouldn't have visitors. Once further up the road, and completely out of view of the road, he waited.

Ten minutes later, he heard the sound of motor bikes racing up the gravel road. He had counted on them to circumnavigate the chain, as they did.

Jeb was the first in sight, riding the dirt bike he'd attempted to escape with when Mark and the FBI had visited him weeks ago. He had endured a long, 3 day period of evaluation by the FBI, and got a release due to the efforts of his lawyer. Also, the FBI had gotten footprint analysis back from the shooting location and had a positive match on boots previously purchased by Franco Hufnagel. From that point on, Sandy and company would focus on Franco, while keeping Jeb in their back pocket, at least for the Echo Ridge case. Jeb's fingerprints still placed him at that location, but it was beginning to look more and more like he had told the truth about the stolen tent.

What Jeb didn't know was that Dan Lawson was about to arrest Jeb for the pot growing activities as there was plenty of evidence to make those charges stick. The feds had suggested if they couldn't keep Jeb off the streets because of the Echo Ridge case, they could at least keep him detained because of the illegal marijuana farming charges, while conducting additional interrogations for both cases. As things turned out, Jeb and Haus were arriving to meet Mark at about the same time law enforcement was visiting the residence of Jeb's father, where Jeb and his wife had been staying after the fire. They would not find Jeb there, as he was now on a mission that would keep him away from that trailer for days.

While speeding up the gravel road, Jeb was wearing the same Red Man hat he'd worn in the surveillance video of the marijuana field, as well as both times Mark had seen him in person. This time, the hat was worn with great intentionality, at Mark's request.

Behind Jeb was Haus, riding his trusty, yet rusty, Indian road bike. He moved slower, finding it difficult to navigate water-runoff ruts in the gravel road. He looked out of place, such a big person on such a compact motorcycle. Haus' wild, unkempt hair flowed freely as he rode. Both of the young men reached Mark, parked their bikes, and dismounted, before walking over to Mark's side of the cruiser.

"Gentlemen," said Mark, by way of a greeting. He tried to remain calm, but even Mark was terrified of what was going down. He suspected Jeb and Haus must also be equally unsettled.

"Ranger Mark," said Jeb as a greeting, and Haus merely nodded.

Now that Jeb was closer, Mark took stock of how bad he looked. He appeared as if he'd been beaten hard by his life's recent events. He would not speak of it, but he was still grieving heavily over the loss of his son. Despite this, he looked at Mark with a laser focus. He was all in for this arrangement. Haus, too, appeared ready and willing to carry out the plans that had been devised between the three of them.

"Let's get this over with," said Mark. Still seated in the driver's seat, Mark handed them a small duffle bag through the car window. Jeb looked inside at what was contained there, then looked at Mark.

"You sure we're gonna know how to use this?"

Mark paused before answering. He knew Jeb had a way of messing things up. Like when Jeb returned to his pot field after the DEA had seized the crop, only to get his face on camera for easy identification. Mark hoped that dumb luck would not follow Jeb and Haus on this mission. Mark's own fate was tied to theirs.

Mark spent a few minutes explaining the device to the two young men. He was glad he took the time and grew confident they would do fine.

"Now I need your stuff," said Mark. With that, Jeb removed a card from his wallet, tossed it into his Red Man hat, and passed the items to Mark through the open car window. He also removed a baggy shirt he was wearing, and gave that to the ranger as well.

"I'll be watching your Twitter account, Jeb. Make sure it's a public message, not just to me. We don't want an electronic trail to link us together. In fact, NEVER send me a direct message. Ever. Just to be safe."

Jeb and Haus did appear nervous, but they were giving Mark their full attention, which gave the ranger confidence.

"Just before you're ready," continued Mark, "you need to tweet:

'Bored. Think I'll Go Shopping.'

I'll be looking for that so I know when to begin things on my end. And then, when you are done with the job, you'll tweet:

'The eagle has landed.'

When I see that, I'll know you have finished and I can stop my masquerade. So, do you both understand? Don't forget those phrases. There's no room for error here."

"Hey, what is that second one, anyway? I've heard people say that before," asked Haus.

"Those are the words spoken by Commander Neil Armstrong when he set foot on the moon... Apollo 11. I know you're a modern day mountain man and all, but Haus, you got to read up on history."

"Hey, about the phone," interrupted Jeb, "I bought an extra charger so I'll have extra juice for the phone. And if we can't get no signal, we'll pay a visit to a McDonald's to use their Wi-Fi until the Twitter goes through. We're all set. We won't mess this up." Jeb sounded confident, and eager. Little did he know how frazzled he would be when it came time to execute.

Mark nodded in approval, and spoke his final words. "Remember, we never met here. Those tweets will not be for me, and if you ever need to answer to what those phrases meant, you will need to tell them you went shopping and found something good, and that's what you meant by 'The Eagle Has Landed.' And after this, we will never talk again, except in case I somehow work on the outstanding case against you. If that happens, we will never speak of our personal involvement ever again. Got that? I'm sorry about your boy, Jeb. Good luck in the future, to you and your wife, and stay out of trouble. Haus, good luck to you, too."

"Right, Ranger Mark. Think about what we're doing here, and you tell me to stay out of trouble?" said Jeb with a laugh.

Mark saw the dark humor in Jeb's comment, and laughed a nervous laugh of his own, though his eyes revealed his concern outweighed his amusement.

Both Jeb and Haus mounted their bikes and promptly departed, with Jeb giving a 'thumbs-up' signal as they glanced at him over their shoulders and then disappeared down the service road.

Mark was left in silence. His stomach was tied in knots. Had he made the right choice? He was suddenly filled with regret. It was far too risky, he wished he'd never thought of this course of action. But it seemed it was too late to turn back now. He kept reminding himself of the pros, rather than the cons, or the risks, but his nerves were getting the worst of him. He leaned his head backwards, and stared at the ceiling of the cruiser.

"Dad, if you can hear me," he muttered, "please forgive me. Laurie, my love, pray for me."

Mark wound up the windows of the cruiser, and removed his park service laptop computer from its docking station on the dash of the passenger side. He placed the computer under his arm and held it against his side as if a football. He exited the vehicle and walked a ways up the gravel road just shy of a trail crossing. It was an unmarked trail, not appearing on most maps since the road was closed to the public, but he had hiked it many times.

Mark located a stream he knew about. He crouched down, and slid the laptop into the deepest water. He could no longer see it at the bottom, but decided to slide a few large rocks in to cover it up for good measure. If someone were to find it in the future, it would be blamed on thieves, and would be totally useless to anyone by then. Before leaving, he grabbed a fist-sized rock with a sharp point to take back to the cruiser.

With the laptop disposed of, he then walked up to the trail, and walked around a bit, making sure his boots left a few traceable footprints. He hoped the tracks would back up his story, about looking for the perps.

Eventually he returned to his cruiser and walked to the passenger side. He glanced around to make sure there were no accidental hikers or bystanders. He could not afford an accidental witness. Then, with all his strength, he smashed through the passenger side window using the rock from the stream. Self-consciously, he glanced around once more, ensuring yet again that nobody was there to hear that noise.

There was one last step. He walked back around to the driver's side, leaned in, and retrieved the hand-held portion of his radio. He called in the theft to the dispatcher. Twenty minutes later, Dan Lawson arrived.

"So Mark, what the hell happened here?" he asked. Mark was nervous to be on the lying side of the equation. He knew Dan had a great mind for investigation, and there was no room to mess up.

"I was driving down to Newfound Gap, and as I passed this service road, I thought I heard dirt bikes up in here somewhere. I still had the combination for the chain from the last time I was out here, figured I'd take a look."

"You didn't hear me on the radio? I was trying to see if you know of Jeb Fields' whereabouts. We were hoping to pick him up for the pot bust later today."

"Nope. Didn't hear that. I must have already been out of the car, and left my walkie-talkie on the seat. So yeah, I drove up here, parked, and then decided to walk up to the Raccoon's Crossing trail just up the road, thinking maybe somebody was partying up there. I looked around for about ten minutes, and didn't find a thing. I came back to find this," he said, pointing to the broken window. "They got the laptop, and a bag full of some other gear."

"Damn. Sounds like maybe they lured you up here with this in mind. What was in the bag?" asked Dan.

"A couple of GPS units, some of my own hiking clothes. Maybe a few water bottles. Oh, and an empty box of Dr. Scholl's arch supports, for my boots. Should have bought those things long before now, you should try 'em out. Miracle workers, I'm tellin' ya."

"Sons of bitches, what's wrong with kids these days? Nobody respects authority anymore. Runnin' off with your arch supports. Let's hope they end up in maximum security for that."

"We always have hope. Oh, and I noticed we have some motorcycle tire marks coming up this gravel road," said Mark, "but nothing looks traceable. I didn't see anything on the dirt trail up there, which is a shame... dirt would have probably revealed some clean tracks if they'd been up there."

"Well, if there's a silver lining, it looks like you'll get one of those newer laptops for a replacement, Mark."

"Can't wait for the day when we get a chip in our brain. That way nobody can break into the office and hack my account during the night, or steal my laptop out of the cruiser."

"Yeah, but then big brother would know your every thought," replied Dan.

"I guess you have a point, there, man."

Mark realized how ironic that statement actually was. Indeed, he would be in quite a bit of trouble if the government could have read his mind at that very moment.

Chapter 27

They gorged themselves on Mexican Pizza from Taco Bell, while driving, hoping to fill their stomachs after neglecting their hunger for most of the day. They had never been on a stakeout before, and had not planned on needing food or water in case their wait was long. Eventually Haus ran across the street from their position to grab a sack of deliciousness. He barely got back to their borrowed deathtrap, a 1978 Bonneville, before the person they were watching exited the bar and took off in his pickup. Haus was still entering the car as Jeb rammed it into drive.

They followed the pickup, but Jeb was driving erratically.

"Bro, keep it on the road, will ya!"

"I knew this was a mistake," said Jeb.

"Look, man, it was your idea to kill the bastard, not mine!"

"Not that you moron. Eatin' while I'm drivin'! I got refried bean shit on the steering wheel now! Gimme a napkin!" yelled Jeb. Haus complied, but the cleanup was done clumsily and they were getting further and further behind the Ford.

"Just keep your eyes on the truck," Haus said, alternating his gaze between the vehicle they were tailing, and the device he held in his lap next to a half-eaten Mexican pizza.

"I'm not gonna lose the son of a bitch," said Jeb. "Not in a million years."

"Of course not," said Haus. "We've got the GPS from Ranger Mark! Franco can't get away from us with that thing on the bottom of his truck!"

"I know," replied Jeb, nervously. "Where do you think he's going next?"

"If I had to guess, he's calling it a night, and is going home to sleep off the whisky," said Jeb, who knew a bit about Franco's habits.

The Bonneville was not in good shape, as it was not hitting on all cylinders and lacking in power. Jeb appeared stressed that Franco would get beyond their sight.

"Don't worry about it," said Haus, holding the tracking console on his lap. "We can track him. You know, this ain't new or nuthin', but this GPS stuff just freaks me out. Communicatin' with satellites up in space while we're driving down the road like this. Just freaks me out."

"What, are you Bill Nye the Science Guy or something? Don't worry about that shit now, we know where he is... he's right in front of us. We don't need that thing no more!"

"Just saying. It's amazing, man."

"Speakin' of the GPS, we can't forget to get that beacon out from under the truck."

"Before or after we bash his head in?"

"I'd say after. Probably a good idea to leave it be until we're done with the son of a bitch."

Both men wore black clothing, which would serve them well if their deeds took place in the dark of night, as it appeared they would. It was 11:30 as they drove, and had no idea where Franco was headed. As it would happen, they would eventually reach Franco's roadside motel just before midnight.

They noticed a bit of a swerve in Franco's ride. It grew worse the longer he drove, and the younger men wondered if he was going to kill anyone in a head-on-collision. Franco's driving spoke volumes about the length of time he'd spent at the *Hacienda*. It was a crappy little bar just north-east of Bryson City. Any normal person who started drinking during happy hour, and stayed for over five hours, might not be able to drive at all. Jeb and Haus could not know how much Franco had been drinking, although they hoped it was a lot. He would be easier to manage that way... if he made it to where they thought he was going.

Once Franco arrived at his short-term residence, he pulled into the lot with his rusting muffler notifying the motel manager of his arrival. As per usual, Franco pulled his truck around the back of the motel. He always parked around the rear because he was paranoid about being located, especially after offing Craig Banister at Steve's Steaks. He needed to lay lower than a snake, and that meant parking out of view. On this occasion, his intoxication made that task more difficult to execute.

Jeb and Haus did not follow Franco into the parking lot. Instead, they drove a short distance up the road, and parked off into the grass. Prior to exiting the vehicle, Jeb used his phone to make a contribution to the Twittersphere. "Bored. Think I'll go shopping." He tossed the phone into the glove box and then both men exited the Bonneville.

Jeb grabbed a baseball bat from the bed of the pickup, and they quickly bolted across the road and through the woods. They sprinted to where they had just seen Franco's vehicle disappear behind the motel. They ran as quickly as they could, getting thrashed by undergrowth as they went. They did not want to give Franco a chance at disappearing into a hotel room. They had to intercept him quickly.

Franco pulled his truck into position along a brick wall. He'd done a poor job of parking, nearly scraping up against the wall. He put the truck in park and reached for the keys. Just as soon as the sound of the muffler grew silent, he passed out with his upper body leaning against the steering wheel, keys still dangling from the ignition, his foot still pressing upon the brake. Jeb and Haus as they exited the woods and found themselves a short distance from the Ford's tailgate.

"Look, he's still in there," whispered Jeb as he pulled the drawstrings tighter on his hood. "Put up your hood."

"I don't want to. I hate hoods."

"But we're going to kill him. We can't be seen. Put up the hood!"

"No man, leave me alone. It messes up my hair."

"Dang if you don't sound like a woman."

"I got better hair than any woman around!"

"Only you got ticks in there the size of quarters!"

"I do not, now shut up, man." said Haus. "Let's just get this done and get out of here. You go first."

"Follow me closely with this, and cover me," said Jeb, removing a pistol from his waistband and handing it to Haus. Jeb planned on using the Louisville Slugger he had retrieved from the bed of their truck.

The brake lights were still illuminated, giving the false impression that Franco was awake. With the bat held in both hands in front of him, Jeb walked slowly toward the driver's side of the truck, careful to look for a face staring back at him in the side-view mirror. He saw nothing. He wondered what Franco was doing, and braced himself for the man exiting the truck at any moment. It was not until Jeb was fully alongside the door that he could hear snoring. He was relieved that the man they came to kill was now an easy target. Or so they thought.

Haus whispered from behind his pal. "Open the door and crack his head with the bat, man!"

Jeb agreed the easy target warranted the baseball bat, but then realized Franco had parked too close to the building. The truck door would only open halfway.

"What the hell are we supposed to do now?" he whispered.

"What do you mean?" asked Haus, whispering as well.

"I can't swing the baseball bat right here! There's no room."

"Well, hell, I don't know. Let's get him out first. We can drag him behind the truck and finish him off there!" suggested Haus.

"You mean beat him with the bat while he's on the ground, while he's unconscious?"

"What the hell else do you think I mean?"

"I can't do that!"

"Why not?"

"I don't know. That's not how I thought it would go. I wanted him to see me hitting him, like how I saw him when he came after me with that damned bat up on that mountain. I want to know he's feelin' the pain, you know! Just like my boy did. I don't want to just kill him when he doesn't know he's being killed!"

"That has to be the dumbest thing you ever said. HE'S DRUNK AS A SKUNK! HE CAN'T FIGHT BACK! Does it really matter if he's in the truck or on the ground when you bean him? You either make him dead or you don't. Nothing else matters."

Both men were wearing on each other's nerves, and they both realized the stress of the situation was to blame. Haus took a deep breath, followed by a controlled exhale while he handed the pistol to Jeb. "Okay, I'll get him out, put him on my back, and carry him over there," he said, "and you keep the gun pointed in case he wakes up. Maybe he'll wake up so you can have your words with him before you bean him in the head. How's that for a plan?"

"Okay, I guess," said Jeb, sheepishly.

"And don't you go shootin' my ass by mistake."

Awkwardly, they opened the driver's door and realized it would be a tight fit to remove the drunk man. Eventually, Jeb entered the truck from the passenger side to push Franco out and twist him around a bit. Haus was there to receive Franco onto his back, and would grab hold of Franco's wrists from over his shoulders so he could carry the drunkard on his back. This was his preferred method of carrying bears in the backwoods, until he could get the fallen beasts into the bed of the truck. He considered the irony that he was now carrying the bear killer in the same manner.

Haus was in the process of lugging the sleeping adversary to an open area when Franco Hufnagel, who'd had one too many whiskey's and Coke, vomited into Haus' flowing mass of mountain man hair. Haus stopped in his tracks, wondering if things could go any further astray. As Haus began dry heaving because of having vomit in his hair, Franco woke up.

Realizing he was no longer in his truck, but instead being carried on someone's back, Franco instinctively wrapped his arms around Haus' throat and pulled as tight as a boa constrictor. Jeb watched as he slowly realized Franco was on the attack.

"Sht, Sht!" yelled Haus, unable to utter the words intelligibly. Jeb knew Haus wanted him to shoot, but Jeb panicked, and was afraid he might shoot his buddy. Dropping the gun upon the ground, he walked around to the back of Franco and lit into him with the baseball bat across the top of the man's right shoulder. Franco immediately relinquished his grip around Haus' neck, and fell to the ground, writhing in pain and holding his right shoulder with his left hand.

Jeb and Haus now looked at him, wondering what they should do.

"Hit him again," said Haus.

"I can't," said Jeb.

"What the hell? HIT HIM AGAIN!"

"I can't kill a man who's lying on the ground like that. Wouldn't be right!"

"Well then give it here!" said Haus.

"No, this is my thing to do" said Jeb.

Jeb watched as his friend walked a few paces and picked the gun back up off the ground. "You better do your thing now or I might beat you to it!"

While the two bickered about their murder responsibilities, Franco quickly leapt to his feet and made a staggered run for it. Still drunk but semi-sobered by adrenalin, Franco continued holding his injured shoulder with his left hand as he ran surprisingly fast.

Both Haus and Jeb ran after Franco as they all emerged into the front parking lot. Jeb, longing to keep the attack way from the parking lot lights, took another swing with his bat and grazed Franco across his back. It did Franco no harm.

Using drunken logic that would be his downfall, Franco staggered into the pool area, with no plan of how to go beyond the surrounding fence. Once inside, he turned to face his attackers who blocked his exit. His face was filled with hatred, as if the look itself would repel another attack.

By now, Jeb had no more reservations about getting the job done, as he was terrified Franco might get away, bringing ruination to their plan, and lives.

"Remember that movie, 'SIGNS' with Mel Gibson?" said Haus, breathing heavily.

"Yup," said Jeb, also breathing rapidly.

"Swing away!"

Jeb did, as the bat thumped heavily across the side of Franco's head, twisting him vertically as his body slumped backwards into the pool. After an initial splash, the body bobbed on its back with the rocking waves of the water. Jeb, shocked at what he'd just done, dropped the Louisville Slugger which bounced its way into the pool. With jaw dropped, he stood motionless, his mind churning away with no thought to retrieve the bat.

"I'm going to shoot him now," said Haus. Jeb looked at him, perplexed, dialing in the reasoning for such a suggestion.

'Why? He's dead!"

"We don't know that for sure," said Haus as he stepped closer to the edge of the pool.

"I… I don't know. That will make noise. People will hear it!"

"Too late to worry about that now!"

Haus, now thoroughly fed up with arguing over the matter, raised the gun, and shot one bullet into the head of Franco Hufnagel. The gun produced just a minor cracking noise. Both of the assailants looked toward the hotel to see if any lights would be turned on in the rooms, or curtains pushed aside as tenants peered outside to investigate. Seconds passed, and no one took notice.

"Let's go, man," said Jeb, bolting for the tree line.

Haus did not comply with Jeb's suggestion to run. Instead, he trotted to the other side of the pool where Franco's blood had not yet drifted, and dove into the pool. He remained under water for about ten seconds, jostling about. Jeb scolded him when he resurfaced.

"WHAT THE HELL? WE HAVE TO GO YOU STUPID ASS!"

"I HAVE to get this PUKE off of me, man. If we get pulled over on down the road, you want me having the dead man's puke on me? There might be puke back there on the ground. The police could find out it's a match!"

"When the hell have you ever seen a cop show on TV where they matched puke? Fingerprints… Shoeprints… Tire tracks… yup. But puke? You're a freaking idiot!"

"I don't own a TV you jerk wad, remember?" said Haus.

Jeb could not argue against that point. "Well then, hurry your ass up!" he said as Haus came up the steps of the pool while placing the hood onto his head so as not to be seen.

As they departed, heading for the woods once more, a lonesome motel manager looked out of the office window, wondering what all the commotion was about.

Once they returned to their Bonneville, they sped off into the night with one hell of a story that they'd never be able to tell another soul.

"Man, I can't believe we did it!" said Jeb. "That son of a bitch is DEAD! And we're gonna get busted, I just know it!"

"Don't start that shit man, we are NOT going to get busted. Just drive." Whether Haus would admit it or not, he too was a little shocked at the fact that they had just killed a man, even an evil man like Franco Hufnagel. His mind replayed that day when Franco pointed a gun in his face, and Haus found himself clinging to that memory as justification of what the two of them had just done.

Jeb struggled with their deed as well. He had done what he swore he would do, avenge the death of his son. Only now that the deed had been done, he realized it wasn't going to bring his son back from the dead. In some twisted way, Jeb had thought this act of vigilantism would set things right, but knew how foolish that idea had been. Instead of being a man who was grieving the loss of his son, he was now a murderer who was grieving the loss of his son.

Within the confines of the vehicle, they could more easily smell traces of Hufnagel's vomit which had not been fully removed from the dip in the pool. Haus wound down his passenger window, and stuck his head out the window, using his fingers to help dry out his hair and, hopefully, remove more of the smell. His fingers found chunks in his hair that he knew belonged to Hufnagel which nearly made him sick. The last thing they wanted to do, however, was stop somewhere to remedy the situation. They were now in full flight mode.

Jeb pulled on Haus' dripping wet belt, urging him to stop hanging outside the window. "Dude. We have to Tweet!" he said, as Haus was once more seated inside the car.

"Oh yeah!" Haus removed his cell from the glove compartment and asked Jeb for the password.

"No, gimme the phone. I don't want your puke hands touching the glass."

"You're driving. I can do it."

"Damnit, you better clean it off when you're done."

"Don't worry about it. What's the saying again? Fly Like an Eagle, or something like that?"

"No, you idiot. The eagle has landed." Haus typed it in, but his fat thumbs urged autocorrect to do its duty. Without noticing his mistake, or AutoCorrect's poor attempt at a fix, he sent the message.

Back in Townsend, Mark Powers was nursing a Happy Amber beer from MadTree Brewing in Cincinnati. Normally a little hometown libation would lift his spirits, but not tonight. He drank to quell the fear of something gone wrong. As he sipped, the hour neared 1 a.m. He sat with the beer in his left hand, his cell phone occupying the right. Despite his casual appearance, he was in torment. Tears streamed down his face. He'd set things in motion much earlier, but now he came to regret his actions.

It was too late, and he impatiently refreshed the display every so often, looking for the message they had all agreed upon. Maybe if he saw things had finally ended, he could begin to bury his anxious emotions, and seek some measure of satisfaction in knowing that Franco Hufnagel would never again kill another human being, or another bear, for that matter. Hopefully he could move on, and grow to accept the part he had played in this conspiracy to commit murder.

He prayed to his deceased father to forgive him for straying from the law, but in the next moment, prayed he would be proud of his son for putting an end to an evil man, a man worthy of execution. He attempted to convince his father through prayer that the important thing was that justice had been served, despite not having gone through the courts. The end had justified the means, in Mark's mind. Still, Mark knew he was not really trying to convince his father, but himself. Something in his very soul knew he was just trying to put lipstick on a pig. He'd screwed up, and no amount of justification could make it right.

He prayed to his departed wife. *Look at me, I'm finally praying! You finally got to me. I thought this was about justice, my dear, please forgive me if it was only revenge. I may have blown it, big time. I pray this won't mean I'll never see you again, in heaven, if such a place exists. Just knowing I'll never see you again will be more than enough hell for me to bear.*

He glanced once more at his phone, and refreshed the Twitter app. He could not believe his eyes. There it was, the Tweet he had hoped to see from Jeb, published for all the internet to see, but for no one to understand except for himself and his two cohorts. He blinked a few times, thinking perhaps the beer had affected his vision, but he was not mistaken. It said:

"The Eagle has Lenses."

Chapter 28

A cold front was blowing into the Nashville area, dark clouds gathering in the western skies, while sunshine retreated to the east. Isabella Lopez could see the darkness in her rear view mirror, like some bluish gray pillows piled against her rear window. She was dragging her way through rush hour traffic, hoping to make it back to her apartment before the rain consumed the town.

Her purple Prius, tagged with a license plate of **N8TR1ST**, was running low on its charge. A distant lightning strike appeared in her rear view, causing her to ponder the viability of electric cars outfitted with lightning strike receptors. She could not fathom the scientific details but considered how great it could be for the environment if a nation of electric car drivers could catch that natural source of electricity and store it for future mobility needs. Surely she would also be in line to be a recipient of an NAEP Environmental Excellence Award with such an idea.

She was listening to NPR on her radio when they broke for a local news update. Normally she would only listen half-attentively while she thought of other matters that weighed heavy on her mind, but this time a story caught her ear. She turned up the radio in time to hear authorities announced earlier that day that Talia Manaia, one of those critically injured during the Echo Ridge shootings, had emerged from a coma and was now being questioned by police.

Isabella's heart-rate kicked up a few paces at the news. She had been so worried about her comrade, but unwilling to visit the hospital for fear someone might ask how the two knew each other. With this news, she hoped perhaps she'd be able to rendezvous with Talia once she was checked out of the hospital. She wanted to share details with Talia about things that had happened while in the coma, such as how the shooting played out on that mountain, the FBI inquiries, Banister's disappearance, etc. It would be important for them to be on the same page when talking to the authorities. Unfortunately for Isabella, Talia had already revealed her own story.

Isabella was temporarily living in an efficiency above the garage of Janet's biggest financial supporter, the man who she'd had a fling with in college. He was divorced, and she knew he had ulterior motives by letting her stay on his property. It would be just a matter of time when he began inviting her over for dinner, then watching a movie, and that of course would lead to what he really wanted. But the key thing for her now, was that she was not tied down in any way in case she needed to flee at a moment's notice. She had limited personal belongings and kept a go bag in the Prius. She would begin seeking opportunities in the D.C. area, and use the money she had gotten from Banister for her part in the shooting to settle into a nice, green condo in the part of town where all the movers and shakers lived.

Her new job was mostly clerical, and boring but also temporary. No longer did she have access to inside information to topple Republican eco-terrorism agendas.

She had operated under the radar then, in a buildup to greatness. Now she flew under the radar to keep from being incarcerated. *This too shall pass*, she thought, knowing her future looked bright. *If I can just lay low for a year or so, this will all just go away.*

She was in the process of retrieving her charging cable from the garage when she heard another vehicle pull into the driveway behind her own. Cautiously she walked out from the garage to see who was there.

"Well if it isn't my favorite little Snowflake!" said Shane Goodwyn while exiting his truck. She was angered that he had the nerve to come onto her turf.

"I'm not a snowflake, I'm not little, and I'm certainly not yours," quipped Isabella as she turned to go into the garage where she pressed the button to close the garage door.

Shane jumped down from the driver's side of his truck which sported wheels that were nearly the size of Isabella's Prius. He was well dressed on this occasion, wearing a sports jacket, bolo tie, nice jeans, a cowboy hat, and pointy armadillo boots. Isabella had hoped she'd never see him again. Not impressed by her cold welcome, Shane moved toward the half closed garage door, grabbed the handle from the outside and gave it a good tug. Instantly the door reversed its direction.

He began speaking to her while his face was still obscured by the rising garage door. "They make these things so they won't accidentally close on a kid, or something. Good thing for me, don't you know?"

"I don't want you here. Leave... Now!" shouted Isabella. "You are breaking and entering. I'll call the police!"

"Holy smokes girl, you really need to take a lesson in southern hospitality from us good ol' boys. I was hoping maybe you'd invite me up to your apartment for a little bit of that Latino food you eat. I could go for some goat-meat fajitas right about now. Protein!" he said, flexing his right bicep, although unseen through the sleeve of his jacket.

"I have a Taser and I will use it on you if you don't leave immediately," warned Isabella as she clutched the device within her purse.

"No match for this bad boy," said Shane, pulling his Houston H9 from a holster hidden beneath his sports jacket. "You know, I love this gun. I went without it for a while, so the feds could test it. Turns out they didn't need to. Wrong bullets, you see. I can tell you, they really wanted me to be guilty, but that didn't happen, now did it? Whoo-hoo, another husband set free from the misguided prejudice of society. But then again, I got a feeling you know a little something about all that. You knew I didn't kill my wife, now isn't that right?"

Isabella was now fearing for her life. Because he was such a gun advocate, she incorrectly believed he would shoot her for sport, if he so desired. She slowly loosened her grip on the Taser within her purse, fearing he would shoot her before she could put it to good use.

"Yeah, be careful there Snowflake, don't go pulling anything else out of that purse that might do me more harm than the Taser."

"Don't be serious. I would never own a gun. Guns are for mentally unstable people, like you."

"Always quick with an insult for freedom loving patriots, just like a true lefty. Where is the tolerance? Where is the love? I'm thinking these days your breed has given up on all that."

"Putting flowers in the barrels of guns was a 60's thing. That didn't work, obviously. So now, to win against haters like you, we must fight fire with fire."

"Oh, so you would use a gun against me even though you hate guns. Just because you say I'm a hater. Sounds logical. Right! It's all just a bunch of cockamamie BS! Look, I don't hate anybody, sweetheart. I just get a little agitated when your kind tells me what I'm allowed to say and what I'm not allowed to say. What I should do and what I'm not allowed to do. Who I want for president, and who I don't want for president. And you're always commanding the language, and limiting freedom of speech. How many amendments is it again that you want to get rid of? I'm starting to lose count."

Isabella still had not removed her hand from her purse.

"Let's just see what you have in there," Shane suggested, as he creeped forward. He flickered his fingers on his free hand, signifying he wanted her to give him the purse. Reluctantly she did so. He kept the barrel of his gun pointed in her direction while he put the purse under his shooting arm, then pulled items out of her purse with his left hand.

"Keys, mm-hmm, lipstick... what is this? Oh, a birth control... now ain't that a little awkward, but we're all adults here. Well, just like I thought, one thing you don't have in here is the gun you stole from me. I knew that would be impossible, and do you know why? Because you left it up on that trail. Didn't you, Snowflake?"

"What are you talking about?" said Isabella, curious as he knew that.

"My experimental Houston H4 Prototype. I have to admit, I was a little confused when I noticed it was missing, trying to think of who would have wanted an old prototype weapon that was never sold to the public. But now I'm guessing you just grabbed whatever was closest to the door that night of our party, since you don't really know shit about guns. Or maybe you grabbed the smallest one, thinking you'd need to keep it hidden, which is pretty smart of you, I'd say. And it didn't hurt that it has a micro suppressor, now did it."

He was absolutely right about Isabella having stolen his gun, but she was not about to acknowledge his statement.

"I bet you had a helluva time getting ammo. Didn't you? The Houston team wanted to make a really small-ass pistol with a suppressor so they even went with a slightly smaller round, an 8mm baby bullet. Very rare these days for a pistol to take anything but a niner. Let me guess, you had to buy the ammo on the internet, didn't you?"

Again, he was absolutely right, although it was Banister who had taken care of finding the ammo, not Isabella. Banister had ridiculed her by saying she should have stolen a gun that had standard sized bullets. Yet Isabella reveled in the idea of killing the governor with one of her husband's guns, and she did like it's small profile. She insisted they use the stolen weapon, in case they could use it to frame Shane for his wife's murder, and with enough persuasion, Banister went along with her plan. In the end it would be her undoing.

She knew it was futile to deny Shane's charges. He knew too much.

"How did you know I took the gun, and not someone else?" she asked.

"How do you like that? An admission of guilt. Well, let me tell you. I'd like to say I had my house wired on the inside with cameras but I did not. You know, I was a bit of a fool to display these guns at a dinner party like that without some kind of security. I guess when you are passionate about something, like I am, you want to share it with people. And I really thought I could trust everyone there that night. Everyone there was a conservative... except for you. But no, there were no cameras. Took me a long time to realize that one of my guns was even gone. I should have paid more attention. But now... yes, NOW I have cameras inside and out. Thanks to you."

Isabella knew he was enjoying this moment, dragging everything out for full dramatic effect, but he still had not fully answered her question. Yes, he knew the gun had been taken at the dinner party, but how did you absolutely know it was taken by her? She crossed her arms and tilted her head, displaying a look that communicated to Shane that she was still waiting to know how he knew she'd taken the gun.

"Do you listen to talk radio, darlin'?"

She nodded in the negative, rolling her eyes in the process.

"Oh, you really should try it sometimes instead of the fake newsy liberal crap you listen to. Just yesterday I heard on a Knoxville talk show about the investigation. Somebody on that show was a real journalist and did some research. I was so proud of them for announcing the coroner found an 8mm 8 X 22 slug in my wife's chest. That kind of detail don't show up in the regular news, you know. It took me a while, but that news finally sank in. I thought to myself, 8mm? *8 X 22? Holy crap, that really is a strange one*, and I wondered to myself what kind of guns might take that kind of a round. And what do you know... the gun that was stolen from me took an 8mm round. Now isn't that a coincidence? An 8mm is pretty rare, and so most likely, I figured whoever stole THAT gun probably shot MY wife. Then I thought, who would have been at that party, AND up on that mountain that day? SNOWFLAKE! Damned if the FBI shouldn't pay me for doing their job, you know what I mean?"

Isabella knew the gig was up, but being held at gunpoint gave her no options. Still she remained silent, and endured Shane's diatribe.

"Oh, and then I thought back on my second interview with that sassy FBI chick, and they told me my wife's last words were 'Shane... did it'. Well, given that I know for sure that I did NOT do it, and I know for sure my wife would not lie about that on her deathbed, I had to think hard about who the liar really was in that situation. I knew it was you and Mark Powers who were with her when she died, right? No doubt it was one of the two of you that twisted the truth a little bit. And let's be honest. I know you hate me. It had to be you. And then it hit me. My wife wasn't trying to say that 'Shane did it,' she was trying to say that 'She did it,' meaning you, little darlin'. Or maybe 'Snowflake did it!' Nah, I'm just kiddin' about that one. But sure enough I would have said it if that was me on the ground, for sure.

"And if all that ain't enough, this morning at a coffee shop, I sat there drinking a plain black coffee, reading the paper, thinking about what I should do about you, and Lordy, Lordy, I found out even more about the murder of my wife on page six. Seems they found the murder weapon on the trail coming down the mountain. A Houston H4, the gun you stole from me. I hope you do realize that gun was never sold to the public. I'm one of just 12 people on the planet who own one of those. So that's the long answer for why I know the gun would not be in your purse just now. Although, there is a chance you came to love guns after you used one for a while, and maybe you have a little something else tucked away in there that you might shoot me with, now that you're cornered. So do you?"

Isabella did not reply. The Taser was all she had. All she could think of was running. But as long as he pointed the gun at her, she was frozen.

"So now what? Is that what you want to know? Am I going to shoot you? No. I'm not, unless you make a run for it. This here is a citizen's arrest. I have the right to hold you until the FBI arrives. And gol-dern-it, traffic must be a little congested because they should have been here by now. No, contrary to what you probably think about us bitter clingers in fly-over country, we're generally not a violent breed. We like to protect ourselves, and our loved ones, our property and in other cases our livestock. And maybe we shoot for sport or to hunt, but we generally don't go out and shoot people just because we disagree with their politics. We may 'cling' to our guns, and we 'cling' to our Bibles, but honey those are good things to cling to, even though you lefties try to tell the world they ain't. Maybe you've heard the Bible calls murder a sin. Now granted, I have committed my share of sins — I'm not as perfect as most people think I am — but murder is not one of them. You on the other hand, well, I'm afraid that's a mighty big sin. That makes you a sinner. I recommend you start praying right about now."

His sermon was over and there was silence between them, but only for a moment. Isabella paused, then replied. "Don't act like you didn't want to do the same thing. I saw you argue with Janet. You hated her, I just know it!"

"So an argument with a spouse is grounds for killing them? Maybe in your world, Snowflake, but not mine. Not even close. I do have an eye for the ladies, that's a fact, but I loved only one, and chose her to be my wife. She loved me for who I am, never tried to change me. Okay, that's a stretch, she did, but only just a little. Seems I have a knack for saying the wrong thing sometimes so she wanted me to be a little more 'reserved' at her political shin-digs. Still need to work on that I guess. But no, I never cheated on her. I may not show my deepest emotions on my sleeve, but Janet was everything to me. And now I know for sure YOU are the one who took her from me."

"So why don't you just go ahead and kill me?" asked Isabella.

"Sounds like you pay a little too much attention to Hollywood movies where killing other people comes a little too easily. Besides, that'd be takin' it a little too easy on you. The quick way out. I wanted to see your face when I told you how I knew it was you. I wanted to see you squirm. And you, my dear, look pretty uncomfortable right about now. For me, this is priceless. There's that, and the fact that I called the FBI is on their way. Might not work out so well for me if I shot you and then they showed up."

Isabella now remained quiet, thinking through all that had transpired, wondering why she had ever volunteered to be the second shooter.

"Snowflake. Tell me one thing. Why on earth would you shoot Janet with a pistol? You HAD to know that the autopsy would show the bullet was not from the sniper, and then they'd be investigating those of us who were on that hike that day. That really improved the odds of you getting caught."

"I thought I could get the gun back into your house, to make it look like you were the one who killed her."

"Looks like you thought wrong, Snowflake."

Moments later, several black vehicles sped onto the scene and agents emerged from their cars with weapons drawn. It was time for Isabella to face the music for her deeds upon Thunderhead Mountain.

Chapter 29

Several Months before the Shooting

On a cold and windy night, individuals gathered at a cabin tucked back in the woods near Cherokee, NC. Winter still held its grip on the region, with gusting winds and flurries threatening to transform the rain into a snowstorm at any minute. Outside by the main entrance was a massive pile of lumber, enough to last throughout the winter, chopped into precise pie-shaped wedges by the cabin's owner. Inside, a fire roared in an oversized hearth, designed for cooking around the fire. Metal racks contained an array of pewter cookware, hanging at the ready, in case a feast were needed to be prepared by fire.

Gathered there was an unlikely troop, some from positions of power, activists, and yet others were employees of the park service. They sat around an impressive wooden table with no chair unused. At the head of the table sat Craig Banister, nervous, but eager, to start the meeting. He had learned long ago never to let anyone know you lack confidence, and to fake it until you make it. He would do that again tonight. He looked at his watch, and was irritated.

"He said he'd be here by dark," said Isabella Lopez, in charge of making contact with their very special guest. "I'd call him but I only have one bar," referring to her phone. She was irritated that Banister lived so remotely, and would have preferred meeting in a more civilized environment. She was uncomfortable with rustic, and preferred cosmopolitan. She had reasons of her own to be nervous. She stood to be a key player in the drama that was being finalized that evening. She'd never killed anyone before, but knew that protecting the region's last remaining wilderness would require drastic measures. Like a delicate egg, Thunderhead was about to be cracked open, and marred by commercial development. She would commit to whatever it might take to keep that from happening. Killing an innocent would be too much to ask, but to kill the primary proponent of Echo Ridge was morally doable. Even if it was Isabella's boss.

Another woman sat across from Isabella. She was more bored than irritated. Her back was aching as it often did, a remnant of having the razor-sharp tusk of a wild boar slice through her rib cage, nearly killing her years earlier. A change in the weather always made it worse. Much of Talia's work had already been done prior to this meeting, as she had been charged with gathering information that ultimately led to their guest's hiring after nearly a month of searching.

"Are we sure this is the right guy for the job?" asked Banister, staring at Isabella, still messing with her phone.

"I believe he is, but don't look at me. You picked him. I don't want the blame if he doesn't work out."

"I'm not trying to pin anything on you, I'm merely looking for reassurances. None of us have killed anyone before. At least not that I'm aware of. It's a little unsettling."

Two other men sat at the table, at the farthest end from Banister. They were the Thompson brothers, with Joe the oldest at 32, and John the youngest at 28. Both were founding fathers of EarthForce1, and both reported to the top dog in the organization, Craig Banister. "It's alright, boss," said Joe, sensing Banister was nervous despite his attempts to hide it. Joe was handsomely sporting an imitation leather jacket, and sat in a relaxed position, one ankle on his other knee. "This is war. And in war there are always casualties."

"You're saying this to a Vietnam vet?" replied Banister. He was not offended, but amused at the younger man's attempt to share such wisdom with a Purple Heart recipient.

"I'm just saying, we shouldn't forget why we're doing this.

"I may be old, but I'm not forgetful," replied Banister.

"Protecting this wilderness is surely worth sacrificing just one of seven-and-a-half billion human lives that are overcrowding the planet and leading to its demise. What's one less carbon footprint to worry about?" said Joe. He was Isabella's lover. The two of them met while forming EarthForce1 along with a number of their faculty, while in college. There they met Craig Banister who was teaching Environmental Studies as an adjunct. EarthForce1 would not have happened without Banister's deep pockets, and his ability to raise money from other high net worth individuals who were passionate about protecting the environment, particularly in the southern part of the United States where they lived.

John took notice of the exchange his brother had just had with Banister and decided to keep a low profile for the rest of the meeting. He was the one who would be orchestrating all of the local protests, and was aggressively opposed to Echo Ridge as anyone else in the room, probably more so.

Banister's German shepherd went crazy and began barking at a sound not yet heard by those around the table. Seconds later, headlights from an approaching vehicle shone through the living room window of the cabin. Banister reached to grab for the dog's collar and held him firmly until the guest entered through the front door. Everyone noticed the temperature drop with the man's entry, yet Franco Hufnagel felt only a welcoming burst of heat.

Isabella rose and went to greet him. Banister would have done the same, but he was occupied with the dog. Everyone rose from the table and greeted Franco with a firm handshake. An extra chair was pulled from below a window sill and placed at the table for their guest, providing him a look down the table at his newest client, Craig Banister.

Once seated, Banister released his dog, who quickly galloped over to sniff the stranger's leg with a low-level growl, followed by a few vicious barks. It occurred to Franco the dog just might be smelling bear. Banister chastised the animal verbally, causing the dog to retreat.

"This is quite a welcoming committee," said Franco. "I've never been hired by a group like this before. I'm usually called because of turf wars, drugs and money. But you people are tree huggers, hiring a hit man. Pretty weird." He said this with a certain degree of mistrust. He knew having too many people involved in a hit increased the risk of being caught. He preferred to get his marching orders from a solitary boss in the Dixie Mafia.

"It's okay, we don't bite," said Banister. "It's a funny set of circumstances that we're doing business, isn't it?"

"I guess. We ain't done the job yet, so I would not say anything is funny. This is serious business as far as I'm concerned," replied Hufnagel.

"For those of you who don't know the story," said Banister, "when Joe submitted this crazy idea, none of us had any clue how to hire a sniper. Talia, here, told me that one of our law enforcement rangers had a long standing feud with Mr. Hufnagel, an accomplished gun runner and pot grower in the area. Now, I was none too happy about hiring someone who's been growing pot in our park, and I'm STILL not happy about it. But I networked with my friends in the so called Dixie Mafia, and who did they recommend? Mr. Franco Hufnagel, who has worked for them many times in the past."

"I'm not into the pot thing anymore, by the way. That was just a part time gig. I'm working with a butcher these days, totally legit!" added Franco. He reminded himself never to mention his poaching activities to the superintendent of the park, as Banister would turn on him in an instant if he found out.

"A reformed pot grower now, he says," said Banister, followed by hearty laughter. "It's okay, Mr. Hufnagel, I've run with shady characters all my life. Started with moonshining when I was a very young tot, right here in the park. It was right after prohibition ended, but there was still a demand for our moonshine. You know professional auto racing has its roots in my people. That's right, we delivered liquor quicker in our souped-up roadsters, and the chase eventually turned into competitions. But I digress... when they recommended you, I did a little checking around, thanks to some info our Talia came up with, we agreed to give you a shot. Literally."

"The history lesson is nice, but I just want to get this over with, if you don't mind, Mr. Banister. Weather's getting bad out there, and I have a long drive back to my place. So can we get started?"

"By all means. Mr. Hufnagel, it's a sorry state of affairs that brings us to this moment. Never in all my years would I have dreamed I'd be paying a man to kill another human being. But our hands are tied. As a group, we'll work as hard as it takes to prevent our little slice of heaven to be desecrated by commercial development. But despite our efforts, politically and with protests, I just don't think it will be enough. I, like everyone around this table, believe Echo Ridge will become a reality without drastic intervention. The governor has already gotten clearance from the legislature and shored up funding. I have opposed this, and still have some latitude for further opposition, yet, my boss is a conservative, and I'm on thin ice with all my efforts to stop the development. I'm working hard to keep up appearances, to appear neutral. I can't let my true colors show, you see. I'll do EarthForce1 no good if I'm out of this particular job, so it's a delicate balancing act."

Franco sat in disbelief that the old man was going on such a long tangent. Hadn't he just been asked to make it quick? But his wait for a payoff was about to end.

"I've not shared this next bit of info with anyone in our group," continued Banister, "but thanks to some reconnaissance from Ms. Lopez, this governor has a special committee researching the idea of fracking and drilling within the park. Just like Echo Ridge, she's blocked the media from having access to planning meetings. Fracking... here. That's right. It seems inconceivable, but it's true.

"And that's not all she has in the works. She has recently voiced intentions to help Monsanto build a new chemical treatment plant in Chatsworth, just 2 miles from the park's border on the south-western side. Oh, yes, there will be plenty of jobs, but there will be risks to the water table. In a few short months, Janet Goodwyn has become eco-enemy number one for all of us in this room.

"If we remove the governor, I believe we can disrupt the machinations of progress on Echo Ridge, fracking, and the chemical plant. She is the primary driver of these endeavors, but if she were to disappear, I believe we can undermine support for her projects. Echo Ridge alone may seem like a trivial reason for our actions to our political foes, but Echo Ridge is just the start. We are the brave ones to draw a line in the sand and refuse to yield to this ill-conceived progress, for it is not really progress at all. Have we not learned the lessons of our mistreatment of our natural resources, time and time again? I'm old enough to remember the strip-mining that took place in our region, and it was devastating. I am determined we will not relive those ecological horrors again. I do not like that we have to take a life. It is an extreme measure, no doubt. If there's a God, I hope we will be forgiven for what we will do together. But I'm not convinced there's anyone up there listening, and thus our destiny is in our own hands."

Banister's speech was effective at inciting more loyalty in the room. Granted, everyone was already on board, and dedicated to their cause; they would have followed him even without the speech. But hearing the F word — *fracking* — sent chills down their spines that the park might someday be sitting on a not-so-solid foundation due to natural gas extraction below the surface. And the M word — *Monsanto* — was the icing on the cake.

Hufnagel, still concerned with getting out before the storm hit, began asking questions about his role in the assassination of the governor. The back and forth went on for more than an hour. One of the discussion points had to do with fallback measures in case he could not succeed with the hit.

"It is our expectation that you will kill Governor Goodwyn with one or two shots," said Banister. "Still, the best laid plans sometimes don't get laid. If some unforeseen incident keeps you from making your way to the shooting location, or if you have equipment difficulties that prevent you from initiating your business, all bets are off. We will have lost an opportunity to make our statement. But there's another scenario to consider.

"Let's suppose you manage to begin shooting, but the governor takes cover. If you find you simply cannot hit your target, your mission will change. We would then want you to continue shooting to generate an environment of chaos. We will have a second shooter embedded within the groundbreaking party, who will remain close to the governor. While you continue shooting, we'll make an attempt to hit our mark at close range. She will make an assessment at the time as to how viable that shot might be, and if it appears too likely that she would be seen or heard by anyone else there, she will abort. Again, this leaves us with a failed attempt. But we have talked this over at length, and feel the rangers who will be on duty at that time will be so focused on defending against a sniper they will not notice a second shooter, if that shooter conducts herself with great discretion. We have the element of surprise working in our favor."

"And who might this second shooter be?" asked Franco.

"Isabella Lopez, here, is the governor's personal assistant. Having her on the inside is a grand advantage for us. She's the logical best choice for a backup shooter. She will be very close to the governor. If she believes something has gone wrong, she will attempt to use a small pistol, outfitted with a suppressor, to kill the governor."

"It's a chance I'm willing to take," said Isabella, proudly. "We have one chance to make this statement, and I will do whatever it takes to make sure the governor only leaves that mountaintop in a body bag."

Banister grimaced at her tone. He was not reveling in their plans to kill the governor. For him it was a very unfortunate, and terrible thing they planned to do, but it needed to be done. He did not like hearing anyone on his team show such crass braggadocio regarding the assassination. On the other hand, perhaps it was a good thing Isabella was turbo-charged, emotionally, to get the job done. He would not want anyone who was wishy-washy about the job to be the one with the gun in their hand.

"I'm still not gettin' somethin' here," asked Franco. "Why not just have the lovely Lopez slip a little something in the governor's drink and take her out that way, long before they are ready to start construction? Why do you even need me? Why are you planning this in such a public way, like it's some kind of execution?"

"Because it IS a public execution. The groundbreaking ceremony would be the ideal time to send a message to developers, and the world, that this will not do. There she'll be, in her moment of political glory, up on that mountain, ready to take the very first incremental step in that development, only to lose her life in doing so. We know there will be media present, so the images will spread near and far. The Thompson brothers, will be in charge of following up with demonstrations all over the state, to bring power to the people. And of course, we will get plenty of ongoing media coverage, that's a foregone conclusion, you see. We will have additional documents to share with them regarding the fracking and chemical plant, all of which the public has not yet heard about. All of this will create the perfect storm, and have a tremendous impact on Goodwyn's backers, and anyone else who'd ever consider a similar scar on the wilderness. We've considered the risks, but the rewards must also be taken into account. The bottom line is that we want it to be public."

"Okay," said Franco, "now that you put it that way, it looks like you do need me. Me and 'logical choice' Lopez over there."

"I AM the logical choice. Do you have a problem with that?" said Lopez.

"Maybe. Have you ever killed anyone before?"

"No."

"Have you ever shot an animal before?"

"No."

"Wow. Okay, how about... have you ever shot a gun before?"

"I've been practicing."

"Well then what the hell? Yes, I do have a problem with this!"

Isabella was telling the truth, but not the whole truth. She opposed guns as part of her world view, but knowing a gun would now further her political ambitions, she was willing to make an exception.

"Ah," replied Banister, "She's been practicing at an indoor facility in Nashville and here on my property, when she can get away. She's a natural. The key will be to fire at close range, if possible, and she will be closer than anyone. She will do fine." He turned to Isabella and said, "Why don't you tell everyone about your weapon of choice?"

With that, Isabella reached into her purse and withdrew a micro-pistol. It was a tiny little thing, and outfitted with a miniature suppressor, or silencer, as it is also called.

"There is a little irony here," she said. "I took this gun from the governor's arsenal, in their home. They have so many guns, they will never know this one is missing. There is a fine sense of social justice in knowing she will be killed with one of her husband's weapons. If it comes down to me to take the shot, my plan is to leave the gun in the woods without being seen, as soon as I can. I can't keep it in my backpack because there's a chance they might search everyone after the shooting. I don't want to run that risk, so I will dump it. Then, whenever the opportunity might present itself, Joe and I will return to find it. I will then slip it into the Goodwyn's home because I know their security code. Then I will notify the authorities. They would then find the gun in his house, match it to the bullet that killed his wife, and he will be arrested."

"It's too complicated," objected Hufnagel. "That'll never happen. You obviously have never planned a hit before because you gotta keep it simple."

"It's alright Mr. Hufnagel," said Banister. "If you are as good as you say you are, there will be no need for her services. Right?"

Franco's expression showed that he felt Banister had made a good point, but he decided to continue with his objections anyway.

"Still, as a contingency plan, she's a horrible choice. Isabella, what if you shoot the governor, and someone actually sees you do it? Then what?"

"She surrenders," replied Banister. "She'll put the gun down, put her hands behind her head, and surrender. We want her to remain alive, and as long as she's in the surrender position, the rangers will not shoot her."

"Mr. Hufnagel," continued Isabella, "we've already discussed a number of scenarios, and that is one of them. Like Craig said, why don't you focus on what you will be doing that day so none of my scenarios are necessary?" Her venomous tone signaled Banister to lighten things up.

"Indeed, Mr. Hufnagel, we have planned this all very thoroughly. Remember, you don't want to be here too late, why don't we return to a discussion on Plan A... your plan."

"Whatever," said Franco. "You're the man with the plan. I'm just glad this dame ain't gonna be near me when I'm doing my job, you can do what you want."

Despite Hufnagel's criticism, Isabella was excited about her role. She tried not to see the governor as a woman, or even as a human being. She saw Janet Goodwyn as a greedy capitalist politician, an enemy of the environment. As she practiced firing the gun in a field next to Banister's cabin, she would envision the glory of ridding the world of such a wretch.

One thing Isabella could not practice was the emotional impact she would experience when she finally did shoot the governor. Franco's concerns were warranted. When it finally happened, the look on the governor's face would send emotional tidal waves through Isabella's body and mind, interrupting her ability to execute her mission as planned. As it would turn out, Isabella would be successful in taking a shot from a crouching position and do so without being seen by anyone. But after the shot, she would freeze in the moment, drop her gun amongst the undergrowth, and inexplicably walk over to where the governor had fallen. Seconds would pass as if she were in a fog, as if totally unaware that she'd neglected to dispense of her gun properly. But just as it had come upon her, the fog lifted and she was aware that she now had to act naturally, as if she had just discovered the governor had been shot by the sniper. From that point on, she was vying for an Academy Award. She realized a good scream would be a natural reaction to seeing her boss shot and dying on the ground, so she let one fly.

Prior to the moment when Mark Powers led the group back down the mountain, Isabella returned to get her backpack and cautiously slipped her gun within. Later, when Powers mentioned the FBI were soon to arrive, she made the suggestion they stop for a 'bathroom break.' She slipped off into the deep woods, relieved herself, and placed the gun under a rock. She took note of where she'd left it, based on sign markers along the trail, and she planned to return with her team members to retrieve the at a later time.

There would be one person to see Isabella shoot her compact pistol: Talia Manaia. That would hardly matter since she and Isabella were on the same team… at least until Talia was pressured to tell the FBI what had really happened.

Banister was trying to restart the conversation, with the focus on Franco's involvement. "We trust you will do your job well, Mr. Hufnagel. It is important that you get a clear shot of the governor. I do need to inform you that we will have two of our own on that mountain who we do not want to be in harm's way. Isabella will be there for sure, and possibly others I hope to invite from the Sierra Club and the EPA. As for me, I plan to take my time getting up that trail, and I intend to play the age card. Hopefully I will not be in that clearing when all hell breaks loose. I wish to avoid standing next to the governor for the photo shoot, especially since you're going to be shooting at her from that kind of distance. I will find reason to delay. Talia will offer to assist me and stay with me along the approach so we never reach the bald. But as for the others, Franco, you are NOT to shoot Isabella or the others I invite. I'll send you their photos from my phone if they accept my invitation. That is, if I can figure out how to do that on my phone. Do you understand?"

"Whatever you say, Chief. You have nothing to worry about. I've got guns that can drop a rhino in the dust from a half-mile out, with just one round."

Everyone in the room loved animals, and his rhino comment just cost him any respect they had given him for starters. After their initial discomfort was over, it was Banister that broke the silence.

"Mr. Hufnagel, I have to be honest with you. I feel as though I'm making a pact with a mortal enemy, as we apparently see things quite differently. But the fact is, we need you. I hope you are right that you can get the job done, and easily. I just plead with you not to pull that trigger until you're assured Isabella, and other guests of mine are a safe distance away from the governor." It seemed redundant, and so Hufnagel affirmed the remark with a nod.

"By the way, Mr. Hufnagel, you had requested we turn over to you the document that was in the possession of Special Agent Mark Powers... your profile he'd been keeping on you over the years. So here you go," said Banister, sliding a USB drive across the table and into Franco's right hand. Franco had no real use of it, but was curious what kinds of details Powers may have found worthy of storage. Franco particularly wanted to read Mark's account of his wife's death, knowing how excruciating that must have been for him.

"It's ironic," continued Banister, "that one of our own has been keeping track of you for decades, and you are the one we've selected for this job. I think you'll be happy to learn he did not have any recent information about your whereabouts. That was unfortunate for us because it was harder to locate you ourselves."

"Then how DID you find me?" asked Franco.

"Did I not mention that you come highly recommended by the Dixie Mafia? They gave me your contact information."

"I do my best to remain invisible," replied Franco. "It kind of pisses me off that they offered me up, to tell the truth. Nobody in this room's gonna say a peep about me, you got that? Don't get me wrong, this is a helluva good payday, I'm just concerned about loose lips. Don't want my name out there, if you know what I mean."

"We all understand that," said Banister. "That goes both ways. No one is to know we have hired you, or that any of us are in affiliation with one another in any way. We are a secret society, to borrow a phrase from the olden days. And... speaking of money, you will leave here tonight with $10,000 in good faith money. Should you succeed with the task, you will receive the full balance within a week from the date. But as we have agreed upon, you will receive only half of that if Isabella pulls the trigger. Is that understood?"

"Sure. I get it. But if I have my way, Lopez over there ain't goin' to see a shiny penny of it. I'm going to drop the gov in her tracks. For this kind of money, I could put a bullet up a gnat's ass on the moon with my eyes closed."

Isabella was beginning to dislike Hufnagel. While she certainly hoped he would succeed in shooting the governor, she considered his failure could result in a major cash infusion into her bank account.

Chapter 30

The next night Mark was at the scene of the crime. He sat in his car along the highway, a safe distance from the motel. He used his binoculars to watch the evidence collection unit do its job. They were there for hours, checking the pool filters, tagging anything that looked like it could be evidence with little yellow, numbered, plastic triangles. But it was not the ECU he was interested in, but the FBI. He plainly saw Sandy Toney, Tom Luken and Jeannine Gallenstein, each taking notes feverishly and speaking to the motel manager. It was well after dark when they left. Only then did Mark, driving his own pickup truck, drive into the parking lot of the motel. He had to see things for himself.

Franco's body was no longer there, but his evil spirit still lingered. There were a few State Troopers present, along with the evidence team who would be busy well into the morning. Mark went to speak to the motel manager, who was in no mood to replay the events once more, until Mark revealed the story of how the victim had killed Laurie. Then the manager had a change of heart and replayed events to him, just as he had to the FBI.

In time, Mark meandered over to the pool and sat down in a lounge chair. He removed his cell phone, cradled it into the claw of a selfie stick. He'd come up with a smokescreen idea, a way that might help keep his peers off of his trail as a co-conspirator. He would shoot another Wandering Ranger video. Why? Because that would be his natural behavior, and he needed to appear as natural as possible.

Many thoughts were flooding his mind. He was wondering where Jeb and Haus might be at that very moment. He thought back to the previous evening. While the two young men were down south, Mark remained in Gatlinburg, waiting for the first tweet: "Bored. Think I'll go shopping." Once it came, he sprang into action.

Before leaving his house, he'd given himself a makeover that he believed was very accurate. He opened the bag he'd been given by Jeb, and did an inventory of what was there. He'd gotten a wig out of an old trunk; a wig Laurie had used several times for Halloween. It was too long, but at least it was the right color. He cut it down, hoping it would look alright, but then he knew that would be a detail easily overlooked. He'd used a marker to simulate the tattoos Jeb had on the upside of his forearms, and used a woman's concealer makeup to cover up his own. He even shaved off strategic parts of his beard, leaving bushy sideburns, and a dainty goatee. Once he donned the Red Man hat, and looked in the mirror, he was amazed at how much he looked like Jeb. It was then he headed for town.

Parked on a back street where he knew there were no closed circuit cameras, he walked to the main strip. He wanted no evidence of him getting out of his truck dressed like Jeb. Along the way he passed a restaurant he knew was once a LUMS location. He remembered they had great steak fries, his favorite place to eat when he was on vacation. He was under a lot of stress, at this moment, and the childhood memory gave him a respite before returning to what he knew was a mistake. He knew he was doing the wrong thing, but proceeded anyway.

He was compromising his core moral principles, but it was too late to turn back.

Mark meandered up and down the main strip, trying to keep from engaging in much eye contact. Now that he was clear of his truck, his goal shifted to seeking out closed circuit cameras which he knew were used to monitor mostly intersections. Thus, he crisscrossed his way numerous times via numerous crosswalks. His goal was to be recorded, even if he was avoiding personal interaction with just about anyone.

Twice that night, with the brim of the ball cap kept low, he used a particular ATM to remove money from Jeb's bank account. He had seen surveillance from that ATM in the past, and it did not have a camera built into the unit at eye level. Rather, the camera was elevated and off to the side. He hoped he'd look just like Jeb, without a direct view of his face.

He stopped the charade at 11:00 pm. He'd been watching his phone, hoping to see a tweet, but it came much later in the night. Still, he'd done his job, or at least he thought he had. If Jeb should be questioned for the death of Franco Hufnagel, there would be evidence that he had been walking the streets of Gatlinburg that night.

Now his mind snapped back into the moment, as he sat next to the pool. He had a job to do. He focused on what he wanted to say in the video. Once he was ready, he began recording.

Video Transcript:
Wandering Ranger #28
(YouTube Channel)

Visual Description:

START VIDEO: Special Agent Mark Powers of the GSMNP talking to camera, poolside, sitting on a deck chair. It is night time, pool area is illuminated by above-head lighting. Other evidence collection personnel are seen in the background, examining the scene of the crime.

Audio Script:

Hello everyone, welcome to the latest Wandering Ranger video. My subscribers know that I do my best to show what the life of a park ranger is like, day to day, and I tend to get a little nostalgic about the Smoky Mountains in the process. But this time we have a situation that is definitely out of the ordinary. It's really gotten me to thinking about life, a little bit. Let me do my nostalgia thing first, then I'll pose a question for you to ponder.

Mark was struggling. He had to put on his happy face, and show the world the same Mark Powers they had come to expect. If he did this right, it might help obscure the fact he was involved with this crime, and keep his fellow law enforcement professionals from suspecting someone within their own ranks.

Let me do my nostalgia thing first, then I'll pose a question for you to ponder.

When I was a kid, my family vacationed in the Smokies every year. I thought it was the coolest place on earth. That's why I moved here, and started my career here. I was even married here, right in the middle of the park.

This was an easy retreat. He had planned on starting in with the details of the crime, but his instinct told him to take a trip down memory lane as he did in many of his other videos.

This would also give him time to feel more comfortable, by discussing memories so dear to him.

Between the ages of maybe five to fifteen years old, or so, swimming pools really had a hold on me. Every campground had a pool, and they were all different. I loved a good pool with a slide, or diving board, and I especially loved swimming at night, when the water was lit up. I can remember the smell of the chlorine, the irritation I felt from opening my eyes under water too much. Then there was the memory of shivering as I got out of the pool at night, and running to my mom to get a towel before I froze to death. I remember the sound of those cheap diving boards bouncing against the rubber thing on the underside, after my sister would execute a perfectly graceful, backward dive. And then me and my brothers, we'd get up there and do a bazillion cannon balls, jack knifes, and crazy, uncoordinated flips. Man, I'm telling you, there was nothing on this planet that welcomed me like seeing that illuminated aqua-blueness at night, with slightly lighter and darker shades of turquoise dancing around on the bottom of the pool, making the surface look like wobbling, blue Jell-O.

Streams were my daytime fascination. On a hot day, there was nothing like going ankle- or knee-deep in a mountain stream, fighting the force of the rapids, or just swimming out into the calmer areas. Sometimes dad would go to the gas station before we left our little town of Erlanger, Kentucky, and load up on inner tubes that us kids could use to ride down those streams like some amusement ride of mother nature. I remember jumping off of rocks into a deep pool of clear stream water, over and over again. I loved streams so much I even got married at one. I have so many great memories of streams.

Now Mark was feeling like he was overcompensating. He'd probably spent a little too much time on the nostalgia.

Now it was time for the heaving lifting. He'd have to talk about the murder, without looking nervous.

> So that's my nostalgia trip. But what does it have to do with this Wandering Ranger video episode? Well, maybe this time I should say this is a Wondering Ranger video, because I am wondering about something and I don't have an answer. It ties into the crime that took place here last night.
>
> Maybe you can see I'm sitting next to a pool. Notice the crime scene tape, twisting in the breeze. I'd like to tell you about what happened here last night.
>
> By the time I've posted this video, I will have made sure this information is safe to release. At this very moment, though, as I'm shooting this video, there's an ongoing investigation which I'm not at liberty to discuss. So, you may be seeing this video long after it's been recorded.

This was all so odd for him to tell this story, not fully understanding what had happened, himself. He had learned about how Hufnagel's truck was parked behind the motel, and how some fresh vomit was found about 10 yards behind that vehicle. *What had Jeb and Haus been doing back there? How did the body end up in the pool?* These were all questions he'd get answers to in the near future, but for now, he would just relay the details as the State Troopers had relayed them to him. And he would try to keep it simple. He wanted to be done with this video as quickly as possible, while still seeming relaxed.

> About 24 hours ago, the manager of this roadside motel heard one of his customers' trucks pull into the lot. He recognized the distinctive growl of the muffler and knew that customer liked to park around the back of the building. He didn't even bother to get up from the chair he was lounging in behind the counter.
>
> Twenty minutes later, though, he heard a lot of commotion coming from the pool area on the far side of

the parking lot from his hotel office. He thought he
might have even heard someone light off a firecracker
or some kind of fireworks. He finished a phone call to
his wife and then looked out his window. He saw two
people in dark clothing running from the pool toward
the woods. There was also a third person in the pool.
The manager thought maybe they were a bunch of drunks,
messing around, because he'd seen plenty of partiers at
his motel in recent months. He almost ignored all of
this, but decided to walk over to remind the person
that the pool had closed for the season, even though
he'd yet to place a tarp over the water. That's when he
noticed the person floating in the water, and blood
mixing with the pool water. Oddly, there was a wooden
baseball bat floating next to him, as well. A nice
Louisville Slugger, barely used, as it looked like to
me, when I inspected it.

Mark knew that whole back story. He had no prior
knowledge that Jeb was planning to give Franco a little
payback for the leg injury, but thought it was a nice touch
of street justice.

The manager was still pretty shaken-up by the time I
got to speak to him. Seems this man and I have a
similar life experience. Some of you who know me, are
aware I lost my wife at a stream... over at...

Here he almost lost it. In part, Mark found it hard to talk
to others about Laurie's murder, but there were other
reasons for getting choked up as well. At this very moment
in the recording of the video, his life flashed before his eyes.
He thought of his dad, and all the sermons he'd given about
taking the high road, and never being a dirty cop. Now Mark
had blown that advice to smithereens. He'd taken the low
road instead, and there was nothing he would ever do to
change what had happened near that swimming pool.

He dwelled on another thought, too, that was
interrupting his train of thought while recording the video.

The presence of the FBI earlier in the night showed him that justice might have taken its natural course had he been more patient. Perhaps his own vigilantism may not have been needed and Franco would have been sent away for the rest of his life, in due time. He panicked, thinking it was all one massive mistake. And to make it worse, it had all been his idea.

Finally, another disruptive thought: what would he do if he were ever found out? He might not survive in prison, given his law enforcement status. Would he evade the law, or stand to take what was justly coming to him? He prayed he would never need to solve that problem.

All of these emotions caved in on him at this moment, producing a convincing display for the viewers of his video who would assume he was merely choked up about the death of his wife.

```
     Sorry for getting a little choked up, I don't think
I can go into much detail about Laurie right now. But
let me get to the point. Have you ever had a great
memory overshadowed by some other horrible experience?
You just heard me go on and on about how great streams
were when I was a kid, but later in life, my wife was
murdered at a stream. I'm telling you, it's a real
effort to keep the horrors out of my head so I can get
in touch with those childhood memories. How on earth
can we expect to reach old age without being jaded by
the darker moments of our lives? Will this hotel
manager ever look at a pool again without imagining a
dead body floating in it? I'm telling you, for as much
as I love nature, and streams, I still find it hard to
go back to where I lost Laurie. I can barely think of
my great childhood memories without the anguish coming
back to ruin it all. What can we do to protect those
shreds of child-like innocence we carry with us through
life from being trampled by the ugliness of the world?
That's what I want to know. If you have an answer to
this question, or just anything else to add, please
```

```
leave a comment below this video. That's all I've got
this time. Peace.
```

Visual Description:		

```
END VIDEO: Fade to black
```

As he turned off the camera, he considered if he would really want to post that video. It would be very helpful to cover his tracks. Then he recalled one of his previous videos, where he reminisced about his sister's T-shirt. The artist wanted to feature the letters of her name along with the picture of a marijuana plant. In that video, he had commented "I suppose some people see the law as dispensable when it's in conflict with their own beliefs or desires," which shook him to his core. He was now one of those 'some people.'

It was getting late and Mark had a long drive ahead of him. He headed for his vehicle, but then had a panicked thought race through his mind. He turned and headed for the back of the motel. There sat the Ford F-350 in the darkness, with yellow caution tape and evidence markers cluttered around the area where it was parked. He stepped over the tape, approached the truck, and quickly shuffled underneath. There it was, his GPS beacon. He cursed Jeb for not having retrieved it. Those were the kinds of details that got criminals caught. He removed it, tucked it in his pants pocket, and returned to his vehicle.

Chapter 31

With days behind him since the hit on Hufnagel, Mark's personal life was marred by regret. Justice had seemed so important at the time, as did preventing Franco from harming another living soul. Mark had lost all self-respect after having participated in such a heinous act with Jeb and Haus. He tried using beer to alleviate that regret, but it only made things worse.

With respect to his career, difficulty arose when the FBI wanted Mark to work with them on the investigation of Hufnagel's death. After all, he'd been the one to keep an ongoing file that helped the FBI find their way to Franco's roadside motel, although slightly too late. It was a particularly anxious conundrum, to investigate one of his own crimes. He knew that Jeb had made a terrible mistake by leaving a baseball bat at the scene of the crime; one of Mark's reports had mentioned how Franco had beaten Jeb's leg with a baseball bat, giving clear motive to retaliate. Had Mark led the investigation, he would have needed to arrest Jeb immediately. Everyone could see how emotional Mark had become after Hufnagel's death, which was really because of the nervousness of being caught. Mark blamed his emotional state on memories of Laurie, and the closure that was brought on by Hufnagel's death. Mark asked that the case be given to the law enforcement officer who'd replaced him in the Echo Ridge case, Dan Lawson. Mark had given all of his files to the FBI, and there was nothing else for him to do, but wait for the day when Dan would learn of Mark's involvement in Franco's death. He prayed Jeb and Haus would not implicate him, and that no additional evidence would arise that would lead to his downfall.

Prior to the deed, he hadn't realized how much of an actor he would need to be, nor understand that this acting role would last for the rest of his life. Anytime Echo Ridge was mentioned by coworkers, he had to evaluate every word he spoke, before it was spoken, so as to never give any indication he'd been involved with Hufnagel's death. It was like a silent sentence in an invisible, mental prison, issued by a non-existent judge.

Several evenings after Hufnagel was killed, Mark popped the metal lid off another MadTree brew, and meandered about his living room, with nothing more than a playlist on a bluetooth boom box to keep him company.

The stress of the present drove him to seek refuge in the past. He leaned upon happier times and nostalgia like he did a cold beer... something to take his mind off of his current woes. He wondered how everything had gotten so complicated. Life in Erlanger, Kentucky, was idyllic compared to what had become of his adulthood. Soon he lost track of time, and drifted backward to his childhood.

He remembered the summers with the most affection. He'd sleep late just about every day, woken only be a cool breeze bouncing the shade against the window's woodwork. Birds chirped outside, welcoming him to a new day. He'd ride his Schwinn 10-speed down the tree-lined Graves Street in the morning until he'd reach the Triple EEE swim club where he'd jump off diving boards and flirt with girls all day. When he'd return home as the sun dipped in the west, he'd ride shirtless, loudly singing every memorized word of the song *The Devil Went Down to Georgia*. Sometimes he'd veer off course and go watch the Lloyd High School Marching Band evening practice, where he'd watch his best friends, Steve and Doug, playing trombone and sax. Other days he'd spend hours competing in miniature golf tournaments at the Putt-putt golf course, go fishing at the Forest Lawn Cemetery, attend summer festivals like the ones at Lion's Park, or cut through the woods along Stevenson road to play a pickup baseball game at Fox Field. And the nights were also great, hanging out late on his buddy Darryl's front porch in Cherry Hill, or staying out way too late to watch crappy B-movies at the Florence Drive-In.

It was all so simple then, and yet, he had no idea how great that life was at the time he was living it. The same was true of his life with Laurie, a thought which brought him back to the present.

After a brief paus between songs, he began listening to *The SteelDrivers'* song called *Heaven Sent*:

> *"I know our days are heaven sent*
> *Lord knows I know not where they went*
> *Shake my head and I wonder how*
> *I'll ever get to heaven now."*

He laughed under his breath at how frequently song lyrics would hit him right where he was living at the moment. In this case, it was the last two lines that struck him. It was just so uncanny, enough for him to wonder if God Himself hadn't orchestrated that song's delivery at just the right moment.

Eventually his restlessness led him to the mantle, where sat Laurie's old Bible, which he had also seen a million times. It had been a dozen years since Laurie's murder. Twelve long years. He glanced at the Bible, which had remained unused since Laurie had last opened it. He noticed how she had marked dozens of pages with colorful sticky notes that stuck out along the edge, each a reminder to Laurie for finding her favorite verses quickly.

He sat his beer down, picked up the Bible and sat in his recliner. There he stared at the holy book under the light of the end-table lamp. He had not considered looking through the book during all those years, partly because he wanted to leave her things exactly as she had left them, and partly because he was mad at himself, and mad at God, for allowing such misery on Earth. He looked inside, doubting anything in its pages could help assuage the way he was feeling about his life, his mistakes, and his losses.

He was remotely familiar with the books of the Bible, but noticed she had placed many colorful notes within the book of Psalms. He noticed something was making the page turning more difficult, and discovered an envelope tucked into the last few pages of Psalms. He removed it and noticed an old, familiar stationery once used by his wife. His heart was racing, realizing it likely contained a handwritten note. To read it would be like hearing from her again. He tried to guess what she might have written before he opened it, and gathered it was probably written just days before her death. He didn't have a letter opener, so he tapped the envelope on the armrest of the recliner, ripped away one end of it, and withdrew the letter to read. There, before his eyes was a transcribed Bible verse, followed by Laurie's own comments.

Psalms 86:5

"You, Lord, are forgiving and good, abounding in love to all who call to you."

Mark, how dare you forget our anniversary! But I forgive you. How can I stay angry with you over forgetfulness when I myself have made far greater mistakes that have been forgiven by our heavenly father? I want you to know that no matter what we do in this world, our sins are washed away in the name of Jesus. Like it says in in this scripture, call out to Him and accept His sacrifice to cover your sin. Even a sin as serious as forgetting our anniversary! (hee hee)

PS – And... do you think it would kill you to maybe apologize? You are a stubborn old goat, but one that I love dearly with all my heart.

The End

Appreciation

I would like to thank a number of people who have helped me in the production of this book. Thanks to, Julie Due, Alex Kuhl, Lisa Due Wayman, Darryl Jouett, and Jenny Feebeck for the big task of proofreading/editing. For my next book, I promise to quadruple your pay. That, and another $4 will get you a happy meal at McDonald's.

Thanks to Darryl A. Jouett, former Air Force serviceman, Erlanger police officer and Detective. He's also a dedicated husband and father, a fellow writer, and a good friend. I can't count how many times I've tapped on this guy to ask him about law enforcement or courtroom procedures. Also, Check out Darryl's cozy novels, the *Bernie Devlin* mystery series (https://www.amazon.com/s?k=darryl+jouett+devil). At the time of this writing, he's got two books finished and a third on the way.

For a constant stream of encouragement sent my way over the years, I'd like to thank my wife, Julie, my mom, Nancy Due, and my brother-in-law, Tom Post. They may have tired of my incessant ramblings about my books over the years, but for the most part, they seldom shown it. And while I'm talking about my wife, Julie, her photography and lettering appear on the cover of this book. Please check out her photography site at JulieDue.com. Traces of my wife's character can be found in that of Laurie Powers, so it was no surprise that Julie was taken aback when she learned Laurie was murdered in this story. LOL. No worries, love... it's only fiction. The murder was just necessary to provide certain motivations for her fictional husband. You're safe with me!

To Nate Post and John Derks, thanks for your insight regarding firearms. Your knowledge is impressive and lends an air of authenticity to the gun details in this story. Now if we can just find the time to get out to John's farm and make some noise!

I must certainly thank Ranger Jamie Sanders of the Great Smoky Mountains National Park (Public Relations). She was quite an asset for me as I attempted to write from the perspective of a park ranger, never having been one myself. I'm also sending special thanks to authors Kim DeLozier (*Bear in the Back Seat*) and Martha Cole Whaley + Marie Maddox (*A Lifetime in Gatlinburg*) for their writings about the Smokies and Gatlinburg. I read these two books while preparing to write *Low Road*, and some of the history and facts presented in their works influenced my own.

Lastly, thanks to those of you who've supported me online, via my Facebook page (https://www.facebook.com/MikeDueAuthor/) or my personal website at MikeDue.com. You inspire me!

Musical References

The lyrics to several bluegrass songs were excerpted in this book. These and other bluegrass artists served as a soundtrack to my writing sessions, to put me in a Tennessee state of mind. I found it very interesting and maybe a little God-inspired when the lyrics would jump out at me as directly related to what I writing about at that moment. It was as if these songs were pleading to be included in the storyline. Please find credit for these fine artists and their works below:

Artist: *Blue Highway*
Song: *"It's a Long, Long Road"*
Writer(s): Normal Blake
Album: *"Lonesome Pine"*
Label: Rebel Records – REB-1719
Release Date: April 25, 2006

Artist: *The Infamous Stringdusters*
Song: *"Soul Searching"*
Writer(s): Josh Shilling / The Infamous Stringdusters
Album: *"Laws of Gravity"*
Label: Compass / Compass Records COM 46782
Release Date: January 13, 2017

Artist: *The Infamous Stringdusters*
Song: *"Gravity"*
Writer(s): Sarah Siskind / The Infamous Stringdusters
Album: *"Laws of Gravity"*
Label: Compass / Compass Records COM 46782
Release Date: January 13, 2017

Artist: *The SteelDrivers*
Song: *"Heaven Sent"*
Writer(s): Christopher Stapleton, Kevin Stephen Welch
Album: *"The SteelDrivers"*

Label: Rounder Select / New Rounder / Rounder ROUCD 598
Release Date: January 15, 2008

Made in the USA
Columbia, SC
15 July 2019